~ Beyond
The Pyrene ~

John Williamson was born in London rather a long time ago, but apart from a brief spell in South Africa, has spent most of his life living in the gentle countryside of Cambridgeshire.

Beyond the Pyrene continues a novel in two parts, together comprising *The Chronicles of Talakhonsu*.

Book I, *Beyond the Black Earth*, was first published in 2016.

Visit   www.johnwilliamsonbooks.com   for further insights into the author, his works and influences.

Also by John Williamson

Beyond the Black Earth
(ISBN 978-0-9955040-0-4)

The poetry of John Williamson
features in the following
collections of verse

Reverence of Rune
(ID: 214845 – www.lulu.com)

Threads
(ISBN 978-0-557-07491-4)

~ Beyond The Pyrene ~

The Chronicles of Talakhonsu
Book II

John Williamson

STOUT
HOUSE

Published by Stout House Publishing
For further information on
other Stout House titles,
visit:

www.johnwilliamsonbooks.com
www.clandestine-books.co.uk

Cover art byTrif TwinArtDesign,
via www.99designs.com

Maps by John Williamson

Beyond The Pyrene
John Williamson

For mum & dad,
and their love of books

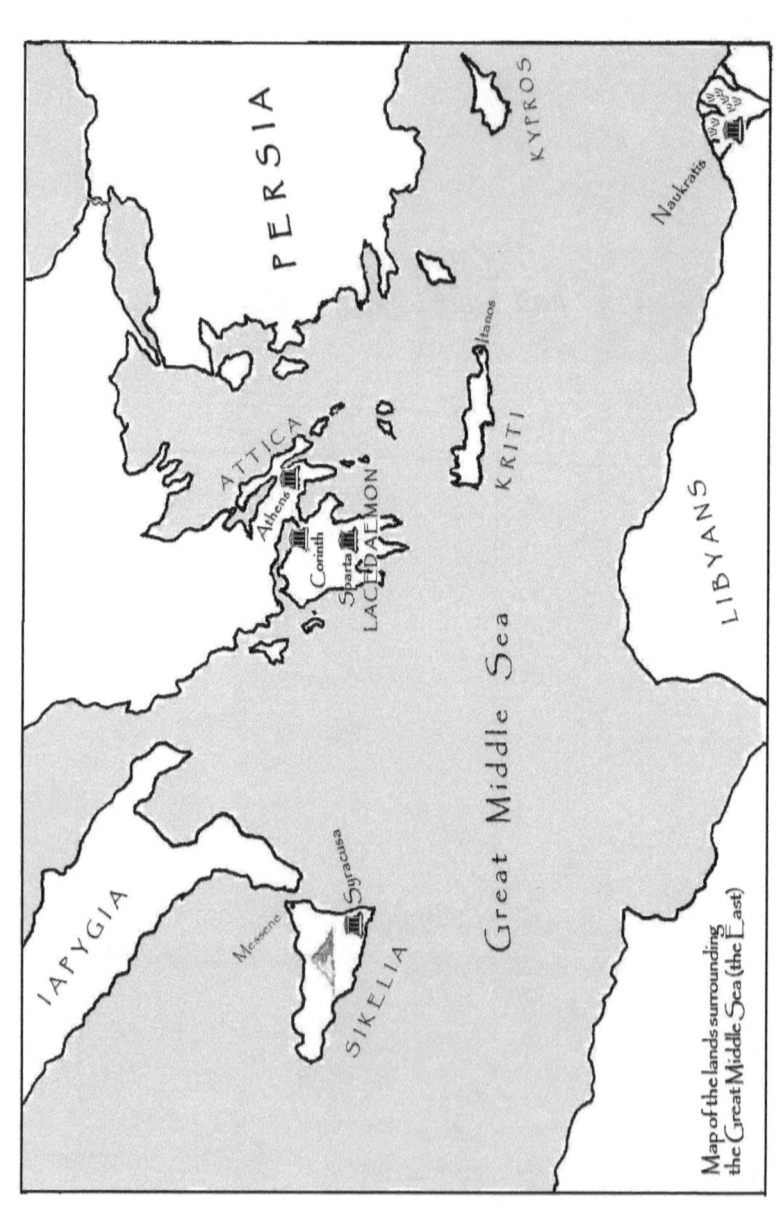

Map of the lands surrounding
the Great Middle Sea (the East)

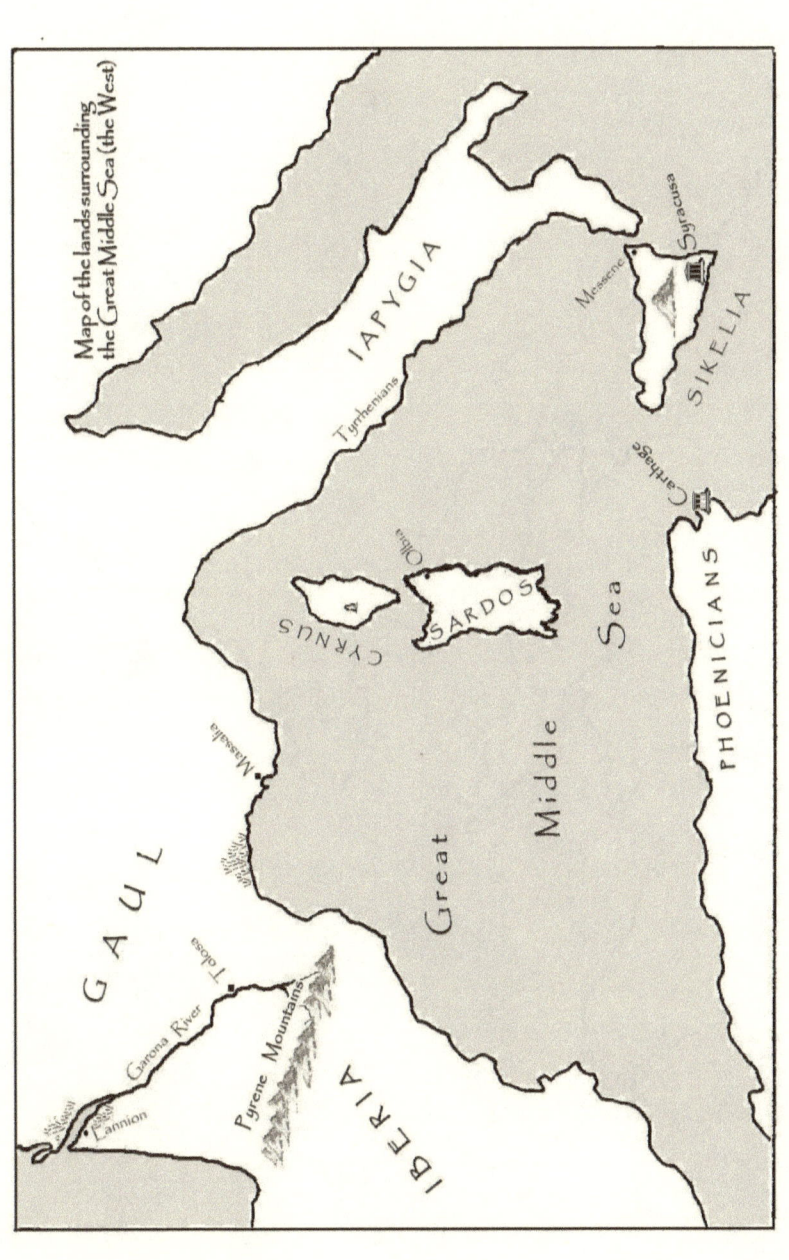

Map of the lands surrounding the Great Middle Sea (the West)

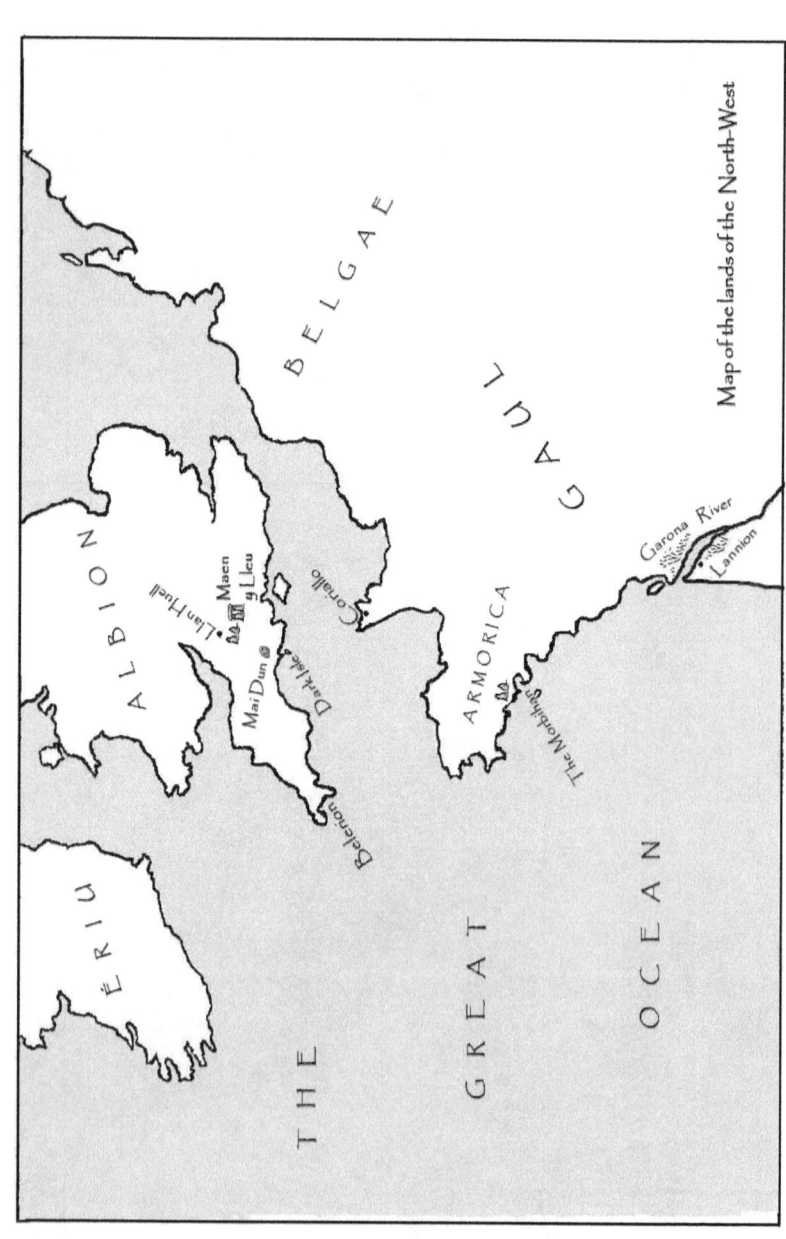

Map of the lands of the North-West

ALBION

BELGAE

GAUL

ARMORICA

ÉRIU

THE

GREAT

OCEAN

Garona River

Lannion

Cornalle

Mai Dun

Maen y Llew

Llan Huell

Dark Lake

Belenton

The Northing

Chapter 1

Ghosts of the Past

At first Talakhonsu's battle with the sea had seemed to go well. He was young and strong, and the cool sea felt good as an escape from the heat of the sun, but still the land grew no nearer, no matter how hard he swam. The wind stirred up the sea so that it rose and fell in small waves that splashed his eyes and stung them with salt. Now he came to curse his former comrades, and call all of the evil fates down on them for abandoning him, yet still he did not give up and he kept on swimming. In spite of his difficulties strangely he was not afraid, or so he told himself. But still he could not help but wonder how long he could keep swimming, and what it would be like to be lost in the sea after the sun had set and darkness had fallen. He struggled on across the dark blue expanse, not daring to look up for fear that the land would grow yet farther away no matter how hard he swam.

When at last he could swim no more, Talakhonsu trod water, struggling to keep his head above the waves as he looked around him.

'Amun help me!' he cried aloud in his despair, yet as he was now adrift on the sea, he was far from the influence of Amun. The god could not help him out here in Poseidon's realm, this much he knew. But why had Leontios deserted him? And why had Hippolytos and Pamphilos not stopped their captain from sailing on without him? These thoughts saddened him more than the thought of his own death as the last of his strength faded away.

The face of his long dead father came to Talakhonsu's mind then and he took a little strength from that, despite the fear that rose steadily in the back of his throat. Korkamani would never have given up, never, and he was Korkamani's

1

son. He had to keep swimming even though his arms and legs were as heavy as stone.

Just then a distant voice found its way to his ear, so distant that he wasn't sure if it was real at first. He listened again but there was nothing, only the wind.

'Talakhonsu,' the voice called again, faintly at first, but then a little louder, 'Talakhonsu!'

He turned about as he trod water, so that he was looking out to sea again, not daring to believe his eyes. There, coming toward him was a ship. The Kallisto!

'Ta-la-khonsu!' Leontios called from the high prow, and Talakh put up a hand to quickly wave back. The ship came up quickly now, her white sail furled again as the oarsmen fought the waves that slapped against her bold, dark prow. The Kallisto's eyes, painted either side of the prow, stared out at him as she drew near and the oars were rested as she coasted closer still. Never had he seen such a welcome sight as this.

'You swim like a dolphin, Napatan!' Leontios said leaning over the side to offer his hand, the worry in his face melting into a wide grin as he saw that Talakhonsu still lived.

'He is Poseidon's own!' the broad face of Hippolytos beamed as he appeared at the captain's side.

Between them the two Greeks pulled Talakhonsu's limp form aboard and in a moment only he was back sitting on the deck rail of the Kallisto, not sure what had happened, nor what would happen next as he was wrapped in a cloak.

'Your first lesson of the sea,' Leontios said solemnly, 'but also a lesson for me.'

'A lesson?' said Talakh, not sure of what the captain was saying.

'Yes, a lesson,' Leontios repeated. 'The sea is Poseidon's and when we bring a new crew member aboard, there is always a trial for him to show the god that all on my ship are worthy of his realm. Sometimes a man may have to step from oar blade to oar blade over the water along each side of the Kallisto, or I may have him climb the mast and drop from the sail arm into the sea.

'In your case I set for you the trial of swimming around the ship. Still, for a good swimmer like you it was plain this was no trial at all, and so it came to me that we would sail off to see what you would do. But what thoughts the gods put in our heads, eh?' Leontios shook his head.

'I thought you had abandoned me, so I swam for the shore,' Talakh said honestly. 'And yet as hard as I swam, the shore came no closer.'

'Aye, it was a stupid thing of me to do, and we are lucky that you survived. But remember this Talakhonsu, we will never abandon you,' Leontios said, clasping his hand firmly. 'We are all brothers now. And as you learnt this lesson, that on his own a man is powerless against the sea, so I have learnt a lesson too. When we left you to show the god your prowess, the wind rose little by little and when we turned about, your dark head was lost to us in the dips of the waves. We furled the sail and rowed back to the shore and yet we could see you nowhere, even when Pamphilos climbed the mast. It seems the current was carrying you away to the side of us.

'Thus Poseidon has taught me to renew my respect for the sea. It is our friend and yet also our enemy and this we forget at our peril, lad. While we are far out here, the Kallisto is our only refuge when Poseidon sends his white horses to race out across the water.'

Talakhonsu looked around him at the dark, sun-dappled sea and it was not hard for him to imagine its beauty turned to such terror. He remembered the storms of sand in the desert he had seen when still a boy. What might such winds do to the wide waters of the sea? A shudder ran down his spine then, in spite of the sun's heat.

'What form does the lord Poseidon take?' he asked, to take his mind from his fears.

'Ah, sometimes he is a man like us, and sometimes he takes the form of a horse, but usually he is said to be a giant who wields a great forked spear. He causes the earth to quake when he is displeased with men. Ah, but when he is really angry, he lifts the land up on his broad shoulders and then drops it, so

3

that even the mightiest of temples fall in ruins! Still other times he might send the nameless monsters of the sea to terrorise the shore.'

'But when he is pleased?' Talakh asked with a fear in his belly. 'What does he do then?'

'Why then he will leave the world of men be,' Leontios said. 'And for that we can all be thankful.'

'I will offer to great Poseidon then in the hope that he will leave us alone,' Talakh grinned. 'And I will offer to my Amun too.'

'Of course,' Leontios nodded. 'You can offer to your Amun without offending us, for he is Zeus and Zeus is he.'

'Zeus is Amun? I don't understand,' Talakh said, puzzled.

'Well, Zeus is chief amongst our Greek gods,' Leontios explained. 'He was born from the earth on the island of Kriti, so the priests say. But still he is the same as your Amun of Thebes.'

'My Amun is of Napata in my own homeland, not the false one of Waset,' Talakh tried to correct him, but Leontios had grown disinterested in talk of such things.

'Ach, the gods are the gods,' the captain shrugged. 'Come on now, back to the oars men. Our journey has only just begun.'

-ϕ-

In the settlement of Llan Huell it was a fine spring evening as Pelia paused in her telling of the story of her father, Talakhonsu the Napatan. She and Cerian were sat outside and it was a joy for them to be beyond the confines of her small hut for once as the dusk came down.

'Did they leave the crocodiles behind when they came to the open sea?' Cerian asked thoughtfully as she gave a shiver in the cool of the evening.

'Ah, that would be telling,' Pelia smiled. 'The secret of telling a good story is always to keep something back, otherwise if the listener knows all that will pass, then their

4

mind will wander off to something else. Such as thoughts of love for instance.'

Cerian blushed a little at that, but said nothing. It was no secret that Tyrnon, a young cousin of chief Heilyn's, had caught her eye, and she his.

'We should go inside and raise the fire again,' Pelia grinned. The cool of the evening colours your cheeks.'

Cerian blushed again, for though in many ways she was a forthright girl, when it came to talk of men she was still shy.

'Tell me again,' she said, seeking to change the subject as they stooped through the low doorway into the darkened hut. 'Why did Isek and Leontios take Talakhonsu aboard their ship?'

'Well for Leontios, as you heard, he owed my father a debt for freeing the Kallisto after she had run aground in the Great River, and the Greeks never forget such things. They see it as a slight on their honour unless the debt is repaid.

'As for Isek, he was a clever man, a wise man above all. Cunning even, some might say. But then if a man is short and not blessed with handsome looks, nor wealth, then he has to look to his brains instead. Still it seems to me that there was also a deep kindness in Isek and that is why he befriended Talakhonsu.

'The fates...,' Cerian nodded. 'When they rowed off and left your father in the sea, he could have been drowned.'

'Yes, the fates,' Pelia agreed as she fanned the embers of the fire back into glowing life and gently placed some kindling onto them. 'They guide us all Cerian, sometimes for good and sometimes for ill.'

A sudden flame flickered amongst the new wood, sending shadows leaping around the hut, and the two women sat in thought by the fire for a while until tiredness took them off to their sleep.

Early the next morning, Aneurin the hunter breathed the chill air long and slow as he crept forward, placing each fur-clad foot softly in front of the other, so that no crack of twig or rustle of leaf would give him away. On this clear morning, a late frost had set in overnight but this was already melting away. Still it was cold enough for Aneurin to see his breath on the slight breeze. This was the time of rebirth across the land, when the young of all creatures replaced the old ones taken down into the earth by dark winter. It was the time too when the heart of the hunter was at once filled with both joy and a tinge of regret.

Aneurin knew this well as he stalked closer to the clearing where a young fawn quivered next to its mother in the weak morning sunlight. It had been born perhaps only the night just past, yet its shaking legs somehow held it up as it suckled from its mother, a roe deer as beautiful as any he had seen. Aneurin knew in his heart that he would not kill this day. Yet still he stole closer still, lowering his bow as he went, and watched as mother roe crooked her neck round so that she could lick her fawn's face with her long tongue. When he was a boy, Aneurin's father had always called him soft hearted and perhaps that was still true of him as a man. But still, he thought to himself, if he had killed the mother, so the fawn would surely die with no doe to suckle it. And only a starving man, or a soulless one, would kill the fawn itself at such a young age. Neither the earth goddess nor Cernunos the hunter god would look kindly on such a wasteful deed. So Aneurin watched, as a cat watches a mouse, but he did not kill.

Pelia too had the skills of a good hunter, though neither the strength to bend a powerful bow, nor to throw a spear very far. Yet just as Aneurin watched the hind and her fawn, so she watched him unseen behind the gnarled trunk of an old oak, hardly daring to breathe. Finally the hunter turned slowly around and returned the way he had come, but Pelia hid and waited until she heard his soft footfall recede into the distance, before she breathed a sigh of relief, smiling to herself at having outfoxed him.

When she returned at last to her hut, Cerian was shivering in the still weak sunlight as she stood outside on the mat of willow twigs that kept the mud and wet from being trodden in. Her long black hair was already braided into the plaits that hung down each side from behind her ears. Though they were not as neat as when Pelia plaited them for her, still they told Pelia that Cerian had been up for some time.

'Where have you been?' Cerian asked, her voice full of worry. 'I thought something might have happened to you!'

'I was restless,' Pelia said honestly. 'I woke early and could not sleep, so I went for a wander to stretch my legs.'

'To the hut of Aneurin?' Cerian asked, mischief replacing the worry on her pretty face.

'No, of course not! I was just by myself.'

'Well, you should have woken me to let me know,' Cerian frowned again. 'I didn't know what to do, whether to raise an alarm, or to look for you myself. A bear could have eaten you! Or a wolf!'

'Be calm,' Pelia said soothingly. 'You are right, I should not have worried you.'

'Next time you will wake me then?'

'I will, though you won't thank me for it!' Pelia grinned. 'The truth is Cerian, until you came along I lived a long time on my own with no-one to watch over my comings and goings.'

'Aneurin watches,' Cerian gave the sly smile that often left boys tongue tied. 'I think he has always watched you.'

'What if he does?' Pelia said haltingly. 'He is a kind man, but I don't love him so that's the end of that. Anyway, let us talk no more of Aneurin. I'll wake the fire up if you will start us some barley broth.'

'Both are already made,' Cerian bowed her head a little, not wanting to upset her friend any further.

'Then let us go inside and warm ourselves,' Pelia smiled

Later that morning Aneurin returned with the hound Sealgair loping along at his side, and passed by Pelia as she carried a heavy jug of water from the spring.

'No luck with your hunting?' Pelia asked innocently.

'No, but my day is always a little brighter for seeing you,' Aneurin said pleasantly. 'You were about early today.'

'I always am,' Pelia said as absently as she could.

'You should not go so far into the forest on your own though,' Aneurin said. 'There are many dangers there as you know. But if you must venture there, then take a spear to protect yourself.'

'The forest?'

'Yes, you followed me this morning.'

'I did not!' Pelia stopped in her tracks to face the hunter. 'Why do you say that?' she said, her eyes of sea-green and gold meeting his.

'Sealgair told me of course,' Aneurin smiled, returning her gaze. 'He said that you followed me from here. Then when I saw a clearing ahead and bade him stay so that I could stalk the deer, he says you skirted around him and hid behind an oak tree without even saying hello.'

Pelia could not help but smile at that and ruffled Sealgair's ear. 'I know he is a fine hound, but he has never spoken to me,' she allowed herself a smile. 'How did you know I was there?'

'You were quiet enough,' Aneurin said seriously. 'I did not hear or see you while you watched me, but still your feet had left prints in the dew and flattened the dead bracken a little. I saw that someone had passed behind me when I went back to Sealgair, so then I too hid in turn. After a while I saw you pass by on your way back here, though it was all I could do to muzzle Sealgair and stop him from barking. It was a simple matter then for me to follow the tracks you had left back to the tree you had crouched behind when I was stalking the deer.'

'You are a clever one, Aneurin,' Pelia shook her head in wonder. 'But I did not follow you knowingly. You see there were some herbs which I had to gather in the morning light for their magical powers and that is why is why I was there,' she lied coldly.

'Oh,' said Aneurin, crestfallen. 'I will let you go, then. The water is heavy and I'm sure you long to set it down.'

Pelia felt bad then for what she had done in hiding the truth from him.

'I am glad our paths crossed though,' she said, the warmth returning to her voice. 'I saw a beautiful thing in what you did when you spared the doe and her fawn.'

Aneurin's deep green eyes brightened at those words, knowing that he had some favour at least with Pelia.

Yet as she carried the water jug back to her hut, Pelia was no longer quite sure what she felt for the quiet, dark haired hunter she had known all of her young life. The truth was that she had followed him out into the forest that morning. Yet when she asked herself why, she did not know.

-ϕ-

The Kallisto rowed toward the west through the breaking chops of the sea, the low lying green coast of Kemet on her left and the hot sun overhead, sweating the men despite the steady breeze that blew from the land. Slowly the few palm trees disappeared altogether and there was then only a lonely marshland bordering the sea, until at last even that expired and the first sands of the desert appeared. That night Leontios beached the ship on that arid coast so that the men could sleep ashore.

The next day and the morning after that, they followed the coast farther west still, until Talakhonsu began to wonder if the Kallisto was sailing all the way to the land of the dead. It was not until after the noon that the captain finally changed her course, back south toward land.

'Abasis, that is where we head now,' Pamphilos said to Talakhonsu as they rowed side by side. 'A surly place,' he grunted, straining against the oar with his slight frame. 'Hippolytos has had cause to bash heads there before now.'

Tall Akakios leant hard against his steering oar to turn the Kallisto's prow and as he looked over his shoulder Talakh saw that they were heading for a narrow inlet. A few low houses clung to the rocky outcrops around it and amongst them a few straggly palm trees gave small relief from the desert's harsh grip over the land. A handful of small fishing boats were tied up here and there, but these were all dwarfed by the approaching Kallisto. Leontios bade the men start up what to Talakhonsu sounded like a chant of battle as they rowed in alongside the boats, but though he did not understand many of the words, he joined his voice to those of the others anyway. If this was a place of trouble, the captain and his crew were making it clear to all that they were fighters who would take no slight from anyone. Some children appeared on the beach as the Kallisto shipped her oars and coasted slowly in under the guidance of Leontios, who had gone forward to call directions from the high prow. Hippolytos meanwhile took his place at the other steer oar to show his brawny arms as the Kallisto slowly slid to a halt, her keel finding the sandy bottom of the inlet.

'Talakhonsu!' the captain barked. 'Over the side and take a rope ashore. Pamphilos! Go with him and show him how to tie her off around the rock over there.'

The two young men lowered themselves quickly down into the water and waded the few feet to the dusty shore. After they'd pulled the rope taught, Talakh helped Pamphilos loop it a few times around the rock, watching carefully as the Greek passed it under itself, so that the rope was caught in its own grip and could not move. All the while, the watching children dared each other to edge closer to the strangers.

'Here, you try,' Pamphilos said, pulling the ropes end, so that the knot came undone again.

Talakh tried, then gave up and started again. It was not as easy as it looked.

'Why are we here then, Pamphilos?' he asked in his broken Greek, as he tried a third time. 'Do we trade?'

'Trade? No, not trade as such,' Leontios answered as he strolled over to watch Talakh's efforts with the rope. 'Tomorrow we sail for Kriti and before we do that, we need bread and water for the voyage.'

'Is it far to Kriti?'

'That depends on the sea god,' the captain laughed. 'If he favours us with a fair wind it will take us two days and two nights. But if the wind turns against us we could be at sea for a week!'

'And that is too long even for a Greek!' Pamphilos joined in.

'Leontios,' tall Akakios called his captain's attention to the approach of a man in the long robes of the desert peoples.

'You learn fast Talakh,' Leontios grinned, choosing to ignore Akakios as he watched the Napatan release the hitch knot he had made. 'You will make a man of the sea yet.'

'Captain!' Akakios called again. 'The headman is here.'

This time Leontios glanced over to where the man in the desert robes stood with some others, but still he did not acknowledge him.

'He wants my silver, and I want his bread and water,' the captain said quietly to Talakh and Pamphilos. 'We will see what deal can be struck. Talakh, you stand behind me and listen well if he speaks to his kin in the Kemet tongue. But say nothing, mind, let him think we don't understand.'

Talakh nodded and followed with Pamphilos as the crew gathered on shore with their spears to make a show for their captain.

'A long day's walk from here,' Pamphilos whispered to him, 'there are magical springs in the desert they say, where sweet water bubbles up from within the dry earth. You understand?'

'Water, from the desert, yes,' Talakh repeated, for he had quickly learnt enough of the Greek tongue to grasp what Pamphilos had said, taking into account the Skyrian's gestures.

'These people make a living by bringing water here to trade with passing ships like us. Then they trade grain and fish back the other way to the desert people who hold the springs for themselves.'

'They must pay for the water?' Talakh asked in surprise.

'Yes, they must pay and we in turn must pay. Water is scarce here where the sands meet the sea and none can live without it.'

Talakh thought to himself now that the world was like a spider's web with threads of trade going to and from places like this to other places, some near, some far and so on. Things passed one way in exchange for things passing the other way, but how big the web was and where it began and ended, he did not yet understand. Nor would he ever, for some things are unknowable. With these thoughts puzzling his mind, Talakh stood behind Leontios, with Pamphilos next to him. Tall Akakios now held Isek's place as the captain's right hand man and his face was stern, implacable as always.

'Captain, welcome...,' the headman began to speak in the Greek tongue, before his words dried up with fear.

'We want bread and fresh water. We will pay you the usual price for each amphora you fill,' Leontios said bluntly in the Kemet tongue.

'I... I am sorry my captain,' the headman stammered. 'Things have changed since last you blessed us with your custom here. The water and bread... they cost more now,' he winced, as if expecting Leontios to strike him.

'How much more?' Leontios asked, his eyes narrowing.

'I... ah... Double the price,' the headman answered fearfully.

Leontios laughed heartily at that. 'You hear that men?' he turned to his crew. 'Double he says! I do not believe my ears!'

Now he turned back and fixed his eyes on the headman, his smile gone, his face pitiless. 'Tell me again your price headman, and do not joke with me this time, or I will think you take me for a fool!'

'No, good captain, never!' the man held up his hands.

'Then honour the old price, you dog.'

'I cannot, lord,' the man dropped to his knees. 'There is another here who sets the price now, not I. Otherwise I would gladly...'

'Enough!' Leontios bellowed. 'Where is this man who seeks to starve my crew?'

'He dwells in the desert, lord, at the place of the spring waters,' the man trembled.

Although he had the colour of the Kemet people in his skin, still his grey, pinched face looked sick with fear as he glanced quickly from Leontios to Akakios and back again. Talakhonsu felt a little sorry for him then, for there was no pity to be had from either of the two Greeks.

'So, I have to go to the desert to take up my quarrel with this other one? Is that what you tell me?' Leontios shook his fist in his rage.

'No lord, no!' the man blurted. 'My master returns here tomorrow, or perhaps the next day after.'

'Then when he does, he will find my usual price and no more, for I will take what I need from you and be on my way.'

'No lord, please! Great captain do not do this or he will kill the children!' the man started to weep.

'So, you are headman here and yet you are not,' Tall Akakios sneered. 'How is this possible?'

'My master is a powerful lord,' the headman sobbed as the tears ran from his eyes.

'So, you threaten me with this master of yours now do you?' Leontios rasped.

The man sank further down onto the sand, and Talakh could see that, had the earth swallowed him whole now, it would have come as a blessing.

'Lord,' he sobbed, 'I do not know what to say, for I have one lion in front of me and another behind.'

'Hmph!' Leontios grunted. He was not an unkind man and though he was angry with what he had heard, still there was also a little pity in him now for the headman's plight.

'Tell me truthfully now,' he said, 'or I will have your tongue. How many fighting men does this rogue have?'

'No Leontios!' tall Akakios hissed, as he guessed what was passing through his captain's mind. 'This is not our fight. Let us take what we need, leave a fair price and be gone!'

'I will say what we are to do here, Akakios, not you,' Leontios said bluntly. 'This man and his dog of a master think to make fools of us! We are men of Kypros you and I, are we to let them dishonour us? Will we leave it to other Greek ships to right this wrong?'

'You turn my words Leontios!' Akakios snapped back.

'Then let me ask you another question, Akakios,' Leontios said hotly. 'Are you the kind of man who would leave innocent children to their deaths at the hands of a thief? No, you are not and neither am I. We either pay the price he asks and live with our shame, or we wait for his master to return and show him what we do with such grasping dregs as he.'

'Aye!' Hippolytos shouted, and his voice was joined by many others in the crew.

Leontios fixed tall Akakios with his eye for a moment before turning to the headman again. 'Now, how many will he come with?'

'No more than three, perhaps four,' the man sobbed again.

'Three or four? Only five then at most, including your master?'

'Yes, but it is not as it sounds,' the headman raised his head to look up at Leontios, who he knew was mocking him then. 'They are merciless and well armed.'

'And we are men of the Islands, so they will not trouble us. By the time I am finished with them, they will be paying me to take your water away!'

When the cool of the evening came, Leontios ordered his men to take some of the long clay vessels the Greeks call amphorae and filled these with water from the caves where the people of Abasis stored it in great stone jars. The amphorae were not light when empty, but when full only Hippolytos had the brute strength to carry them with ease.

'Why are there so many empty amphorae in the Kallisto's belly?' Talakh asked Pamphilos as they carried one between them by its long handles.

'We use them for many things, Talakh. You see the ones that have a cross marked on them?'

'Yes?'

'Those ones were full of oil, and when we return to Kriti we will fill them again.'

'What happened to the oil?'

'Ah,' Pamphilos said, 'the captain traded that in Thebes.

'The place you call Waset,' he added as Talakh looked puzzled. 'Yes those ones had oil, whilst those without marks, they had wine. Hippolytos drank most of that!' he joked. 'They are just for weight, to make sure the ship doesn't roll over in a storm.'

'They won't be used again for more wine?'

'No, they stink too much for that! The wine would sour.'

'Did the wine too come from Kriti?'

'We buy it there yes, but where it comes from, that is a different matter. It may come from Sikelia or from Kypros.'

'Hey, you two!' tall Akakios called to them as they struggled back toward the ship. His face looked stormier than ever after his crossed words with the captain. 'Stopper that amphora and stow it, and then I want you to scour this rat hole for ballast stones.'

'Aye, Akakios,' Pamphilos quickly answered for them as he knocked the wooden bung into the mouth of the amphora and then scooped a little water onto it. 'See Talakh?' he said. 'The water without and the water within will make the stopper swell to keep a good seal.'

'That's clever,' Talakh nodded.

'We Greeks are certainly that,' Pamphilos laughed. 'Now, we must do what Akakios asks. He's in as foul a mood as always.'

'What are we meant to be looking for?' Talakh asked as they wandered over to some rocks.

'Ah, you do not understand ballast?'

Talakh shook his head.

'It is the same as the amphorae full of sand, to stop the ship from rolling over in a storm. You see the Kallisto was built to carry heavy things, but when too many amphorae are empty, like now, there is not enough weight in her belly. What happens when she is not weighted down?'

'She rises up?' Talakh said quickly.

'Exactly, she rises up. This is not a good thing when we are at sea, for the salt in the water makes her rise up all the more. If we do nothing about it, she will topple over in the first storm. So, we need to load heavy rocks…'

'To weight her down again?'

'That's it, to weight her down some more, now that we've

left the river. Then when we reach Kriti and load a new cargo no doubt we'll throw them back onto the quay for some other captain to use!' Pamphilos laughed again. 'Who knows where they might end up then?'

'I don't know,' Talakh scratched his head. 'There must be a better way than this? Why do we not exchange one heavy cargo for another heavy cargo? Why not take something good back to Kriti instead of stones?'

'Aye,' Pamphilos nodded. 'That is just what we should do, but we would have risked too much to linger in Kemet with the Persians at our backs.'

'So we are stuck with the stones and the empty pots.'

'For now yes, but next time will be different. Now, I'll take this one and you take the big flat stone over there.'

It was hard work carrying the heavy stones back to the ship, and by the time tall Akakios was content that enough ballast had been taken on board, Talakh thought he must surely be back labouring in the fields of Siamun the overseer.

That evening around a fire on the beach, Pamphilos told one of his stories of the heroes of Greece and their voyages across the sea in a mighty ship. This then was the gift of Pamphilos. He was not the strongest of young men, but as a teller of stories he had few equals.

Talakhonsu listened keenly, piecing together the still strange words of the Greek tongue, and though he missed some points, still he made out enough to hear of hideous monsters and giants that beset the ship's crew at every turn.

All the while the great double headed axe of Hippolytos glinted in the firelight as he honed first one blade and then the other in turn with a sharpening stone. The others too were sharpening spear points and long daggers as they listened intently, so Talakhonsu found his own short knife and started at that with a flat, hard stone he picked up from the beach. Looking around him as his crewmates clapped and cheered Pamphilos on with his story, it was easy to think that they also were heroes. Tomorrow they would face their own unknown dangers in these strange lands, when the headman's master of the deserts returned.

That night when the fire had burned low and the men were snoring, wrapped in their cloaks for warmth, it seemed to Talakh that only he could not sleep. There were no mosquitoes to trouble him in that dry place, only a doubt in his own mind that if it came to a fight the next day, would he be able to swallow down his fear and win the respect of Leontios with his courage? He searched his mind in vain for the face of Ketet, but that night her smile was lost to him even when his dreams finally came.

'Come on idle bones,' Hippolytos said, poking Talakh in the ribs with the toe of his sandal. 'There is work to be done.'

The Napatan rubbed the sleep from his heavy eyes and blinked in the early morning light.

'Here,' Pamphilos offered him some fresh bread.

The flat loaf was still warm and it tasted good washed down with some fresh, cool water.

'What will we do while we wait?' Talakh asked.

'The captain wants us to practice our arms,' Pamphilos said in an untroubled voice. 'This is something we do often when we beach the ship in foul weather, for at sea there are those who would kill for the ship and its cargo. Can you use a spear, Talakhonsu?'

'I never have until now, no.'

'A bow then? Can you shoot?'

'No, I have only my knife and my throwing stick.'

'And we saw you strike the crocodile with it too!' Pamphilos grinned.

'Try the wooden swords,' Hippolytos said as he strolled by, tossing his axe in the air and catching it as if it were no more harmless than a stick. 'Not that there will be any fighting for you two today,' he grinned. 'My axe will finish any trouble well before it starts!'

So Talakh and Pamphilos took the advice of Hippolytos and fetched the wooden swords from their stowage in the ship. In truth, these were just lengths of old spear shafts, with a hide grip and a guard for the fingers, made from pieces of bound ox rib. Pamphilos took the lead in showing the sword skills he had learnt.

'Aim for my ribs Talakh!' he urged.

As Talakh stepped forward, Pamphilos flicked his own sword arm down and across, knocking Talakh's thrust to one side.

'Try again,' he nodded, but when Talakh lunged, the result was much the same as before.

Talakh aimed another blow, but it seemed that he was just not fast enough to beat Pamphilos.

'This is harder than it looks,' he shook his head in frustration.

'It is, but imagine that the sword is made of iron. The weight of a real sword makes it harder still to wield. Now you try to block me.'

This time as Pamphilos moved slowly forward, Talakh flicked his arm across to push the sword thrust away, just as Pamphilos had done.

'Good,' Pamphilos nodded. 'But without a shield, you must keep your free arm out of the way. Are you ready? This time I will be quicker.'

As Pamphilos swept forward Talakh flicked his arm across and down again, but this time Pamphilos had only feinted his blow and he came forward again in a short step that brought the rounded end of his sword under Talakh's ribs. The blow was not hard, but Talakh knew what it meant.

'You would have killed me,' he shook his head again. 'You are too good.'

'And yet I am not good at all compared to Akakios or the captain. Kleisthenes and Demosthenes are better still,' Pamphilos shrugged his shoulders. 'But don't worry, it will come in time with enough practice. Now, try again.'

And so, while fair haired Kleisthenes looked on, Pamphilos showed Talakh the other sword moves he knew. There was the cross cut, which could slice a man's guard arm open. Then was a parry, where the defender stepped to one side and hacked down at his attacker's hamstrings. Finally, the downward slash, where the sword was swung from overhead with both hands to cut through hide and shield.

'That is the most dangerous move of all for the attacker,' Kleisthenes said coldly. 'Your sword Talakhonsu, give it to me. Now Pamphilos, attack me as you did Talakhonsu, but do not spare your strength, or I will crack your head!'

Pamphilos nodded. 'You are ready?'

'Hah!' Kleisthenes cried, his muscled arm swinging the wooden sword in a wild arc just above the head of Pamphilos.

The young Greek accepted the challenge, raising his sword to block Kleisthenes' next blow, then lunged forward himself with a stabbing thrust.

As Kleisthenes stepped backwards to dodge the blow, he seemed to stumble and fell on his back in the dirt. Yet as Pamphilos raised his sword to bring it sweeping down, so the older man rolled to one side and swept his own wooden blade across his attacker's ankles. Pamphilos was not hurt, but Kleisthenes had made his point.

'There is an important lesson for you both,' Kleisthenes said, his blue eyes piercing them as he stood up and brushed the dirt from his shoulders. 'Remember that an opponent is not beaten just because he is on the ground. To try to kill me Pamphilos, you opened your guard. If our fight were real I would have taken your ankles then and you would have died on your knees.'

'What would you have done O Kleisthenes, if you were in my place?' Pamphilos asked him respectfully.

'Lie down on your back in the dirt,' Kleisthenes ordered him.

'Now,' Kleisthenes said as he cast a shadow over Pamphilos, 'the safest way is either to hack at your enemy's feet, or to quickly circle round if he is stunned and strike from behind his head. Like this!'

Pamphilos winced as the wooden sword fell from out of the blinding sun toward his eyes, but Kleisthenes pulled up the blow just short of his nose.

'Although a man's feet can kick or trip you, they cannot hold a sword,' Kleisthenes said as he gave Pamphilos his arm and pulled him to his feet again. 'Strike at his feet and you may not kill him, but he will be wounded. And if he cannot stand, then he cannot fight you. After that it is just a matter of time before you strike the fatal blow. But strike at his body and you may be the one who ends up spitted.

'Here Talakh, take back your sword and go on with your practice. Next you must learn to use a shield. Someone else will teach you that. I don't use one myself,' the Greek warrior said without the trace of a boast.

So Talakh saw that this was no idle play, but was the warrior's art, where practice and skill could save a life or take it. Much as he did not want to become a killer of men, he saw too that the path he was now taking might sooner or later lead him towards that end. For better or for worse, this was the world of men that he had been fated to join.

Midday came and went with still no sign of the return of the mysterious tyrant of Abasis, and as the heat of the day grew steadily greater, so the men of Leontios grew first restless and then languid, as they came to think that perhaps there would be no reckoning that day.

'Only a fool or a madman would have started their journey in the desert heat,' Talakh heard Leontios say to tall Akakios.

'Then if he does not come before morning, we should leave our coin and our curses, and to Hades with him!' Akakios said angrily.

'Yes, yes,' Leontios answered thoughtfully. He saw then that Talakh stood close by talking with an old man from the village.

'Talakh,' he called him over. 'Though you look nothing like Isek, when I hear you speak the Kemet tongue it reminds me of my old friend and his wisdom. What words would he have for us now do you think?'

'Never mind the boy,' Akakios said impatiently. 'Isek is not here and that is that. My advice to you Leontios is this. The air is still and the moon will be full tonight. We should sail for Kriti before dusk. That is the wisdom of Akakios, for what it is worth.'

The face of Leontios grew dark and Talakh saw from his set jaw that the words of Akakios did not sit well with him.

'And you Talakh?' he said coldly. 'What do you think?'

Talakh looked from his captain to tall Akakios and back again, conscious that he risked making an enemy of one or even both of them. But his loyalty lay with the captain and it was this that shaped his thoughts.

'Captain,' he said, 'Akakios is a man of experience and I think his way is the safest way for us.'

At this a satisfied smile spread across the narrow face of tall Akakios, but it quickly turned to a frown as Talakh continued to speak.

'Perhaps one of the people here has warned their master? It may be that he has not come here yet because he gathers more men to him so that he can outnumber us. Or he may be waiting us out to see if we sail away. But either way I think that it will do us no good to dwell here now.'

Leontios growled almost like a dog at this, thinking Talakh to be siding with Akakios, but still Talakh continued, his words aimed at salving the pride of Leontios.

'But captain, your honour is clear in this matter all the same,' he said. 'This man chooses not to come here because he fears you, while you have only dealt fairly with his people by paying their usual price. Therefore, the dishonour is only with him. These are only my thoughts, but I would be surprised if anyone else thought differently of you,' he said boldly.

'You presume to speak for all?' Akakios said testily. 'You are just a boy, a pup amongst men here!

'Enough!' Leontios spat. 'This is my ship and my crew, Akakios. All amongst us are free to speak, you know that is my way.'

'But he is just a stripling!' Akakios insisted.

'As you and I once were,' Leontios said firmly. 'It is the things we did, not the years that passed us that made us men. So it is with this young one. Already he has shown us that his boyhood is behind him, for he can put a bend in the oar as well as any of my men. Do not forget either that it was he who pulled us off that mud bank, not with his brawn, but with his brain! A man he may not yet be, but he knows the meaning of honour and because of that he deserves our respect.'

Talakh could see anger starting to boil in both men, but as he feared they might come to a fight, a cry came up from a far rise, where Leontios had posted Kleon.

Leontios stared hard at Akakios for what seemed like an age before he reacted.

'To your arms!' he shouted finally. 'Quickly now!'

The men formed themselves into a loose, broad line that bristled with bright, sharpened iron from between their simple shields, as Kleon came running quickly across the sands from the ridge, his feet kicking up the dust as he grew closer. Though Talakh reckoned himself to be a good runner, still he doubted he could have bested the Greek in a race that day.

'What do you see Kleon?' Leontios called to him as he drew closer

'Horses,' Kleon rasped back with what little breath he had left.

'How many?

'Two or three, no more than that,' Kleon gasped as he ran up to them, and doubled over to get his breath back, his chest heaving.

'There may be more on foot behind them,' Leontios grinned. 'You!' he called to the headman, who had come from his house to see what the noise was about. 'You complain that this man you call your master has treated you harshly. Well, this is your chance to do something about it. Will your men stand up for themselves? If your master wants to fight, will you join my warriors to be rid of your enemy?'

'Good captain,' the old man trembled, 'our pride has been taken by that one, for he is an evil man. We cannot fight. If we lose, he will take all from us. None will be left alive here, man, woman or child.'

'Then I must fight for you?' Leontios said harshly. 'I must fight for your freedom?'

The old man bowed his head in his silent shame.

'Hippolytos!' Leontios called the burly Kretan to his side. 'Take this wretch and his kinsmen to the strongest house there is here and bar them all in. Pamphilos! Talakhonsu! You stand guard on them with spears and let none of them pass. Whether or not they despise their master, I do not trust them.'

The three of them did as the captain ordered and rounded up those men and older boys who had not already fled with the women. In the end they found that only two men of fighting age still remained. The rest were old men and boys, and these they stripped of their knives. They were a sorry sight and gave no trouble, for their spirits had long since been beaten down.

'I return to Leontios,' Hippolytos said, his eyes set hard in his brawny face. 'If any of these ones try to leave, let them taste the iron of your spear points.'

'Aye,' said Pamphilos, 'you can rely on us.'

With a wink of his eye, Hippolytos swung his great double headed axe over his shoulder and strode off to where the Greek line protected their ship. Yet still the horsemen did not come.

'I hope I will live to tell the story of this day,' Pamphilos said with a brave grin as he watched over their captives. 'It will be a good tale and we will be part of it.'

'I'm still not sure why Leontios stayed so long when he could easily have sailed off and not looked back,' Talakh frowned.

'He has his reasons,' Pamphilos said thoughtfully. 'Many things have happened to the captain, and sometimes he resents the gods for this. They took away his wife and son, you see, so how could he not?'

'Still, the men...' Talakh spoke quietly. 'They are glad to follow him, even when he leads them into a fight.'

'They are,' Pamphilos grinned. 'This is the life that many of us dreamt of as boys, to sail the seas under a captain like Leontios who laughs when he faces danger. To follow in the footsteps of our ancestors and have our names remembered around the fireside on winter nights. It is in the nature of my people to be like this you see, to follow men like Leontios.'

'But you Pamphilos, you use your brain first before your brawn. What is your story? How did you come to join the captain at such a young age?'

'Ah,' Pamphilos said, his eyes distant. 'Two summers ago I was fishing with my father close by our island home of Skyros in the Aegean sea far to the north from here. A storm came up and blew us far out to sea... soon our small boat was lost amongst vast waves, each one like a wall of water hanging in the dark sky above us before it crashed down.'

Pamphilos grew silent then as he relived those moments in his mind's eye, but after a while he spoke again, his voice heavy with sadness.

'Our boat quickly filled with water and before we had time even to think of it, she sank away beneath us and we were swept into the churning waves. My father was a small man like me, but brave and thoughtless for himself. I was his only son and my mother had died bringing me into the world. I was all he had...,' the young Greek grew quiet again.

'I am sorry,' was all that Talakh could think to say, as he thought of the murder of his own father, Korkamani.

'The storm drove us apart,' Pamphilos continued his sad story. 'My father was taken high above me on a swell, while I was swept away. As I looked back, the swell fell away from underneath him and then the sea took him under. That was the last I ever saw of him.'

'I lost my father too, when I was a boy,' Talakh said then. 'I know that sadness well.'

'But the gods spared us to live to be men, eh?' Pamphilos said with the brightness of spirit which was never far from him.

'Aye, they did,' Talakh nodded. 'But how did you come to be saved from the seas?'

'I saw one of the oars floating close by and I clung onto that as the storm raged around me,' Pamphilos said, his face pale as he remembered his ordeal. 'It did not float well and so many times the waves pushed me and my friend the oar under, but Poseidon did not want me that day and so I was spared. I was cold and exhausted though, ready to give up hope, when above me great Zeus himself must have reached down to part the storm clouds. I saw a patch of blue sky high above me and quickly it grew until the sun's rays danced again over the sea and the clouds and rain were blown away off into the distance just as quickly as they had come.

'The winds abated, but the seas were still heavy and I resigned myself to die just the same, for I was lost from all sight of land. How long I clung to the oar I do not know, but the darkness closed around me as the sun set. I thought I would go mad then with terrors of the creatures that lurk in the deeps. Perhaps only my fear kept me alive that night under the blazing stars.'

Again Pamphilos grew silent for a while and a hardness came over his face, his knuckles white as they gripped his spear. Talakh waited for him to speak again in his own time.

'Before I lost all hope,' the young Greek said at last, 'I used my belt cord to tie the oar across my chest. In this way, when sleep took me I didn't slip away under the water.

'When I awoke again it was as if I was still in a dream. I was numb with cold, even though the sun had risen again high into the sky again and my mouth was cracked with the sea water that washed over me. It can send you mad you know Talakh?'

'The sea?'

'Yes, take in its waters and they will dry your brain, just as salt dries fish. You go mad first before it finally claims your life. I had swallowed some of it during the night and I started to dream then, though my eyes were wide open. I imagined I saw things, all kinds of strange things,' Pamphilos said, his voice far away again for a moment.

'Then I dreamt that I saw a ship with a piercing eye on its high prow, and a broad white sail. A graceful ship full of dread warriors from long ago, and they bore me up out of the sea and laid me down on its deck. The great eye of the sun fixed me with its glare, but the men put up a shade to keep its rays from me and they told me to sleep.'

'The ship was the Kallisto?'

'Yes, the same, and the captain was Leontios,' Pamphilos

said as the light returned to his eyes. 'The gods had guided him there and it was their will that I joined his crew. That is why I serve him with no thought for myself.'

'But you were just a boy. He would not return you to your home?'

'Without my father, there was no home and no kin of mine to return to. Of course Akakios would have dropped me off on the next inhabited island we came to, but as you have seen he and the captain do not agree on many things,' Pamphilos grinned. 'So after I had told them of the storm and my father's death, Leontios said that though I was still just a boy, the gods had brought me to them for a reason. In spite of Akakios, he said that I would stay until I had had enough of this life of the seas. And so here I am, still here!'

'And the ship is a happier place for it I think,' Talakh smiled.

'I hope so. We are not so different you and I Talakh,' Pamphilos smiled then. 'The gods brought us both to the captain's care, but only they know to what end, eh?'

'Aye,' Talakh nodded. 'But let me ask you this, Pamphilos. Why does Akakios stay with the captain when they never agree?'

'Ah! You noticed that then?' Pamphilos grinned.

'Who could not?'

'Yet for all that they quarrel, they share the same blood. They are cousins you see? This is why they will not seek each other's blood, though the gods know that they fight enough just the same. Akakios is the only real kin that the captain has left you see.'

'Ah,' Talakh nodded.

'When Isek was with us things were better between them. Isek was always ready with a joke and some wise words to make them think before they spoke too hastily.

'But look!' Pamphilos said, readying his spear. 'There! Horsemen are coming!'

The two young men watched as a fast moving cloud of dust came down from a far ridge, and out of it rode a group of three horsemen, while behind ran a band of men clothed against the desert heat, their faces covered against the dust, their spear points glinting in the sun.

'We outnumber them, but not by much,' Pamphilos said as his keen eyes picked out their enemies. 'They have come to fight!'

The men and boys crept forward a little from the darkness of the house, anxious to see what was happening outside.

'Back!' shouted Talakh in the Kemet tongue, as he thrust his spear point at them. 'Back, or the jackals will feed on your corpses!'

It was the most bloodthirsty thing he could think of, but his words were harsh enough to send the frightened captives scuttling back into the shadows.

As Talakh watched, the horsemen slowed to a walk and then stopped to let those on foot catch up. Finally one of the horsemen shouted a challenge.

'Why do you Greeks stay on here in my master's lands?' he called in the Greek tongue, though his words were thick with an accent Talakh had not heard before.

Leontios stepped forward with his hands on his hips, unimpressed by the horseman's boldness.

'What way is that to speak to your master's guests?' he called back cheerfully. 'We have silver in payment for his hospitality, that is all.'

'Then leave your silver and go,' the horseman called back.

'Yes, get back on your ship and be grateful I don't kill you all,' another horsemen called out in the Kemet tongue. His horse was the colour of dark honey, taller than the others, and by his finer clothes he was obviously the leader of these men. 'You Greeks!' he called out mockingly, though he would not or perhaps could not use the Greek tongue. 'I will take all of your silver!'

'You can have it all,' Leontios shouted across the sands in the man's own tongue. 'I will stuff it into your mouth until you choke on it, dog of the desert!'

'Your words are brave, Greek,' the horseman answered, but I have seen how your kind run from the Persians.'

Leontios was silent for a moment, but when he spoke there was a cold rage in his words.

'No man may dispute my honour as you have done,' he said through gritted teeth. 'Get down from your horse and beg for your life in the dirt. Do that and I may let you keep your head.'

What happened next took Talakh by surprise such was the speed of events, even though he knew a fight was now certain. At first the horseman wheeled his horse away as if he might retreat, but then he harshly reined its head round, ramming his knees into the beast's flanks as he slapped his drawn sword across its rump. The horse shot forward its eyes wild with terror, and Leontios threw himself to one side just in time to avoid the scything sword blade that swept down like death toward him.

'Stay here!' Pamphilos shouted and ran off toward the coming battle, shouting his war cry as he hefted his spear onto his shoulder.

The horseman wheeled sharply away from the Greek line, urging his men forward, but the two other horsemen hesitated and this was their undoing. In an instant one of them slumped backwards on his horse, wearing a Greek arrow. The horse bolted forward, carrying the dying man off toward the sea and this was enough for his companion, who wheeled his horse about and galloped off towards the desert. Yet for all this confusion amongst their enemies, Leontios was still in danger as his opponent charged again.

It was then that Hippolytos ran forward, shouting his own battle cry and with both hands gripping the shaft of his great double headed axe, he threw it over his head with all his might.

To Talakh it seemed almost as if the heavy axe hung in the air like a bird as it arced toward the horseman, before hitting him square in the side with such force that he fell heavily to the ground. Yet still he was not dead, for only the blunt top of the axe head had struck him, not one of the blades. Despite this crushing blow and the fall from his horse, somehow the man rolled to his feet again and sprang for his sword which now lay glinting in the dirt. In an instant, he and Leontios warily faced each other as the line of Greeks came forward and the enemy spearmen ran for their lives under a rain of arrows.

With his crewmates forming a ring around Leontios and his foe, Talakh could no longer see what was happening. Though he had his orders, something told him he must go to the fight.

'Stay here!' he ordered his captives. 'If you leave this place, my captain will chase you down and kill you all.'

Though he did not mean them, still his own words made his blood run cold as he ran to join the men of the Kallisto, who were urging their captain on. Looking over the shoulder of Pamphilos, he could see only the horseman's back as he bravely blocked blow after blow from Leontios' own short sword. The horseman's shoulder was slumped, broken either from the axe blow, perhaps from his fall to the ground. With one more slash of his sword, Leontios beat the man back and he fell to the ground with a roar of pain as his injured shoulder jarred against the sun baked dirt.

'Finish him!' cried tall Akakios, as Leontios stamped on the man's wrist with one foot and kicked away his dropped sword with the other.

Yet Leontios was already the victor. Would he take a brave man's life in such a way, when he no longer posed a threat? No, this was not the captain's way. This much Talakhonsu already knew of him.

'You should die as my men say,' Leontios said calmly, fixing the fallen man with his killing eye. 'But you fought well stranger,' he paused, a grim smile crossing his face. 'Swear that you will leave this place and not return. Swear this on your god, who weighs your sins in the afterlife and will feed on your soul if you break your oath. Swear on your Amun too, and I may still show you mercy.'

'You threaten me with my own gods?' the man raged at Leontios in his pain. 'You dare? I spit on your mercy, you Greek pig! May all the gods curse you! May the seas drown you and your ship, every last one of you!

It was then that he did something that none of those gathered were expecting. He laughed. Not the shrill laughter of a madman, but a deep, long laugh that spoke only of hatred.

That was enough for Leontios. To have his ship and his men cursed in such a way was more than he would stand and without another word he raised his sword over his head with both hands, his face taut with rage. The blade hung for a moment, a flash of death in the bright sunlight as Leontios gathered all of his strength for the final blow.

It was only then that Talakhonsu saw the stranger's blood caked face. Only then that he recognised the pain-twisted features of an old enemy, a face that had haunted him all of his life. It was the face of Khaemwaset.

Chapter 2

The Fate of the Evil One

'No, captain!' Talakhonsu shouted. 'Don't kill him!'

The sword of Leontios hung in the air above the bloodied head of Khaemwaset, twitching as if it were alive in the bright sunlight.

'What?' Leontios barked angrily at Talakhonsu, a blind rage in his eyes. 'Why should I not kill this bastard son of a whore? Who are you, boy to tell me this?'

All fell silent now, waiting for the Napatan to explain himself, but when Talakhonsu spoke it was not to Leontios, but to the man who lay beaten in the dust.

'I know you,' he said, his voice shaking. 'You are Khaemwaset. Khaemwaset, the evil one.'

'It is a long time since I have heard that name boy,' the man said. 'The evil one you call me? I like that!'

'Murderer!' Talakh cried. 'You do not remember me, but I know you!'

'Who is this man Talakh?' Leontios asked impatiently. 'What is he to you?'

'He is a murderer,' Talakh repeated with hatred full in his voice. 'A slave taker. Killer of children and old men. Defiler of women. His men slew my mother, but above all of these things he is the coward who murdered my father Korkamani in cold blood. Murdered him whilst he was tied and bound and weak with thirst.

'My father was a brave man,' he spat at Khaemwaset. 'Yet you stuck him with a spear like an animal while he was on his knees. His death was a slow agony, and for that your life belongs to me.'

As Talakhonsu spoke these words, the captain nodded.

'I will give you that,' he said gravely. 'Your words ring of the truth and so your claim on him is greater than mine.'

Talakhonsu took the heavy spear that Pamphilos offered him and held its point at the throat of Khaemwaset, searching the evil one's dark eyes. He must have been in great pain, but underneath the blood and dirt his skin looked smooth and untroubled. He seemed not to have aged one day, and Talakh felt sick now at the thought of how long Korkamani's bones had lain in the earth because of him.

'You remember me?' Talakh said through gritted teeth.

'Why should I remember you?' Khaemwaset sneered. 'I have taken the lives of many men, but your kind? You are less than animals to me and a man does not remember the prey he hunts down.'

Talakhonsu shook with rage as he looked at the laughing face of Khaemwaset and he drew back the spear, steeling himself to thrust it through the murderer's throat.

'Don't give him an easy death Talakh,' the voice of Kleisthenes called to him.

'Kleisthenes is right,' Leontios said, placing his hand on Talakhonsu's shoulder. 'This dog owes you a debt that the simple taking of his life will not satisfy. Added to that he has cursed us all, so it is right that he should die a slow death. A coward's death.'

'Coward? I am no coward!' Khaemwaset spat at Leontios.

'Shut up you,' Leontios said leaning hard with his foot on the evil one's broken shoulder. But though he grunted with pain, still Khaemwaset would not cry out.

'We have his horse,' tall Akakios said. 'We should bind him and let it drag him over the ground until his skin has been flayed from him and his bones are broken!'

'No,' Talakh said firmly. 'All of you are right, he does not deserve an easy death. Pamphilos, I have thought of your story, of the terror that you felt when you were alone on the open seas in the night waiting for the sea to claim you. Of my own fear too when I thought the Kallisto had left me adrift.'

'Then what will you do, Talakh?' Leontios asked grimly.

'I will not do as he did and spear a man I did not beat in a fair fight,' Talakhonsu said with iron in his words. 'I will not murder as he murdered. No, we will take him with us when we sail and when night falls we will cut his bonds and leave him to the sea. His own curse that we be drowned will come back upon him.

'It will be for the sea god Poseidon to decide your fate Khaemwaset, not I,' he spat at the evil one. 'But in the darkness as the waters wait to take you, then you will know fear. When the sea fills your lungs and drags you to the bottom, you will be alone. The beasts of the deep will feed on your body as it rots there until there is no trace left of you, not even your bones. This is my revenge upon you for what you did to my people.'

As Pamphilos explained these words of Kemet to the other men, Khaemwaset remained silent for a moment, but then a smile broke on his face.

'The boy priest!' he said with a gentle laugh. 'The boy priest, yes I remember you now. So! I speared your father on the battle field while the Greeks ran from their Persian enemies! And now the poor little boy will have his revenge on me?' he laughed again.

'I have heard enough of your poisonous tongue,' Leontios growled, kicking Khaemwaset hard in the ribs with the flat of his sandal.

'Strip him of his clothes and bind him,' he turned to Hippolytos. 'Gag him too.'

Hippolytos and Kleon dragged Khaemwaset to his feet, but though he struggled, Hippolytos soon put a stop to that with a fist to the stomach that folded him in half. As they stripped the once noble of Waset of his clothes and his dignity, Leontios turned to Talakh and placed his hand on the young man's shoulder again.

'We will do as you wish Napatan,' he said, his face still dark with anger. 'By tomorrow this man's life will be at an end, but still, though you will have your revenge, it will not bring your father and mother back to you. When the deed is done, you must let the hatred pass from you if you can. Otherwise it will gnaw away at your insides all your life.'

'I know,' Talakh answered as he looked on the evil one with eyes that burned with anger. 'My father will be avenged and that is all that matters.'

'Good,' Leontios nodded. 'Now go and help Pamphilos. The weather looks fair and the sea is calm. We set sail for Kriti before the sun sets.'

As the sun began its slow descent toward the west, Leontios and tall Akakios bade farewell to the village headman and his people, who were pitifully grateful for the removal of Khaemwaset. The evil one's oppression had caused them much harm and they were glad to see him taken away, though they still feared the return of his men. Leontios told them, they now must arm themselves and defend their own interests against men such as these otherwise they would never be free.

In the evening light the Kallisto left the small inlet of Abasis behind them, rowing out to a calm sea. A favourable breeze filled her broad sail, boding well for the voyage ahead. With the wind pushing her along, the men shipped their oars as soon as they were safe away from the coast.

Leontios had Talakh stand next to him at the steering oars, the two of them silently keeping the ship on her course as they contemplated the fate of Khaemwaset who had been thrown into the prow.

'The time has come,' Leontios said quietly as the light started to fade into a golden sunset in the west and the sea took fire.

Talakh stared intently at the bound figure of the evil one. 'Yes, let it end here,' he said coldly.

'Aye,' Leontios said grimly. 'We will do this between us, for of all the men on the Kallisto we two have the most cause.'

The two of them passed forward to the prow and loosed the rope that bound the feet of Khaemwaset.

'Get up you louse!' Leontios aimed a kick at him.

Khaemwaset had been lying in the bottom of the ship for a long while by this time, but stiff and bound though he was, he still struggled as Leontios and Talakh pulled him upright.

'I wonder if he can swim?' Leontios asked Talakh as they

pushed his bare chest against the ship's side.

'I don't know,' Talakh said absently. He had never dared to hope that this moment would ever come, but now that it was here it seemed as if he was in a dream.

'Well, we will know soon enough,' Leontios grunted as he dealt the evil one a sickening blow to the kidneys with his heavy fist.

Khaemwaset's knees gave way as he groaned with pain through the gag.

The captain pulled out his knife and cut the ropes tying their prisoner's wrists. Khaemwaset's broken shoulder slumped down then as he grimaced with pain, his arm useless to him.

'Now!' said Leontios 'Pitch him over the side, but be careful he doesn't try to drag you after him.'

Khaemwaset struggled in spite of his pain, but as the crew watched in solemn silence, the two of them pulled his legs from under him and pitched him over the side with a great splash.

'Man over the board!' Hippolytos cheered, but the rest of the men of the Kallisto said not a word as they leant over the side to see whether the once noble would sink like a stone, or rise back to the surface. It was no easy thing for sailors to watch a man left to drown, enemy or not.

'He is gone,' Leontios said, putting his hand on Talakh's shoulder. 'Your father is avenged.'

Yet as the Kallisto glided onward with the gentle breeze, Talakh saw a head appear between the low swells and a hoarse voice called back to them.

'A curse on you all...,' the evil one called out. 'I will wait for you at the bottom of sea. Before the year is out you will join me there! I call on the gods to drown you all. Cowards! Women! Daughters of swine!'

The curses of Khaemwaset called to them, ever fainter on the breeze and a shiver ran down the spine of Talakhonsu, as it must have done with all aboard the Kallisto.

'So he can swim then, even with a broken arm?' Leontios said trying to lift the mood of his men with a joke. 'Much good it will do him out here.'

Talakh gave a wry grin, but said nothing. He had his revenge over Khaemwaset at last, yet this was no sweet victory. A bitter taste was in Talakh's mouth and his heart was heavy, for now he understood the price that revenge hangs around a good man's neck. In killing his enemy, a part of his innocence also died that day.

-ϕ-

Pelia and Cerian sat in silence on the hewn logs that served for seats outside the hut, Cerian's mood now sombre following the tale of the death of Khaemwaset. Pelia stirred the embers of the small cooking fire, for though it was the last of a fine evening and the sun was only just set, she felt a chill in her bones.

'A terrible way to die, even for one who had so much evil in him,' Pelia broke the silence.

'Yes,' Cerian answered, 'but if a man commits so many evil deeds in his life, then what can he expect when death comes for him? Your father did the right thing, do you not think?'

'It was the only way for him,' Pelia nodded with a heavy sigh. 'He wanted a part in the evil one's death and yet he could not bring himself to plunge in the knife in cold blood.'

'Your father gave him more of a chance than Khaemwaset gave Korkamani. He left it for the fates to decide, and though you and I know that meant certain death, it was a just revenge for the death of his father and mother, and all the others he caused.'

'You're right,' Pelia said with a rueful smile. 'I know it anyway, but still it's good to hear it from someone else.'

'But there must be more to tell about how Khaemwaset came to be in the desert, far from Waset?' Cerian asked. 'How had he escaped from the battle when the Persians attacked? Surely them it must be that he killed Broken Nose?'

'These things we will never know, for my father did not

speak to Khaemwaset on any of these things. In truth I don't think he would have told my father anything anyway, so we can only guess at the fate of Broken Nose.

'Anyway, it will be dark soon enough. I must go and see how little Fionna is.'

Fionna, the youngest daughter of Miraine, had been taken ill with a fever just a few days before, and Pelia had needed to practice her healing powers once again. Now she lay in the small fever hut, where she could be nursed by her mother apart from the other children of the family. For everyone knew how easily the bad spirits which caused such things could leap from child to child.

Earlier that day, Pelia had given the girl a draught made from the bitter bark of the willow tree and now it was time to give her some more in the hope that the vile taste would make the spirit leave, as it often did with those that caused headaches.

'Should I come too?' Cerian asked as Pelia wrapped her cloak around her shoulders.

'No, it will make less fuss if I go alone this time.'

When Pelia returned some time later, she found Cerian asleep in the darkness of the hut, her own cloak wrapped around her so that it covered her dark hair and her graceful features. Thankfully she did not awaken, for the news was not good. Fionna's fever had grown worse and her body burned like the embers of a fire as her mother wept over her. By morning the child would likely have crossed to the world of shadows and another innocent young life would pass away unfulfilled. Pelia felt utterly helpless, as she always did in these times, but she steeled herself with her own mother's wise words.

'Though we can't save all, or even many, still we can help to save some,' her mother would often say, as Pelia had learnt her ways.

Pelia knew that to be the truth, but still her cheeks burned with tears as she lay waiting in the darkness for sleep to come.

The next morning, Pelia awoke early and leaving Cerian to her rest, she went in the small dawn light to the old fever hut where the stricken child lay.

In the gloom within, the shadowy figure of Miraine lay at her daughter's side, though she started awake as Pelia stooped inside through the low doorway.

Pelia placed her hand comfortingly on the older woman's arm, but did not speak. She felt the sick girl's pale white forehead, which shone in the dim light, like the face of a ghost against the darker skin of Pelia's hand. Fionna's forehead was cool, but not cold and her breathing was deep and even. Pelia felt a surge of happiness and hope within her. 'The Mother be praised,' she whispered. 'I think the fever may have broken at last.'

'My little one is safe then?' Miraine asked, bewildered in her tiredness.

'If the bad spirit has left, then we can hope, yes. She is weak and not out of danger yet,' Pelia cautioned, 'but there is at least hope now.'

'Oh, thank you,' Miraine wept with gratitude, as she held Pelia's hand. 'I will not forget what you have done.'

'It is nothing. You must let her sleep for now, then feed her some warm barley broth when she wakes,' Pelia said. 'But no meat until she says she is hungry. And tell me straight away if the fever returns or her breathing becomes harsh.'

'I will,' Miraine nodded. 'I will send word when she wakes. Thank you again for all of your kindness.'

Pelia returned to her own hut again, little Fionna's face in her mind's eye. She was a pretty thing with her pale skin and fair, straight hair, even though she had been born with the cloven lip that often made other people afraid. As these things went, it was not bad, but time would tell if she would ever find a husband. Pelia thought on how harsh the fates could be to give her such fair looks, yet blight them in such a cruel way.

Cerian stirred when Pelia pushed open the leather door flap, hooking it aside to let light flood into the hut.

'How is Fionna?' she asked, rubbing her eyes.

'The fever seems to have broken. She will recover I think,' Pelia allowed herself a smile. 'Though these things are never certain.'

'Goddess be praised, that is such good news!'

'Yes, for now at least she sleeps peacefully. But we will still need to watch her carefully as she recovers her strength. When the body is weakened, other things can easily bring a fresh ill.'

'Ah, but still. Such good news,' Cerian beamed. 'How is the day?'

'Fair. And warm too.'

'Then why don't we go to the forest pools and bathe there?' Cerian said brightly, as she sat up. 'We could air our clothes if the weather stays dry. Maybe even wash them!'

'And wash the smell of the hearth from our hair!' Pelia added with a laugh, before she thought again of the sick girl. 'But we should not be far from Fionna and Miraine though, in case they need us.'

'We will not be long,' Cerian said brightly. 'Fionna will sleep while we are away, but if need be we can return quickly enough.'

Pelia thought for a while. Her conscience said she should stay, but the winter had been long and she yearned to have some fun. Yearned to leave behind the high walls of Llan Huell for a while.

'Oh, why not!' she said. 'Let's see if anyone else will join us.'

Of course most of the women of the village had children to attend to, while others were forbidden by their husbands to go to the forest with Pelia. Still, three of the older girls who were on the edge of womanhood were keen to come, though when chief Heilyn heard of what was planned, his wary nature came to the fore.

'If you are to go at all, then two of the men should go to guard you. But then, which of them would you trust not to look when you bathe?' he asked testily.

'We will sharpen some ash rods for spears, O chief Heilyn,' Pelia said, 'you don't need to spare us your own sworn men.'

Heilyn scowled, for he knew that though Pelia's words were

respectful enough, still she did not like him.

'The forest is a dangerous place,' Heilyn shook his head. 'Many beasts roam there. Some have four legs, but the worst of all have only two.'

Pelia smiled at the young chieftain's wit, despite herself. Though he was a clever enough man, he was not often given over to such things.

'So, Pelia,' he continued smugly, 'while I cannot stop you going your own way, still I will not let you put those other girls in the way of such dangers.'

Pelia was not surprised, for Heilyn was ever a cautious man and he had a deep resentment of her too. Pelia's honey coloured skin spoke of her father's bloodline and the fact that, but for the Napatan's help, his own father Huell would not have become chief. This was a constant wound to his pride.

'Your words are wise, O chief Heilyn,' Pelia said, biting her tongue. 'But we are at peace with our neighbours now and have been a long time, so it would be a waste of time for the men on such a thing. If we cannot bathe without fear in our own forest pools at times like these, when will we ever be free to do so?'

'I have spoken on this,' the chief said firmly. 'You must live with respect for my word and my ways Pelia. If you do not... well then you know what you must do.'

'O chief Heilyn,' Aneurin the hunter stepped forward and spoke, his voice quiet, but firm. 'Your words are indeed just and wise. It would invite danger for our women and girls to linger in the forest with only sharpened stakes for protection. But if Pelia has no objection, I will accompany them with Sealgair. My bow and Sealgair's teeth will protect them if need be. As well as two men could, at any rate.'

Heilyn was irritated by this challenge however respectful it was. And yet as Aneurin had only returned the chief's own wisdom, he could not easily say no.

'Perhaps they would not trust a lone man not to watch them,' he said irritably.

'My chieftain,' Aneurin answered calmly. 'That would be for them to say, but I do know that if I so much as glanced at his mistress while she bathed, Sealgair would tear my throat out.'

The girls laughed at this and Heilyn saw that he would not win this argument, so he laughed too so as not to lose face, though his laughter was bitter as gall.

'I am content to put my trust in Aneurin,' Pelia said, trying not to smile. 'He is my oldest friend.'

'Then do we have your agreement, chief Heilyn?' Aneurin bowed his head so that his eyes would not challenge the chieftain.

'Aye,' Heilyn answered quickly, though his forehead was ploughed by grim furrows of anger. 'But remember this Aneurin. You are responsible for them all, not just Pelia. If a hair on any of their heads is harmed, you will answer for it before all the men of my hall.'

'That is fair, my chieftain,' Aneurin said lifting his head so that his clear green eyes met those of shrewd Heilyn. 'It shall be as you say.'

'Thank you Aneurin,' Pelia said as they walked with the others along the woodland path toward the deeper forest. 'You need not have given up your day for us.'

'Ah, I had nothing much to do anyway,' Aneurin smiled. 'It is the hunter's moon tonight, and tomorrow too, if the sky stays clear. I will take Sealgair out then to see what I can catch.'

His was a gentle smile Pelia thought as she looked up into his face, but always it was tinged with a little sadness too. Aneurin always kept his feelings deep.

'But when will you sleep?' she asked.

'Oh, there will be time for that when we return home. The moon will not rise until late into the night, so I will wake when you are all asleep in your beds.'

'Then we will go to bed later and you must have supper with us before you take Sealgair out,' Pelia offered.

She looked away and smiled, happy in herself at the small victory over chief Heilyn as Cerian and the other girls walked on ahead, waving their makeshift wooden spears at each other in pretence of warriors. It was good for them all to feel so free again.

By and by, the clearings of the nearer woods gave way to the deeper forest, the greening of the trees forming an emerald canopy above them in the keen sunlight. The milder airs of spring finally breathed the land awake now, bringing with them great drifts of fragrant bluebells that could take even a hardened warrior's breath away with their beauty. The birds sang their secret songs high in the trees and Pelia wondered then what it must be like to be in love, as Aneurin the tall, thin hunter strode along quietly by her side.

After a while they came to a place where a forest stream tumbled down a small drop into a deep, calm pool. Pelia's mind instantly leapt back to her childhood, to a time when her mother would sometimes bring her here to bathe. It seemed like only yesterday and she could see her mother's bright face, her golden hair shining in the sun.

'I will wait behind the bank up over there,' Aneurin interrupted her thoughts as they stopped at the top of a rocky track that led down amongst the smooth, moss covered boulders.

'But take Sealgair with you,' he said, addressing them all. 'One of you should keep a keen watch with him in case bear or boar pass this way.'

'Bears?' one of the girls said excitedly.

Aneurin nodded. 'They are hungry after their winter sleep and the smell of the flowers sometimes brings them here. They dig them up to eat their roots you see.'

'I have never seen a bear!' the girl said nervously.

'You should hope never to see one either,' Aneurin said seriously, 'At this time of year they are driven mad by hunger and so they will sometimes attack people.'

'Don't worry, we will be on our guard,' Pelia turned to the hunter. 'Only come if we call you.'

The colour came to Aneurin's cheeks at that.

'Of course,' he said with a bow of his head. 'I will be just over there.'

So, leaving Aneurin behind with his long bow and iron

tipped spear ready by his side, Pelia took up Sealgair's lead and led the others down to the shaded pool that lay hemmed in by dark, fern covered rocks. Pelia unfastened her broach and hung her cloak over an overhanging branch.

'Are you not afraid Aneurin will watch us?' Cerian asked with a giggle. 'You know he likes you.'

'Aneurin? No!' Pelia laughed as she untied her waist cord so that her long tawny dress hung loose from her shoulders and breasts. 'He is not that kind of a man as well you know, and besides he can't see us down here. Even if he did, he would never boast to the other men.'

'How can you know that?' one of the girls giggled. 'He is a man after all.'

'I've known Aneurin, since we were both children,' Pelia answered as she pulled the dress over her head and kicked off her sandals. 'He is a gentle soul, not like those other boars.'

'He still likes you well enough though,' Cerian teased her, as she too stripped naked.

'And another one likes you,' Pelia teased her back.

She dipped her foot in the water and found that it was cold enough to burn the skin. Still, Pelia knew that if she did not go in, then perhaps no-one else would either. She braced herself and then took the plunge, leaping into the dark cold water with her fingers pinching her nose closed.

From his perch above the dale, Aneurin heard a shriek and started upright in an instant, pulling an arrow over his shoulder from the quiver that was slung across his back as he ran for the rocky path. 'Pelia!' he shouted at the top of his voice.

'She's fine,' he heard Cerian call back over the barking of Sealgair. 'It's just the water. It's so cold! But you must go back Aneurin!'

'You are sure?'

'Of course.'

Next it was Cerian's turn and after she had unplaited her hair braids she too jumped in with a gasp. The water was fresh from its journey down from the hills where winter had not long departed and it burned Cerian's skin like fire.

'It's not cold!' she managed to say through chattering teeth to the other girls, who hesitated at the water's edge, while Sealgair padded around them.

At first, he too was reluctant to do more than paddle around the edge until finally he jumped in, showering them all with a great splash.

After much goading, the others jumped in too, adding their own cries to those of Cerian and Pelia. Gwyna, who had the full body of a woman already, started to sing a song. A teasing song for Aneurin to come and swim with them.

'Gwyna!' Pelia scolded her. 'I think the cold goes to your head. 'Aneurin is a grown man, not a boy,' she said as she climbed from the pool and wiped the water from her body with the palms of her hands, her long wet hair now hanging almost straight. 'You should not sing such things to a man. Not until you are old enough to take a husband.'

But though she stopped her singing, Gwyna still hummed the tune to herself mischievously.

Pelia did her best to ignore the girl. After she had wrapped her cloak around herself, she took her under dress to the smooth stones at the edge of the pool to gently wash it.

'You see?' Cerian said as she hung on to the rocks in front of her friend. 'Aneurin has an admirer there and perhaps Gwyna is not the only one. He is a good man, the best hunter there is and he has the respect of the warriors. If you won't claim him, another surely will and perhaps sooner than you think.'

'Ach, Gwyna is too young for a man like Aneurin,' Pelia shook her head, but Cerian was not to be put off.

'You should steal a kiss from him, that is my advice,' she said. 'Then as your lips part, your heart will tell you what you should do.'

'Cerian!' Pelia huffed, her cheeks flushing. 'So now you know the ways of love better than I, do you?'

'Oh, Pelia, will you not even try with him?'

'I don't know. Why should I want to?'

'Why should you not? I won't get out of the water unless you say you will kiss him,' Cerian teased her. 'Do you want me to catch the cold and die?'

'That is a terrible thing to say,' Pelia shook her head. 'I will only kiss him if I want to. Now, don't tempt the fates. Come out of the water before the cold gets into your bones.'

Cerian climbed out of the pool then, her body whiter than any ghost, and Pelia was reminded again how different her own colour was from the others. Perhaps this was why Aneurin liked her, only because she was not the same as the others. She thought of the hunter, waiting patiently high above them, his straight, black hair tied back with a piece of cord, his dark beard cropped close. Soon he would use a small knife he kept for the purpose to shave it off altogether, as he did every so often. Aneurin had a slight drop in his left shoulder this was true, yet though he was not a thick set man, still he was as strong as any and he stood tall. His deep-set eyes were the dark green of the leaves of late summer and they always looked warmly on her, that much she knew. He was a kind man and she felt her heart warm at the thought of him then, wondering what it would be like to hold him close again like they had as children, now that they were both grown up.

'Your eyes are far away,' Cerian said, joining her friend to wash her own under dress.

'It's nothing,' Pelia shrugged. 'I was just thinking how beautiful the day is.'

Darkness fell aboard the Kallisto, but though there was no moon that night, it was not quite the darkness of the desert either, for the faint starlight reflected on the dark swells of the sea. While the breeze carried the ship on her way north to the great island of Kriti, Pamphilos told a story to raise the spirits of the men and to pass the time, there being little else to do. The Greeks liked to remind themselves of their heroes and the glory of past battles, though as the crew all came from different places, they often knew these stories in different ways.

Hippolytos cheered the loudest as Pamphilos told of the feats of Heracles. He had reason to be in good spirits because after all it had been his double headed axe that had knocked Khaemwaset from his horse in the first place and Leontios owed him much for this, perhaps even his life.

As for poor Talakhonsu, he was on his knees with his head hanging over the ship's side.

'The sea sickness,' Leontios nodded, placing a fatherly hand on the Napatan's shoulder. 'Don't be shamed by it. Even we Greeks who are born to the sea suffer sometimes!' he laughed, though Talakh felt so miserable he could see nothing funny in the matter.

'You will get used to it,' Leontios reassured him. 'Now take my cloak and try to rest.'

Talakh mumbled his thanks and wrapped the cloak around himself, huddling down against the ship's rail.

'See you don't puke on it though,' Leontios grinned, 'otherwise it will be you who goes over the side.'

The night air was colder than any that Talakhonsu had known, colder even than the desert nights of his own lands, so the cloak was a great comfort to the Napatan, since his own was not much more than a thin and threadbare rag. Yet though his stomach settled a little, and though he was weary beyond words his mind would not let him find sleep, filled as it was with the bitterness of his revenge against Khaemwaset. He thought of the girl Ketet, trying again to picture her face. He thought of Isek too. Talakh missed him greatly and could well imagine how Leontios must feel at the absence of his old friend.

When finally Pamphilos had finished telling his stories, he came and found Talakh in the darkness. It seemed already from the short time they had known one another that they were to become firm friends.

'How do you feel?' he asked.

'I have felt better,' Talakh managed a smile.

'There is no moon tonight,' Pamphilos said. 'When the dawn comes you can fix your eyes on the horizon, and that will help to steady you. Even then, many get sick until they are used to the sea. You were fine earlier, so you are halfway there!' he laughed.

'I hope so,' Talakh said, feeling a little better at that thought. He had not felt like talking, but it took away the darkness in his heart a little.

'Tell me Pamphilos,' he asked in his broken Greek, 'how does the captain know which stars to follow for Kriti?'

'Well, the gods placed our heroes amongst the stars to lead our way. When the sun sets, they rise up into the sky to set their fires ablaze. Up there is mighty Heracles, who is the greatest hero of them all. And there is the most important star for we sailors,' Pamphilos pointed. 'The North Star. You see it?

Talakh nodded, making a careful note of its place in the roof of the night sky.

'It is not the brightest of them,' Pamphilos continued, 'but it is our guiding light, the sailor's star. It is the only one that never moves, no matter what time of the year it is, so if you are facing toward it then you are facing north, always.

'So you see, as the captain knows that Kriti is northwest from Abasis, he can work out our heading from the North Star. That is, as long as the skies remain clear.'

'I will remember it well.'

'Aye, but besides that there is much to navigation that only time will teach you,' Pamphilos said. 'The captain knows that the currents and winds can push us off course, so even though Kriti is a very large island, it would be easy enough for us to sail right past it if our course is not true.'

'And what then?' Talakh asked with a worried look, his stomach churning again.

'The ship would reach land eventually, but long before then thirst and hunger would set in. Have no fear though Talakh, Leontios is rarely wrong. Now I will leave you to your sleep. It has been a hard day for you.'

Talakh nodded and closed his eyes, but when sleep did finally come to him it was fitful. From that night on, whenever the wind sighed and moaned around the ship a certain way, he would often imagine he could hear the voice of Khaemwaset, calling out his curses upon them all.

When dawn broke on his first morning aboard the Kallisto, Talakh was already awake, as were most of those aboard. The ship had few enough comforts to help a man find his rest, that much was true.

But for the Napatan, at least his sea sickness had faded at last and after eating a little bread and fish, he rowed with the others, glad to feel the warmth of the sun on his back. The men had no need for Leontios to tell them to put their backs into it, anxious as they were to cross the open seas as quickly as possible. For they knew that, though the wind followed them and the skies were clear, still the weather can change quickly upon the open seas. This was perhaps the biggest lesson of life at sea for Talakhonsu, since in both Napata and Kemet the weather changed little and the skies were clear and sunny almost without fail. At sea, he was to find that storm clouds could billow up all too quickly to hide the sun in their dark menace.

The time came for Talakh to leave the oar benches and take his turn at the steering oars and, still not feeling himself, he was glad of that. With the wind on his back, the warm sun on his face and the dark blue sea all around him, life was good again! Ahead lay unknown lands and adventures to be had, things that one day he hoped to tell Ketet as they walked together in the shade of the palm trees in Isek's village. Just then a fish bigger than any Talakh had seen before shook him from his thoughts as it leapt from the sea at the Kallisto's bow wave.

'What was that?' he asked Hippolytos, who had taken the other steering oar while Leontios and tall Akakios rowed with the men.

'A dolphin!' Hippolytos grinned broadly as more of the sleek creatures appeared and rode alongside the Kallisto, their shining backs curving up out of the water.

'Ah, I have heard of them. But why do they come so close? Do they want to be caught?'

'Caught?' Hippolytos scowled. 'They are the messengers of the sea god boy! Only a fool would do harm to a dolphin. It would bring terrible luck on us all'

'I am sorry Hippolytos,' Talakh said hastily, 'I meant no harm. I have not seen a dolphin before. They seem to fly half in the water and half out. Are they a fish then?'

'A fish? No! Have you ever seen a fish breathe the air like us?' he gestured, not sure if the Napatan understood his gestures.

'Breathe air? No,' Talakh said, though in truth he had sometimes seen them come up and gulp air in the shallows of the Great River.

'The dolphin is a wondrous creature!' Hippolytos said and as if to prove him right, one of them leapt clean out of the water ahead of the Kallisto's prow. 'See there! He blows air out the top of his head. Go forward and see!' he beamed. 'I will keep the oars straight.'

So Talakh edged forward between the banks of oarsmen and climbed into the high prow so that he could look down on the dolphins.

'Today is a good day Talakh!' the voice of Leontios called from behind him.

'Aye captain,' he called back.

'The dolphins lead us on our way to Kriti,' Leontios shouted again above the stiff breeze. 'All will be well for the voyage!'

Talakh smiled to himself and leant over the side. The dolphins at times came so close that he might almost have reached out and touched them, yet he dared not try for risk of angering the sea god. The creatures swam over and underneath each other, now and again cresting the water so that he could see the blow hole that Hippolytos had spoken of. Their dark eyes watched him as he watched them.

'They are friends to we sailors,' Leontios said as he shipped his oar and came up to the prow. 'They will push a drowning man back up to the surface if Poseidon wills it, for they do whatever he bids them.'

Talakh nodded, but these last words troubled him. What if

the dolphins had been bidden to save Khaemwaset?

Leontios guessed what had crossed the young man's troubled mind.

'Don't worry, they would not have helped that wretched son of a dog we pitched over the side, that much I'm sure of. Put it from your mind now and go to the oars,' he said clapping Talakh on the back. 'A spell of rowing will cure any man of his worries.'

This time Talakh sat at the head of the men, next to Kleon and when the captain gave the word, it was they who gave the call to start rowing again, setting the stroke with one of the familiar chants Talakh had learnt from his crewmates. Rowing gave the men purpose, stopped them from quarrelling and kept the strength in their muscles for the days when they must fight against the stormy seas.

So the Kallisto and her crew passed the rest of that day and two more besides as they crossed the seas to the land of Kriti. Talakh was sick no more by day or by night and he thanked mighty Poseidon for this blessing on him. But when the sun rose into a clear sky on their fifth day at sea, the mood of Leontios grew dark, despite the calm seas and following winds that still helped them on their way.

'We will not be long now before land is sighted,' Kleon said to Talakh as they sat across from each other at the oars. 'The captain always gets like this at the end of a long voyage. He starts to doubt himself I think, but he is rarely wrong in these things. Mark my words, we will see the mountains of Kriti before noon.'

Leontios rested the men and called on Pamphilos to climb the wooden pegs to the top of the mast so that he could see further with his sharp eyes, but after he had been up there a short while, the captain called him back down.

'We can see the horizon without climbing the mast,' Talakhonsu said to Kleon, 'and there are no mountains on it. Can Pamphilos see further from up there?'

Kleon frowned in surprise. 'Well, of course!' he said shaking his head. 'The mountains are beyond the horizon, so you have to climb the mast to see them. You understand?'

'I'm not sure,' Talakh puzzled, wishing he had not asked the question.

'Isek was a clever man,' Kleon said. 'He explained it to me like this, you see. Though it seems flat enough, the earth is like a great round shield, a little higher in the middle and curving away gently to its edges, around which the great Ocean flows.'

Now he made a curve out of his hand to show Talakh what he meant.

'You see, if the Kallisto is here on the back of my hand, and the mountains of Kriti are here on the tips of my fingers, then if our mast were tall enough, we would be able to see them over my knuckles, would we not?'

'Ah, I see now,' Talakh said, though in truth he was only partly convinced. For if the earth was like a great curved shield, then how was it that the waters of the sea did not run off its edges?

The Kallisto sailed onwards, as Talakh pondered these things, while the captain grew evermore restless and impatient as time passed. Poor Pamphilos climbed up and down the mast pegs so many times that, light as he was, even he grew weary of it.

'Talakhonsu!' Leontios called out. 'You must have a good eye with that throwing stick of yours. Go aloft and keep look out.'

Talakh remembered how keen were the eyes of Meketra, the Kemet warrior he had known as a boy, and he knew that his own eyes were not so good. Yet he did not want to disappoint his captain, and so he climbed hand over hand up the mast pegs, trying to match the grace of Pamphilos, though it was not as easy as it looked. The mast swung about with every pitch of the Kallisto's hull as she rode the gentle swells, forcing him to grip it with his knees as well as his hands. He had climbed palm trees before that were taller still, but to climb the Kallisto's smooth mast as it swayed to and fro and the seas heaved about, this was a test indeed. Just below the mast top there were two bigger pegs, one on each side and Talakh felt the mast bend a little as he heaved himself up and settled his feet on these, holding on grimly.

'What do you see?' Leontios called up to him.

Talakh looked from left to right and back again, shielding his eyes from the bright sun with one hand as he clung on for his life, not daring to think what would happen if he fell. 'Nothing!' he called back. 'No wait... a sail! I see another sail!'

'On what quarter?'

'Ahead, over to my left a little!' Talakh called back, pointing with his arm. 'It is a long way off captain. I cannot tell if it comes toward us or heads away.'

'Then we will head for her. Akakios!' Leontios cried. 'Bring us round to follow Talakh's arm. This ship will either be heading to Kriti or coming away from it, I'll stake my fortune on that. Kriti lies that way!'

With the wind still favouring her and the crew rowing steadily, the Kallisto brought Talakh's eye closer to the sail and then what at first he had thought were dark clouds on the horizon showed themselves to be mountains. The mountains of Kriti!

'Land captain! I see land!' Talakh called out.

'I knew it!' Leontios cried above the cheers of the crew. 'We'll sleep ashore tonight, the gods be praised!'

Talakh stayed aloft, though his arms and legs were starting to ache, until at last tall Akakios called out from the steering deck that he too could see the mountains low on the horizon. Soon they could all see the sail too and it was plain that the other ship was also heading for Kriti.

'We will follow her,' Leontios said, clapping Talakh on the back as the tall Napatan returned to the deck, his long legs quivering from his efforts. 'At this time of the afternoon, she will be making for a safe haven to beach for the night.'

For once though, the judgement of Leontios was not quite right, and as afternoon wore into evening, they had gained little on the other sail. Still there was no safe beach or settlement in view as they passed a large barren island just off Kriti, and ran northeast along the coast.

'We will anchor off the shore,' Leontios said, disappointment in his voice.

'Aye Leontios,' tall Akakios said, 'Better one more night on the Kallisto, if it means we can bring her safely in tomorrow.'

The Kallisto furled her sail now and the crew rowed on until they came in the failing light to a wide, rocky bay with high cliffs that sheltered them from the wind. There they dropped two great anchor stones, which took the sweat of two men to heave over the side, and these they tied at her prow.

'Ah Kriti, home of my ancestors,' Hippolytos grinned. I cannot wait until the dawn!' he said, taking off his sandals and tunic so that he stood naked as the day he was born, only much hairier.

'Talakh, Pamphilos,' Leontios called the two young men over to him. 'Go with Hippolytos and make sure no harm comes to him,' he said with a wink. 'He swims not so well these days.'

So as Hippolytos jumped off the Kallisto's side rail with a great splash and a cheer from the others, so Talakh and Pamphilos also stripped down and dived over the side, soon catching him up as he laboured through the lapping waves. It was not long before the three of them waded ashore and Talakh planted his feet on the shores of this strange land for the first time. Though he had travelled far along the Great River, from his home in Napata to the edge of the sea, this was another world again and he knew that all that was familiar would be left behind him here.

'Ah, it is good to be home!' Hippolytos grinned broadly, as he sunk to his knees and filled his fists with the rough sand. 'Soon we will be in Itanos and then I will hold my wife and my children in my arms again. Ah, life is good!' he laughed heartily. 'You have heard of Itanos, Talakh?'

'Yes Hippolytos, Isek told me of it often. A great port, so he said,'

'Aye, a beautiful sight is it not Pamphilos? Ah, but all of this we will see only tomorrow! You two should head back to the ship now, or you'll miss your supper.'

'But what of you Hippolytos? Will you not come back with us?' said Pamphilos.

In a while lad,' Hippolytos said contentedly. 'I will rest here for a bit and look at the stars as they brighten. You go on ahead and I will follow.'

The dark sea had grown calm now, for the tide was ebbing and it was easy enough for Talakh and Pamphilos to swim back toward the dark shape of the Kallisto, marked out as she was with a torch to guide their way. Talakh turned onto his back and kicked his feet while he looked up at the stars as they started to appear overhead. Tonight Poseidon rested easy and the seas were so calm and peaceful he felt he could swim forever, all the way back to Kemet if he had a mind to. Soon enough though they came to the ship, whose dark prow eyes watched them as they hauled themselves up the anchor ropes, a race that the lighter Pamphilos won easily.

'Where is Hippolytos?' Leontios asked.

'He wanted to be on his own awhile I think,' Pamphilos answered him. 'It is not far, captain. We will keep a look out for when he starts back.'

'Be sure that you do,' Leontios growled. 'I value all my men, but him I value more than most.'

The moon rose behind the dark cliffs as Talakh and Pamphilos ate their bread, watching for Hippolytos. When at last he made his return, they could see him easily enough as his rough strokes rippled the silvery water.

'Put out an oar,' Hippolytos puffed as he drew close.

Pamphilos ran the oar out, while Talakh added his weight to it as Hippolytos reached out and grabbed the oar blade. Between the oar and a rope that was hung over the side, the burly Kretan scrambled breathlessly over the ship's rail.

'Poseidon's spies!' Hippolytos cursed. 'Those things make my skin crawl, swimming around a man's feet!'

Talakh looked over the side as he helped Hippolytos up. Just below the surface, strange forms glided about, the moon catching their large, silvery eyes. The sleek bodies of these mysterious creatures seemed almost to glow in the darkness.

'What are they?' he said, recoiling in fright, for though the creatures were only half a spear length, they had a great many writhing arms that coiled around themselves and then shot out like striking snakes to grab at each other.

'Don't worry yourself Talakh,' Pamphilos laughed. 'They're only squid. They are harmless to us.'

'Harmless they may be, but still I wish they would take themselves off somewhere else!' Hippolytos grumbled as he pulled his tunic over his head and stomped off to talk with the captain.

Talakh stared over the side again, straining his eyes to see more of the squid. 'Are they the spies of Poseidon as Hippolytos says?'

'Who can say?' Pamphilos shrugged his shoulders. 'All the creatures of the sea live in Poseidon's realm, so perhaps Hippolytos is right about them. Anyway, when the sea is calm and the moon is bright like tonight, they come up from the deep in swarms, like bees. They like the light of our torch too. Now watch and I'll show you how I used to catch them with my father when I was a boy.'

Talakh looked on while his friend sought out his spear and dangled it over the side. Suddenly the shoal of squid became restless as the bright iron glinted in the dark sea, their many arms tugging at the spear head. Pamphilos pulled the spear back up with two of the creatures still holding on to it, but though one quickly dropped back into the sea with a splash, the other would not let go, even when it was hauled aboard. Talakh shuddered at the sight of the slimy creature as it spat out some black liquid that stained the wooden spear shaft.

'If we were going ashore I would kill it and roast it over a fire to eat, but this one is lucky. I will let it go,' Pamphilos grinned.

Yet as much as the young Skyrian tried to shake lose the creature, it would not loose its grip until he had stunned it by banging the spear against the side of the ship. Even then Pamphilos had to prize its arms loose. Talakh watched as it flopped back into the sea and sank out of sight followed by the rest of the shoal.

'Where do they go to now?' he asked as he stared into the dark water.

'Back down to the depths out of the reach of any man,' Pamphilos said. 'In Kriti I sometimes hold my breath and swim down amongst the rocks looking for them, but I have only ever seen octopus and fish there.'

'Octopus?' said Talakh repeating the strange word.

'Yes, they have eight arms attached to their heads, much longer than those of the squid. It is for this that they are named. They're good to eat too.'

Pamphilos told Talakh more of the octopus and a great many other strange creatures of the sea as the two talked late into the night, sometimes in the Kemet and sometimes in the Greek tongue.

The next morning, tall Akakios roused the men early, though in truth most were already awake, stretching their stiff limbs after spending another night in the cramped hull of the ship.

After they'd hauled in the heavy anchor stones with much grumbling and cursing, the men took some dry bread and water before they set to rowing, as the wind was not favourable. Leontios took his turn at the oar benches again and led his men in their chanting as they proudly rounded the lonely coast of Kriti until at last they saw a shepherd boy who called and waved to them from the cliff top. All the crew were happy now, for even if Kriti was not home to them all, it was close enough for them after the voyage into the heart of Kemet.

The cliffs dropped away to gentler slopes and as he rowed alongside Pamphilos, Talakh had his first view of the island's vast interior with its rugged hills and the mountains beyond. The Kallisto pulled around a headland to find a coast of gently curving beaches and shallow bays, where the deep blue of the sea gave way to a brilliant blue-green. Here were scattered settlements and many small fishing boats that hailed them as the Kallisto drove her high prow on through the rolling waves.

'Over there is Roussolakos,' Pamphilos gestured with his head to a large settlement of stone houses that gathered about a sheltered, sandy cove. 'This is where the captain beaches the Kallisto every winter,' he continued, 'and where he has his home too. You will get to know it well Talakh when you stay with us.'

'Why do we pass it by?' Talakh grunted as his oar blade broke through the top of a swell.

'Ah, for now we have cargo to trade, so we head further along the coast to Itanos, a much bigger place.'

By the time they came to the great port of Itanos in its sheltered bay amongst the low hills, Talakh had seen at least a little of the character of this strange island of Kriti. Yes the land had a rugged wildness to it, but still the hand of man could be seen in the narrow ledges etched into the hillsides where small trees gave shade to the farmers as they tended their crops. Further inland were a range of mountains taller than any he had seen in his young life, their outlines fading as they marched into the distance. Here perhaps was a place to forget the troubles of his past life at last.

'So many ships!' Talakh thought aloud, as the Kallisto rowed toward the wide harbour. And indeed there were, some bigger yet than the Kallisto.

'War galleys,' Pamphilos pointed to a line of three ships that were moored side by side on their left. 'See their rams?'

'Aye,' Talakh nodded. He had heard how the Greeks used such prow rams in battle, to hole the ships of their enemies so that they quickly sank.

'They are the ships of Hermokrates, a great chieftain who rules here.'

'Who does he fight?' Talakh asked.

'Because he has ships and men, he does not need to fight anyone,' Pamphilos grunted as he pulled on the oar. 'The pirates and raiders find easier meat elsewhere, as long as Hermokrates' ships guard these waters. That way the trade comes to his port and he grows richer still.'

'Itanos is his?'

'There are many people in Itanos, many clans, many traders,' Pamphilos said between oar strokes. 'But all the ships trading here must pay him a tax in silver coin. So yes it is his in all but name.'

'Then why does the captain not take his cargo somewhere else to trade?'

Pamphilos laughed at that. 'You are always full of questions Talakh!'

Leontios, who had overheard the two young men talking as he returned to the steering deck, answered for himself.

'Because Itanos is the safest port in these parts,' he said clapping Talakh on the shoulder. 'Here are the richest traders, secure under the protection of Hermokrates, and so here is where I will get the best price of silver for my cargo. For that, it is worth my while to pay Hermokrates his tax, just as a shepherd throws meat to his dog. The teeth of Hermokrates watch the flock and keep the wolves at bay.'

At the order of Leontios, the Kallisto shipped her oars and coasted toward the low wooden quay that was built out alongside a headland. Still there was no space for them alongside, so instead they moored her abreast of some smaller boats. In this way, as the crew tied fast her prow and stern, there were two boats separating her from dry land. This did not seem to bother Leontios at all, and he and tall Akakios climbed over the Kallisto's side, using these other vessels to cross to the quay.

'The captain has ordered that we stay here and guard the cargo,' Kleon said to Talakh and Pamphilos, while Hippolytos and the others followed their captain over the boats.

And so, with nothing much to do and the grumble of hunger in their bellies, the three of them sat under the hot sun and talked about what the days ahead might hold. While they sat, Talakh cast his eyes about the port to form a view of it.

Strong, stone built storehouses lined the left side of the harbour nearest the quay where the Kallisto was moored, whilst squat houses separated by narrow streets made up much of the rest of the port. A few of them were whitewashed with flat roofs, not unlike those in the land of Kemet, but most had pitched roofs of thin stone flags laid one over the other. Others still had their doorways painted with bright patterns of sky blue or oxblood red. There were low, craggy hills hemming Itanos in against her harbour and a few houses straggled up toward their slopes, though these were not as big, nor as well tended as those nearer the sea.

Beyond these Talakh could see an earthen bank topped with a stone wall that protected the landward side of the port. A few scattered buildings lay beyond this defence near the summit of the closest hill, but what they were Talakh could not guess at, as they were beyond the strength of his eyes. Such was the lie of the port of Itanos.

It was late in the afternoon by the time Leontios and tall Akakios returned with some of the others, though Hippolytos was not amongst them.

'He has his head stuck in a flagon of wine before he returns to his wife,' tall Akakios said sourly when Kleon asked after him, for Akakios was no drinker himself and he did not like it much in others.

With them came the masters of the two boats the Kallisto was moored alongside. These ones were old friends of Leontios and had agreed to make way for him so that the Kallisto could be berthed against the quayside, the better to offload her cargo and to take on a new one. So the Kallisto threw off her lines and was poled out a little into the bay where she held station with her oars until the other captains had hauled their boats out of the way. At last the Kallisto finally brought her flank against the quayside and the crew could begin to unload her, though this was no light task as to take on a heavy new cargo, they needed to first unload some of the flat ballast stones that sat in her keel.

After much sweating, the stones were at last piled at the back of the quay, where if they were not taken up by another ship, they would be used by the townsfolk in strengthening their walls.

It was almost the evening before Talakh finally set his feet back on dry land. Still though, his work was not done yet.

'Pamphilos!' Leontios called. 'You and Talakh will take the cargo to the storehouse of my good friend Solon over there. You know what to do.'

The small cargo of scented wood and incense Leontios had pointed to was placed in a handcart, together with the captain's small chest of dark wood in which he kept his silver coin and other treasures.

'The captain trusts us well,' Talakh said quietly as the two young men pulled the hand cart along the quay. 'What if someone tries to steal the silver from us?'

'We are safer here, than on the sea,' Pamphilos said cheerfully. 'But still the captain went ashore first to make sure all was well. He has many friends here Talakh, you can be sure of that. All in Itanos know Leontios and the Kallisto.'

But as the two young men pulled the cart along, Talakh felt his legs wobble and quake underneath him. 'I think I am getting sick, Pamphilos,' he said with a worried frown.

'Sick? Are you sure? You look alright to me.'

'My legs won't walk straight. It's as if they have a mind of their own.'

Pamphilos laughed heartily at this. 'Don't trouble yourself Talakh, it's just your sea legs.'

'Sea legs?'

'Aye,' Pamphilos grinned. 'As the sea moves the Kallisto up and down, and side to side, so your legs push one way and then another to keep you upright. When you come back to the land, your legs still try to wander about under you.'

'But will it pass?'

'Maybe,' Pamphilos said seriously. 'No! I joke with you, it will go soon enough. Now, here is Solon. He will store the cargo for us until it is sold.'

'The silver too?'

'Aye. It is too heavy for Leontios to carry everywhere. It will be safely barred inside Solon's storehouse, until the captain exchanges it for more cargo.'

'Young Pamphilos!' the man Solon greeted them, his small

stature and wiry hair reminding Talakh of his old friend Isek.

'Still you have not filled out then, eh? Who is your dark skinned friend?'

'He is called Talakhonsu, a Napatan from Ethiopia.'

'Ethiopia?' Talakh said, puzzled by the word. 'I have not heard of that name before.'

'Ah! It is the name we Greeks know your land by,' Solon smiled. 'Now, come inside and have a little wine with me while we count the captain's silver.'

And so between them they carried the cargo up the stone steps at the side of Solon's storehouse to the small door that opened onto the upper floor. Inside was a simple enough dwelling with a raised sleeping platform at one end, a low table, and some small stools to sit on. A woman, long past the beauty of her youth, stood up as they entered and bowed her head in greeting to them.

'My wife Hermea,' Solon introduced her. 'You know Pamphilos of course. And this is his young friend, Talakhonsu,' he added, struggling with the strange name.

The woman gave a slight nod, but said nothing.

'She is mute,' Pamphilos whispered to Talakh, so that she would not hear, as Solon lit a small clay lamp and led them down a flight of stone steps that descended to the lower floor, where he had his store.

In the dim light of the lamp, Talakh could make out the strong bars girt with iron that held the heavy doors fast against attack or robbery. They stacked the cargo in one corner, for it was not much, and then climbed the stairs again to where they had left the chest of silver. It was bound with cord and Leontios' own knot by way of a seal. Pamphilos cut the cord with his knife, satisfied that it had not been tampered with since the captain had placed the chest in their care, and then emptied it out onto a piece of cloth which Solon had placed on the table.

There was more silver than Talakh had ever seen, some in coin of different sizes, some in small bars that shone brightly in the shaft of light from a narrow window slit set high in the wall.

The hoard was from many places, as Pamphilos explained. Silver from Sikelia, the great island of the smoking mountain far to the west. Silver also from the mainlands far to the north, where the Greeks had discovered it in mines deep under the ground. Pamphilos sorted the coin and bars into piles of their like, counting these in turn into stacks of ten at a time. Then when all was done, Talakh watched in awe as his friend then counted each of the stacks into one total, a large weight of silver.

'You are agreed?' he asked Solon.

'Ah, you have a quick mind,' Solon smiled. 'And your numbers are the equal of mine. We are agreed at that, you can tell Leontios. His treasure will be safe here until he calls for it again, less of course my usual small fee.'

So Talakh came to know better the ways of trading amongst the Greek peoples, and how a man's wealth was counted not in head of cattle as it often was in Napata, but in silver and gold.

That night he and Pamphilos were put up at the favour of Leontios in the house of an old widow, who made her living from lodging and feeding sailors. The rest of the crew stayed with their friends and kinfolk.

The old woman's snores woke Talakhonsu early the next morning and as he came to, he found himself confused for a moment. The very ground beneath him seemed to swell up and down as if he were still aboard the Kallisto, even though he knew he was not. The spell of the sea was on him now, something that never truly leaves a sailor so they say, no matter that he may spend many years ashore. And now Talakh learned another side of the sailor's life.

'What will we do today?' he asked Pamphilos as they ate the fresh cakes the old woman had baked for them, a welcome change from the dry bread they had taken to sea.

Pamphilos gave a puzzled look.

'Do?' he said. 'We can look around Itanos, though that will not take long'

'Will we go back to sea soon do you think?'

Pamphilos laughed at that.

'You are keener than the rest of us Talakh, but you must remember that we were aboard the Kallisto a great many days before you joined us, so we are all glad of the rest.'

'Yes,' Talakh nodded, feeling foolish for his words.

'Besides, the captain and Akakios will take their time in getting the best price for our new cargo.'

'What will we take do you think? And where will we go?'

'Ah, there is always wine and fine oil for Kemet. Much wine is shipped there from Kypros, but though the Persians have long held that island, still in Kemet they are fond of the wine from Kriti too.'

'But the Persians are your old enemies?'

'They are, true enough. Yours as well if you think yourself a free man now. You see, the Persians are the enemies of all that do not kneel to their king,' Pamphilos said with a quite anger in his voice. 'They can never be content with what they have, for each new king tries to outstrip the last in his achievements.'

'But you trade with them all the same?' Talakh pursued his point.

'We Greeks have always traded in the land of Kemet, since long before the Persians came, so why should we not trade there now?' Pamphilos said testily. 'We will never kneel to them, never. When they came to our northern lands to do battle, we beat them on the plains of Marathon and the world saw then that their old king Darius was not so great. We sent him back to his own lands in defeat.'

Talakh saw then that though he was gentle in many of his ways, Pamphilos still had the pride of his people about him. If the Persians came again, he would not be the last to join the fight.

'Then what of king Xerxes?' he asked as Pamphilos pulled on his sandals. 'He took back Kemet when the nobles rebelled against him. Will he not bring his armies to your northern lands as his father did?'

'Yes, Xerxes will be hungry for revenge,' Pamphilos accepted, his eyes keen. 'He will come in the end, I am sure of it, but we will defeat him just as we defeated his father.'

-φ-

The more commonly used paths around the settlement of Llan Huell were sticky with mud from the recent heavy rain, whilst the gales that had brought the storms had torn a clump of thatch from the roof of Pelia's hut. But still it was spring all the same in the land of Albion and Pelia was glad of it. She and Cerian fixed the roof in the bright clear sunshine, spreading some of the old reed a little and patching over it with young willow shoots, bracken and turves. When the autumn came, there would be reeds enough off in the marshes to do the job properly.

'And when the Kallisto left Kriti again,' Cerian asked Pelia as they worked, 'where did she go then?'

'They sailed a new cargo of wine and oil back to Kemet, and then returned to Kriti, this time with a store of Kemet grain. You see, the harvest of Kemet always comes earlier by far than that of Kriti.'

'Did they go to the home of Isek? Did Talakhonsu see his Kemet girl again?' Cerian asked eagerly. Love had come into her own heart and now she always looked for it in the lives of others.

'No, no,' Pelia shook her head. 'The village of Isek lay away from the trade routes and so was out of the Kallisto's path, unless Leontios had chosen to go there to see his old friend. So, it was as Isek had said for my father and Ketet. I'm sure he would have thought of her often, but he knew it was unlikely he would see her for a long time.'

'The days must have passed by so slowly for him,' Cerian sighed, turning on her back to gaze up at the white clouds as they coasted along in the sky.

'All the more so for the girl Ketet I think,' Pelia smiled wryly as she too lay down on the roof and closed her eyes to the sun.

'As you can imagine, every day must have been a new adventure for my father on the open seas, and he had the friendship of his crewmates to take his mind off such things. They would always have been doing something or other. Even when they were ashore, Leontios had them all practice their fighting skills.'

'Did they fight the Persians in the end?' Cerian asked, sitting up in her excitement.

'We will come to that in good time. For now, the Kallisto plied her trade to and from Kemet until the heat of the summer gave way to autumn, and the first of the winter storms began to trouble the seas. Then came the time for Leontios to beach his ship until spring, at this place in Kriti called Roussolakos where he had his home. His men went back to their homes and their wives, but he kept my father and Pamphilos by him. They had no family of their own, so where else were they to go?'

'What did they do then?'

Pelia smiled to herself. Cerian had the questioning mind of the young, always wanting to know more.

'Well,' she said, 'while the winter storms of Kriti are not as cold or wild as they are in our land, still it is too dangerous to venture a ship out onto the open seas.

'So they helped Leontios to make good the Kallisto while she was hauled up out of the water. Leontios did this each year to stop up any leaks between her planks so that she was kept watertight. They scrapped the moss and sea shells from her hull too, so that she would ride the sea swiftly the next year.

'Then they laid down her tall mast in the shelter of her hull and put her ropes in a dry storeroom to keep them out of the weather, but her sail they put to good use in covering over the Kallisto to stop the rain water sitting in her bottom. As for the oars, these they stored in the bottom of the ship, oiling them well to stop them cracking as the blades dried out.

'After all these things were done, they were at their ease for a while and Leontios took them hunting in the hills for wild boar.'

'Wild boar?'

'Yes, many of the animals on the isle of Kriti are the same ones we know here. But my father, he was a strange sight to the people of Roussolakos. Even so he learned their tongue well and so despite his dark skin and his unusual height, slowly most folk came to accept him and smile and greet him when they saw him coming along.

'By day, when the weather was calm enough, Talakhonsu and Pamphilos would take out a small boat to cast nets for fish, though they never went out far. And in the dark of the winter evenings Leontios would sit with them and tell of his adventures on the seas.'

'What stories did Leontios tell of?' Cerian asked, sitting up on her elbows.

'There is only one that I know from my mother and it is this. One day, when Leontios was a young man sailing with another captain, he had been on an island of the Greeks far off to the north. The morning dawned fair and yet his captain would not put to sea.'

'There were omens?' Cerian asked. 'Signs?'

'None that Leontios could see,' Pelia frowned, 'but then, like you, the young Leontios was impatient. He could not see why his captain hesitated, and the man would say nothing to his crew other than that he was uneasy and that they would not put out to sea that day. He was an old man and though they did not say it, some amongst the crew thought that perhaps he had grown too old for the sea. And so they sat idly playing at bones and dice in the fine morning sunshine, bored and restless.'

'And then?'

'Well,' Pelia continued. 'As the sun reached its highest into the sky, a faint ring the colour of the rainbow appeared around it and the sky grew a little hazy. Some of the younger men thought this to be a good omen, but the captain and those who had more years said not. They knew that rain was on its way you see?

'Sure enough, as the afternoon wore on, great towering clouds rolled toward them from the north, darkening the sky as the gathering wind started to blow hard. The men were all for seeking shelter, as it seemed that this was to be a great thunderstorm and they all feared the bolts of lightning that their thunder god, mighty Zeus, was sure to hurl from on high.

'The old captain would have none of this and told them to stand their ground, though some of them cowered in their fright. It was then that Leontios saw something with his own young eyes, the thought of which would send a chill down his spine for ever after. Out at sea the black clouds grew ragged and hung low as they were whipped by the rising wind. Suddenly in their rage the clouds dipped down to the sea and drew up a thin stream of water, taking it high up into the darkened sky!'

Cerian covered her eyes now with her hands at the thought of what Pelia had said, not wishing to anger the gods of the sky with her stare.

'So,' Pelia continued, a tremor in her voice, 'the stream moved slowly across the water, widening into a great spout that even drew up shoals of fish from the depths, so they found afterwards. To their horror those on the shore could do nothing but watch as it bore down on a small fishing boat. When the spout had passed, the boat had gone. The old captain said that Zeus had sucked it up into his mouth, as he did such things when he grew annoyed with the vain pride of men.'

Cerian shuddered at the thought. 'What became of the fishing boat?'

'Nobody knows,' Pelia shook her head sadly, 'But you can be sure that the fishermen who were on it were never returned to their kin, alive or dead.'

'That is a horrible story!' Cerian shuddered again. 'I'd rather hear no more of those.'

'Well, you did ask,' Pelia said with a wry grin. 'Alright, while the sun still warms us a little, I will continue the story of Talakhonsu and his time aboard the Kallisto if you are still happy to listen? Well then, it is now my father's first winter in Kriti. His first winter at all really, as all his life he had never known true cold.'

'Was there snow in Kriti then?' Cerian asked as she lay back again, her eyes closed to the bright sun. 'Was it as cold as our winter?'

'Yes, at least in the high mountains of Kriti, the frosts would come and sometimes snow would follow them, though never as far as the coast. Still, even by the sea it was almost too cold for my father to bear at first. He spent some of the silver that Isek had given him on a thick woollen cloak that kept him warm by day and by night, as he and Pamphilos slept in the small stone built house of Leontios. He was not used to the weather, nor to the shortening of the days, as in Napata and Waset the length of the day had been much the same all the year round.'

'How strange,' Cerian frowned. 'I wonder why that should be? Is it because their sun god is stronger than ours?'

Pelia laughed at that.

'Your mind will never be dull Cerian,' she said, 'you are always full of questions.'

'Do you not know then?' Cerian asked cheekily.

Pelia shook her head. 'There are many mysteries which we will never know. I can tell you of what my father heard when he was in Kriti though, concerning the winter.

'You see the Greeks have a story about the great island of Sikelia which lies far off in the western seas. I will tell you more of it when the time comes in my father's story, but anyway Sikelia is the place where the earth goddess of the Greeks makes her home. An old woman of Kriti told my father that the winter comes because the goddess pines for her beautiful daughter who lives under the earth with her husband, the god of the underworld.

'With the coming of every spring the daughter returns to her mother for a brief while and so the goddess gives life back to the land in her joy. But then with the coming of the autumn, the daughter must return to her husband under the earth and so the goddess pines for her all over again until the next spring.

'So, finally the spring came to my father on the island of Kriti, his first spring in that place, and it was as welcome to him almost as bread is to a starving man. If I close my eyes Cerian, I can try to see in my mind what he would have seen. The green and blue of the sea, the golden sands of the beach upon which the Kallisto rested her dark hull, waiting for the day she would slip back into the sea again. I can see the fields beyond the beach coming to life again with flowers in the corn, and the distant mountains grow peaceful once more as they lose their stormy caps of cloud.

'Try to imagine these things now and I will tell you of when the crew of Leontios returned to their captain in the spring and of what happened next.'

-ϕ-

Hippolytos came back to Roussolakos with the spring, the first of many happy reunions between captain and crew, though in truth he did not have far to come from his home along the coast. Tall Akakios was soon there too, looking thinner and sterner than ever, so Talakhonsu thought. As for the others, they arrived in their ones and twos as the moon waxed and then waned again, but then they had farther to come from their homes across the fickle seas. By the time of the next new moon only Demosthenes had not arrived and nor would he, for he had taken ship with another captain from his own island, so Leontios came in time to hear. Still, Leontios was pleased.

To lose only one man was good and Demosthenes was soon replaced with another, a young man named Jason from the island of Carpathos, who had come to Kriti in search of adventure. Jason fell in with Talakhonsu and Pamphilos, the three of them becoming firm friends. Jason was the youngest of three sons and so there was nothing for him at home. He had crossed words with his aging father once too often, and already his elder brother wanted to force him out as he became head of the family. Such is often the way for younger sons.

Before they returned the Kallisto to the sea the crew practiced much at their arms and tall Akakios drove the younger men on relentlessly in this. In the deep of the winter, Talakh had cut himself a green branch from an oak tree and stripped it of its bark before carving it into a wooden sword, which as it dried, hardened like stone. Around the handle, he bound a strip of hide so that he could grip it better and he then rubbed bees wax into it so that it would not crack. Of course this wooden sword had no edge and was much lighter than one of iron, but it served him well in practicing with the others. He had made a spear too in a similar way, but this was a true weapon with a point of bright iron spliced into its tip.

With these weapons, Talakhonsu practiced with the others on the sands near the Kallisto. But while most of the men tried out the bow, he left this to one side. He had his heavy throwing stick, and now that he was almost a full grown man he could throw this harder and further than ever. Talakh thought of Korkamani at such times, and of Meketra and Broken Nose who had between them saved him from the evil of Khaemwaset those many years ago in far off Kemet. He was probably the equal of Meketra now in height and strength. Somehow though he still doubted his throw was the better of the two.

As the spring weather settled and the sun's strength was restored, Leontios had the men raise the Kallisto's mast and rig her again with her ropes and tethers. Finally they brought out the oars and passed them into their locks in the ship's flanks. The men looked on with pride now as Pamphilos painted the eyes afresh on either side of her slender prow, so that the ship's bold gaze was restored to her.

'She is ready!' Leontios said with a satisfied grin. 'Tomorrow we will return her to the sea and place her in great Poseidon's care once again. But tonight we will feast around the fire in celebration of the good times to come. Ah, it is a fine thing to be alive with the open sea before us, is it not?'

'Aye, it is. To you and to us all!' stout Hippolytos raised a cup of wine.

Talakhonsu had a broad smile on his face then as he and the others cheered the captain. The wide world awaited them all and the blood coursed through his veins with excitement at the thought of the adventures that lay before them.

In the afternoon the men gathered together driftwood from the shore and made a fire as the sun set in the west behind the distant mountains, turning the sky a rose pink. As night fell, they feasted on roasted goat with fresh bread, dried fruits and honey with curds of milk, washed down with good wine brought to them by the daughters of Hippolytos, whose family had come to see him away to the sea again. All knew that in the nights to come they would find themselves far away from home, their fate placed in the lap of the gods once more. Adventures awaited them, danger too, but for tonight they drank each other's health, safe from the seas and those who would be their enemies.

Talakhonsu woke in the first of the dawn, as he always seemed to, his mouth dry and his head still fuzzy with strong wine. He had fallen asleep on the beach with his crew mates, most of whom still snored and grunted around him, while Hippolytos and his wife, their daughters and their young son were slumbering a way off by a small fire of their own. Only Leontios and tall Akakios were not there. Talakh guessed they had gone back to the house of Leontios, the more comfortably to rest, for it was true that in the months to come they might sleep on many a beach before the Kallisto rested her oars for the winter again.

The young Napatan yawned and reached for a jug which he hoped would have water, but it lay unstopped and so empty, its contents still damp on the sand. Another jug lay out of reach by the grey ashes of the fire. Sighing to himself, Talakhonsu unwrapped his long cloak from about himself and crawled over to it, thankful to the gods to find this one stopped up, thanking them all the more that it was water and not wine within. The cool water revived him as it ran down his throat, and he sat awhile in the dawn as the gentle waves lapped the shore, gazing out to the dark, silver-grey sea beyond. All was peaceful and still in Poseidon's realm.

Talakh sat there on his own for a long time before Jason, the fair haired Carpathian, came over and crouched next to him.

'You cannot sleep either?' Jason said.

'Not today,' Talakh grinned. 'Soon we will be out there on the seas, with the wind to carry us along if we are lucky.'

'And the oars if we are not,' Jason grinned back.

Talakh glanced at Jason, wondering how the Carpathian would be at the oar. He was the same height as Pamphilos, though stockier. His muscles would not be used to rowing though, so Pamphilos would probably outstrip him for a while until he was hardened to it. Talakh guessed that Leontios would have these two rowing together and that he himself would be moved up the benches to replace Demosthenes. This thought saddened him a little, as Pamphilos was his friend, and yet he would also welcome it because it would mean he would be amongst the first rank of Leontios's men. He knew he was ready as he looked about him at the others. Ready to leave the last of his boyhood behind him.

The sun was risen when Leontios and tall Akakios came down to the beach and by this time all of the Kallisto's crew had roused themselves and eaten what they could find. Most of them now spent some time stretching their stiff limbs, as they knew well what would come next. Their captain scaled the ship's side and stood in the high prow as his men gathered on the sand below.

'Men of the Kallisto!' Leontios addressed them all. 'The long winter is finally over for us today. It's time to return the ship to her home, put your shoulders to her now!'

The men were well drilled in launching their ship, the strongest at the front, the weakest at their backs, all bringing their combined weight to bear against the bulk of the ship. Yet she would not budge.

'We will have to rock her a little,' Hippolytos called up to Leontios.

'Aye, you take half the men. Akakios, you take the other half,' Leontios nodded.

So with half of the crew on each side of the Kallisto they heaved with all their might first one way and then the other to break the grip of the sand.

'Try again,' Leontios commanded, but still the ship refused to move, hard as the men grunted and swore their curses.

It was then that Talakh had an idea.

'Captain!' he called up. 'The wind is off the shore.'

'What of it?' Leontios fixed him with an irritated glare.

'We could hoist the sail. Perhaps it will be enough to help us a little?'

'Hah!' tall Akakios laughed harshly. 'Listen to the boy! I think you are still drunk from last night's wine,' he sneered.

Leontios thought for a moment, feeling the wind through his fingers. 'There is nothing but a gentle breeze,' he said finally, 'but it will do no harm to try your plan Talakh.'

Tall Akakios did not like this at all and glared at Leontios, though he said nothing as several of the lighter men scrambled aboard and unfurled the sail.

To Talakh's disappointment the heavy sail was hardly stirred at all by the breeze and the smile returned to the face of Akakios, who shook his head as if at a child. Talakh gritted his teeth and ignored him, though he felt like punching the older man's grinning face to wipe that smile away. Instead he prayed to his god Amun that he would whisper a wind from across the great Middle Sea and the deserts beyond. As the men strained, still no wind came and Talakh wished he had made more offering to Amun during the cold months of winter.

'I don't understand this,' Leontios shook his head. 'It is as if the thumb of Zeus himself pins her to the sand. Strip out the oars!' he bellowed in a rising anger, 'over the side with everything!'

The crew did his bidding but still the Kallisto stubbornly refused to move, even when Leontios himself added his strength to theirs. The captain had the men rest and drink some wine to recover their spirits as much as their strength, but Talakh would not join them. Instead he searched the shoreline for flat stones and placed these in a row in front of the ship, to form a track that lead down the shallow beach toward the sea. Jason and Pamphilos joined him once they saw that there was sense in his plan. If only they could get the Kallisto off the sand and onto those stones she would move far easier.

'Ah!' Hippolytos said as he came to look over their efforts. 'You use your brains Napatan, when the rest of us bash our heads in with our stubbornness!'

'Thank you,' Talakh bowed his head a little, for to be praised by Hippolytos was a worthy thing.

Wiping the sweat from his brow, he wished he had cut his hair. It had grown thick and bushy again over the cold winter. With this thought in his mind he found himself gazing inland toward the distant mountains. There were dark, heavy clouds over the peaks, and they were rolling slowly but surely toward the coast. Hope rose in him as the breeze cooled and freshened on his face. A storm was coming! Great Amun had answered his prayer! The Kallisto's sail filled a little before sinking, and then filled again with a loud crack as the wind caught it and pulled the tether ropes taught.

'Captain!' Talakh called. 'A storm comes!'

The men did not need orders from Leontios and they sprang to their feet as the Kallisto's mast began to creak with the strain of the rising wind. With the weight of the men against her and the wind in her sail, the ship finally began to move, slowly at first but then once her hull found Talakhonsu's path of smooth flat stones she seemed as light as a feather and glided forward with ease. They dropped the sail again and stopped her half in and half out of the sea so that they could feed her oars back into her locks and take back on board those things they had cast over the side to lighten her. Only when they had loaded some ballast stones aboard her was she fit to enter upon the sea fully.

'Pamphilos! Talakh!' Leontios called to them. 'Come aboard and take the steering oars.'

'Why not ourselves?' tall Akakios scowled. He liked to stand on the steering deck, looking over the men as they strained at the oar.

'Those young men watched well over my ship through the winter, Akakios,' Leontios said, not rising to the other's ill mood. 'And once again Talakhonsu has used his brains to free the Kallisto. Between them they have earned the right to see us back upon the sea.'

Akakios said nothing, but his jaw was set with annoyance. He stood with his arms folded in the prow, tall and vain in his pride while the men below him pushed the Kallisto the last few feet into the sea.

Talakhonsu and Pamphilos grinned at each other as they stood on the steering deck and lowered the steering oars down against their stops into the chopping waves that had sprung up in the wind. There they stood ready to turn the Kallisto about and steer her out to sea, but Leontios wisely ordered the men dig their oars into the sand to keep her prow up against the beach until the squall had blown over. These spring squalls were rarely long, but they could be violent and there was no sense trying the goodwill of the gods when they had shown already they did not want the Kallisto to put to sea.

Of course, sullen Akakios did not move from the prow, left to stew as he was by the rest of the crew. Whilst he had not made an enemy of Akakios, Talakh knew that the tall Kyprian would like him even less now. For though they were both tall, the similarities between them ended there. Talakh was from a different race of men, but even so he was still more popular with his crewmates than Akakios and he had shown himself to be resourceful too. Perhaps this last thing rankled with Akakios most of all, for the older man no doubt saw that Talakhonsu had the ear of Leontios, just as Isek had done before him.

There were many aboard the Kallisto that Talakh would trust his life with. But, he decided then, tall Akakios would not be one of them.

Chapter 3

Enemies Made, Friends Found

When the squall had safely passed and the sun had returned to the sky, the Kallisto at last backed off from the beach at Roussolakos, turned about and headed out once more onto the open seas. With the wind against her course, the sail remained furled, but soon enough she was surging forward through the chop of the seas at every oar stroke, the warm spring sunshine on the backs of the men as they rowed north along the eastern coast of Kriti on the short voyage to the port of Itanos. Talakhonsu felt the fresh salt breeze on his face and thanked great Amun, who had preserved him for days like this. To be alive was a good thing, he thought to himself as he leant against the steering oar alongside his friend Pamphilos.

They soon rounded a rocky headland and saw Itanos ahead of them once more, so Leontios and tall Akakios shipped their own oars and went to stand in the ship's high prow. For though he was not too proud to bend the oar, still Leontios was the captain and there were many that knew him in the busy port.

Talakh looked on past the two Kyprians as he and Pamphilos strained to turn the ship landward, while the choppy waves slapped against her prow, sending up plumes of spray to wet the men's backs. Leontios had already sent word to his friend, the merchant Solon of Itanos, that he wanted a cargo of oil and wine readied. It was always oil and wine for Kemet, since even when the floods of the Great River did not come and the harvest failed, the tastes of the wealthy were always well provided for.

'The warships of Hermokrates must be out on the sea,' Pamphilos said, looking around the harbour.

'Perhaps we'll see them when we put back out?' Talakh answered.

One of Hermokrates' ships had already been seen off the coast of Roussolakos a few days before, rowing along at a pace as her crew tested their strength against sea and wind. They were raiders, the wolves of the sea, and it was well to be on the right side of them, as any ship that had no business in the waters of eastern Kriti would soon find out. The fate of the crews of such ships would depend upon where they were from, but Phoenician ships had the greatest cause to fear. As the allies of the Persians, these men were hated by all of the free Greek peoples and their ships would be taken from them whenever they strayed too close to Kriti's waters.

Once the Kallisto was safely moored up at the quayside, the crew went ashore to stretch their legs and shake the stiffness from their arms and shoulders, while Leontios sought out Solon. The winter had been long enough for their muscles to forget the strain of rowing in a heavy sea and already they were stiffer then they would have wished, though their pride would not admit it.

After he had spoken for a while with Solon, Leontios gave the order for some of the men to fetch the new cargo he had bought. The captain ordered Talakh, Pamphilos and Jason to stay behind to unload the ballast stones that kept the Kallisto's hull down in the water. It was a hard afternoon's work for all concerned, the more so after the effort that had gone into launching the Kallisto that morning, yet Leontios was in no mood to stay that night in Itanos.

'Pamphilos,' he called the young Skyrian over. 'Take Jason with you and buy bread enough for four days. We will sail before sunset.'

The crew took fresh water aboard the Kallisto in clay jugs to keep it cool and fresh, as the sea calmed itself and the wind dropped to a gentle whisper. Even so, Talakh wondered at the wisdom of the captain, for they would have to row hard to leave Kriti and the small islands to the south safely behind them before darkness fell. By the time the bread had been baked for them and Pamphilos and Jason had returned with great stacks of the hot, flat loaves, the sun was almost upon the horizon.

'We go now!' Leontios said impatiently from the steering deck as the men climbed aboard. 'Ready the sail!'

'The men should be fed first, do you not think captain?' Hippolytos said with a worried look on his face, for he liked his food better than any man.

A brief anger crossed Leontios' face, before he relented. 'The front four ranks will row first,' he agreed. 'That way those behind you can eat their bread. Then they will row so that you can eat, my friend.'

Hippolytos took this with good grace and went to his oar bench happy, though he still had the eyes of a hungry man as he looked at the loaves again. Talakh took his new place next to Kleisthenes the fair haired, who nodded a welcome to him. Except for tall Akakios, all now viewed Talakh as a grown man, deserving of their respect the same as any other.

When the captain gave the word, the ship cast off and after the oarsmen had turned her prow to face the open sea once more, Leontios called those not eating to their oars. Hippolytos struck up the chant, and those at the oar filled their lungs, their voices rising at the pull of each stroke as Itanos slowly receded behind them. Talakh thought of Ketet, the pretty daughter of Isek, at her father's side in far off Kemet and his heart warmed at the thought that every oar stroke brought him a little closer to her home again. Yet whether he would see her before the winter came again, this was something that only the gods could know.

When all the men had eaten and taken some water and a little wine to keep their spirits up, they rowed on into the fading twilight, before that too was gone and the Kallisto was alone under the vault of the night with its countless stars. Still the men rowed on, their effort keeping them warm in the chill breeze that played idly with the sail. In the deep of the night, a sickle moon rose low over the horizon, laying the faintest of silver shadows across the sea, and it was only then that Leontios had the men rest at last. Some tried to sleep, though in the laden ship there was little enough room to lie down. Most leaned against the side, or doubled over their shipped oars, wrapped in their cloaks against the cold. Only Leontios stood on the steering deck, guiding the Kallisto away from the North Star, on their course south across the whispering seas. Talakh went to join him, as with his tall frame he was more uncomfortable than most in the cramped ship and he could not sleep. The captain's bearded face looked grey and a little sad in the faint light of the moon

'A fine night,' Talakh offered. 'Your Greek heroes look down on us brightly from the stars.'

'Perhaps,' Leontios said quietly. 'I'm not sure that I believe in them as much as I used to. But still, they show our way to the south,' he nodded, cheering himself a little. 'We will see what waits us there, friend or foe.'

'Aye, let us hope it will be only friends,' Talakh said, remembering their last flight from the Persian soldiers, what seemed so long ago now.

'Friends may be in short supply for a Greek ship in the land of Kemet,' Leontios said, his frown returning. 'Solon told me the latest news. There is much talk of a fresh war in the north.'

In truth there was always talk of war between the Persians and the powerful Greek city states, yet this was different. Talakh could see that much in the grim face of Leontios.

'For a while the Persians were content to let the strongest of us be, while they nibbled away at the weakest,' Leontios continued. 'They saw no threat in us as we were too busy fighting among ourselves to trouble them, so they bided their time to take their revenge on us. But all that changed last year when the rulers of Athens put aside their differences with Aegina.'

'Aegina?' Talakh asked.

'Aye. It is a powerful island off the coast of Attic Greece and so a close neighbour to Athens. They fought for many years, but now they are allies again you see. Together with others they now seek to form a great alliance of the Greeks and it is this amongst other things that will bring Xerxes of Persia to fight now.

'Not that he fears them of course, his armies are too vast for that. But Athens has thumbed its nose at the Persians in the past and so Xerxes sees their growing power as an insult to him. He will try to divide Athens from her allies with threats and bribes. That is the Persian way.

'So you see Talakh, Xerxes will not be content until Athens is burnt to the ground, just as the Athenians went to Asia and burnt the city of Sardis after they had defeated his father, Darius. Now Sardis was not even a Persian city really, but still Xerxes wants to avenge this slight against his rule.'

'But if the armies of Xerxes are as mighty as they say, will the Athenians not also have to bow to him in the end?' Talakh asked. 'Surely they cannot think they will win against him?'

'Greeks bow to Persians? Hah!' Leontios laughed harshly, causing one of the men to stir in his sleep. 'Well in truth it has happened with the Ionians who live along the Asian coast, though at heart they still hate Xerxes as much as any of us. But Athens? Never! The Athenians are far too proud for that.'

'Then can they win again against such a strong foe?'

Leontios rubbed his bearded chin.

'Can they win?' the captain said thoughtfully. 'Xerxes will bring more men and ships than his father Darius ever did. He will want to make absolutely sure of victory, and his men will swarm over the ground like ants, but that may also count against him.'

'How so?'

'Well, the more men he has, the more mouths he has to feed and the harder his armies will be to organise. They will expect to win easily, but if they suffer setbacks and victory evades them, the seeds of doubt may be sown in Xerxes' mind. His men will be fighting a long way from home in a strange land against a fierce enemy who are determined not to give in. And you must understand that those warriors of Athens would rather die by the thousand than turn and flee from the field of battle.'

'Because they fight for their honour?'

'Aye, the warrior's pride,' Leontios nodded as he drew

himself up to his full height, his eyes burning bright in the darkness. 'How many amongst the armies of Xerxes would do the same for him? Perhaps some, it is true, but you see the Greeks have only not to lose, Talakh! If they can avoid outright defeat, then the Persians will have no victory and they will return home disheartened and in shame, as happened last time. Still, as I have said before, Darius the Great once under-estimated us. Xerxes would have to be a vain and foolish man to make the same mistake.

Talakh nodded as he tried to understand all of these things.

'But then,' continued Leontios darkly, 'as well as the war on the land, there will also be war on the sea. Xerxes will need a great many ships to bring his men across from Asia into the mainland of Thrace, and to keep them supplied afterwards. If they cross the path of Athenian ships or those of Corinth, or Chalcis, then the Persians will regret it.'

'Aye,' Talakh nodded in agreement. 'I have heard it said many times that the Persians are cowards when the water is under them.'

'Yes, men say that. But much as I dislike them, they are not cowards just because they don't like the sea, Talakh,' Leontios said his mood calming. 'They come from deep within the land of Asia, so the sea is not in their blood as it is in my people. Because of this they rely on their allies, the Phoenicians, to do their work for them when it comes to matters of the sea,' he spat over the side.

Talakhonsu had learned already that if there was one thing that the Greek peoples despised more than a Persian, it was a Phoenician. 'Will Kriti be safe?' he asked, fearful for his new home.

'Aye, Kriti will be safe,' Leontios gave a satisfied nod. 'The seas protect us there. All of Greece would need to fall before the Persians could threaten Kriti. But when will Xerxes strike against the Athenians? That is a good question to think on. Perhaps he will wait till just before the harvest is due? His armies will eat all in their path and he will need the harvest of the lands to feed them. It will be this year, you can be sure of that. You see, besides gaining revenge for his father, there is another reason for Xerxes to make his move soon. You have heard of a man called Themistocles?'

'From the city of Athens?'

'Aye, that one.'

'He is a famous man.'

'He is, and wise too,' Leontios nodded. 'When the Athenians discovered their silver mines in the mountains, he persuaded them to build a fleet of ships with it, rather than squander it on riches for themselves.

'You see they knew that one day soon the Persian armies would return and so they sought advice from a famous oracle at Delphi in the north. She speaks with the voice of a god and through her, that god told them only a wall of wood could protect them. Now, stupidly they thought this meant they should build a stockade of wooden pales around their great city. As if that would protect them when the armies of Xerxes arrived at their gates!'

'Aye, the Persians would burn it surely?' Talakh agreed

'Exactly! Only Themistocles was wise enough to see the truth in the oracle's words. He told the Athenians that the wall of wood she had spoken of was not on land, but at sea and that the god meant that they should build themselves a great fleet of ships with their silver for this purpose. Eventually he persuaded them, and so it has been done.

'But who knows what fate the gods will choose for the Athenians when the time comes?' Leontios said, his mood turning darker again. 'Perhaps their wall of wood will not be enough.'

Talakh left him to his thoughts then, and tried to find what sleep he could while the Kallisto coasted on over the calm seas.

Over the next few days as they crossed the seas to Kemet, the wind favoured the ship of Leontios and so there was time for the men to rest from their rowing, though in the cold of the morning they often rowed anyway to warm themselves up. At times like this, Talakh remembered well the hardships of life at sea, when the voyage could be long and the weather cold and wet. It was easy to forget these things when the sun warmed your back and you were chanting the rowing songs with your friends, but they waited for the Kallisto all the same.

As they continued south, there was much talk amongst the men of the Persians and what the armies of King Xerxes would do next, so that when finally the Kallisto came again to the heat of the Kemet coast, all aboard her were on their guard against what might await them there. They rowed slowly along the coast, passing other vessels, some suspicious of them, some more friendly. One such ship, a trading ship with a bigger sail and far fewer oars than the Kallisto, drew near them as it headed westward.

'Leontios!' the ship's captain called out as his ship slipped past. 'Leontios of Kriti!'

'Leto, you old dog! Can it be you?' Leontios called back as he leant hard against the steering oar to turn the Kallisto's prow.

The man Leto took the wind from his sail, while Leontios had the men row hard on one side and back oars on the other so that they turned quickly about. Soon enough the two ships came alongside each other again as the Kallisto shipped her oars.

'You look as if you are in a hurry,' Leto grinned, as Leontios climbed aboard and the two men embraced as old friends.

'It is good to see you Leto!' Leontios beamed. 'If I judge by the grey in your beard, then many a year has passed since we last crossed paths!'

'Ah this is true. But those same years have been good to you Leontios my friend,' Leto laughed. 'At least if the breadth of your belt is anything to go by!'.

'What news do you have?' Leontios asked after the two men had exchanged enough of their friendly jibes.

'Not news, but advice my old friend,' Leto said, his smile turning to a frown. 'Keep a careful watch for Phoenician raiders! They took a ship from Kypros a week past and left only one survivor out of the seven aboard to take his chances in the sea. Luckily for him he was a good swimmer and the currents carried him to the barren coast. He was nearly dead from thirst when a passing ship happened to beach there for the night, and so he was saved in spite of all.'

'The Phoenicians,' Leontios spat over the side. 'They grow bolder as the Persians grow more warlike.'

'It was always their way,' said tall Akakios, who had gone across to join the two captains.

'Aye, since the days of the old races of men,' Leontios agreed. 'I will let you be on your way Leto old friend, but let us hope that we will meet one day soon on dry land, so that we can drink to each other's health in comfort.'

'That will be a good day for me Leontios,' Leto said as the two men locked arms in farewell. 'Go well Kyprian, and watch out for those Phoenician dogs.'

'They had better watch out for me!' Leontios boasted as he climbed back over to his own ship. 'Pity the Phoenician that crosses my path.'

And so the two old friends drew their craft apart again and went their separate ways.

For all the talk that passed between Leontios and his old friend Leto of war and raiding, the Kallisto's return to the land of the black earth remained untroubled as she passed into the serpentine mouth of the Great River. There at least, the minds of the Persian rulers were for the present only on wine and women, for they had long since crushed the resistance of the few nobles of Kemet who had once dared oppose them. There was still good trade to be had for any ship full of wine and oil that came early to the Kemet shores after the winter storms had at last abated. Even tall Akakios was a happy man when he saw the silver coin filling Leontios' chest after they had unloaded their cargo at the port of Naukratis, a short journey along the river. Yet though many other Greek ships and merchants were there, still these were Persian lands, enemy lands now more than ever. Leontios would not dwell long here, that was sure in Talakhonsu's mind.

'Will we see Isek again while we are here?' he ventured to ask Leontios as they took more stores aboard.

'I know you would like to see his daughter,' Leontios said, shaking his head, 'and it would gladden my heart to see Isek and know that he is well, but no, we must return to Kriti. You know that many men here speak the Greek tongue you have learned so well, Talakh?'

'Aye?'

'Well, they might seem harmless enough, but a lot of them are no friends of ours. There are Ionians from the coast of Asia and even some of my own countrymen from Kypros who kneel to Xerxes now. The time will come soon when they will be forced to bear arms for him whether they like it or not. Then they will fight those like us who should be their friends. Greek will fight Greek, Talakh, and that is why we do not linger here. We bring our cargo, take our silver and then we leave. One day soon it will be too risky even to do that.'

Talakh could do little but hope against hope that perhaps things would change and that the voyages to Kemet would continue until he saw Ketet again.

Before they started their return, the Kallisto took on a cargo of fresh spring grain at Naukratis, as in Kriti the harvest was still many months away. So the Kallisto settled into a familiar pattern for a while, returning to Kriti with grain and then bringing wine and oil back to Kemet time and again as the heat of summer grew and the muscles of her crew hardened at the oar until they were like iron.

All this while fresh news came of the preparations made by the armies of Xerxes and of the Greek allies who would oppose them in the coming war. Talk grew too of the boldness of the Phoenician raiders who had taken many Greek traders captive. In truth the Greeks of the northern and western islands were doing much the same where they could, but whoever was at the root of it, these were anxious times for any captain sailing the open seas. Leontios was no different and so whenever the Kallisto beached or moored for the night, he would drill his men in their fighting skills, even though most were already formidable fighters. Talakhonsu, who had once been destined to lead the peaceful life of a priest, now took his place as a warrior too, though he had yet to be bloodied.

One morning, as the Kallisto sailed north from the coast of the land of the Libyans, Leontios had the men battle each other two at a time in the prow of the ship, whilst the others watched. They fought with wooden swords and spear poles and it was good sport, though not always fairly matched. Still there was little bad blood between any of the men and so those that were beaten were not battered.

'Talakh, go and test yourself against Kleisthenes,' Leontios said when the Napatan's turn came. 'Let us see your sword arm, Napatan!'

But as Talakh took up his wooden practice sword, it was tall Akakios who stepped forward first.

'I am a closer match for Talakh than Kleisthenes,' he said with the trace of a smile on his thin face. 'Let him test his long arm against my own reach, Leontios.'

Talakh looked to the captain, half hoping that he would refuse Akakios. A part of him did not want to fight the tall man who had taken a dislike to him and yet there was also a dislike in Talakhonsu for tall Akakios too. And so when Leontios nodded his agreement, Talakh was more pleased than not as he gripped the wooden sword hilt in his hand and walked past his opponent to the prow of the Kallisto. Tall Akakios followed him, with a wooden sword of his own and drew himself up to his full height. Without a pause, Akakios lunged forward hoping to catch his opponent off guard with a sharp thrust, yet Talakh was ready and swept the sword easily aside as he stepped back. Without thinking, his own sword feinted forward, not with any real force but still it was just enough to force Akakios back.

With an angry shout Akakios lunged again, as did Talakhonsu and the two men exchanged blows at a fierce rate, blocking and slashing with the wooden swords. Talakh felt his heart in his throat and the taste of iron in his mouth, yet strangely he was not scared and instead anger blazed in him as his youth and vigour started to tell on the tall Greek. While the crew cheered them on, Akakios fell back breathing hard as Talakh pursued him relentlessly. Yet Akakios was not ready to yield and he picked up a coil of rope and threw it at the Napatan's legs. Before Talakh knew it he was tripped, and as he fell forward Akakios was on him in an instant, beating his back with hard swinging blows of the wooden sword.

'Akakios!' Leontios bellowed as the crew's cheers grew quiet, but it was the strong arm of Hippolytos who stopped the beating as he grabbed Akakios from behind and held him fast.

'That is enough!' Hippolytos growled, as Akakios struggled in vain to free himself. 'You beat the boy as if he is your worst enemy. What has he done to you?'

'Let him go Hippolytos,' Talakh said defiantly as he got to his feet. 'I will fight him again.'

'There will be no more fighting!' Leontios thundered as he pushed past Hippolytos and stood between Akakios and Talakhonsu. 'What do the two of you think you are doing, eh? There are enemies enough for us out here on the seas without us making more amongst ourselves!'

'This one has never shown me any respect!' Akakios spat. 'He ...'

'Enough!' Leontios cut him short. 'Respect is given where it is due Akakios, you should know that!'

'He is above himself!' Akakios retorted angrily. 'You favour this Napatan more than you would one of us!'

'One of us?' Leontios said through gritted teeth. 'Talakhonsu *is* one of us! He has the heart of a Greek and he has proven himself to me, proven himself to all of you, more than once. You have a short memory Akakios, and too much pride besides.'

'You take his side?' Akakios spat.

'I take no sides,' Leontios growled back. 'But I will have no enemies on my ship. The two of you will shake hands and bury your differences, or I will put you both off the Kallisto when we are back in Itanos.'

'What?' Akakios hissed, as Hippolytos let him free. 'I cannot believe my ears! My own kin!'

'I am captain before all such things,' Leontios said firmly. 'All are equal in my eyes on my ship. Now you have my terms. Make your choice.'

'I will do as you ask,' Talakhonsu spoke up. 'I would not defy you captain, after all that you have done for me.

'Akakios,' he turned to the tall Greek. 'I offer my hand. I will forget our differences and you will have my respect. All I ask is that you judge me fairly in return.'

'Hah!' Akakios sneered. 'You would give me terms boy? Well I spit on that!' he said, turning his back as he spat over the Kallisto's side.

Leontios caught his arm as Akakios brushed past him. 'I will put you both off, Akakios,' he said quietly. 'Think on that while your hot head cools.'

But Talakhonsu knew just as well as Leontios that tall Akakios would happily cut his nose off to spite his face. He would not back down and neither would Leontios, for the captain had spoken and his word was his word. It seemed to him then that the favoured time he had spent at the side of Leontios was coming to a sudden end just as quickly as it had begun. With a heavy heart he went back to his oar bench and slumped down next to Kleisthenes, his back stinging from the blows Akakios had dealt him.

'Here, have some water,' Pamphilos said, passing him a cup from the barrel. 'I will try to speak with Leontios, Talakh. Perhaps...'

'No Pamphilos, do not trouble yourself,' Talakh shook his head. 'You are a good friend, and the captain is a good man. I owe him much, but you know as well as I do that he has given his word and he cannot go back on it without losing face.'

'All the same, I will speak with him,' Pamphilos said as he went back to his own bench.

'You hide your pain well, Talakhonsu,' Kleisthenes said when Pamphilos had moved on along the benches. 'Are you hurt?'

'It will pass,' Talakh shrugged his shoulders.

'Not for a few days though. You'll feel it tomorrow when the bruises come out.'

'I am a Napatan,' Talakh smiled grimly. 'We don't bruise easily.'

'Your dark skin hides the bruises, that is all. They are there just the same, this I know,' Kleisthenes fixed Talakh with those piercing blue eyes of his that made him look angry even when he was not.

'Aye, that is true.'

'It is. But whatever happens next, don't give up hope just yet Talakh,' Kleisthenes reached across to clap his shoulder. 'The fates brought you from your own land to sail with us. They will not be done with you for a while I think.'

Talakhonsu nodded. If nothing else it was good that he had the respect of a man like Kleisthenes, who did not give such things lightly. If the time had come for him to leave the Kallisto, he knew he could do so with his head held high.

The ship of the Greeks sailed north now on a fresh breeze, the men put hard to the oar so that their minds would not dwell on the fight between Akakios and Talakhonsu, as the Kallisto's keen prow surged through the swelling seas.

It was some hours later, whilst they were resting for bread and water that they first saw the dark outline of a ship, far off and distant to the horizon from them.

'A sail, captain!' Pamphilos shouted as he leant against the prow to stretch his back out.

'Where does she lie?' Leontios called back, for like Talakh his sight was not as keen as Pamphilos, who had the eyes of a hawk.

'Away behind us and off to your right a little!'

Leontios rubbed his stubbled chin as he looked in vain for the ship.

'Pamphilos!' he called. 'Bring your eyes back here and keep a keen watch on them.'

As the south-westerly breeze carried them gently on, the dark sail of the other ship drew slowly closer.

'We will leave her to her own seas,' Leontios called to the crew, as he and tall Akakios leant on the steering oars to change the Kallisto's course a little.

'Probably another trader,' Akakios muttered. It was clear he would not have changed course if he had been captain, but Leontios was in no mood for his advice.

'Everyone back to the oars!' he ordered. 'Friend or foe, we'll leave them to their own business.'

Leontios began a chant to set a fast stroke and soon the men were straining every sinew as their oars pulled hard through the chop of the sea. The captain pushed the pace higher still until Talakhonsu no longer felt the bruises on his back, only the burning in his arms. The men's backs soon began to shine with sweat as they waited for their captain to relent, but Leontios urged them on, looking behind from time to time with a dark look on his face.

'They follow us,' Kleisthenes rasped in between strokes.

'Follow us?' Talakhonsu breathed hard. 'The ship?'

'Aye, the ship. A Phoenician. Or Ionian perhaps. Some of them are our enemies too.'

'What do they want?' Talakh gritted his teeth as his arms felt they would pull from their sockets.

'To slit our throats and take the Kallisto, most probably,' Kleisthenes grinned. 'They want a fight!'

Talakh saw from his face that these were no idle words. Fear rose up in his throat and now there was no pain in his arms, only a tingle that shuddered through his whole body. All tiredness was banished and the wooden world of the Kallisto and her crew closed in around him, but still Leontios drove them on. Some of the men were close to the limit of their strength and their strokes started to become more ragged. Talakhonsu thought they would surely be driven on until they died of exhaustion when suddenly Leontios cried out for them to stop.

'Prepare to fight!' he barked without warning.

As the men hung over their oars, sweat dripping from their brows, Leontios jumped down from the steering deck and unwrapped his sword from the oilskin that kept the rusting sea spray from its iron blade.

'Listen to me, men!' he summoned them as he stood, sword in one hand, spear in the other. 'That ship is lighter and faster than us, with a bigger sail. We can't shake her loose.'

'Lighten the ship,' Akakios said grimly. 'Over the side with the cargo, I say.'

'And you are captain now are you?' Leontios spun to face him so that his nose almost touched that of Akakios. 'They want our silver and our ship and they will catch us still, cargo or not.'

'Leontios is right!' Hippolytos spoke up. 'They have too many oars and too much sail for us.'

'Thank you my friend,' Leontios said, then turned to face the crew again, a defiant look in his eye. 'Listen to me well. They mean to take our ship, and as for us, we will either be over the side to Poseidon, or taken as slaves. But we are Greek! No-one takes our silver without a fight! Are you with me?'

'Aye!' the men shouted as one for their captain.

'Then drop the sail and ship the oars!' Leontios shook his spear in a battle rage. 'We will catch our breath while they draw near and then we will make them wish they had never set eyes on the Kallisto!'

While the others readied their weapons and young Jason gave them water, Talakhonsu hefted his own spear and slipped the wooden sword he had made in the long winter through his belt. But whereas those of the crew who had them took up their shields, Talakh instead gripped his heavy throwing stick, the same one he had made on the farm of Siamun in far off Kemet. It was only then that he caught sight of the enemy.

'Phoenician by the look of her,' Kleisthenes said quietly as he leant out over the ship's rail next to Talakhonsu, straining his sharp eyes. 'She has fifty oars,'

'Fifty?' Talakh repeated, his voice dry.

'Aye, fifty. But fifty oars doesn't mean fifty fighting men. Some of them could be slaves and they'll be chained at the oar. As for the rest, those long beards wouldn't stand up to you or I in a fight.'

'Aye,' Talakh agreed, though in his heart he was very far from sure of himself. He had seen men fight, seen them die, but he had never fought for his own life. Now a moment of truth awaited him. There was no other way of it.

'Bowmen in her prow!' Pamphilos shouted urgently from the stern.

'They will come up under a rain of arrows,' Leontios warned his men. 'Take up your shields and be ready.'

Jason, the young Carpathian had found an old shield and held it above his head while he crouched down against the ships side, a fearful look on his face. Talakh looked from him to the other Greeks as they called upon their heroes to give them courage. It was for every man to find his strength for the fight ahead, but Jason was young and untested. In his mind he had not readied himself for times such as these. Still the Phoenician ship drew ever closer, while the men of the Kallisto waited in grim silence.

It was burly Hippolytos who first found the voice of battle, roaring from the depths of his belly as he held up his heavy war axe in one hand and shook it at their enemies. The shouts of the others quickly joined him even as a dark smudge of arrows soared into the sky like living smoke.

'Shields!' Leontios shouted, and Talakhonsu ducked under the side of the ship as the arrows thumped home on shield and deck, though many also hissed into the sea either side of the Kallisto.

'They will fire again, and then they'll be on us,' Leontios called again. 'Be ready for them! When you hear my word, we take the fight to them. Are you with me, men?'

'Aye!' the crew of the Kallisto shouted as one.

'Then let those dogs hear our voices! Let them hear our chants of war! Let them see the iron behind our words!'

Talakhonsu had learnt much of the Greeks and their ways in his time with them. They were brave and bold yes, but above all it was the fear of shame that gave them the courage to fight so boldly. This was their strength, for no man would back away while his friends still fought on. Talakh looked around him at the bared teeth and snarls of the Greeks and thought of his father Korkamani watching him from the after world. For himself, he would fight for the memory of Korkamani, for Leontios and for his crew mates.

The arrows came again just as Leontios had warned, clattering harmlessly against the ship's side and her crew's shields, yet even before the rain had died away, Talakh sprang to his feet and ran up onto the steering deck to challenge the lump of fear that rose in his throat. An arrow hissed past him like a striking snake as he stood there cursing in his Napatan tongue, his spear at the ready. It was then that he saw almost his reflection, for another of his race stood in the prow of the Phoenician ship. A tall, dark man with a great bush of hair and a beard that hid most of his face, he held a short throwing spear in one hand and a sword in the other. Both of them glinted death in the bright sun.

Talakhonsu took all of this in, even as the Phoenician ship ran quickly up to the drifting Kallisto, shipping her oars and readying boarding planks as she closed.

'Now!' he heard the voice of Leontios, and this time a few Greek arrows shot past him toward the Phoenician ship. Though they were only a handful, two found their mark and cries of pain rose up from their enemies, but they came on nonetheless. The dark one in the prow did not flinch, his eyes staring intently along the Greek line. The eyes of a killer of men.

Talakhonsu knew fear then, though he gritted his teeth and tightened his grip still further on his spear.

'Step aside lad, he is not for you,' Hippolytos' gravelled voice came to him as if from a dream.

'No, I will fight him!' Talakh found himself saying in a voice that was not his own.

The Phoenician ship was almost on them now, bristling with men and the glint of honed iron, the sea parting either side of her sleek prow with its two great unblinking eyes. As the Phoenicians closed and the curses and threats of his own crewmates grew louder still in his ears, Talakh drew back not the spear but instead his throwing stick. Like a whip, he snapped his long arm forward and the heavy weapon spun out of his hand like a striking snake. Flying straight and true with a terrible force, the dark throwing stick struck the man's sword as he brought up his arm to block it and glanced up full into his face. With a crushing blow it broke the man's nose, taking his senses from him as he fell backwards amongst his crewmates. A roar went up from behind him but there was no time to think of what to do next, for in another moment the Phoenician's prow crashed into the Kallisto, smashing a steering oar and shaking Talakh's footing so that he almost fell himself.

'Now!' he heard the voice of Leontios again, and with a great roar, Hippolytos leapt from the steering deck onto the Phoenician ship as it ground along the Kallisto's side. Without thinking, Talakhonsu jumped after him, though Hippolytos almost felled him as he swung his huge axe wildly, left and right amongst the bearded Phoenicians who came on to challenge him. A sword flashed bright in front of the Napatan's eyes, just missing his nose as he swayed back. Instinctively he lunged forward, grasping his spear in both hands. The iron point grated into the chest of a squat man, snapping his ribs.

'Pull your spear! Hippolytos roared, as he put his foot against the man's stomach and pushed him backwards.

The bearded Phoenician fell back with a cry of pain that turned to a low groan as Talakh instinctively twisted his spear so that it came free. Now the gush of blood from his chest became a river and the bearded man could only look surprised as his life left him. For a moment Talakh felt sorry for what he'd done, before the spear thrust of another of the enemy snapped him to his senses. He stepped back without thinking and swept the blow away, then rammed his own spear down into the man's leg. This one was taller than the other and his eyes narrowed in pain as Talakh pulled the spear point free. Luckily for him there were no barbs to the wicked iron point, so it wounded and withdrew easily like the strike of a snake. In the blink of an eye, Talakh brought his spear point up to the tall man's chest and jabbed forward. The rage on the Phoenician's face had turned to fear now and he backed away, swinging wildly with his own short spear. A blur of dull iron flew past Talakh and struck the man full on his chest with a crack of bone that knocked him flat on his back. The great throwing axe of Hippolytos.

Only now did Talakh draw breath to look at his enemies as they backed away between the ranks of ragged, cowering men who were chained at the oar.

'Slaves,' Leontios muttered as his shield pushed past Talakh's arm. 'Finish them!'

For a brief moment the Greeks and Phoenicians stared at each other, whilst Hippolytos calmly strode past Talakh and picked up his heavy, two headed axe from where it lay next to the tall Phoenician, who moaned in agony as he tried to get to his feet. Hippolytos kicked him hard in the face with his sandaled foot and the man fell back to the deck unconscious, which was just as well for him.

Leontios spoke then, though Talakh could not understand his words. It was clear enough though that he offered the Phoenicians death to a man if they did not lay down their arms.

One of their number came, a broad man with an arrogant look that reminded Talakh of Akakios.

'We outnumber you,' the man said in perfect Greek. 'Why should we yield? Give yourself up to us, and perhaps we will spare your lives!'

Leontios stepped forward and pointed with his sword at the man.

'In the sea,' he said coldly, 'there are two kinds of fish. The tiny ones that shoal in their hundreds and the bigger ones that eat them by the dozen. My men are handpicked killers, every one of them schooled in the art of killing and you are no match for us. Lay down your arms or you will die, all of you. That is the word of Leontios.'

These things Leontios said with a steady, dread voice, that drew the colour from the face of the Phoenician's makeshift leader as his dark eyes flitted about nervously. Here was a man used to having the upper hand, but now that he was faced with armed warriors he was not so sure of himself.

'Leontios? I have not heard of you,' the man shrugged his shoulders as dismissively as he could.

'Those who cross me don't live to tell the tale,' Leontios growled, taking another step forward.

Another Phoenician whispered to their leader then, as did another. It was clear they too were losing their nerve.

'It seems that you are fighters like us, not traders,' their leader said, his voice unsteady. 'We will let you go back to your own ship, and we will go our separate ways,'

'So that you can go free to raid others?' Leontios spat back. 'No, no. Throw your arms over the side and we will let you live. Otherwise my friend, you will be the first to die. I will take your head myself!'

The Phoenicians squabbled amongst themselves now, speaking in their own language for it seemed they too knew enough Greek to understand the harsh words of Leontios.

'How do we know we can trust your word?' the unwilling leader said, fear in his rising voice.

'Ach, I am sick of his bleating,' Hippolytos said, raising his axe above the head of the man he had kicked to the deck. 'Let's just kill them all!'

Though Talakh knew Hippolytos was at heart a good man who would not slaughter for the sake of it, the Phoenicians did not. Without warning one of them climbed over the side and jumped into the sea rather than face the stout Greek with the thirsty, double headed axe. This was enough for the rest of them, who lost all heart for the fight and one by one they dropped their weapons into the sea. All this while, the slaves who were tied to their oars had remained silent, but now they could see their freedom might be finally at hand and they cheered for Leontios with all their hearts.

'Get to the stern and turn your backs!' Leontios snapped at the Phoenicians. 'We will see how well you like being chained at the oar,' he added under his breath.

So it was that Talakh fought his first battle alongside Leontios, and gained his first real scar, though in the heat of battle he had not noticed the score on his arm from a Phoenician spear.

Whilst his men went amongst their enemy and made sure they were disarmed, Leontios and Talakh freed the slaves from their bonds.

'You have nothing to fear from me,' Leontios said to a Greek who had thanked him. 'From your accent you are Kyprian like me I would guess.'

'Yes,' the man croaked, his voice cracked from lack of water. 'My name is Sikinnos. I am from Kypros and I owe you my life, captain.'

'Any man of Kypros would do the same for any other,' Leontios said, his voice heavy with emotion. 'We have all suffered at the hands of our enemies. Now tell me,' he knelt close to Sikinnos. 'Who leads these men? I will take his life for the things he has done.'

'It was the Ethiopian. The one he felled,' he glanced up fearfully at Talakhonsu.

'You have no need to fear Talakhonsu here,' Leontios reassured the man. 'He is one of my crew, and as Greek now as any of us.'

Talakh held out his hand and helped Sikinnos to his feet. The man could barely stand, weak as he was from hunger and thirst.

'I thank you captain,' he said as he leant against the side of the ship to try to straighten his stiff back. 'You have saved the lives of many good men today.'

'Aye, but I will take a life before the day ends,' Leontios said bluntly. This I swear.'

With that he left his men to guard the Phoenicians and made his way to the prow. Talakh and Hippolytos followed him, past the bodies of two more Phoenicians. These ones Talakh had not even seen fall in the heat of the fight, and he gave silent praise to Amun for sparing his own life. In the keel of the ship, the Ethiopian as Sikinnos had called him, lay moaning. He still lived, though Leontios had a mind to send him to the underworld soon enough. The man looked pale despite his dark skin, his face and bushy beard caked with blood from the crushed mess that had once been his nose. Already his face was swelling, closing up around one of his eyes so that he looked like a beaten animal. And yet there was something familiar about him, Talakh thought.

'Your throwing stick finds its mark well,' Leontios said solemnly. 'Give me your spear Talakhonsu. I will finish him.'

Talakhonsu gave up the bloody spear to Leontios's outstretched hand, and the captain took it up, holding its sharp point above the man's fast beating heart.

'A quick death is too good for you,' Leontios muttered, readying himself to strike. 'Now your own men will be lashed at the oar in place of those you enslaved. Breathe your last, and pass from this world without honour.'

Yet even as the captain drew back his arm to make Talakh's spear kill again, the dark man opened his one good eye and stared up at them. It was only in that moment that Talakh finally knew him.

'Stop!' he cried grabbing the spear shaft, though the strength and battle fury of Leontios pulled it free in an instant.

Leontios glared at him, his eyes narrowing in anger. 'Once again, you stay my hand!'

'I meant no disrespect captain,' Leontios said quickly, 'but I know this man.'

'Again you know my enemy?'

'Yes, again,' Talakh nodded sadly. 'He was a friend to me long ago when I was a boy. This is the one called Meketra I told you of. The one who taught me how to find my mark with the throwing stick.'

'The one who saved you?'

'The same one,' Talakh nodded. 'He risked his own life for mine when Khaemwaset murdered my father.'

'Hmm,' Leontios nodded, thoughtfulness replacing his anger. 'And now, just as with Khaemwaset, this one crosses your path again too? To be felled by the same weapon in which he taught you? Truly the gods play with the lives of mortal men,' he laughed harshly. 'Still, I swore to that poor man over there that I would kill this Meketra. Would you have me dishonoured Talakh? Would you have me break my oath?'

'No, I would not captain,' Talakh lowered his head. 'And yet I owe him my life...'

'He released you from that debt when his ship chose to attack us,' Leontios spoke solemnly, placing his hand on the Napatan's shoulder. 'Perhaps he was a good man once, but that was a long time ago. Look around at these poor men he chained at the oar. And what of those others he had no use for? Those that grew too weak? They would have gone over the side, dead or not.'

Talakh nodded his agreement. He knew that Leontios was right, but still his heart was heavy as he remembered the Meketra of his boyhood, long ago in Kemet.

'Go and see to the captives,' Leontios ordered him. 'I will give your Meketra a quick death.'

'Aye captain,' Talakh nodded, but as he turned away he saw Hippolytos tip one of the dead Phoenicians over the side. 'What of his... what of his body?' he turned to ask.

Leontios's face grew dark with anger again. Killing a wounded man was a grim task, all the grimmer now that the battle was ended. But when he looked into his own heart and remembered the story of Talakh's youth, the captain relented.

'He let you bury your father,' Leontios nodded. 'If it is your wish, you can bury him with the rites of your people when we reach land. That much you owe him.'

'I thank you Captain,' Talakhonsu lowered his head. 'My mind will rest easier for that.'

With that he went astern to help his crewmates bind their Phoenician prisoners and free the rest of the slaves. Talakhonsu did not hear the death blow, for Leontios was true to his word and had struck the man unconscious before burying the spear in his heart. This then was the close of another memory for Talakhonsu, his heart heavy at the death of Meketra. For though the Kemet warrior had turned to evil ways in the end, he had once been a different man. A man who had risked his own life for that of a Napatan boy and his dying father.

Chapter 4

The Story of Huell

The death of Meketra and the overthrow of his men brought great cheer to the freed captives of the Phoenician ship and as they told their stories to Leontios and his crew it was clear that they had suffered greatly. But of Meketra, even his own men knew little about him, other than that he had made his home in their lands some years before and had bought his great ship with gold and silver. He was a great warrior they said, one who took joy in the slaying of other men. He had fought for the Persians, who reward well all who are loyal to them.

This then was the fate of Meketra, taken from his father's farm by Broken Nose and his war band many years before in the land of Kemet. Instead of learning how to bring corn forth from the earth at his father's side, he had learned only how to fill it with the bodies of men. Talakhonsu shuddered at that thought, for in some ways it seemed that his own path might one day lead him to the same end.

'You fought well, Napatan,' Kleisthenes gripped his shoulder.

'Aye, he did that!' Hippolytos grinned as he bound one of the Phoenician's arms tightly through the eyehole of an oar shaft. 'Did you see how he elbowed me out of the way so that he could get at them first? The cheek of it!'

'A born warrior,' Kleisthenes agreed.

Such praise was high indeed for Talakh and in spite of himself he felt his heart swell with pride.

Soon all of the Phoenician prisoners were bound securely and their former slaves took much sport in humiliating them. Leontios stood on the steering deck of the vessel and called the ragged men to heed him.

'Free men!' he shouted. 'Now your lives are your own again.

Where are you from? Where will you return too? What will you do now?'

The men turned to face Leontios and grew quiet until one of them stepped forward to speak. He was filthy with sweat and grime, his dark hair knotted and wild.

'I am Ionian,' he said, a thick beard hiding his mouth. 'From the southeast coast of Asia. My name is Diokles and I owe you and your warriors my life, good captain.'

Another spoke. 'I am from Kypros captain, a trader of the seas.'

'As am I,' said another.

'Hmm,' Leontios murmured, rubbing his chin. 'How many from Kypros? Show me your hands.'

Out of the forty or so men, perhaps a third were from Kypros or close by. The rest were either from the Greek colony of Bubastis at the delta of the Great River in Kemet, or from Ionia. Also, there were two men of Kemet, and one strange looking one unlike any of the the others who said he came from far to the west, beyond the setting sun.

Leontios rubbed his chin again in thought and then talked quietly, first with tall Akakios and then with Hippolytos. When he spoke again, his words were for his own men as much as for those they had freed.

'I have the right of captain to this ship,' he declared boldly. 'Does anyone here dispute that?'

Talakhonsu saw that the face of Akakios grew darker still at this, but he said nothing and neither did anyone else.

'You are our captain!' the freed men joined together to cheer Leontios.

'Then I will tell you what is to be done,' Leontios continued. 'My kinsman Akakios and the great warrior Hippolytos here will sail with you to Kypros. There you will be free to find your kin, or to return to your own lands if Kypros is not your home.'

There was much murmuring from the former captives and the Phoenicians alike at this as they thought on the words of Leontios. Then the man who had been put forward as the leader of the Phoenicians spoke up for his men.

'But what of us, captain?' he said plaintively. 'Kypros is not our home. We have no welcome there.'

'Shut your mouth, dog!' Leontios bellowed at him. 'Think yourself lucky that you don't follow your dead friends over the side to feed the fishes.'

The Phoenicians hung their heads low at this for they could see little enough mercy in the face of the Greek captain.

'This ship is my prize,' Leontios continued, thumping his chest to make his point, 'and when she reaches Kypros, Akakios and Hippolytos will sell her for me. But!' he held his finger up, 'you men have suffered greatly and I will not see your suffering continue when you leave this prison ship. Therefore, the price of the ship will be divided in two. I will have half of the silver for myself to share with my crew. The rest will be shared equally among all of you freed men. Hippolytos will see to this and you may trust him, as I do, with your life. This is my command and you will all swear to it.'

'We are your men, captain,' Diokles the Ionian thumped his bony chest too. 'We will gladly do as you ask. Your name will be held up to all that we meet as Leontios the brave, Leontios the just!'

'Aye!' the others cheered as one. 'Leontios the just! Leontios the brave!'

'Then we will go our separate ways and part as friends,' Leontios smiled. 'May the gods watch over you until you see your loved ones again.'

Talakhonsu and the others of Leontios's crew followed their captain back aboard the Kallisto at that, but this was not the end of the matter as far as tall Akakios was concerned.

'You are a fool Leontios!' he cursed. 'Why should we give those men anything? They are without honour. They gave up their freedom rather than fight the Phoenicians and now you reward them for it?'

Leontios strode up to Akakios until his nose almost met the taller man's chin.

'Who are you to judge them Akakios? You did not see them captured. Perhaps they were tricked. Perhaps they fought with honour and were overwhelmed, or perhaps they gave in too easily. But still, they are the enemies of our enemies and so that is why I help them!'

'Help them yes, but reward them too? You take silver out of our pockets and food from our mouths so that you can act as the generous lord,' Akakios sneered.

'None have ever gone hungry on my ship for long and without my ship there is no silver at all!' Leontios seethed at this fresh insult. 'You have long since forgotten that Akakios, and it is only due to our kinship that I do not strike you down now for your fresh insult! You remember when you fought with Talakhonsu?

'I said then you were both finished on the Kallisto,' Leontios continued, his eyes bulging with anger. 'Well, he has redeemed himself to me with his bravery and he will remain in my crew. But as for you, when the Phoenician ship has been traded off, your time with me will be at an end. You will have your share of the silver as I have said, but not a measure more. Hippolytos and these poor men you brand as cowards will see to that!'

As the crew of the Kallisto looked on in silence, Talakhonsu thought for a moment that Akakios would challenge the words of Leontios with more of his own. But though the tall man was foul tempered and though he often misused his kinship with Leontios, still he was not foolish enough to challenge him outright. Akakios muttered something under his breath as Leontios climbed back aboard the Kallisto, but it was clear enough that the captain would not forgive him, kin or no kin.

'Jason!' Leontios called to the young Carpathian. 'Take Akakios's belongings to him and then help Talakhonsu to bring the Ethiopian's body aboard.'

After these things had been done, Leontios spoke to Hippolytos in private one last time and the two men hugged, thumping each other's backs as such old friends do on parting.

'Captain Leontios,' a voice called then from the Phoenician ship. One of the former slaves, the strange man from the west with hair the colour of fiery bronze, had come to the side to speak for himself. He looked like he had suffered much under the harsh glare of the sun, for his red skin was covered in many sores amongst the brown freckles on his bony chest.

'My name is Huell,' he said in a voice like splintering wood. 'I come from a land too far away to even think of it now. Far to the west beyond even the smoking island, which your people call Sikelia. If I go with the others to Kypros, that would take me further east still, so instead I would come with you if you will have me.'

Leontios looked him up and down. This was the man of the setting sun who had spoken up before, and he was an odd looking one, with his light blue eyes and tortured skin.

'But still, why would you come with us?' he said after a pause. 'We go north to Kriti, not west.'

'Even so good captain,' the man Huell spoke up again, 'north is better than east for me. There is nothing for me in Kypros.'

Yet despite his pleadings, it was plain for Talakhonsu to see that Leontios was not in the mood to see things Huell's way, for he still burned with anger from his words with tall Akakios.

'I owe you my life captain,' Huell said humbly, 'grant me this favour and I will row for nothing and ask for nothing but a little water. When we reach Kriti, I will do any task you set me until my debt to you is paid, for it is plain to see that you are a fair man who would not ask me for anything that was not due.'

Leontios was touched by this and at last he agreed.

'I could use an extra man at the oar,' he nodded. 'Come aboard. You will take the place of Hippolytos and then we will see what is to be done when we make our landfall.'

After the ships had pushed off from each other, the crew of the Kallisto shouted their farewells to Hippolytos, though not a one called the name of tall Akakios.

'Unfurl the sail!' Leontios shouted, and with the wind at her back the Kallisto careened through the swells on her way north to Kriti, whilst the other ship rowed to the east and Kypros, her former masters the ones to be flogged at the oar now.

After their flight from the Phoenicians and the battle that had followed, Leontios rested his own men from rowing, though their mouths did not rest much for there was much talk amongst them of the prowess of Hippolytos, Talakhonsu and the captain himself. Much talk too of the parting of the ways with tall Akakios, who was not well liked amongst them in any case. Talakhonsu left them to it and took Leontios some water as the captain leaned against the steering oar, a distant look on his face.

'Some water for you captain,' he handed up the cup.

'Thank you Talakh,' Leontios nodded. 'How is your wound?'

Talakh held up his arm to look. A scab of blood had clotted around the ragged spear cut, though it still gaped and would no doubt leave a livid scar on his dark skin until age darkened it.

'It is nothing captain,' he shrugged his shoulders.

'All the same, watch it carefully,' Leontios said darkly. 'I have seen men die from their wounds long after the fighting is forgotten, so do not neglect it. Keep it bound to close it up and bath your arm in fresh sea water every day lad. The salt will keep the foulness at bay, the gods willing.'

'I will captain,' Talakhonsu nodded, then he added quickly, 'I am sorry for Akakios.'

'Hmm,' Leontios grunted, turning his dark eyes on Talakhonsu. 'I think not, Talakh. You and he never saw eye to eye.'

'I meant ... he was your kinsman.'

'He *is* my kinsman,' Leontios corrected him, 'but he abused that bond. Akakios has always been a bitter man, and when Isek left us to return to his family he thought he would fill Isek's place. The truth is that though Akakios was twice the height of Isek, he was only half the man,' Leontios chuckled at his own words.

'Isek was a wise one,' Talakh agreed. 'What will Akakios and Hippolytos do with the Phoenicians? Will they set them free when they reach Kypros?'

'No, Hippolytos has a mind to put them over the side on the shore of a small island near there.'

105

'To see which of them the gods would drown?'

'What?' Leontios laughed. 'Could you believe that of Hippolytos? No, as fierce as he is in battle, Hippolytos would not see them drown. They are our enemies, but bad as they may be they are not your Khaemwaset. On the other hand, neither does he want to show them any comfort. The gods will decide what is to become of them and it will be no easy thing for them to find their way to their own lands, if they get off the island in the first place.'

Talakh nodded, thinking on this. He doubted there would be water on this island of Hippolytos', so these men might die of thirst, unless they could swim to the mainland or were rescued.

'Do not trouble your thoughts with those thieves and murderers Talakh,' Leontios clapped him on the shoulder. 'They would have killed or enslaved us all if we had not beaten them. No, they chose their own fate when they took to raiding the ships of honest men.'

'You are right captain,' Talakh said. 'I will think on them no more and when I bury Meketra, I will forget him too.'

'No,' Leontios said with a shake of the head. 'Only forget the man he became, not the man that he was when he saved your life. It is difficult to do this I know, but that is my advice to you Talakh,' he said, rubbing his bristled chin thoughtfully.

'Well, the sun grows low in the sky and I am hungry. Bring that red man Huell to me Talakh. I will rest and hear his story, while you keep the Kallisto on her course.'

So Talakh called the man Huell over and took the remaining oar while Jason brought more water and some bread for the captain. This Huell was taller than most men and thin with hunger, yet like Talakhonsu he was sinewy and so was perhaps stronger than he looked. A long, bushy red beard hung from his chin and it was no easy thing to guess his age.

'Come,' Leontios said to him. 'Sit and take some bread with me.'

'Thank you captain,' Huell bowed his head, 'but I will not go back on my word and take bread from the mouths of your crew.'

'Ach, you speak our tongue well enough to be one of them,' Leontios said cheerfully. 'So take some bread man! You are my guest and I will be offended if you do not.'

Reluctantly, Huell took the flat bread from the basket. It had been hardened by the sun, even though as was good practice the loaves had been wrapped in fresh leaves to try to keep them fresh. Still Huell ate it down quickly.

'Starved as well as flogged, eh?' Leontios frowned. 'Have another.'

'Thank you captain,' Huell bowed his head. 'But yes it is true enough that they starved us,' he said between mouthfuls. 'They would only feed us at the end of the day, like animals. Those who had not the strength to pull the oar, they would not feed at all.'

'What was to become of you?'

'They told us that if we rowed well and did what we were told, they would find good masters for us at the end of the trading season when they laid their ship up. But we all knew in our hearts that we would die long before then. The weaker men did not last long,' Huell shook his head. 'I saw three in all thrown over the side.

'But you survived to tell your tale.'

'Yes,' Huell said, hanging his head. 'I did not try to fight them, but instead I fought myself. When my arms felt as if the oar would pull them from out of my shoulders and I would die of thirst, then I gritted my teeth and pulled harder. For as long as I remained on their ship there was a chance I might yet escape. Above all, my will to live stayed strong and so I rowed for that evil dog Meketra as if with a willing heart, though it shamed me greatly.'

Leontios shook his head. 'What else could you have done?'

'If I had tried to escape I would still have my honour, but not my life.'

'Yes...' Leontios grunted as he rubbed his chin looking for something to say. After all a man without his honour is a worthless thing in the minds of the Greeks.

'Yet now your life is your own again,' the captain said at last. 'Tell me Huell, where are your own lands? Where must you return to?'

'I come from a place you Greeks call the Cassiterades, far out to the northwest,' Huell said with a simple pride.

Those crew of the Kallisto able to hear Huell's tale grew silent at this, for all of them had heard something of those far off lands of mist and dark gods, where the valuable metal tin was mined from the depths of the earth.

'You have heard of it captain?' Huell asked.

'All who sail the wide seas have heard of those islands,' said Leontios, 'but I never set eyes on anyone from there, nor has any man I ever spoke to. Are all there like you?'

'No, no,' Huell laughed drily. 'Not many have my colour, though most are pale skinned compared to the peoples of the Middle Sea.'

Pamphilos spoke up then. 'Is it true that the hottest part of the day in your western lands is in the evening?' he asked.

'The evening?' Huell frowned. 'What makes you say that?'

'Our wise men say that the sun touches the edge of the earth when it sets in the west. It follows then that because the sun is closer to the earth when this happens, the evening must be the hottest part of the day in the west, just as the morning is the hottest part of the day in the far east. That is what our wise men say, or so I have heard.'

'I will not say your wise men are wrong my friend,' Huell smiled, 'but in my own lands at least, things are not so. No, the hottest part of the day comes when the noon sun is overhead, just as it does here. But the sun is much weaker all the same, the more so in winter.'

'In my own home of Napata, the sun is hotter still than it is here,' Talakh added. 'Far hotter.'

'All this talk of the sun and the earth!' Leontios shook his head with a laugh. 'I have sailed far and wide, and heard many wise men talking to the gathered crowds on such matters, but the truth is that no-one knows for sure why these things should be as they are. The gods make them so and that is all there is to it.

'Huell, tell us instead of how you came to be here. What drove you from your own lands? How did you come to speak the Greek tongue so well?'

'It is no easy task to tell you these things,' Huell said, his face lined with the memories of his hardships, 'but I will try at least.

'I left my own land four years ago when I was not much more than a boy,' he began. 'I was the son of a chieftain who had defended our people's lands over many years, fighting off raiders that came inland from the coast to take our cattle. Though I was only the second son, I was still the boldest and my father favoured me to succeed him over my brother.

'Then one day my father was struck down suddenly with a fit that left him unable to speak or move. His trusted men were at his side with my brother Cadno and me, when one of them whose name was Dubhain spoke up. He said it was clear my father would soon join my mother in the afterlife and so it was important that this news be taken to the people in our eastern lands, a day's walk away. They needed to be shown that our chief had chosen me to replace him, or so Dubhain said. The others agreed that this was a wise thing to do, so I kissed my father's forehead for the last time and with tears in my eyes I went with Dubhain and one other of my father's warriors, a man called Liathain.

'That night while we camped in the forest around a fire, we were attacked by a small band of men and it was then I realised I had been deceived, for Dubhain joined them in killing Liathain who was truly my father's man. They hacked him to pieces with their axes, though he fought with all his strength and wounded the dog Dubhain in the leg when he saw that he had been betrayed. He was a good man, Liathain. A brave warrior, and loyal to my father's memory to the last drop of his blood.'

Huell paused, his eyes closed as he no doubt saw the slaughter in his mind's eye.

'But as for me,' he continued, 'they circled around me and

closed in as I tried to slash at them with my knife. One of them got behind me and struck me down so that my senses left me. When I awoke, I was bound and lying in the bottom of a boat that was headed out across the seas, south as I soon saw by the sun. Dubhain was not there, just the raiders.'

'This was your brother's work?' Leontios guessed.

'I have thought about this much, and I can come to no other view than that he was behind it,' Huell shook his head. 'What has happened now, I can only guess. Perhaps my brother is chieftain, or perhaps it is Dubhain? One day if the gods will it I will see for myself and then I will have my revenge on all those who were against me.'

The crew of the Kallisto all murmured their agreement at this, for to be betrayed by your own blood in such a way was a terrible thing to them all.

'What happened next?' Pamphilos asked eagerly. He was a great lover of a good story, and Talakhonsu could imagine him telling this one to his children in the years to come when he had given up the seas.

'Well, it seems they had been sworn not to kill me,' Huell said bitterly. 'This much I overheard, but I can only guess why. Perhaps Dubhain thought he owed my father that much. Or perhaps he feared that my father's spirit would pursue him in the afterlife when he passes over? Whatever the cause, I am still here,' he laughed harshly.

'The raiders took me in their boat as I have said, and by evening we came to the shore of the Armoricans, as they call themselves. There they sailed along a while until we reached the mouth of a river and the boat rowed up that until we came to a small settlement. The raiders were known there and they had soon paid another boat to take me further still away from my own land. These others took me aboard, still bound hand and foot, and the next day they set their sail back down the river and out to sea to the west. They were traders these men, traders in the tin that comes from the land of Kernow, far to the west of my father's own lands. From what I could make out they were bound for the land of the Iberians, farther still to the south.

'After a few days on a calm sea, we rounded a fierce cape where the currents and winds were stirred violently by the gods, and from then onwards we headed further and further south along the coast. The hot sun parched my throat, as they gave me little enough water and no food, so that I soon grew weak, despairing at my fate. My eyes misted over and I thought surely death was coming for me.

'Then, when I thought I could stand no more of it, a cloud shadow came overhead and the air turned cool. A fresh breeze blew up and if this was a welcome thing for me, the unease I heard in the voices of my captors was more welcome still. I opened my eyes and saw that great black clouds were swallowing the last of the sun. A storm was coming!' Huell's cold blue eyes bulged wide as he spoke.

'I will admit that fear gripped me then too, yet it was a good fear, a fear that returned the strength to my body. My blood warmed as I saw the terrified faces of the traders, for the wind rose and rose until the storm began to howl like a wolf. The sea heaved and fell, taking the boat high into the air and then dropping it back down time and again, while a heavy rain started to fall. Despite my pains I lay there on the bare timbers that dug into my back, catching the rain in my parched mouth and swallowing all that I could.

'You see, for me the storm was a relief from my suffering, though it made my captors fear for their lives. There was nothing that they could do but keep their sail aloft and run before the driving wind, until the sail itself was ripped to pieces and the mast tethers tore free to lash about in the gale like striking serpents.

'The boat started to founder as the waves broke over her, and now the captain ordered his men to throw the tin cargo over the side to keep her afloat. This they did frantically but to little effect and soon they wept for their wives and small ones that would never see them again, praying to the gods to spare them.

'But as for me, I was strangely calm. For many days, I had

felt death creeping around me and I dared him to come now if he must. The crew forgot about me, for only their own lives were in their minds, so I struggled against the leather straps they had bound me with. Now, with the salt water filling the hull where I lay, my bonds were soaked through and I found that I could stretch those about my ankles a little. I had almost managed to free my feet when there was a great crack as the steering oar was broken by the storm's might! The end of the boat came quickly then as the wind pushed her stern round until she was sideways on to the fury of the storm,' Huell said, his thin arms waving wildly.

'And then?' Leontios asked, as the rest of the crew listened intently.

'Well, the next wave that came was not as big as those that had already broken over us, but it fell right into the boat, filling her completely so that the sea rushed in after it and she sank away beneath me,' Huell croaked, his voice grown hoarse.

'The next wave swallowed me down to follow the boat as the sea god claimed us for his own, but my father's voice spoke to me then and told me it was not yet my time to die. A hunger for revenge against those who had betrayed us filled my heart and I kicked with all my strength until my legs came free and I struggled to the surface again, just as I thought my lungs would burst. Now, the storm was still raging and my arms were still bound, for though the tethers had loosened a little it was not enough to pull my hands free.'

Huell paused then, a distant look in his eyes as Jason placed another cup of water in his hands.

'When I was a boy,' he continued at last, 'my father taught me to swim in a pool in the forest. At first I was scared, but he showed me that he could lie upon the dark water on his back, as if it were a bed. 'Hold the air in your lungs,' he said, 'and keep your arms loose.' This I did, as he held me up just with one hand and by and by as I closed my eyes, I felt my body go light in the cool water while I breathed long and deep. After a while I realized my father's hand was no longer at my back holding me up and when I opened my eyes he was sitting on the bank with a grin on his face. So I lost my fear of the water and now that I could float, I became a good swimmer.

'This memory came back to me as the storm raged its fury upon the sea, so I kicked my legs out and took in a great breath of air so that I floated on my back. The waves lifted me up into the sky and dropped me back down again until they rose around me like great green mountains over and again. But though much of the time the sea rushed over my face, and though many times the waves turned me over, somehow I righted myself each time this happened and breathed when I could. Gradually I worked my hands free from their bonds and though my arms were stiff and lifeless at first, I began to swim on my front to keep myself warm against the cold of the sea.'

'What of your captors?' Leontios asked, as Huell again paused in his story to take some more water.

'I looked around for them, but there was no sign. They were surely drowned, but though I was glad of their fate in some ways, I knew that now I was alone in the vastness of the seas. It seemed the gods had spared me from the wreck of the ship only so that they could give me a slow death as the cold sapped the life from me. But then as I started to lose hope, the gods sent me a sign, for they tore a hole in the clouds above me so that a warm beam of sunlight shone down on my face. The winds eased and the swell of the sea faded into a gentle calm. I turned on my back again and let the sun warm my body a little, but still as the time passed the cold of the sea drained what little strength I had left, until darkness came over my eyes and I felt my end was near...

'I thought of many things while my spirit wandered between this life and the one which comes after, my anger at the spite of the gods slowly slipping away from me. How long did I drift upon the great sea like this? Perhaps it was only a few hours, but it seemed like days.

'I dreamed of voices that called to me from far away and then I saw the light of the sun, red through my closed eyes, and cool water trickled into my parched mouth. I slept on, dreaming still of many strange things until one morning I awoke to find myself on dry land again, an old man looking down on me. I thought that I was dead and that he was a spirit, but as my senses returned to me I saw he was a fisherman, a simple man of the sea. Though he spoke a very different tongue to me, some of our words were the same, so that with signs from our hands we could more or less understand each other.

'I later came to know that the same storm that had wrecked my captor's ship had caught up his own small boat and he and his son had found me clinging to life and pulled me aboard, though with much difficulty. So it was that I found myself amongst these kind people and their kin.'

'It is clear that Poseidon did not want you my friend,' Leontios nodded thoughtfully. 'Surely it is a sign that you can only bring good fortune to my ship.'

'Thank you O captain,' Huell lowered his head. 'I hope that will be so.

'To continue,' he said after a pause. 'When my rescuers knew of my betrayal at the hands of my father's trusted man, they offered what help they could to take me back along the coast a way, by sea. Yet after my ordeal I could not face such a thing, so instead I asked them which way I must go across the land to return to my own people. They warned me of warlike tribes and mighty rivers that would bar my way, but I hungered for revenge and my ears were deaf to them. With a little bread, some dried fish and a skin of water, I left these kind people behind me and turned inland, where the hot sun burned my skin until it blistered. Still I did not care and I rushed blindly on, thirsting for the blood of my betrayers even though back then I was not much more than a stripling. The people I came across turned aside from the wild thing I had become and I spoke to no-one.

'After many days, I saw high mountains in the distance and made for them with all speed, keeping them to my right as the fisher people had directed me. It was then that I came across the first of the warlike tribes I had been warned of, and I fled for my life before their spears. Many times I tried for the north, but even at night there were vicious dogs and other wild beasts that pursued me. I became lost, driven blindly on until after many days I saw the sea again...

'I know now that this was not the wide ocean that flows beyond the Pillars of Heracles, as you Greeks call the mouth of the Middle Sea. No, it was the same Middle Sea that we sail upon now, the sea of the Greeks and the Phoenicians, though far to the west from here.'

'It is our sea alone,' Leontios broke in. 'The Phoenicians have no place upon it, as you saw earlier.'

'Aye,' Huell said bitterly, 'but still they ply their trade where there are no Greek ships, as I found to my cost.

'Still, when I saw the sea it was such a beautiful thing for me to behold, even though I was half starved by that time. I wandered down amongst the cliffs to where a sandy bay of clear blue and green water called me to swim to escape the unrelenting sun. Then I drank the last of the water from my goat skin and found some shade where I fell asleep on the sand in the cool evening breeze. It was here that my fate took an even worse turn, when a Phoenician ship came ashore whilst I lay there. I awoke from my troubled dreams to find a spear point pressed against my throat while these strange men with babbling tongues took me for their prisoner.'

'There is no shame in it,' Leontios said. 'You had no weapon, so what could you do?'

'Aye, and so I was taken. Once they had bound me, they took me aboard their ship and sailed away the next day into the east. I will not dwell on what happened to me from that time on, for the memory of it is too painful to me, but it is enough to say that I was traded by these men as a man might trade an animal. I passed through the land of the Libyans and then to the edge of Kemet, where I was made to work the meagre land. It was there that I was eventually traded to Meketra, to row aboard his ship as a slave with the other Greeks. From them I learned your tongue as they told me their own desperate stories.'

'He was a man full of evil this Meketra,' Leontios shook his head. 'Why would one man use another as a slave? There is no honour in that!'

'He enjoyed having the lives of other men in his hands,' Huell answered. 'He thought this made him a big man who others would fear, and in this he was not wrong. But now thanks to you and your crew, he is dead and I am a free man again.'

Talakhonsu hung his head then, feeling bad that Meketra's body still lay under the steering deck. It would start to smell soon and then all would want to be rid of it. Besides, it was bad luck amongst the Greeks to have blood spilt on your own ship, this much he knew. There seemed no end to the blood that drained from the corpse, staining the Kallisto's deck. And yet still he owed his own life to the Meketra he had known as a boy. Above that he owed Meketra for helping lay to rest his murdered father, Korkamani. These things he could not easily forget, despite the terrible story of Huell.

-ϕ-

'So you see,' said Pelia, as she finished combing Cerian's long black hair with the younger girl's comb, 'that was how my father Talakhonsu came to meet Meketra again after all those years, only to have to take the life of the one who had once saved him.'

'How strange the fates are,' Cerian shook her head sadly. 'So Meketra was a bad man after all?'

'There is good and bad in everyone,' Pelia shrugged. 'We cannot know what befell him after he fled Kemet. Everything that he had known there was gone and, like my father, no doubt he found himself to be an outsider. Perhaps without Broken Nose to lead him, the only way he could see for himself was one of violence.'

'But to take other men as slaves... that was a shameful thing to do. A cowardly thing.'

'Yes, and he died for it in the end, so it did him no good.'

'Aye,' Cerian said thoughtfully. 'Still, I feel sad for his death in spite of all. But what happened to tall Akakios after Leontios had cast him off? And what of Hippolytos? And this one Huell too?' she asked. 'So many things have changed now... you must tell me what happened next!'

'I will,' Pelia smiled. 'You will hear the story right to the end. That is if you don't take Tyrnon for your man first. It will not be long before you are gone from me I think.'

Cerian's pale white cheeks flushed red, just as Pelia had intended. She loved to tease the younger girl.

'Tyrnon is still a boy,' Cerian said, trying to sound disinterested. 'Besides, his father is strong and in good health. He has a young man's eyes and so it will be many years before he passes on and Tyrnon has land of his own. All he has to offer is what he catches in the hunt, and that is not much. He is not as good a hunter as your Aneurin anyway,' she grinned.

'So you have at least thought of taking his hand if he offers?' Pelia smiled back, not to be deterred from her own fun.

'No more than you have thought about your Aneurin.'

'Ach, I am happy as I am, you know that,' Pelia shrugged her shoulders. 'Aneurin has his ways and I have mine, so while I will not deny that I love him, it is a sister's love for a brother. Not the kind you have for Tyrnon.'

Even as she said these last words though, Pelia doubted them. Soon enough her young friend would leave their hut to live with Tyrnon, she felt sure of it. Then Pelia would be alone again when night came and the beasts cried out in the forest. She thought of Aneurin again, and the image of his naked chest lying next to her on her furs came unbidden into her mind. The thought of a man's warmth close against her in the chill winter nights made her feel comforted. And yet, also uneasy.

'You are looking far off again,' Cerian said gently.

'I was just thinking that the goddess smiles on us,' Pelia said as she placed another branch carefully onto the dwindling coals of the fire. 'The summer lies before us and we have food enough too. The land is at peace. No tribe lifts its hand against another.'

'It is good,' Cerian agreed, feeling the thrill of youth run down her spine like a shiver. 'We must make the most of it Pelia, you and I. We are young and the eyes of the men follow us when we walk by!' she laughed. 'Now, while we still have this time together, will you tell me more of where the ship sailed next and what new adventures Talakhonsu had?'

'Aye, I will if it makes you content,' Pelia smiled, while Cerian laid aside the winter boot she had been patching and listened intently.

-φ-

With the sad tale of Huell fresh in their minds, the crew of the Kallisto sought rest where they could, but it was an uncomfortable night for all of them as a fresh breeze brought a chop to the sea that made the ship's timbers creak and groan as her hull slapped the water. The next day passed slowly too, as the same favourable wind meant there was nothing to be gained in putting the men to the oar, but after another sleepless night the keen eyes of Pamphilos made out the coast of Kriti in the first light of the dawn. All aboard the Kallisto were glad for that.

By noon they were safe in the harbour of Itanos, where one of the galley ships of the warlord Hermokrates lay alongside the quay. The Kallisto moored behind it. Then, much to Talakhonsu's surprise, Huell helped him and Pamphilos in carrying the now stinking corpse of Meketra ashore.

'You don't need to come any further,' he waved the red man away.

'No, I will help you,' Huell answered. 'I have reason enough to hate him and to wish that the crows feast on his rotten eyes, but then I am indebted to you also. I respect your wish to bury him in the earth.'

'Make a litter and drag his body as far from here as you can up into the hills,' Leontios said as they lay down the dripping corpse on the dry earth. 'Let his spirit wander up there alone if it wishes, where it can do no harm.'

'Aye captain,' Talakhonsu nodded.

'And make sure you bury him far from any stream!' Leontios called over his shoulder as he returned to the Kallisto.

A kind old man who knew Pamphilos and Talakhonsu lent them a small axe to cut some strong poles from a tree on his land and with these and some smaller branches tied together, they made a litter onto which they bound the body of Meketra.

But the flies! There had been none until the Kallisto had drawn close to the shore, but then they had come, a few at first and then in their droves. Now they swarmed all over the dead man, feeding on the dark blood that caked his bloated limbs. It was a task not pleasant, and hard work too, to drag Meketra's body away from the harbour and up into the hills. There, the paths were rocky and uneven and it was some hours later that Talakhonsu fixed upon a shady hollow under a low cliff. In the heat of the day the three men sweated greatly as they used flat stones and sticks to scrape out a trench, and in it they laid the body of Meketra. Though Talakh had not planned it, the thought came to him to gather some bright flowers that grew nearby and these he cut with the small knife Meketra had left for him those many years ago under a rock on the farm of Siamun in far off Kemet. He placed these at the tall man's feet so that his spirit might be cleansed by their goodness. When the grave was filled back in, they laid large stones over the top of it, both to keep the wild beasts out and also to stop Meketra's spirit body from wandering the earth in its anger.

'Do you have any words for him?' Pamphilos asked quietly when they had finished.

'Yes,' Talakh answered quietly, holding his palms upwards to the sky as was the custom of the people of Kush. The words he spoke were in his own Napatan tongue, as he sought a blessing from great Amun of Napata, that in this distant place far from his father's lands the spirit of Meketra would find peace. Talakhonsu shed no tears then, though his heart was heavy. With the death of Meketra, it seemed the last of his troubled boyhood was now left behind him, yet so also was the last human tie he had with his own poor murdered father, brave Korkamani.

When at last the three young men returned to the harbour, they found the crew of the Kallisto gathered around Leontios, all of them shouting and waving their arms about, whilst Solon the merchant, friend of Leontios, stood by shaking his head sadly.

'What's going on?' Huell asked. 'Are they always this excitable?'

'I don't know,' Talakhonsu frowned. 'O Solon,' he called to the trader. 'What has happened?'

'The Persian king has bridged the waters of the Hellespont with ships and crossed from his Asian lands into Thrace,' Solon said above the din. 'Xerxes marches on Athens to avenge his father!'

'Then it is war,' Pamphilos said, his usually cheerful voice now as dark as winter clouds.

'War, yes, for those who will not kneel to Xerxes,' Solon answered with a grim smile. 'But not for the men of Kriti, and not for those of Sikelia. Here we are beyond the reach of the Persians.'

'That may be true for now,' Leontios raised his voice, whilst his men fell silent, at last remembering his place as their captain. 'But when the Persians have finished with the strongest, Xerxes will then turn his gaze to the rest of us and he will not rest until all of the Greek peoples are under his heel. Only then will his pride be sated.'

'Then what will we do?' Pamphilos asked. 'Will we sail to the mainland and help the Athenians?'

'Aye,' a few of the men said, raising their fists.

'You are young, Pamphilos,' Leontios said, clapping his hand on the young man's shoulder, 'and brave too. I have no doubt you would fight well, but any help we might give is as nothing. What is important is that the Spartans of Lacedaemon come together with the men of Athens, Aegina and Corinth. If they can bury their differences and act as one force, then many others will gather to them and they could yet turn back Xerxes' army. But if their squabbles continue as they have done, then we are all lost. My advice to you all is to wait for news of what alliances the Athenians form, for unless all are united our cause will be lost from the start.'

'We wait, yes,' Kleon said, 'but what do we do in the meantime? It will no longer be safe to sail to Kemet. More Phoenician raiders will replace Meketra's black ship, now that there is war.'

'You forget that there are many of our peoples like the Ionians who have pledged themselves to Xerxes,' Pelagios spoke up. 'They are still welcome in Kemet, so perhaps we can carry on our trade there? The Persian king has no quarrel with the men of Kriti yet.'

'No,' Leontios butted in, 'not yet. But one day soon he will if the Athenians and Lacedaemonians are defeated. If Xerxes plants one foot in Sparta, he will quickly plant the other one here in Kriti, and for this reason I have made up my mind on this. I will ply my trade west to Sikelia for the moment, and then if Xerxes burns the Attic harvest as I suspect he will, we will trade Sikelian grain into Sparta. Through that back door will be the best way for us to help the Lacedaemonians and Athenians in their struggles.'

Some of the men said, 'Aye!' to this, but not as many as Leontios might have hoped, and the captain stomped off away from his crew in a dark mood. He was a proud man and did not welcome his advice being questioned, or worse still ignored.

Talakhonsu wished at that moment for the return of Hippolytos. The Kritan was always staunch in his support of his captain and when he spoke, his words carried the men with him. For the first time, Talakhonsu saw that without old Isek, without Hippolytos, without even the troublesome Akakios to bolster him, Leontios with his gruff ways had lost the hearts of some of the men. These ones who had not given their 'Aye!' now had war on their minds and feared for their island homes far to the north in the Aegean Sea. These thoughts drove Talakhonsu to speak.

'Our captain Leontios speaks wisely on this,' he said boldly. 'We have sailed the seas far and wide together and he has never led us wrong yet. I put my trust in him above all else.'

'What you say is true Talakh,' Kleisthenes said, 'there is no better captain sailing the seas than ours. But it is not your homeland which is under threat, and not Leontios' either.'

Talakhonsu wanted to speak again, but he held his tongue. In truth he knew that though Leontios spoke with a clear head, these men would listen to their hearts first, as he himself would have done if he were in their place. When a man's family comes under threat and their backs are against the sea, he must do all he can to protect them, even if he is one against thousands and death is certain. So he said no more as the men talked and argued amongst themselves.

Later, as the evening drew the sun down behind the distant western mountains of Kriti, he sought out his friend Pamphilos. The young man was sitting alone on the rocks where the harbour ran round into a headland, throwing pebbles into the becalmed sea.

'Will you return to your island now?' Talakh asked, as he sat next to the young Skyrian.

'It is strange,' Pamphilos said quietly, without turning his head. 'I have lived happily these past years with Leontios and he has been as a father to me. And you as a brother too, Talakh, since I have known you. But though I have no kin left on Skyros, still I must go back there. It is where I was born and my father before me. It is the land of my forefathers. If the Persians threaten it, then I must be there to stand with the men of my island.'

Talakhonsu nodded, but again he said nothing. The legends and heroes of the Greeks were strong in the heart of Pamphilos and though he was not a warrior by nature, it was perhaps this as much as a love for his Skyros that called upon him to fight.

'I will do everything I can to return to the Kallisto when the Persians are defeated,' Pamphilos said determinedly. 'Do you think Leontios will hold this against me Talakh?'

'He will be angry... but no, when he looks into his own heart he will see he would do the same if he were in your place, I am sure of that. All the same you should talk with him tonight, Pamphilos. Tomorrow, who can say how many of the other men will drift away to their own islands. You should not be seen to stand with them, or Leontios will feel his trust in you is betrayed. Tell him of your plans tonight, before he has too much wine. That is my advice.'

'And it is good advice. I will miss you, brother.'

'And I you brother,' Talakh shook the young Greek's shoulder. 'And I you.'

That night there was much wine drunk amongst the men, too much for some, and the next morning there were many sore heads amongst those who had slept on the sands around the headland. The men had been through a battle against the black ship of Meketra and the uncertain times ahead only added to their need to forget themselves a while.

In the morning, Solon the merchant came early to them and summoned all to their captain, for Leontios wanted to speak plainly with them. Leontios stood on the steering deck of the Kallisto as the men gathered around her on the quay.

'I will get straight to the point,' he said bluntly. 'I expect Hippolytos to be here in no more than seven days, but whether he is here or not I will sail after that. Who sails with me and who amongst you will remain behind? I must know now so that I can find other oarsmen if need be.'

Leontios cast his eyes around his crew, fixing each one of them with a piercing gaze.

Talakh was first among them to raise his voice.

'It is my honour to serve on your ship, O Leontios,' he said with his hand on his chest. 'The Kallisto is all the home I have, and whilst you have a use for me I will serve under you.'

'As will I,' Kleon spoke up.

'Aye, you are our captain O Leontios,' said Pelagios.

Nine in all of the crew raised their voices, but Pamphilos, and Kleisthenes were amongst those who did not. Young Jason too, hung his head and said nothing, though perhaps that was no surprise as he had shown great fear in the face of Meketra's men.

'So it will be,' Leontios said solemnly. 'But know this. I will take on others in your place, and if you then come back I cannot say that there will be a place for you in my crew.'

The eyes of Leontios fixed upon Pamphilos as he said these last words. There was a deep sadness there in the eyes of the younger man and yet a resolution also that he had to do what he thought was right.

'If you sail to the west captain,' Huell stepped forward, 'then I will row for bread and water only, until you have no use of me.'

Leontios grunted, with a brief nod of his head. The captain's pride was too wounded to give his thanks to the red man.

So it was that the crew of the Kallisto, who had held fast to their captain and each other through thick and thin, were split apart by the actions of a great king from a distant land.

After seven days had passed, Leontios paid off those men leaving the Kallisto with their share of silver coin, for none of them had changed their minds. Still Hippolytos had not returned and so the remaining men of Leontios readied the Kallisto and its cargo of spices and incense from Kemet for the journey to Sikelia, that island of great riches far off in the western seas. Pamphilos came to say his farewells, and though few words were said, it was a sad time for Leontios, for whom the young man was as good as a son to him.

'I hope Skyros is spared, but if you have to fight, then fight well,' Leontios said in parting. 'Remember this only, Pamphilos. If the cause is lost, then save yourself if you can. The gods have greater things in mind for you than to die needlessly. I will offer to them that they keep you safe.'

'I will heed your advice captain,' Pamphilos lowered his head in respect, though also because his eyes welled with tears. 'When all is done I will return to this place and seek out the Kallisto and her crew, and we will share stories late into the night. This I swear to you.'

'Be sure that you do,' Leontios nodded and there was a tear

in his eye too. He said no more and stumped off to the steering deck.

'Keep your eyes keen and use that wit of yours to stay out of trouble,' Talakh said as the two young men clasped arms. 'I will ask my god Amun to keep you safe.'

'And I will offer to my gods for the Kallisto and her crew,' Pamphilos said earnestly. 'Go well my brother.'

As he turned his back and walked away along the quayside, Pamphilos looked older now to Talakh. The boy had finally stepped from behind the shadow of Leontios to face the world as a man.

When the crew of the Kallisto pushed her away out into the bay with their oars, the heart of Talakhonsu was heavy. This would be a strange voyage, sailing to the far west with so many of his trusted crew mates and friends missing. Now there were new men on the boat, men he did not know well, if at all. Only time would tell if they were any good. There were no songs and no chants as the Kallisto rowed clumsily out of the bay and around the headland under the gaze of a few of their kin, who watched from the rocky shore. The eyes of Talakhonsu were turned now upon the west, away from Kemet and the south. Away too from young Ketet and the love he had pledged for her. And so a new turn in the Napatan's uncertain life had begun.

The Kallisto sailed the northern length of the great island of Kriti, staying always within sight of the coast as the wind sometimes helped them and sometimes did not. For much of the time, they had to row in order that the wind would not blow them onto the rocky shores, and this was made all the harder by the new men who had not yet learnt to row as one. There were many oar clashes and much swearing from the more experienced men, Talakh included. After a while Leontios called him to the steering deck, for the wind was testing even his strong arm as he leant on one of the great steering oars.

'The men are tired,' Leontios said wearily. 'As am I. Hopefully we should find a sheltered beach to put her ashore when we near the western coast.'

'Aye, Leontios,' Talakh nodded. 'Will you give the new men the trial of Poseidon as you did me when I first came on board your ship?'

Leontios laughed a little at that, as he recalled Talakh's own trial which very nearly lost the Napatan to the sea forever.

'Perhaps tomorrow before we set sail again,' he said. 'Though perhaps not. In truth Talakh, I am in no mood to play games for the sake of the sea god.'

Talakh nodded, but though he thought it unwise of his captain to talk so casually of the gods, he said nothing. Leontios had lost much in the last few days, despite gaining Meketra's ship and Talakh knew that above all of the silver in the captain's hoard, he valued his men more. Hippolytos, Pamphilos, Kleisthenes, even the quarrelsome Akakios, none of them were aboard the Kallisto now and the vessel felt strangely empty without their laughter, stories and curses, though there were men enough to take up the oars.

'The wind blows hard toward the land, Talakh,' the captain said. 'What would you do if you had the steering oars?'

Talakh turned his gaze toward the land. The northern coastline of Kriti had beautiful bays along some stretches, whilst along others it was rough and ragged, with the swells of the sea foaming white around jagged rocks. Only a few small fishing boats braved these waters and Talakh had not seen a ship of the Kallisto's size for some time. These were dangerous seas for any vessel, let alone one with a patchy new crew.

'We could row out at an angle to the coast and then let the wind crab us back in under sail,' Talakh said. 'If we kept crabbing out and back we would make more headway. But...'

'But?'

'To sail in that way, the crew would need to know each other well and row as one. No, this is a coast with teeth, captain. Who knows what hidden rocks there may be close in, waiting to tear open the Kallisto's belly? Better for us to put right out to sea until Kriti is just on the horizon. Out there, away from the heat of the land we may find a better wind.'

'Or a worse one,' Leontios rubbed his chin. 'The choice is yours Talakh.'

'Then we take the Kallisto full out to sea,' Talakh said firmly.

'And then?'

'We keep the land just in sight, but when evening comes, if the weather is fair we sail on into the dark. Better to not risk beaching her at all with a tired crew.'

'Hmm,' Leontios rubbed his chin again.

'There is a moon tonight to silver the sea for us if the sky stays clear,' Talakh continued. 'Yes, if the weather stays fair we should push on for the west.'

'Good!' Leontios said, his mood brightening. 'That is what I would do myself. Give the order.'

So, Talakh shouted for Kleon and Pelagios to furl the sail and called the other men to bend their oars as he leant against the steering oar to bring the Kallisto's proud eyes round to face the wind. Kleon sang out a rowing chant and one by one the new men joined in as they strained at their oars. The waves slapped the ship's prow and her progress faltered at first, as the oarsmen struggled to find their stroke.

Leontios shook his head. 'They have a way to go.'

'They will learn captain,' Talakh grinned. 'As I did.'

'Aye,' Leontios gripped his shoulder, 'Though few of them will match you lad.

Talakhonsu's heart was full of pride at those words. The respect of a great sea captain was a thing indeed for a young man to have.

Slowly, steadily, the Kallisto made some way against the wind until she had gathered enough speed for the knife edge of her slender prow to slice through the waves, sending up great showers of white spray that cooled the backs of the men, though the salt stung their blisters. Talakh looked over their heads down the length of the ship and beyond, out toward the dark blue horizon. He breathed the air deeply and felt the full strength of youth coursing through his body. At times like this, he could forget the bitterness of the past and live for each passing moment.

'Soon we will be beyond the reach of the land, and the wind will turn,' he said to Leontios. 'I am sure of it!'

So after a while it came to be, as the wind became at first fitful and then finally made up its mind to favour the Kallisto. Talakhonsu quietly mouthed his thanks to his great god Amun, who caused the wind to blow in distant Napata and Kemet, vowing to make a small offering to the god when they came to land again.

'Unfurl the sail!' he called out to Kleon, while Leontios nodded with satisfaction at both the Napatan's growing knowledge of the broad seas and his command of the men, as the two of them worked the steering oars to bring the Kallisto's prow back around to the west.

The Kallisto made good progress now with oars shipped and the wind cracking the sail as it flapped and billowed, yet even so Leontios put his crew back to their benches from time to time as the afternoon wore on, so that the new men could learn their trade whilst Poseidon still smiled upon them. When the evening drew near, the skies were clear and the cool wind still favoured them, so the Kallisto sailed on toward the setting sun of the west, while Talakhonsu waited for the heroes to show themselves in the night sky. The breeze was fresher now, foretelling that it would soon grow cold aboard the Kallisto out there in the vastness of the great sea.

'There will be no stories tonight, Talakh,' Leontios said sadly, his stubbled face lit up in the last of the setting sun.

'Perhaps Huell will tell us more of his adventures?'

'Aye, but there is much sadness in his tale,' Leontios shook his head.

'Perhaps. You must not blame Pamphilos, captain,' Talakh said quietly. 'Nor the others. They are brave men, who do what honour demands to defend their lands.'

'I know, I know...,' Leontios tailed off. 'You are right of course Talakh. I feel suddenly grown old. I have long forgotten what the others still feel deep in their hearts, the need to fight for what they believe in. To fight for their honour, rather than just for the gain of wealth.'

'Your honour is just as deep as theirs captain. You do what you think is best for the Greeks of the mainland, even though they are not your kinsmen and in fact you owe them nothing at all. This is why you would take grain to the Spartans, in spite of the danger that might bring.'

Leontios grunted, but said nothing. He was not ready to be convinced.

'If you had gone to fight with Pamphilos and the others,' Talakh continued, 'I would have followed you, for all that you have done for me and all that I owe to you. But you made the right decision captain. That I do not doubt.'

'Thank you lad,' Leontios said, turning to Talakh as they rested themselves against the steering oars. 'Your words are a comfort to me. But,' he grinned at last, 'still I feel old all the same.'

With the last of the sun now gone and the oars shipped, Leontios posted a look out in the prow of the ship. In the gathering dusk, Pelagios manned the steering deck, so that the captain and Talakh could join the rest of the men in some supper. There was bread, fresh cheeses and some baked fish that had been wrapped in leaves back in Itanos and stored between the jugs of water, to keep it cool. This would be the best supper that the men would have until they touched land again, for tomorrow and the day after there would only be hard bread, dried fish and some duck eggs that had been baked hard. Still for that night there was wine the colour of blood to wash their meal down, and fresh water to slake the thirst that came after that, so that those of the new men who were not sick with the motion of the sea soon found themselves in good spirits.

'It will pass,' Talakh said to Hylias, a young, dark haired Kritan who had been sick over the side many times already that day. 'Here, take a little bread and a little water, and look always to the horizon,' he said, remembering the advice Pamphilos had once given him. 'That will help you.'

'But how will I see the horizon now that the light is dying?' Hylias moaned.

'Ah, when the moon rises in a while you will see it clear enough. Until then, remember you are a man of Kriti and a Greek. The sea is in your blood. You will find your sea legs soon.'

'Thank you Talakhonsu,' Hylias managed a weak smile in the fading light. 'We have heard of you in my village,' he said after a while. 'The Burnt One', some call you,' he said nervously.

'Only some?' Talakh laughed. 'Ah well, it is not the first time I have heard that said of me.'

'They say you come from far in the south, where the sun scorches the land and all of the people there. Is that true?'

'Aye, my home was once in a land called Napata, where the sun is hotter than in your own Kriti, far hotter. Yet there is a great river there which brings life to our lands all the same. When there is peace, then there is much for my people to thank our gods for.'

'Do you miss it, your Napata?'

'Ah...' Talakh thought for a moment. 'It has been so long, Hylias. I was only a boy when I was taken from there...'

'Will you ever return?'

'That I cannot say,' Talakh shook his head. 'But you will also have heard of the land of Kemet, Hylias?'

'Yes, of course. There are great temples and strange gods there, so they say.'

'And they are right,' Talakh smiled. 'There is a girl who waits for me in Kemet. Perhaps when I return to her one day we will raise children together, but whether they will grow to be of my skin or hers only time will tell. I will love them all just the same.'

'What is your girl's name?'

'Ketet. Little Ketet, and she is as beautiful as the rising sun,' Talakhonsu smiled broadly, his heart lifting as Ketet's face came to his mind's eye. 'You have a girl yourself, Hylias?'

'There is one who my mother wants me to marry, but I like another.'

'Then you should follow your heart,' Talakhonsu grinned.

'After all it is you who will have to lay with her, not your mother!'

The two young men laughed at that, and for a brief while some of the old cheer was restored to the Kallisto.

'One day you will be a captain yourself I think, Talakhonsu,' the red man Huell said when the Napatan joined him and Leontios as they talked together. 'You have a way with the ship and a way with the men I think.'

'A captain? No, that is not for me,' Talakh shook his head, embarrassed by this praise.

'Huell is right, Talakh,' Leontios agreed. 'You were not born to this life, but the sea is in your blood now just the same. You have all the makings of a leader of men, so one day perhaps you will have a ship of your own. Though she won't be as beautiful as the Kallisto,' he added proudly.

'There is no other ship like her, captain,' Talakh agreed.

'Aye, no other,' Leontios grinned. 'How is the new lad Hylias? He still feeds the fish?'

Talakh laughed at that.

'Aye, he does. When we touch land again he will be the first ashore no doubt!'

'Hmm,' Leontios rubbed his chin as he leant on the deck rail. 'When that will be is not easy to guess, for even though I have sailed these waters before, it was long ago and I was under another captain then. Still, I will show you where I think we are now and then you will know what I know.'

Talakh and Huell listened intently, keen to learn the lie of these northern seas, as Leontios held out the palm of his hand toward them in the last light of the dusk.

'Imagine my hand is the long island of Kriti,' he said. 'Where the knuckle of my wrist is, that is Itanos on the south western coast, yes?'

'Well then, so far we have sailed across my wrist to the base of my thumb and then rounded the cape of Sidheros that brought us to the northern coast. Now we sail westward toward the end of my fingers and the last of Kriti. You understand?'

131

'Aye,' Talakh nodded.

'Up here,' Leontios held his other hand up high, fingers pointing down. 'My fingers and knuckles are the Peloponnese where the Lacedaemonians have their lands in Laconia. Their hoplites are the greatest warriors of all we Greeks, and their city of Sparta is here, on my knuckle, while north of them are the Arcadians.

'Further north still, there is a narrow bridge of land or isthmus as we call it and this links the Peloponnese to the lands of Beotia and Attica, with the city of Corinth nearby. They say that at its narrowest, a hundred men could join their shields and bar the way across this isthmus, though I have never been there to see it with my own eyes. It is to Attica that Xerxes will march first, so that he can take his revenge on Athens.'

'But then they have their wooden wall of ships,' Talakhonsu nodded, remembering what Leontios had told him of the Oracle and the man Themistocles, whose silver had paid for the great fleet of Athenian warships.

'Aye, that is right,' Leontios said. 'They will bloody Xerxes' nose for him if his own fleet crosses their path.'

'And Sikelia, captain?' Huell asked, 'Where does she lie compared to Kriti?'

'Many days sailing to the west far beyond my fingers of Kriti, that is where Sikelia is to be found,' Leontios answered, gesturing with his map of the hands. 'But before you can think of Sikelia, I will explain the other lands that lie before her. Here along the coast above the fingers of the Peloponnese is the island of Cephallenia. Then west across the sea from her are the narrow lands we call Iapygia. Along her southern coast there is a narrow spit of land and almost joined with that is Sikelia. She is a big island, as long as Kriti I think, but much broader.'

'Aye,' Huell nodded. 'That is as I have heard it too.'

'You know of these other lands, besides Sikelia?' Leontios asked.

'Some of them,' Huell answered flatly, a bitterness hardening his narrow face. 'My captivity took me to many places around the Middle Sea.'

'Well, that part of your life is ended now,' Leontios placed his hand on the red man's shoulder. 'You will go to Sikelia a free man.'

'I thank you again for it,' Huell said, a worn smile returning to his face. 'May the gods always look upon you well for all that you have done for me.'

'Ach, it is nothing. Here, have some more wine,' Leontios filled Huell's cup. 'And you too Talakh! Let us drink to a safe passage.'

'Yes, a safe passage,' Talakhonsu nodded, taking a warming draught of the red wine.

'We will cross to the Peloponnese when we pass Kriti's westernmost point, and from there along as I have shown you, past Cephallenia and across to Iapygia,' Leontios continued. 'It will take longer than if we were to cross the open seas straight to Sikelia, but with many untried men amongst the crew it will be safer in the long run. Besides, I want to beach my ship when I can, and the new men will thank me for that at least. They have much to learn.'

And it was true that they did. That night there were many grumbles as men more used to solid ground under their backs struggled irritably with sleep that would not come to them, while the sickle moon silvered the dark seas.

The next morning in the first of the dawn light, Talakh could just make out the last of Kriti, a neck of land that Leontios had spoken of which jutted north into the sea. It had been a long night for the Napatan, keeping watch at the Kallisto's prow for rocks that might gouge out her belly if they ventured too close to shore. Now, he went to the steering deck where Leontios stood, his eyes sunken with tiredness.

'You look how I feel, Napatan,' the captain said with a wry grin. 'You should get some rest after you have had your bread.'

'And you captain?'

'I have the care of these men too much on my mind,' Leontios said. 'So there can be little enough sleep for me until we beach again. You saw the last of Kriti?'

'I did. It is time for us to turn to the north?'

'Aye it is. Take the other oar and help me bring her round.'

While the two men leant against the steering oars, weary Leontios called the other men to their oar benches, ready to row at his command. The wind was light, as was the sea, and the Kallisto's prow swung easily round to the north. Now that they were on their course, Leontios set half the men to row whilst the other half took their bread and filled their stomachs with whatever of their own food they had left.

'We will run with the noon sun at our backs,' Leontios turned wearily to Talakhonsu. 'We should make the coast of Lacedaemon soon enough.'

'Perhaps you should try to rest captain, while the open sea is before us?' Talakhonsu said, sensing that this was perhaps what Leontios had in mind.

'You are more tired than me,' Leontios blustered still.

'I am, but I can sleep when we reach Lacedaemon, whereas none but you can guide us along those shores.'

'Well, perhaps you are right,' Leontios relented. 'I will close my eyes for a while amongst the cargo. Follow this course and you will see a small island soon enough, off to our left. Pass to the left of that and head on until you see a much larger island. Pass to the left of that too and wake me when we are close on it. Have you got that?'

'To the left of the small island and then also to the left of the large island, aye. I will wake you when we have the large one in sight captain,' Talakh repeated.

'Good. And be sure to wake me if we sight another ship or the wind changes.'

'You can rely on me captain,' Talakhonsu lowered his head.

'I know lad, I know,' Leontios clapped him on the shoulder and stepped wearily from the steering deck, his legs stiff from standing so long at the steering oar.

Talakh watched as the captain wrapped himself in his cloak and bedded himself down in the cramped hold. Only now did he truly understand the weight that rested on the shoulders of Leontios. For without Isek, Hippolytos and tall Akakios, there were no others aboard the Kallisto with his skill at navigating the ship. No others who could steer her surely from one land to the next, as she crossed the wide seas. He saw that it was his place now to help where he could, for although the captain had said nothing to his face, Leontios was relying on him for this. That much the young Napatan knew.

Sure enough, as the morning breeze picked up a little and a chop set in on the sea, Talakh very soon brought the ship to the small island, though it was off to one side and the men had to row across the wind to bring them to it. The same thing happened when the Kallisto came to the larger island, which again was not far off, but by this time the captain had rested for at least a while.

'You have done well,' Leontios said, rubbing the sleep from his eyes after Talakh had called him awake. 'I will take her from here. Get some rest yourself now.'

Talakh did as Leontios asked and wrapped his cloak over his head and shoulders to keep the light from his eyes. He had long been used to the heaving of a ship at sea and he fell into a deep sleep almost as soon as his eyes closed, so tired was he. Amongst his nameless, shapeless dreams, the voices of the men drifted distantly as they sung a low rowing chant against the lullaby of the waves.

Chapter 5

Island of the Smoking Mountain

It was late afternoon when Talakhonsu woke again, his senses stirred by a change in the motions of the ship upon the sea.

'Zakinthos!' Leontios called to him cheerfully as he got to his feet. 'It is many years since I was last here. Hah! I was not much more than a boy then!'

Talakh squinted in the bright sunlight, trying to hold his eyes open. The sail was furled now and the wind had dropped to almost nothing. Ahead of them lay a wide bay on the shores of a large island, green with trees that clung to the craggy hills inland. The Kallisto made her way to the westward side of the bay, nearing a smaller island thick with pines where the crickets called to each other noisily in the tree tops. There the sand was pure white, dazzling in the heat of the sun, and lapped by the calm, blue sea.

'A lovely place, is it not?' Leontios beamed.

'We will land here?' one of the new men asked.

'No, not here,' Leontios shook his head. 'If there was water maybe, but on this isle there is none.'

They rowed deeper into the bay to where a smooth sand beach beckoned the Kallisto to rest her keel on its gentle shores, sheltered by the white cliffs of a headland. A small settlement of stone huts stood back from the sands amongst the shady trees, a few fishing boats drawn up before it. Yet as the Kallisto drew closer, the children playing in the shallows amongst them were hurried inside by their mothers. A few men in the light tunics that were common to many of the Greek peoples walked down onto the sands and stood there boldly, leaning on their light spears.

'Hold your oars!' Leontios ordered the men. 'Talakh, you are

the best swimmer of us all. Swim ashore and see that there are
no rocks in the shallows for us to ground on.'

Talakh did as he was bid and dived into the cool, clear
water. It was only when he rose back up to the surface that a
thought crossed his mind that the men on the beach might
mean him harm. Still, he did not want to show weakness and he
knew his captain was behind him, so he swam slowly on
toward the shore and the waiting spears.

Back on Kriti, Pamphilos had taught him to dive down
through the water to search among the rocks with a small spear
for octopus. Down there he had sometimes opened his eyes
briefly against the stinging salt water, and though it was not
pleasant, still it let him see the wonders of the sea even if they
were blurred. Now he lowered his face into the water to look
out for rocks that might tear out the Kallisto's belly and found
that here the sea was saltier than on Kriti, and blurred his sight
all the more. Still he could make out clearly enough that there
was only sand and clumps of sea grass such as often grew in
these shallow bays. A shoal of fish darted in and out of the
grass, their golden eyes glinting in the sunlight as they turned
on their sides to look up at him. Talakh's heart leapt then, as it
always did at such sights and for the briefest of moments he
forgot about the men on the shore. He could not hold the air
within his lungs for long though, and when he surfaced and
wiped his stinging eyes clear of the salt water, he saw the
menacing shapes of the men waiting still with their spears at
the water's edge. It was only a few short strokes until the sea
grew too shallow for him to swim and he felt the sand under
his feet as he walked ashore. Wiping his eyes again, Talakhonsu
took a few steps forward onto the soft sand and bowed low,
before addressing the men.

'My captain would like to beach his ship here for the night,'
he said carefully, polishing his words as much as he could so
that he might sound as a Greek native does, rather than a
stranger.

One of the men stood forward.

'Who is your captain? What is his business here?' he asked

with a hoarse voice that sounded as if his throat had been cut long ago.

He was older than the others this one, a small wizened man with a short, grey stubbled beard and dark wrinkled skin, yet he was clearly their leader and he looked the kind who would not shirk from a fight.

'He is Leontios of Itanos,' Talakh said, raising himself proudly to his full height. 'A famous captain.'

'I have not heard of him and I know of no Itanos,' the older man said in his scraping voice. 'Where is this place you speak of, stranger?'

'Kriti,' Talakh said bluntly, knowing that the man would not respect any weakness in him.

'Than you are a long way from home, dark skin,' the man narrowed his eyes. 'What brings you to my shore?'

'We sail for Sikelia,' Talakh answered firmly again. 'We have trade there. But from your shore we need only fresh water. That and sand under our keel for the night.'

The man's eyes narrowed still further and Talakh was sure now that they must be closed, but from his grizzled throat no words came.

'We are traders...' Talakh began to say, but the scraping voice interrupted him.

'You look more like a ship of war to me, a raiding ship,' he said, his hand resting on his dagger hilt. 'You have many men aboard. Too many for a trader.'

'The seas can be dangerous,' Talakh said, rubbing his chin. He wished then that he had not shaved his bushy beard off in Itanos, for in truth he felt a little naked without it. He breathed in deeply, pushing out his chest to its full extent and spoke with the pride of a warrior who has made his mark in battle.

'My captain likes to be ready for a fight if need be,' he said. 'You can be sure of that.'

'He does, does he?' the man rasped again. 'But you are not ready, are you dark skin? Where is your knife? Where is your spear?'

'When I come upon the shores of the Greek peoples, I have

no need of such things, for then I am amongst friends,' Talakh replied, thinking quickly.

'Hah!' the man laughed hoarsely, clapping his hands together loudly. 'You have your wits about you stranger, I'll give you that,' he smiled thinly. 'As a brother then, you and your ship can land here. That is if I have the word of your captain that you come in peace and will cause no trouble.'

'You will have his word on that,' Talakh placed his hand on his heart. 'I swear to it.'

'Good,' the grizzled man nodded his head, satisfied with Talakh's oath. 'What is your name stranger?'

'My friends call me Talakh.'

'Talakh,' the man said. 'Not a name I know. But who is your father?'

'Korkamani. Korkamani of Napata,' Talakh said proudly.

'Well,' the man said, 'you are welcome here tall one. Tell your captain he is welcome too as long as he and his men stick by your oath.'

'Thank you,' Talakh bowed, then turned and waved to the Kallisto. The ship looked a thing of great beauty out in the bay with the blue sky above her. Alive almost, he thought, as the shimmering sea dappled the painted eyes of her prow with light.

At the command of Leontios, her oars dipped into the water and though some of the newer men caught their blades now and then, still she came on smartly.

'She is a lovely ship,' the man said, as he stood alongside Talakh to watch beach. 'What name has she?'

'Kallisto,' Talakh answered proudly.

'After the beautiful nymph?' the man asked.

'No, the captain's wife,' Talakh answered. 'She is in the after world now.'

'Everything alright?' the deep voice of Leontios called across to Talakh, echoing from the low cliffs behind the beach.

'Aye captain, no rocks,' The Napatan shouted back.

As she closed on the shore, Leontios had the men ship their oars so that the Kallisto glided silently in until her prow slid up and out of the lapping waves and her flat keel grounded fast in the shallows. Leontios leapt over the side and into the water with a great splash, striding from the sea like a hero from Pamphilos' stories.

'I am Leontios,' he offered his hand to the hoarse man with a warm smile, his teeth white against the black of his stubbly beard.

'Welcome, captain Leontios,' the man rasped. 'I am Amyntas. I am head man here.'

'I thank you O Amyntas,' Leontios tilted his head a little. It was not a bow, but still by doing this he showed the older man respect. 'We spent last night aboard my ship,' he said cheerfully, 'but hardened as I am to that, many of my men are new. They will rest well tonight on your beach, if you would allow that.'

'Your men are tired,' Amyntas said, with a tilt of his own head. 'I would not turn them away.'

'Thank you. You will feast with us tonight?'

'I am not as young as yourself captain, and I need my sleep too, but I will share a cup of your wine if you have any?'

'Of course, we will be honoured to drink the health of you and your kin.'

'Good, I thank you. Now, your man Talakh here mentioned water. There is a spring at the foot of that low hill behind the village,' Amyntas pointed. 'The water is sweet and you can fill your jars there.'

So, the new men were put to work carrying jugs of fired clay to collect the fresh water in. Talakh laughed with Pelagios as they watched two of the men stagger from side to side while they hefted a full jar between them. The motion of the sea does strange things to a man's legs when he is new to it, they knew.

When night fell, the islanders laid two fires on the sand that soon blazed merrily enough. One, the high fire, was for Leontios and his guests. The other, a way off, was for the rest of the crew.

Leontios bade Talakhonsu, Pelagios, Kleon and the red man Huell to stay with him when Amyntas came to join them in the early evening. The grizzled head man's eldest son strode alongside him and after Leontios had offered them his welcome, two old women of the village served them all dishes of fresh flat breads with small fish and some cakes sweetened with honey. Even so, despite his hospitality Amyntas was old and wise enough to know that trusting a stranger with your beach was a different thing to trusting him with your young women, for there were none of those in sight. No doubt they were safely hidden in the hills for the time being.

'We will have roasted goat in a while,' Amyntas said in his gruff way. 'The women cook it slowly over the embers so that it falls off the bone!'

'We thank you for your kindness, O Amyntas,' Leontios smiled. 'I have a gift for you in return. Two jugs of our best Kritan wine and some incense from far off Kemet for you to offer to the gods if you wish. Or your women if you prefer,' he winked.

These things were well received by Amyntas, for the wine of Kriti was known well for its quality amongst all of the Greek peoples. So, the two men drank each other's health, whilst the son of Amyntas, and the captain's companions sat by respectfully.

'What of the Persians?' Leontios asked as he broke bread with Amyntas to start the feasting. 'Do you have any news of Xerxes' army?'

'There are many rumours, many stories,' Amyntas grunted. 'But which of them are true I ask myself? One of my kinsmen told me a Persian raider was rowing ashore to attack us earlier this very day, and yet if that were true his name is Leontios and he now sits before me sharing his wine!' he laughed gruffly. 'Still, the people of these islands are worried, all the same, even if the danger is far from us here.'

'Aye,' Leontios raised his cup, 'and long may it remain so.'

'You sail for Sikelia then?' Amyntas asked after they had all drunk to that.

'We do, though this is the first time I have taken my own ship there. For many years my trade has been with Naukratis at the mouth of the Great River of Kemet, sometimes beyond that even to the place the Kemet people call Waset, though you may know of it as Thebes. Those waters are too dangerous now for a lone Greek ship I think.'

'That is so?'

'Aye. On our last voyage we were attacked by a Phoenician vessel as we returned to Kriti.'

'You did well too escape them!' Amyntas said with a wry grin.

'Escape them? No, there was no choice for us but to fight. The gods favoured us that day and my men showed great courage. We took their ship from them instead, killed their captain and freed their slaves including this man here, Huell. He is a Celt, from the place they call the Tin Isles far off to the west.'

'A Celt you say? Well I never thought to see a Celt on my beach!' Amyntas laughed heartily, slapping his bony knee. 'Ah, but now at least I know why you have so many men for a trading ship. And now Sikelia?'

'Aye, Sikelia.'

'Well, the Phoenicians will not trouble you in those waters. You know of Gelon, the tyrant of Syracusa? He has a mighty fleet, perhaps two hundred or more fighting ships, though they say he will not help Athens against the Persians even so.'

Talakhonsu listened intently, the wine stirring his blood as his mind's eye saw the massive trireme ships he had heard of, gathered together in a great formation on the calm sea. Each one's three banks of oars dipped and rose as they ran forward, ready to ram and sink any enemy that stood in their way! His crewmates often spoke of these giants of the sea and Talakh could imagine himself standing high up on the fighting platform of one such ship. Without doubt, he thought now, they would see many triremes when they came to Sikelia.

'I hear Gelon has a good many men too that he can call to him,' Leontios said. 'Yet he has enemies of his own to the south.'

'The Carthaginians? Pah!' said Amyntas, the wine firing his

temper. 'They fear him far too much to give Gelon any trouble I would think. The tyrant is a clever man, clever indeed. First, when the last tyrant, Hippocrates died, he helped that man's sons to defeat their enemies. Then after helping them, he usurped them! Yes it is true!

'After that, he won Syracusa too through his guile, and this was a place that even great Hippocrates had never ruled. Syracusa is now the most powerful city in the west! As great as Carthage, so they say! So you see that though Gelon has enemies, they will not move against him lightly.'

'And yet still he will not help the Athenians and their allies,' Leontios shook his head. 'One day perhaps he will regret that if Athens and Sparta fall, for then nowhere will be beyond Xerxes' grasp, not even Gelon.'

'It is the same with my own people,' Huell spoke up. 'Always amongst them there are petty squabbles, as one man will not give way for another, nor help him either. So it is that we often become easy prey to raiders from both the north and the south. '

'It is that way the world over, except perhaps in the conquered lands of Xerxes, where they will no doubt have some kind of peace under his heel. Yet despite all these things there is still hope for us. We have Leonidas, King of the Spartans. He will fight to the last drop of his blood for Lacedaemon!' Amyntas shook his yellow-knuckled fist as he worked himself up into an indignant rage that brought on a fit of coughing.

'The Athenians too will play their part,' he nodded to himself after he had recovered his breath a little. 'It must be ten years now since Darius the Great was defeated on the plains of Marathon by the Athenians. Ten years and now this whelp Xerxes comes looking for revenge. Well, he will not have it! This, I Amyntas of Zakinthos swear!'

'Aye,' Leontios raised his cup, though by now he looked a little bored with the older man's wine bluster. 'We will all drink to that.'

After the tender goat had been served and devoured, after the last cup of wine was drained, and after the fire wood had burned down at last to grey ash, Leontios and his men slept well on the soft sands of the beach, while the waves lapped gently on the shore.

Talakhonsu woke early the next morning, but he was not the first to greet the dawn light. Huell crouched on the shoreline, the gentle waves lapping around his ankles.

'Poseidon favours us with a rising tide,' he said to the red man.

'Aye, it will be an easy thing to launch the ship today,' Huell nodded.

'You could not sleep?'

'Oh, I slept well enough for me, but always now I awake at the first of the dawn. When others rise from their sleep, I must be ready for what they might do, good or bad. That is the hard lesson that life has taught me.'

'I see that,' Talakh nodded, remembering Huell's story of how he was captured by the Phoenicians. 'But now you are amongst friends. We all keep a look out for one another.'

'But still for me it is a lesson not to forget and a habit not to break.'

'Aye, it is much the same for me and for the same reason too,' Talakhonsu nodded, thoughts of his own enslavement coming to his mind. 'You were thinking of your homeland?'

'I was, Talakh. Strange as it seems it gives me a comfort to rest my feet in the sea. The water that laps around them now might once have washed my own shores.'

'How do you mean?'

'Well, the sea never rests,' Huell said casting his blue eyes to the distant horizon. 'It is always moving with the storms and tides, on the currents and in the waves. Though the Greeks say that great Poseidon is master of the sea, still even he cannot bid it to remain all in one place.'

He bent down now and cupped some water in his hands.

'Who knows where these few drops will go when I release them?' he said quietly. 'Perhaps far to the west, beyond the pillars of Heracles. Further still even, to my own shores? It is a strange idea I know, but it comforts me all the same.'

Talakh watched as Huell let the water trickle from his hands back into the sea. He had never thought of such a thing before, but he saw that Huell was right all the same.

'You and I, Talakh, we are alike in many ways I think. I am the red man, as your captain calls me, and you are the black. We are both strangers here amongst the Greeks, do you not think?'

'Me, a stranger? No,' Talakh shook his head. 'Leontios is my captain. These men are my brothers...'

'I meant no offence. But your own lands? Your own people? Do you never long for them?'

'No, there is nothing for me in Napata. No-one waits for me there.'

'I am sorry for that. Still, no matter that you have learned the Greek ways and mastered their tongue, I think you will always be an outsider to them, just as I am.'

'Maybe to those who don't know me,' Talakh shrugged. 'But on the Kallisto at least, my crewmates are as good as my kin. I have their respect and they have mine. We have fought side by side to defend each other and would do so again to the last of our blood, that much I know.'

'I meant no offence, Talakhonsu,' Huell said, his cold blue eyes as impenetrable as always. 'Perhaps we are not so alike after all. Yet times change, as surely as the tides of the sea. As Leontios has seen already, those who we count on today may not be there tomorrow. We must all be ready for that.'

'I am always ready,' Talakh gave a wry grin. 'Life has taught me that lesson too, many times over.'

When all had risen and taken their bread and water, Leontios drilled the new crew members in their arms on the beach, to see what they could do with sword and spear. No doubt, thoughts of the Persians and their Phoenician allies were much on his mind.

Old Amyntas came to watch as the men fought and he urged them on with his harsh voice, waving his staff as he no doubt relived past fights in his own mind. His son watched too, eagerly stepping in every so often to show the younger Greeks his own prowess with spear and shield.

When enough bruises had been despatched amongst his new hands and the tide had reached its highest, Leontios said his farewell to Amyntas and climbed aboard the Kallisto.

'Talakhonsu,' he called. 'You can launch her today.'

'Captain,' Talakh answered, proud at being given this task. Six of the best oarsmen he ordered aboard so that the Kallisto would not drift when she refloated. The others he divided in two, half on each side of the ship's high prow with its unblinking eyes that always looked for danger. A slight swell approached the shore and as it broke and then started to retreat he gave the shout, 'Heave!'

Deftly the Kallisto slipped back into the water and after the men had pushed her a little way back, they started to clamber aboard.

'May Hera watch over your ship,' Amyntas said, invoking the goddess's name as he gripped Talakh's hand. 'You and your captain are welcome here again, dark of skin.'

'Thank you O Amyntas,' Talakh grinned. 'We will bring more wine next time.'

With that he waded into the sea and reached for the arm of Huell, who was waiting to help him aboard. Slowly, the Kallisto backed out into the bay with her oars, turned smartly about and then rowed out past the island, back into the open sea once more. The salt breeze on his face, Talakh hoped they would soon return to this happy island. But whether or not this was in the mind of Leontios, he did not ask, for the captain was lost in his own thoughts.

They soon left all sight of land behind them as the Kallisto headed westward, carried out into the vastness of the open sea by an eager wind that cracked the raised sail like a whip. It seemed to Talakh that the gods favoured their voyage to be an easy one, yet the face of Leontios grew dark and he would let no other take the steering oar but him.

'What is it captain?' Talakhonsu eventually plucked up the

courage to ask.

'A storm comes Talakh. I feel it stalking us,' Leontios spoke quietly, not wishing to trouble the new hands in his crew.

'A storm?' Talakh looked to the far horizons. 'But I see no storm cloud.'

'The sun,' the captain said. 'There is a haze of rainbow around it, do you see? Faint though it is, this is a sure sign of bad weather to come.'

'Bad weather, yes, but some way off do you not think captain?'

'You are talking from what you have seen before, but this time it will be different, I feel it in my bones Talakh. This storm will not come tomorrow when we are safe ashore, it will come today,' Leontios said with such surety in his voice that it made the young Napatan's blood run cold.

'But what...?'

'I dreamt of this moment long ago,' Leontios cut Talakh's question off short, 'I had forgotten it, but now... Now I remember again, just as it is happening. Do you believe in the Fates, Talakh?'

'We are all in their hands captain, it is true. But, you should not talk of such things as this. To do so is to tempt the gods to come against us.'

For a moment the face of Leontios grew darker still, though just as suddenly the darkness passed, replaced by a faint smile.

'You are right,' he said at last with a heave of his shoulders. 'It was a dream after all, nothing more. Let the men row for a while Talakh. We will race this wind, faster than Poseidon's white horses.'

And so the men were put back to their benches, and their voices rang out once more in their rowing chant as the Kallisto surged across the shimmering seas, swift as a dolphin, driving up great plumes of white spray from her high prow. Much was the sweat that ran from the men's shoulders and much was the water that had to be baled from her hull as she ploughed on through the swells, but she was a tight ship and the old hands of her crew, knowing her well, were happy in their work.

They made good speed now, crossing the wide seas between the isle of Zakinthos and the far mainland of Iapygia to the west, but as Talakh pulled on the oar and joined the rowing chant next to Huell, he too now had an eye on the sun. A haze was growing in the sky and the rainbow circle around the disc of fire was now clear for all to see. The afternoon wore on, and the wind grew troublesome as it swung first one way, then another, until it finally resolved to blow hard across them from the south.

'Furl the sail!' Leontios shouted above the rush of the wind and the spray. 'Talakh! Take the other steer oar.'

Talakh drew in and raised up his own oar, making it fast so that it would not foul the others, and struggled past the grim faces and gritted teeth of his crewmates up to the steering deck. Picking his moment he leapt up onto the deck and grabbed the other steering oar so that he could help Leontios with the ship's course.

'You were right captain, the storm comes!' he shouted above the wind that battered his ears. 'What will we do?'

'To make a safe landing in these seas...' Leontios said darkly. 'That will be no easy thing Talakh. Yet if the storm catches us out here, the waves will overwhelm us.'

'We could run north before it?' Talakh shouted back as he worked the oar.

'The seas to the north are unknown to me,' Leontios shook his head. 'There could be rocks or islands there that might wreck us before we even saw them. No it is better that we make the crossing as soon as we can before the rain comes and the light fails.'

The Kallisto pressed on, and Talakh's bones grew cold in the heavy spray that soaked his tunic and stung his eyes. He wiped them as best he could against his forearm, blinking away the salt while he clung to the steer oar with all of his strength for fear of being washed over the side. Quickly now, the hazy sun disappeared and the sullen sky grew dark with racing clouds as the sea by turn dropped away under the Kallisto's oars, only to rise again in the next moment to swamp them again. Leontios called two of the newer men to bale water from the bottom of the ship, though as fast as they baled, still more water was washed in by the white horses whipped up by the rising gale.

Talakh felt it now and saw it in the wild eyes of the men. Death was stalking them all across the raging seas, screaming their names in the howling wind and as the Napatan glanced at the grim face of Leontios, he knew that unless they made the shelter of land soon they would all go to Poseidon's realm under the sea, never to return.

'Amun,' the god's name came unbidden to Talakhonsu's lips. 'Amun save us all.'

The rain started then, a harsh stabbing rain like the winter torrents that fell upon the high mountains of Kriti. Soon the dark sheets of rain took the horizon away and closed around the Kallisto like a cloak until Talakh could hardly make out the ships prow.

'Find your stroke!' Leontios shouted against the wind. 'Find your stroke!'

Though fear was in his heart, Talakhonsu knew that others of the crew, the newer men, were now in dread of their lives. He started up a rowing chant, shouting out the words as loud as he could, until one by one the others joined in as they renewed their struggles at the oar in spite of the wild pitching of the ship. They were brave men then, brave men all, their voices joining together to defy the gods who sought to drown them in the dark gloom of the storm. Brave even when the great god Zeus himself hurled his spears of lightning down around them. But bravery alone will not keep a ship afloat when the great storm comes.

'Talakh!' Leontios called to him above the roar of the wind. 'When the time comes, save yourself. Think of no other.'

Talakh shook his head. 'Captain...' he started to say, but he had no words.

'We will meet again one day, you and I,' Leontios shouted again, a grim smile showing in his dark stubble as he strained against the steering oar with all his strength. 'If not in this world, then in the next. Remember that, Napatan.'

In the years that were to come, Talakhonsu often thought back to that moment as he remembered the sad loss of the man who had been as a second father to him. For this was the last memory that he had of Leontios, alive or dead.

-φ-

'Then Leontios did not survive the storm?' Cerian asked, wiping a tear from her eye.

'No,' Pelia shook her head sadly. 'You see, the Kallisto was sunk by a great wave that reared above her like a mountain of water, so my father was later told. When the wave broke over her, the ship was filled with water and sank into the deep at once, taking down all aboard. Talakhonsu struck his head, and so he remembered nothing beyond what I have told you.'

'Then how was he saved?'

'This I will have to tell you tomorrow. Your Tyrnon is back from the hunt with his father I see and I would not want to keep you from him.'

'Let him come to me,' Cerian said boldly, though Pelia knew her too well by now to fall for her feigned carelessness of Tyrnon's affections.

'At the midsummer feast, your hands will be bound together and he will be yours and you his,' she smiled. 'You will be happy together, but from that time, even though we will always be friends, you will be his wife first.'

'And he will be my husband above his own kin,' Cerian retorted.

'Yes, this is true. You will all have to find a way together, for though they must give their son up to you, still they deserve your respect.'

'I know,' Cerian gave a sigh. 'Sometimes it all seems to be coming too soon.'

'It is only natural to have a doubt or two,' Pelia said, patting her hand. 'This step will be the biggest one you ever take, but it is plain to see that Tyrnon loves you deeply. You are a good match for each other.'

Cerian gazed up into the blue sky of early summer. 'You are right, I know Pelia. But if I could only have two lives, then my life would be complete, for then I could have a life with Tyrnon and then another to be your friend. To be like you are.'

'Like me?'

'Yes, to know what you know. To be at no-one's call but my own. To learn the mysteries of the earth magic.'

'Ah,' Pelia smiled kindly, 'but there is only one life for each of us, you know that. Only one time to walk the earth in our bodies, before they grow cold and we go on to the spirit world. And though there may be many times when love comes to our hearts, still as you have found with your Tyrnon, if your heart is true then there is only one man you can think of spending the rest of your life with.'

'Your words are wise as always Pelia,' Cerian sighed again. 'You know me better than you know yourself I think.'

Pelia looked away, seeing that there was an unintended truth in Cerian's words. Out at the edge of the forest she saw the familiar sight of Sealgair her great hound bounding along toward the settlement gates, and behind him at a distance strode Aneurin. One day she too would have to choose, as Cerian had done, between freedom and love.

-ϕ-

Talakhonsu dreamt a dark dream of an unending night. He was cold and alone in this dream world of his, naked to his dark skin as he crouched down amongst harsh rocks, just a young boy again. Tears came from his eyes, because he knew in his heart that he was alone, banished to this place of sadness. The tears and the cold would go on without end it seemed and his heart grew weak and hollow. He became as one of the rocks that surrounded him, cold and lifeless, still and unheeding of the storm clouds that raced overhead. And yet now and again for a fleeting moment he felt a presence close by him. An invisible hand touched his shoulder then, though he did not know who it belonged to, nor if it meant him good or ill.

'Talakh,' he heard somebody call his name, though it was too faint for him to recognise who spoke it. A great many memories came flooding back to him then. Prainke the wise old holy man who had been his teacher. Korkamani, his father, who had taught him far more even than the old priest had. His gentle mother and all the love she had borne for him. All of these things came back to him and the darkness began to lift a little, as though it were dawn and the sun were about to rise.

'Talakhonsu,' the wind spoke to him again and Talakh opened his eyes as he returned to the realm of the living once more, though at the time he did not know it. He found himself in a darkened hut lying on a soft fleece while strange voices carried to him from outside in a tongue he could not make out.

In a new terror he thought he must have passed over to the spirit world. But not the world of his ancestors, for though his head was spinning with pain, still he knew he was a long way from his homeland and the spirits of those that loved him. There would be no Korkamani here, no mother, no Prainke. No-one to offer him solace for the loss of his life in his earthly body. With a hollow heart Talakhonsu slipped back into a troubled, restless sleep.

When he awoke again, it seemed to Talakhonsu that much time had passed, but in the darkness of his confinement it was difficult to be sure. It was only then that the memory of the wreck came back to him. The ship. The sea. The storm. All of these things rushed at him until a cry rose from his throat.

'It is alright Talakh, you are safe,' a familiar voice came to him.

'Huell?' Talakhonsu opened his eyes. Sure enough, the red man was crouched down next to him in the dim light. He looked older than Talakh remembered, his face lined and drawn.

'Here, drink some water,' he offered a cup to Talakh's dry

lips. 'I thought you would never wake.'

Talakh took a sip and his dry throat welcomed the water like the sands of his desert home. 'Thank you,' he croaked with a voice that did not sound his own. Even the dim light of the hut hurt his eyes and he closed them again quickly. 'My head...' he managed to say.

'You struck it hard,' Huell said. 'You had a fever for many days, but you are over it now I think. You will be well again once you have eaten and your strength returns.'

'Yes, I am hungry,' he realised, but as he tried to sit up a wave of sickness came over him and the precious water he had just drank came back to his mouth again with the bitter taste of bile. He spat it on the earth floor of the hut.

'Do not worry, it will pass,' Huell said calmly. 'I have had such a knock to the head myself when I was a boy.'

'The others? Talakh asked. 'Where is Leontios?'

Huell hung his head, his face grim.

'I am sorry Talakh,' Huell said sadly, his pale blue eyes bright in the gloom. 'They were all good men, none more than the captain.'

'All of them? Dead?'

Huell lowered his head again. 'The sea took them all,' he shook his head. 'Only we two survived when the ship went under.'

Talakh did not speak, for the shock was too great for him to bear.

'I know,' Huell said again, and it was clear that he too felt a great pain in his heart at the loss of the others. 'I will bring bread and water in a while, but for now you must try to rest. When your strength returns you will be able to make a little more sense of what has happened.'

Talakh sank into a troubled sleep soon after Huell had left him, his heart heavy as stone. It seemed an age before he awoke again.

'How do you feel?' he heard Huell's voice. 'Your head is better?'

'It is still tender,' Talakh touched the side of his temple, 'but at least the pain has gone.' He struggled to sit up, though that was no easy task, for his back ached and his arms felt only just strong enough to hold him.

'Stiff eh? You have lain there a long time. Here, try to take some bread.'

Talakh no longer felt ill in his stomach and he quickly devoured the bread along with some water. 'The ship...' he said, after they had sat in silence for a while. 'I must know how Leontios... how the others died.'

'You remember nothing?'

'I remember the storm,' Talakh shuddered. 'I was with Leontios on the steering deck when it struck, that much I know. He spoke to me then as if he had foreseen what would happen. I tried to tell him all would be well, but I think he knew in his heart that his time had come. I saw it in his eyes.'

Tears glistened on Talakhonsu's dark cheeks as he saw again the resigned face of Leontios. 'After that, I remember nothing more.'

'Who knows what thoughts the gods may plant in our minds,' Huell said gently. 'Leontios was a brave man, that much I know from the little time I sailed with him. He was not one who would easily give himself over to fear when danger loomed, so perhaps he did have the sight of what was to come. But what none of us knew when the great wave struck the ship, was that if the fates had been only a little kinder we might all have been saved.

'You see we were not far from the shore at all by that stage, though with the wind and the rain we could see nothing of it,' Huell said sadly. 'When the ship was sinking, a wave rolled her over and I was hurled out into the sea. The others, they were not so lucky. Some I think were drowned there and then, yet the ship floated still, upside down like the back of a whale. All the while the waves tossed me high in the air the one moment and then reared above me the next as I fell back down between them. I thought I saw the head of Leontios come to the surface for a moment, but then he too was gone like the others.

'It was only then that I saw you, with your arm around a

broken piece of the mast. I managed to reach you somehow, though by then you were barely alive. I clung on to the mast with you and kicked with my feet so that I managed to keep us both afloat, but for how long we were like that I cannot say.'

Huell paused for a moment in his story, his blue eyes wild and fearsome as he relived the terror of the wreck.

'Then,' he said at last, 'just as suddenly as the storm had come upon us it was gone. The sky cleared again and I saw we were almost upon the shore of a sheltered bay. The sea had calmed itself by now and as I kicked the water with my legs, so the swells pushed us slowly into the shallows of the gentle beach. When we washed ashore I could finally tell myself I was saved, though I thought that by now you must surely be dead.

'I dragged you out of the waves with the last of my strength and it was then that I heard the shout of a fisherman and his son who came to help us. They had beached their own boat there when the storm came and they gave me a little water and bread to revive my spirits. It was they who brought us in their boat to this place close by, and they who laid your body over a bed of flat stones, warmed in a fire, to drive the cold out from you.

'Then they are kind people,' Talakh said, humbled to find such goodness in strangers. 'I owe them much and I must thank them. But you Huell, you saved me from the sea. To you I owe my life.'

'As I surely owe you mine for freeing me from the Phoenicians,' Huell gave a grim smile.

'No,' Talakh slowly shook his head. 'That was Hippolytos and Leontios as much as it was me. But what you did for me, you did alone. When my grieving is done and my strength has returned, I will repay that debt many times over.'

Over the next few days, being a young man in his full strength of life, Talakhonsu recovered quickly. But though his stomach was full enough with good bread, still he felt hollow inside.

Huell took him along the coast when his strength had

gathered enough, to see the wreck of the Kallisto. The poor ship, vessel of the dreams of Leontios, lay broken on her side. One of her unblinking prow eyes stared forlornly up at them as they stood on the cliffs above and all Talakh could do was look away, out over the gentle sea that lapped the shores so gently. The sun, high in the clear blue sky warmed his face but he shuddered still as he thought of his dead friends down at the bottom of the sea.

'I have been here every day since the storm to look for them,' Huell said sadly. 'I found only the body of the boy Hylias. He is laid in the ground over there, well away from the sea.

Talakh looked toward where a small cairn of stones marked the boy's grave.

'Then it is true,' he shook his head in disbelief. 'Just as Leontios foresaw...'

'I know,' Huell said. 'And yet, though we have both lost much in our lives, still time and again the gods have spared you and I for other things it seems Talakh.'

'Spared us? Perhaps they have spared you Huell, but my heart is empty. Only anger lives there now,' Talakhonsu said bitterly. 'Perhaps it would have been better if I had not survived.'

'And yet you are a rich man now.'

'Rich?' Talakhonsu turned to meet Huell's cold blue eyes with his own. 'How am I rich when I have lost these men who were like brothers to me?'

'I know, but the chest of silver which Leontios carried is yours now,' Huell said grimly. 'It was lashed in the bottom of the ship along with a great many other things which I managed to salvage from her. These things now belong to you Talakh. I did not know your captain long, but I do know he would have wished you to have it.'

'I want none of it!' Talakh shook his head.

'That is your choice,' Huell looked away back out to sea. 'But remember that this silver was the work of Leontios's life. He risked much and worked long and hard to gain it. If he had lived to grow old, he would surely have given it to you and Pamphilos when he passed on. To disown it now would be to disown his memory.'

A sudden rage grew in the heart of Talakhonsu as those words stung him, and he lashed out at Huell with his fist, though still weakened as he was, the blow did not fall hard.

Huell wiped the blood from his split lip and glared at Talakh, but he did not strike back.

'I am sorry,' Talakh said as a deep shame replaced his rage. 'You spoke only the truth and yet I struck you out of hand.'

'Ach, it is nothing,' Huell shook his head, though his bloodied lip said otherwise. 'Terrible things have happened Talakh, but you cannot let them lay you low. Leontios would not have wanted that for you.'

Talakhonsu took a deep breath and thought for a while before he spoke again. 'You are right, red man,' he nodded. 'Now that I am recovered, will you continue your journey back to your own lands?'

'I will,' Huell said. 'I must. That is where my fate will be decided once and for all, when I confront those who betrayed me.'

'Much time will have passed. You may be only one against many.'

'I don't doubt it, but the gods of my people will decide who will prevail. If they are with me I will be chief. If not, then Dubhain and my brother will end me there and then. But either way, I can do nothing else but to face my fate.'

'Then I must go with you.'

'I cannot ask that of you,' Huell shook his head.

'I must repay my debt to you all the same, or I would dishonour myself. You will have a quarter of the captain's silver and after we have rewarded the fishermen for their kindness, the rest I will share with Pamphilos and the families of the crew. That is if my god Amun wills it that I should ever return to Kriti.'

'No Talakh, you don't know what it is that you pledge,' Huell shook his head. 'My land is far away. So far, that I don't even know if I can reach there myself.'

'Then we will find that out side by side.'

'But, it may take many years for you to return to Kriti, if you ever do. There will be many dangers,' Huell said grimly.

'Then that is how it must be,' Talakh said wryly, 'for it seems that just as you have your fate, so I now have mine.'

The two men locked arms to seal their brotherhood in this quest of Huell's, then turned their backs on the sad wreck of the Kallisto for the last time, for there was no saving her now even if they had wanted to.

As the two men walked away along the cliff, the long forgotten face of the evil one, Khaemwaset, came to the mind of Talakhonsu and he shuddered in spite of the sun's warmth. They had thrown him over the side to his lonely death in the darkening seas. How he had cursed them with the last of his breath that day, cursed them all to join him at the bottom of the sea. At least in part, the last curse of Khaemwaset had come true.

'You are unwell Talakh?' Huell asked. 'Does your fever return?'

'No, I am fine,' Talakh lied. In the years to come the curses of Khaemwaset would often trouble the Napatan's dreams, for when a cruel deed repays a cruel deed, only more evil can come from it in the end.

Over the next few days, Talakhonsu's strength returned and so did something of his old spirit as he said goodbye in his heart to Leontios and the others, resolving with the last of his tears to remember them only with happiness for the adventures they had shared aboard the Kallisto. He found too that the sea had not taken everything from him. Huell had salvaged a cloak each for both of them where these had washed up along the beach. But there was something else just as useful to them in this strange land of Iapygia. As had been the way on the ship, the spears and the bright sword of Leontios had been wrapped in oiled skins and were securely wedged between her timbers still when Huell had found her run aground on the rocks.

The leather-bound handle of Leontios's sword was whitened with salt, a reminder of the captain's watery fate, but despite this Talakhonsu fought back thoughts of his loss and strapped the sheathed sword to his waist. He took also a heavy shafted spear, as did Huell. But the thing that was more precious to him than either of these weapons in a way was his own heavy throwing stick which had also been wrapped in the skins for safe keeping. This had been with him since his boyhood and had almost been lost many times over when he had thrown it in anger. And yet after everything that had happened, here it was again before his disbelieving eyes.

The two men spent much time between them polishing the tarnished iron of the weapons with stone and oil until they shone again in the sun, then sewed the silver coin into heavy cloth belts that they wore under their tunics for safekeeping. All this while, the honest fishermen who had given them shelter left them be until the time came when Talakhonsu was strong enough to leave. The carcass of the Kallisto, they left to their hosts, for though her sad hulk was too badly broken on the rocks to repair, still her timbers would be of great value to them in repairing their own boats and their huts. He gave them a gift too of some silver coin for their care and kindness, and in return the fishermen offered good advice for their onward journey to the west. But though Talakh offered them more of his silver to take the two of them along the coast by boat, none of the fisherman would accept, for they feared that the sea god might try to claim the stranger's lives again.

So it was that on a fair sunny morning, Huell and Talakhonsu set out on foot, laden with skins of water, bread, dried fish, and other good things to eat. In the heat of the afternoon they rested and took turns to sleep, then walked on into the cool of the evening, before bedding down for the night wrapped in their cloaks. In this way they carried on for the next four days, stopping for water and directions where they could. It had been some time now since they had heard any news of the war in the Greek mainland, but no-one they passed in this land of Iapygia could tell them much that could be relied upon.

Talakhonsu longed to hear whether or not the Athenians had withstood the hordes of Xerxes and he thought often of Pamphilos, Hippolytos, and even of tall Akakios, wondering how they fared, hoping they were safe and well. When Hippolytos finally returned to Kriti, he would ask after Leontios, but there would be no word of the Kallisto. As the time passed from months into years then he would know that fate had caught up with Leontios at last. Talakh thought then that he should have returned to Kriti, so that Hippolytos and Pamphilos could know of the captain's fate, and he quietly cursed himself for having already given Huell his sworn word. This he could not take back and so he said nothing to the red man, though he swore to himself that one day he would return to Itanos.

By and by Talakhonsu and Huell came one morning to the end of a long headland, where a fair sized port sat down below them. Opposite it across a narrow strait there lay another great mass of land.

'That is the island of Sikelia I think,' Huell pointed across the strait.

'An island?' Talakh asked in his surprise as he looked across the sun dappled water to the distant cliffs.

'Aye it is,' Huell answered. 'Look there! Do you see that peak on the horizon?'

Talakhonsu squinted against the bright sunlight. Like Pamphilos, the eyes of Huell were sharper than his, but still Talakh could clearly make it out. 'The cloudy peak?' he asked.

'Aye, but that is no ordinary cloud,' Huell stared intently. 'The Greeks say a god of the underworld lives within it. When he is angry he rains fire down from its peak, but most of the time he sleeps and belches out clouds of smoke from his troublesome belly!'

'Ah, I had heard something of this,' Talakh nodded, remembering the words of Leontios. 'Let us hope the god stays asleep while we pass by.'

The port below them they found to be named Rhegion and a Sikelian merchant there advised the two travellers to cross the straights to the neighbouring port of Messene on Sikelia. From there he said, they had more chance of finding a trading ship to the north, so this is what they decided to do. There were a few boats in the harbour making a living by ferrying folk to and from the island, so it was no difficulty for them to join one such vessel as it filled up, for just a small price of silver. As they went to the prow of the boat, Huell struck up a conversation with another man, an old but tall and still unbowed Greek in a long tunic, who sat down across from them.

'Friend,' he asked, 'we need to make passage to the far north. Where would be the best place to take a ship from?'

'North?' the Greek asked with a suspicious look on his lined face as he looked at their spears lying in the bottom of the boat. 'To the north of Sikelia there are many islands, many places. I could not say.'

'Then have you heard anything of the war in the east?' Talakhonsu asked the man. 'The war of the Greeks and the Persians?'

'The war in the east?' the Greek repeated Talakh's question, again with the same suspicion in his eyes. 'We have had our share of war right here in Sikelia young man.'

'War here?' Talakh said in surprise. 'That we know nothing of, but I have friends who went to fight against the armies of Xerxes. We have heard nothing of the fate of the Greeks of the mainland for many weeks now.'

The cold look in the old man's eyes warmed a little at that.

'I am Xenagoras,' he said, reaching across to grip Talakh's hand in a bony handshake. 'As luck would have it, some news came to me yesterday from an old trader friend of mine. He sailed from Lacedaemon a week ago, but as with all things, the news he brought me may not be the whole truth of the matter.'

'I would be glad of it all the same,' Talakh gripped the man's arm in friendship. 'I am Talakhonsu of Kriti and this is Huell. He comes from...'

'My lands are far to the north in the western seas,' Huell jumped in. 'The place I am from, your people call the Cassiterades after the tin ore that is found there. It lies far beyond the Pillars of Heracles.'

'Then you are a long way from home indeed,' the man Xenagoras said quietly.

'That I am,' Huell nodded. 'I will return there, if the gods will it.'

'Then I will tell you where best to find a ship,' said Xenagoras. 'But first you should hear of how the Persians fared when they came up against the warriors of Sparta.'

So, as the boatmen rowed and the sail flapped listlessly on a fickle breeze, Xenagoras began his story, while all aboard the ferry boat paid him heed.

'There were over a thousand ships in the mighty fleet of great Xerxes that came to invade Attic Greece,' Xenagoras said as he warmed to his task. 'A thousand and more! But Xerxes it seems had offended the gods with his vainglorious ambition to rule over the whole of the earth, for Zeus himself caused a great storm to break upon the Persian fleet whilst they rode at anchor to the north of Athens. Thunder pealed and great Zeus himself threw down his bolts of lightning as the Persians and their allies cowered below! The seas raged in the storm, smashing a good half of their fleet. Half is what they say! Half of the thousand ships of Xerxes! And so Xerxes lost a lot of men and a lot of supplies too in that great storm.

'Well, as you can imagine this heartened the Athenians and their allies greatly, since they now saw that as well as Zeus, Poseidon of the sea and Boreas of the north wind favoured them against the Persian invaders. As it was, the gods had preserved the Greek fleet intact for the coming battle, so now though the odds were still against them, they were at least evened a little. This, together with the favour of the gods gave the Greeks new heart!'

Xenagoras paused now, smoothing his grey hair back over his temples, as he looked about him at his intent audience. He was a good storyteller, better perhaps even than Pamphilos, Talakh thought.

'So,' Xenagoras continued, his voice deep and resonant. 'You may think that mighty Xerxes was disheartened by the fate of his fleet, yes? Well, in his gut perhaps he was. And yet,' he raised a long finger in the air, 'the Persian fleet still outnumbered that of the Greeks by two to one. Two to one, mark me! Added to that he had a huge army in the field that marched toward Attica to threaten Athens herself. They say he commanded more men under arms than the total of all the Greek peoples added together, women and children included. This is how big his army was!

'Now, it so happened that Leonidas, king of Sparta, had taken it upon himself to leave his own lands in Lacedaemon and march to a narrow pass in a bid to halt the Persians there. But, though he sought to rally the Greek armies to him...' Xenagoras shook his head as his words petered out in sadness.

'They say,' he began again, 'that he commanded only a few hundred Spartan warriors, plus a few thousand others from various states who bravely followed him. This against the might of the Persian army, but still he did not shirk the fight. When battle was joined the long spears of the hoplite warriors inflicted a heavy toll on the best that Xerxes had to offer, so that the ground ran red with rivers of Persian blood! For three days the fighting raged, with Leonidas foremost amongst his men until finally he was surrounded by hundreds of the enemy and fatally wounded, though he fought on with the strength of ten men until his last breath had left him.'

'Long may the name of Leonidas live on!' one of the other passengers called out.

'Aye, he was a great hero,' said another. 'The greatest of all the Spartan kings.'

'So he was,' Xenagoras nodded gravely. 'You see while Leonidas stood forth, there was hope for the Greeks warriors at the pass of Thermopylae, but with him gone their defeat came swiftly. The Lacedaemon hoplites fought on to the last man until they were utterly destroyed by the Persian hordes, who had found a way through the pass to outflank them. A great battle! A great death upon both sides! Truly Leonidas had inflicted a mighty blow on Xerxes, for though the Persian king left the field as victor, he also left his finest men there, slaughtered in their thousands at the hands of the Lacedaemonians.'

Xenagoras paused again and gathered himself for the next part of his story, while Talakh bit his tongue, for he dearly wanted to know what happened next.

'Now,' the old man continued, 'you might think that with the way clear into Attica and Athens beyond, this would have been the beginning of the end for the Greeks, no? Yet this was not the case, for by pure chance during the three days that the battle lasted upon the land, another great battle was taking place upon the sea at a place called Artemesium. Now this battle of the Greek and Persian fleets almost did not take place at all, as the commanders of the Corinthian ships were all for fleeing. It was only after the Athenians had bribed them with silver that their loyalty was finally secured.

'Whilst all of this was going on, the Persians decided to split their fleet in two and send half around behind an island to try to surround the Greek fleet. How foolhardy was this of them?' Xenagoras laughed harshly. 'They had not heeded the lesson that the gods had taught them before, and so Zeus punished them again by sending another great storm as night fell. The half of his ships caught out at sea were either wrecked or blown to the four winds, so that the fleet of Xerxes was further diminished. Even after all of this though, still the Persians and their allies outnumbered the Greeks!

'The next day the sea battle proper was joined with heavy losses on both sides and so this continued for three days. By the fourth day, they had had enough of each other and both sides withdrew, since they had fought to a standstill with neither the outright winner. It was only then that the Athenians heard of the death of Leonidas and so in spite of them denying the Persians victory at sea, still they were greatly disheartened, for they knew that the way was now open on land for the Persians. The Greek fleet did what they could to evacuate the people but the army of Xerxes fell upon Athens, quickly took it and put it to fire, burning the sanctuaries and temples of the gods.'

'Athens burnt? Then surely all is lost for them?' Talakhonsu could not help the words that came from his mouth.

'All lost?' Xenagoras answered him. 'Yes, I am sure that's what many of the commanders of the Greek fleet felt. In fact some were all for retreating back to Lacedaemon to defend Sparta itself. But in the end they could not agree the best course of action and so delayed their flight for too long. You see the Persians were not stupid, they knew where the Greek fleet had retreated to and a few days later they managed to surprise and encircle them without the Greeks even realising it. When finally they saw that the Persians were upon them, they had no choice but to launch their ships from the beaches and fight for their lives. Against all the odds, they managed to rout the Persian ships, many of which were rammed so that they quickly sank. Others still were set afire or boarded by the warriors of Athens and their allies. Soon enough the seas ran red with the blood of the Persians and Phoenicians. The Greeks had won a great victory against them all!'

'That is fantastic news!' Talakhonsu jumped to his feet and punched the air in his excitement before the ferryman gruffly told him to sit down.

'Good news indeed,' Huell grinned. 'Let's hope that our friends still live. Most likely if they fought, it would have been aboard the ships.'

'Aye,' said Talakh. 'I pray to Amun for that. But tell us O Xenagoras, what now? Does Xerxes still hold Athens?'

'Ah, for the moment it is finished... And yet still it is not finished, stranger. Xerxes has retreated back to the shelter of his allies in Thrace. You see although he still has a mighty army in the field, they are a long, long way away from their homes. Without their fleet, they could easily be trapped. Without supplies, they will quickly starve when the winter comes.'

'Xerxes is defeated then?' Talakh asked as the ferry boat finally came under the cliffs of Sikelia.

'Defeated?' Xenagoras repeated the question, while he rubbed his chin thoughtfully. 'Yes young man, I think perhaps he is. You see, he came to Greece with his best men and his best ships and yet despite all of his long preparations still he failed. I don't think he will try there again. And now, here is Messene. It is time for me to go to my friends and my family.'

'Thank you for your welcome news,' Talakhonsu said, the darkness lifted a little from his heart for the first time since the death of Leontios.

'Aye, thank you,' Huell added. 'But you also mentioned war here in Sikelia?'

'That I did, young man! I will tell you quickly before we land. As the fates would have it, western Sikelia was invaded by Hamilcar of Carthage and his Phoenician allies almost to the day it seems that the Persians invaded Attic Greece! Of course Xerxes and Hamilcar were no doubt in league, but it has done neither of them any good. Our Sikelian forces under Gelon of Syracusa won a great victory against them at Himera off to the west from here. Hamilcar was killed and his army routed completely, so Sikelia is safe, at least for now. The gods be praised for that!'

'Aye,' Huell said. 'The gods be praised. Now O Xenagoras, you were going to tell us of a ship that might take us on from Sikelia?'

'Ah yes, you must forgive an old man his bad memory!' Xenagoras laughed lightly. 'It is all this excitement, it's not good for my heart! But yes, I will walk with you to see a nephew of mine. He has sailed far and wide and what he doesn't know of the trade routes north from Sikelia is not worth knowing.'

'But when I was... I mean when I first came to Sikelia, I came from the west, not the north,' Huell frowned.

'Well,' Xenagoras answered, 'The best way for you to return to your people may not be the way that brought you here, do you not think? Better to travel through safer waters, eh?'

The old Greek looked into the red man's eyes then and Talakh saw that he had perhaps guessed something of Huell's former captivity.

For an instant Huell's face flared red as his hair, but just as quickly he sighed wearily and his temper cooled again.

'You have the wisdom of your years, Xenagoras,' he bowed

his head. 'We will listen to what your kinsman has to say.'

When the ferry boat beached itself on the gentle sands of Messene, Xenagoras led Talakhonsu and Huell towards the fishing boats and trading vessels that were gathered in the lea of the northern end of the bay.

'He is not here,' Xenagoras frowned. 'Wait while I ask after him.'

Huell and Talakhonsu looked on while the old man strode over to some fishermen who sat mending their nets.

'He will be back before long,' Xenagoras said when he returned. 'Until then you will be my guests. Follow me.'

As the old man strode off at a good pace, Talakh and Huell looked at each other, shrugging their shoulders at this strange turn of the fates.

'It can do no harm,' Huell said. 'Let us follow him.'

Xenagoras led them back along the beach, stopping to talk to folk every so often, for he seemed to be known to one and all there. In a short while they came to the place of Messene itself with its tall traders storehouses gathered around a shady square and there the old man sat himself down on a weathered block of stone under a shady tree.

'Come, sit,' he gestured to Huell and Talakh, who sat on some smaller blocks facing him.

A young, fair haired boy, evidently the old man's grandson ran up and greeted him with a hug that brought a broad smile to the face of Xenagoras.

'Ah you have grown a little more, young one. And I have only been away a few days!' he joked with the boy. 'Soon great Heracles himself will be in your shadow if you continue in this way! Now, go and fetch some water for my guests. And kiss your mother for me!' he called after the boy as he ran off.

'My grandson, also called Xenagoras,' he beamed proudly. 'You have children?'

'No, though I hope to one day,' Talakhonsu smiled.

'And you, friend?' Xenagoras turned to Huell.

'I will need sons when I gain my birthright,' Huell answered with a distant look.

'Daughters too, to marry off to your rivals and keep them close by your side,' Xenagoras said shrewdly.

'Aye, daughters too if the gods will it,' Huell agreed, the rare trace of a smile on his lips as he thought of what might be if the fates were kind.

'I have been lucky to have both,' the old man nodded. 'My daughter Euterpe brought forth young Xenagoras there to be a comfort to me in my old age, and for that she is my favourite above all of my sons,' he chuckled. 'But tell me my friends, what is your story? How do you both come to be here, so far from your own lands? And how do you come to speak the tongue of the Greeks so well?'

'We were shipwrecked off the coast of Iapygia on the way to trade here in Sikelia,' Talakhonsu answered sadly. 'We were the only two survivors of the crew, and I lost many friends. Our captain was as a father to me.'

'What was his name?'

'He was Leontios of Kriti, a brave and generous man.'

'I do not know of him,' Xenagoras rubbed his chin. 'It is difficult, I know. I see the grief in your eyes, young Talakhonsu, but it will pass in time. All things do in the end.'

'Aye they do,' Huell said resting his hand on Talakh's shoulder. 'But still we will remember him well, for he was a good man as you say. I will never forget those men who won me my freedom.'

'That is well said,' Xenagoras nodded. 'And your own lands?' he turned back to Talakhonsu. 'You are not from the Cassiterades I think, nor are you from Kriti. You are from the place we Greeks call Ethiopia?'

'Aye, the land of the burnt people, as you have it,' Talakh nodded.

'I meant no offence to you friend,' the old man held up his hand. 'It is an ignorant name, but clever and cultured as my people are, still we are ignorant of many things in this great world of ours.'

'I take no offence, O Xenagoras,' Talakh shrugged. 'When I first saw the Greeks and the other sea peoples, I thought your pale colour very strange too. But since you ask, I was born far to the south of the land called Kemet, where there is a mountain temple to the god Amun in my home of Napata.'

'I have not heard of Napata, but Kemet you say?' Xenagoras' dark eyes grew wide with excitement. 'You have been there? You have been to Kemet?'

'Aye, I sailed the Great River from my own land, right through Kemet and out into the great Middle Sea,' Talakh said proudly.

'Ah Kemet...' the old man sighed. 'Or Egypt as we Greeks call it. I have heard stories of the great pyramids there that touch the sky, so that the gods may step down upon them.'

'It is true. I have seen the wonders there with my own eyes. There are many temples, watched over by great statues of the gods. And yet I am not sure that the gods still dwell in those places.'

'Why do you say that?' Xenagoras gave Talakh a quizzical look.

'If they did, surely they would not have allowed Kemet to be overthrown by the Persians?'

'Hmm, perhaps,' Xenagoras rubbed his chin again. 'Yet their worship still goes on?'

'It does, but the priests there are mostly rich men who use their position for their own ends.'

'It is the same the world over,' the old man nodded. 'Though not so bad in our own Greek temples, we would like to think!' he added hastily. 'And you Huell? I will not ask how you came to be so far from your northern lands, for I guess that yours is an unhappy tale. Now you return there though, and Talakhonsu goes with you?'

'Huell saved my life in the shipwreck, and so I owe him a debt,' Talakhonsu explained. 'I will lend him what help I can to reclaim his birthright.'

'You are well armed for that at least,' Xenagoras gave a shrewd look. 'You are warriors both then?'

'We know how to fight,' Huell nodded.

'Hmm,' the old man nodded. 'All the same you should be

wary here, for in the aftermath of the battle at Himera not all are as trusting, nor as friendly as I. There are men on Sikelia with the taste for blood now, men who would gladly cause trouble for outlanders like you. But, here comes my nephew, and little Xenagoras with him. Let us take a drink and we will talk of your journey to come. Then we shall see what is to be done.'

Chapter 6

Beyond Sardos

The nephew of Xenagoras was a smallish, wiry man with a little grey in his black curly hair and darker skin, not like his uncle at all.

'I am Kharopinos,' he introduced himself with a firm handshake that spoke of many years hard work.

Xenagoras beckoned for them all to sit again and the four men refreshed themselves with the watered wine that his grandson had now brought for them, while the old man briefly recounted the story of the two travellers.

'It is as my uncle says,' Kharopinos agreed. 'Even though the Carthaginians are defeated, the way across the western seas is not for you. It is north that you must go. Here, I will make a drawing of Sikelia and the lands and seas you must cross.'

Talakh and Huell watched intently as Kharopinos took up a stick and started to draw it across the dusty earth at his feet.

'Here is Sikelia,' he said, marking the shape of the island, which was like the haunch of a bull. 'We are here, near the northeast point, whilst here across the strait is the mainland of Iapygia.' Kharopinos then scribed two more shapes, one above the other.

'Far to the north there are two large islands,' he pointed, 'Sardos and Cyrnus they are called. Sardos here, they say is the largest island in the world, though I doubt that! Cyrnus lies just to the north of it, here and is also very big. The mainland follows them along over at the east like this, and then curves round above them to the north up here somewhere. It is to this far northern coast that you must find passage I think.

'Now, once there were a number of wealthy Greek colonies on these islands, but they are no more since they warred with the Tyrrhenian tribes on the mainland. Still perhaps you may

171

find a few familiar voices amongst the people there, for not all of the Dorians left, so they say. When you cross from Cyrnus to the coast of the northern mainland, you should follow the coast until you come here to the port of Massalia, and from there turn inland toward the foot of the mountains of Pyrene as they are called. They say these mountains are taller by far than the pillars of Heracles.'

'Aye, eagles soar there, big enough to carry off a man in their claws!' Xenagoras pitched in.

'This is what we hear of those mountains,' Kharopinos nodded, 'But even if it is not true, then you can be sure that wolf and bear will await you there,' he added grimly. 'All in all, it would be better by far for you to steer clear of the mountains of Pyrene altogether I would say. Keep them on your left as they march west and head north away from them as soon as you can. From there onward I have no real knowledge of the land or the sea. All I can tell you is that your land of the tin isles lies far to the north, perhaps up here somewhere,' he dragged his stick through the dust again.

'How many days sailing is it to this Massalia?' Huell asked. 'Is there a captain here in Sikelia who would take us there?'

'No one captain will take you to Massalia, or anywhere close to it,' Kharopinos shook his head firmly. 'It is too far for one voyage. Your best chance is to take a ship to Sardos. From there you can easily cross to Cyrnus, and from Cyrnus a ship to the northern mainland and Massalia should not be hard to find. That is if you have something to pay for your passage?'

'We have silver enough for that,' Talakhonsu answered, though as soon as he did he wondered if this admission was wise.

'Silver carries a good value here in Sikelia,' Xenagoras jumped in ahead of his nephew, his eyes screwed up in a shrewd grin. 'For that reason, keep that which you have close to you, if you take my meaning. Messene itself may be a lawful place, but as I said earlier in the aftermath of battle there are some on Sikelia who would gladly lighten your load for you if they saw their chance.'

'Thank you again for your advice,' Talakhonsu bowed his head in turn to Xenagoras and his nephew.

'Aye, it is well given,' Huell added. 'But pity the man that picks a fight with Talakhonsu here!' he laughed.

The veiled threat in his joke was not lost on Kharopinos.

'You can rest easily on that friend,' he said lightly. 'No man hereabouts will pick a quarrel with a friend of my uncle's. He is too well respected for that. Now, let us get down to business. You need to make for Sardos and I have a boat that could take you safely there. I can ready her within a day or two at the most if your price is right, though it must be a good price to make it worth my while. We Greeks are not so welcome in Sardos these days.'

So Kharopinos and the two travellers set to bargaining a price in silver coin for the passage to Sardos, whilst old Xenagoras sat by, his eyes half closed like an owl as he seemed to nod off. In the end it was the wily old man who spoke to seal the bargain.

'If you will give Kharopinos the silver he asks for,' he said with a gesture of his hand, 'then he will take you not just to Sardos but across to Cyrnus too. There he will deliver you to the first port that you come to. Is that not a fair offer?'

'I believe it is a fair price,' Talakhonsu said, glancing at Huell as he shook the bony hand of Kharopinos.

'Just one other thing,' said Xenagoras. 'The price will remain here with me when you sail.'

'But how do we know you will honour our bargain?' Huell said, a sudden anger rising in him.

'And how do I know you won't refuse to pay my nephew when he has brought you to Cyrnus?' the old man answered coolly. 'You are fighting men you two, are you not? But yet I trust you with the life of my nephew, as does he himself. Is it then too much for us to ask for the silver in advance?'

'Perhaps it is,' Huell snapped. 'Perhaps we would be best to cross back to the mainland and follow the coast all the way up here to Massalia,' he pointed to the drawing that Kharopinos had made in the sand. 'Then we would save our silver.'

'You would be mad to tread that path,' Kharopinos shook his head. 'You will find no friends there, only enemies.'

'Perhaps they will receive us just as well as Messene has?' Huell countered, the trace of a sneer on his face.

'Enough!' Talakhonsu said, clapping his hands together loudly, just as he had seen the elders of his own people do to halt a quarrel when he was a boy. 'My friend means no offence, but he has been betrayed before and so it is no easy thing for him to trust a stranger.'

Huell glared at him then, but said nothing.

'We will accept your terms, Xenagoras,' Talakh continued, 'You are a wise man and a man of your word, that is plain to me, so we will sail with Kharopinos and put our trust in him. On the morning we leave, I will hand the silver price to you for safekeeping.'

'So it will be,' the old man nodded, 'May the gods watch over your journey until you are safely home.'

That night the two travellers slept as the guests of Xenagoras on the floor of his tall house while the old man climbed the ladder to the upper floor where he slept alone, for his wife had died many years ago and his children lived with their own families. When dawn broke their host rose early, as is the way with the very old, whose itchy bones will not let them rest for long.

After young Xenagoras had brought a simple breakfast to them, his grandfather spent much of the day telling them something of the land of Sikelia. He told them first of the snows that capped the smoking mountain in winter, and the legends of the race of one eyed giants who were said to live on its slopes where no man dared to go. There they battled each other, making the earth shake and tremble as their clubs struck the ground. At night, fire sometimes rose from that place, filling the darkness above the mountain with a livid orange glow. This was when the people of Sikelia feared the mountain the most, Xenagoras said. For then the god who lived there would send rivers of fire tumbling down its slopes in his anger, to burn all in their path.

Yet despite these dangers the Sikelian Greeks had striven to build the great city of Syracuse on the eastern coast of the island, off to the south. Xenagoras spoke proudly of this place with its many beautiful temples and great wealth. The most powerful city in the known world he said, and if this was perhaps an exaggeration, still Talakhonsu had heard its name spoken of often enough during his travels aboard the Kallisto to know there was some truth in the boast. The young Napatan found himself longing to go and see Syracusa for himself, but he knew that this was not to be, for his fate was now tied to that of Huell and the red man was anxious to continue his journey north.

'We should be on our way as soon as we can,' Huell said to Talakhonsu when their host had left them alone for a moment. 'These people may have won their battle with Carthage, but have they won the war? The Carthaginians will thirst for revenge no doubt and I have no wish to be here if they return. I have my own battles to fight.'

Talakh could not argue with that. Still, while they waited for Kharopinos to ready his boat, he thought his time on the island of the smoking mountain should not be wasted. Xenagoras had told them of a bay of great beauty, a day's walk to the south along the coast, and though Huell had no desire to see the place, Talakh decided to walk part of the way there anyway. The loss of Leontios and his crew mates weighed heavy on him whenever he sat with his thoughts for too long. Never again would they chant at the oar together while the Kallisto surged across the deep blue seas, and this saddened him greatly when he thought on it.

So Talakh left the house of Xenagoras in the bright sun of the next morning, taking with him a skin of water against the heat of the noon to come. It felt strange to be alone as he walked to the sandy beach, where the fishermen mended their nets in the shade of the rocky headland that guarded Messene from the sea.

'Where do you go dark man?' a small voice called after him. It was young Xenagoras, the grandson of the old man, who now

175

came running up to him across the sand.

'Just for a walk,' Talakh returned the boy's bright smile.

'Will you come back?'

'I hope so,' Talakh laughed.

'Then I will walk with you.'

Talakh stopped and looked down at the boy for a moment. 'You can walk with me for a while, but not far. And when I say go back you must go back, otherwise your mother will look for you. You understand?'

'Alright,' the boy nodded as he offered Talakh his small hand. 'I will show you the way.'

Talakh let himself be led by young Xenagoras, reminded of his own boyhood when he used to play with his friends in the shallows of the Great River, and this lifted his sadness a little.

'Why are you so tall?' the boy asked, cocking his head to one side so that he squinted up against the sun.

'Well, my father was tall,' Talakh chuckled. 'I take after him in that I suppose.'

'And was his skin like yours too?'

'A little lighter I think. But my mother, she was as I am. All of my people are much alike in that.'

'I like you anyway, even though you are funny,' the boy said. 'I have decided I will grow tall like you. Then I will see further then my friends, because my eyes will be higher than theirs, as if I am up a tree!'

'And how will you make yourself grow tall?' Talakh laughed.

'I will hang by my arms from a branch,' Xenagoras said seriously.

'Ah, that is very clever.'

'Yes,' the boy said earnestly. 'I saw a man stretching a goat skin in such a way once, so I know it will work if I can hang there long enough.'

'Hmm, I have an easier way,' Talakh crouched down. 'All you have to do is eat all of the food your mother puts in front of you, and go to your bed when she tells you. Do these things and you will grow taller.'

'As tall as you?' the boy looked up.

'Perhaps,' Talakh stood up again, ruffling the boy's hair as the two walked on.

They had only gone a little further, when young Xenagoras spoke up again. 'Where is your home, Talakhonsu?'

'Far off across the seas to the east,' Talakh pointed. 'It lies a long way from the sea though, along a mighty river. It is from there that I came with my friend Leontios, who was a great sea captain.'

'Can I meet him?' Xenagoras asked excitedly. 'Will he come here to Messene, like you did Talakhonsu?'

'No, he will not come,' Talakh shook his head. 'He is with the heroes now, up there among the stars in the night sky.'

'Was he brave?' the boy said, looking up at him with awe in his dark eyes.

'The bravest!'

'Then one day I will build a ship and be like you and Leontios,' young Xenagoras said with a boldness that brought a smile to Talakhonsu's face again. 'I will sail with my men across to your homeland and we will go everywhere!'

'Perhaps you will, young one, perhaps you will,' Talakh ruffled the boy's hair again. 'But for now you have come far enough. Go back home to your friends now.'

'But I want to hear about Leontios and the faraway places,' the boy frowned.

'Perhaps if Huell is there you could talk to him?' Talakh offered. 'He has many stories to tell too, stories of his home in the far north where they say the sun sleeps all the winter long.'

'But I don't like him,' Xenagoras said with the honesty of the young.

'You need not fear him,' Talakh smiled. 'Huell is a good man too. He saved my life you know, when I would surely have drowned in the sea.'

'That is good, but still I don't like him,' the boy frowned again. 'His eyes are scary.'

'Never mind about that,' Talakh said firmly, trying not to laugh. 'You must go back now. Go on with you!'

With that young Xenagoras hung his head and reluctantly trudged off back along the beach toward the houses of Messene.

By himself again, the Napatan chuckled at the boy's nature and wondered if one day he too would have a son like young Xenagoras. His thoughts turned to the face of Ketet and her smile that warmed his heart. Far away in the land of Kemet, she would be waiting at her father's side for him, he was sure of that. Not for the first time or the last, he wished that he had not given his oath to Huell, but there was nothing to be done. He shook his head and carried on walking, as he gazed out across the calm, untroubled sea, trying in vain to resolve these unhappy thoughts. Huell, Ketet, her father Isek, all of them depended on him to honour his word. But the fates, only they could decide what would become of him next, and if he would ever return to Kemet to find his love again.

After a few more idle days that tried Huell's patience, the boat of Kharopinos was at last readied for its journey and the time came for the two travellers to leave the company of Xenagoras the elder. Though they both liked the tall old man well enough, still they were both glad to be at the start of their travels once again. For Huell had his birthright to win back, whilst Talakh could think only of what would come after the red man had avenged himself on his enemies, so that he could release himself from his oath. That is if he lived to tell the tale.

It was in the cool of the morning that they finally departed Sikelia under the watching eye of wise old Xenagoras, who stood on the shore, whilst his young grandson swam after them in the shallows, waving and smiling. Talakhonsu watched them out of sight until the fair southern wind carried the boat around the northern tip of Sikelia, out into the wide open sea. The vessel was not small, but by no means was it large either, for it was crewed by three men only: Kharopinos and his kinsmen Periphetes and Akrisios. The steering deck, such as it was, was really big enough only for one and Kharopinos as captain stood there tending the two steering oars. It was his boat after all.

The other two Greeks tended to the ropes and the sail, though really there was not much for them to do in the favourable breeze that gently coasted them along northwards. Talakh and Huell leant against the boat's sides looking out at the islands that appeared before them like the tips of steep mountains poking out of the sea.

'Some of these are fire mountains too,' Kharopinos said, following their gaze, 'though they only grumble and smoke instead of throwing out fire and rocks.

'They are strange places though,' he added. 'Only a madman would live there.'

'What causes them to smoke?' Talakh asked out of curiosity. 'Is it the gods? Is there a fire on their peaks?'

'Not as you would think, no,' Kharopinos shook his head. 'They say that there is a great hole in the summit of such places that reaches down to the underworld itself. Creatures live down there that eat the very rock of the earth, but those rocks they don't like, they spit out in a rain of fire and smoke.'

'Then the ones under the great mountain on Sikelia must be giants indeed,' Talakh said quietly.

'Giants yes, and dangerous too. Amongst these smaller fire islands we are safe, but if I were ever this close to the great mountain on Sikelia, I am not afraid to admit that my knees would be knocking in fear.'

Kharopinos may not have been worried by these dark, smoking peaks that rose high out of the sea, but Talakh was glad to see the back of them all the same as they slowly faded into the distance. Still, there was a strange mood aboard the boat, a sullen air that hung over them in spite of the bright sun that shone overhead. Kharopinos was a man whose mind was only on his work, now that Sikelia was behind them, whilst his kinsmen seemed not interested in talk either. They spoke only with each other and then only the odd word as they pulled the sail taught or loosened it again.

Huell too said little. Ever since they had planned the journey back to his own land in the Isles of Tin with old Xenagoras and Kharopinos, the red man's mood had changed. For now every

179

day that they travelled north brought him closer to the time of truth when he would have to regain his birthright or die in the trying. The same went for Talakhonsu, his fate too now tied to that of Huell. These thoughts ran through his mind as the wind carried the boat of Kharopinos on and on across the deeps away to the north, until by and by they came closer to the distant western coast of the Iapygian mainland itself.

'I will run us ashore for the night,' Kharopinos said at last, just as Talakhonsu was about to ask that question.

'A wise choice,' Huell nodded. 'If we don't get in soon, then there may be a breeze from the land once the sun goes down.'

Kharopinos frowned at that, but he said nothing. Talakh knew that for a man of the sea, and a Greek at that, such advice was rarely welcome. The Sikelian would know well enough himself about such things as the evening breezes.

'Who is your boat named after?' Talakh asked, seeking to change the subject.

'She is called Zosime and she is my first love. After my wife and my daughters, of course,' Kharopinos added, with the briefest of grins. After all, he was not a man of good humour.

'The Zosime,' Talakh repeated, mulling the name over in his head. It was a name of meaning this one, which if he remembered it right was, 'a one that will survive', or 'a one that will be steadfast'.

'A good name for any vessel,' he nodded.

'Aye. She has served me well... brought me good luck too,' Kharopinos said with a quiet pride. 'There are bigger boats, but not many are better. Your feet will not be drier in any other ship you may board.'

'Aye,' Talakh nodded. It was true enough that the Zosime was tight against the water. There was almost none to speak of in the bottom of her hull.

'Built of Sikelian oak,' Kharopinos added. 'Already she is seven seasons old and yet the worms have not made their way into her.'

'They don't like the taste,' observed his kinsman Akrisios wryly.

Kharopinos brought them slowly closer to shore, steering the Zosime toward a small sandy bay sheltered by steep cliffs. By now the sun hung low in the western sky.

'We will run her ashore here,' he said with satisfaction as he leant and pulled in turn against the steering oars to bring the Zosime's prow around.

'You know this place?' Talakh asked.

'Aye,' Kharopinos answered. 'As long as we take her straight in to the middle of the beach, there is only gentle sand to ground us. No-one will trouble us here,' he said, and it was easy to see why. There was no easy way to reach the shore from the rugged cliff tops high above them.

As Talakh and Huell watched keenly, Periphetes and Akrisios furled the sail and then ran out oars to row her in. Like all of the seagoing Greeks, they knew their craft well and brought her in straight and true until her prow pushed up against the soft sand. Talakh stepped past the two oarsmen and leaped over the side with a rope to help pull her ashore. Huell joined him and together they strained at the rope while the others shipped their oars and they too jumped over the side. With the Zosime five men lighter, it was an easier task for their pooled strength to drag her prow up out of the water so that she would not drift away in the night while they slept. Kharopinos tethered her to the rocks just the same.

When she was at last secure, the five men sat and drank some watered wine that Huell had brought aboard and watched the red disc of the sun slip slowly into the dark sea. There was talk, though not the cheerful banter of his crewmates on the Kallisto, for here there was no cheerful Hippolytos with his jokes, and no Pamphilos to fill the empty night with the stories of the heroes. Talakhonsu stared into the dark eyes painted on the prow of the boat, but they did not look into his soul like the eyes of the Kallisto's prow had once done. Already those days of the great ship of Leontios seemed far away from him. As the last of red sun filled his eyes with its dying light, the Napatan wondered how long it would take to reach the land of Huell and how long then to return to Kriti? How long after that before he might return to Kemet?

'You are quiet, Talakh. Are you well?' Huell asked him.

'Ach, I am just tired,' the young Napatan answered.

The red man turned to look at him then, his cold blue eyes glimmering with an unnerving light of their own that pierced the twilight. 'You can go back,' he said quietly. 'It is still not too late to return to Sikelia with Kharopinos.'

'I gave you my oath,' Talakh said holding the other man's gaze.

'Yes you did, but I would not hold you to it. You saved my life too, and I do not forget that. No Talakhonsu, you do not have to go on. Much as it will make my task more difficult, I release you from your oath. Now it is for you to decide again what you wish to do. You could return to Kriti? Your brothers wait for you there.'

'I hope so. But now you are my brother too.'

Huell smiled. 'I take a pride in that my friend,' he said. 'But what about the girl you told me of? The one who waits for you in the land of your enemies?'

'The land of my friends too, now,' Talakh corrected him, thinking of old Isek, father of Ketet. 'Yes, I think of her often it is true, but...' he hesitated. 'There is something that draws me on. If I turn back now I think I will always regret it.'

'Regret it? Why?'

'Because I know it is the right thing to do, Huell. If Leontios were alive to see me abandon your cause, I think he would be disappointed in me, as would my father. That shame would never leave me. If I meet them in the life that comes after, I hope to look them in the eye and know that I faced the fates like a man, for better or for worse. For all of these reasons I will go on.'

'Then it is good!' Huell shook Talakh's shoulder as they clasped arms. 'But rest easily on this Napatan, I now give you my oath that I will guard your life better than I would guard my own, and if I cannot take my birthright back, then I will return with you back to the land of Kriti.'

'So it will be,' Talakh took a draught of wine from the flask that Huell now offered.

'So it will be,' Huell answered as he received the flask back.

That night, in spite of a chill breeze that made him glad of his woollen cloak, Talakh slept better than he had for many a day. When he woke the next morning it was finally resolved in his mind what he must do and why he must do it. He felt at last his old self again, ready for the adventures and even the dangers that he knew would surely lie ahead of them.

The next morning after a breakfast of dry bread and cheese in the still of the dawn, the five of them pushed and poled the broad hull of the Zosime back into the gently lapping waves. Soon they were safely away from the land, but that day and the next, the sea was rough and the wind not favourable, so they made little headway. At night they would put in carefully at some small bay, and each morning put out again knowing that there was little to be gained from it. Even though they rowed her as best they could, the Zosime was a stable craft, not a fast one.

When finally the wind changed and got behind them a little from the east, Kharopinos decided that they had hugged the Iapygian coast long enough and so they struck out across the open seas toward the setting sun and the island of Sardos far to the west. With the dusk soon passing into night, Talakhonsu found himself once more sailing under the stars on an open sea, as he had often done in the time of the Kallisto. In spite of the dark, the spirits of those aboard the Zosime rose now, for she carried them over the swells on an adventure toward a strange land of many legends. At such times as these, all felt the watchful gaze of the heroes and gods high above them.

The crossing to the island of Sardos took three days in all, a short time said Kharopinos, for the wind was their fair friend most of the while. Still, they were all tired to a man when the keen eyes of Akrisios finally sighted land, far off in the first light of dawn. They had all slept little enough, whether they had been on watch or not, as the swells of the sea had been too much for them to rest in any comfort. Now that land was in sight, it was plain that neither Kharopinos nor his men knew Sardos at all well and so were wary as to where they might safely put in.

Finally they resolved to carry north along the rugged coast, as that is what the wind still favoured. Here and there a fine bay of white sand would beckon them, but Kharopinos was not keen to venture ashore whilst no other boats were in sight, as there was no telling what dangers lurked under the breaking waves. At last they came upon a small boat with just a fisherman and his son aboard, rowing out against the breeze from one such bay. Yet as Kharopinos tried to draw the Zosime across toward him, so the fisherman sought to row away again.

'Friend!' Kharopinos called across to the man. 'Is there a safe way into that bay?'

'Safe? No,' the fisherman called back in the Greek tongue.

'But, you have just come from there,' Huell shouted.

Now the man looked fearful, Talakh saw as he stood in the prow. 'You don't need to worry about us,' he said in as friendly a way as he could. 'We come from Sikelia and our captain here seeks only fresh water and a little rest in your bay.'

'Aye, we are peaceful traders,' Kharopinos added. 'I am Kharopinos of Messene. This is my boat and these are my men. If you will guide us into the bay and show us fresh water, I'll make you a generous gift.'

'Aye, I will show you the way Messenian,' the fisherman answered, seeing that he had little choice but to help, whether he wanted to or not. Still, he glanced from Talakhonsu to Huell with deep suspicion in his eyes.

As the Zosime coasted along across his path, the fisherman stood at his oars and paddled his small craft about, to head back in. Kharopinos now hauled hard on the steering oars, so that the Zosime's prow hauled round toward the land, though the wind made her crab sideways.

'Furl the sail!' Kharopinos called out. 'Put out the oars! Quick now!'

Talakhonsu and Huell did not need to be asked twice and quickly ran the oars out, pulling hard as they hauled against the chop of the waves. Yet though the sail was quickly furled, the wind still pushed against the side of the Zosime. Even with Akrisios and Kharopinos rowing with the steering oars as well, it was hard work for them to bring the boat safely around the rocky headland and into the shelter of the bay. At last the sea grew calm as they entered clear shallows that were the colour of the summer sky, led on by their reluctant fisherman guide.

'We could have made our way in here easily enough, without his help,' Huell grumbled as he and Talakh stood up to watch for rocks.

'We could,' Talakh agreed, 'but that would not have been without risk. Besides, it is always good to make friends in strange lands where we can. The fisherman will tell us something of this island at least.'

And so it proved. The fisherman lived with his family and a few others of his kin in a small settlement around the beach, yet although they claimed Greek descent, they were in many ways very different in their words and their customs. Still after the Zosime was safely beached and Kharopinos had made him a gift of a flask of wine, the fisherman was helpful enough in the advice he gave them. From him they found that they had met the Sardonian shore a day's good sailing from its southern tip, whilst the northern tip of Sardos was no more than two sailing days away. There he told them, was the city of Olbia, which had been a Greek colony long ago. Now all but a few had left and Olbia was full of strangers, Tyrrhenians mostly.

While Talakh waited with Kharopinos and Periphetes, Huell and Akrisios were shown the way to a spring in the wild forests away from the shore, so that they could fill their water skins.

When they returned, Kharopinos called them all aboard, for he was keen to be under way even though they had not rested and it was still only the midmorning. As they poled the Zosime back out into the shallows with the helping shoulders of the fisherman and his brother, Talakh put any doubts in Kharopinos behind him. Though his boat was only a small vessel, and though he himself was not an imposing man, the Messenian was a good captain all the same. For when the wind is set fair, only a fool fails to make the most of it.

They made steady progress as the day wore on, though for the steersman it was hard work. The wind slyly pushed them toward the shore a little, even as it carried them on northwards. Akrisios and Periphetes took turns with Kharopinos to rest his aching arms, while Talakh and Huell also rowed in the prow to keep the Zosime straight. As evening closed in, so the wind dropped to no more than a faint breeze and this time they were able to make the shore of a small, deserted bay with ease, for the waters there were clear and still. There was no settlement and no folk to be seen or heard, only more dark, silent woods and rugged, scrub covered hills, as seemed to be the nature of the mysterious island of Sardos. Even so, once night had fallen Kharopinos kept a keen look out while the others slept in their cloaks on the soft sands, until his kinsmen took their turn on watch.

They sailed early the next day and by the afternoon the steady breeze at their backs brought them to a great inlet, where suddenly they were amidst many other trading boats. More worrying for all on the Zosime, there were warships too, rowing back and forth along the sound.

'The sound of Olbia,' Kharopinos confirmed what the others were thinking. 'The city lies deep into the channel I have heard, but we had best avoid that by the look of those ships. We will keep on until we see the coast of Cyrnus.'

They came now to a shallow sea of the most brilliant sky-blue, dotted with countless tree clad islets, so beautiful that they took Talakhonsu's breath away as the Zosime picked a careful path between them. There were many dolphins too, chasing the fish that escaped the fishermen's nets, every now and again leaping clear of the sea and high into the air with a flick of their sleek tails. Not for the first time, Talakh wondered what thoughts were in the mind of Poseidon's messengers as they looked keenly about them with their dark eyes, their jaws seeming almost to laugh as they played and chased each other around the fishing boats.

The Zosime coasted slowly on across these calm seas, time

and again sighting what they thought must be the coast of Cyrnus, only to find that it was some lesser island that loomed out of the gathering dusk. The last of the evening light found them with no choice but to carefully beach for the night on the sands of a small, deserted island where no folk lived, nor ever had as far as they could tell.

The next morning, after an untroubled night the Zosime at last broke away from the Sardonian coast and out into the open sea, for there across a deeper sound was surely the neighbouring island of Cyrnus itself, its rugged hills and mountains rising from the deep blue sea. Like Sardos and Sikelia, this Cyrnus was no small land.

'The eastern coast is controlled by the Tyrrhenians, so I have heard,' Kharopinos said to Talakh and Huell while he took a rest from the steering oars.

'The tower folk?'

'Aye, Talakh. Their name comes from their dwellings, perched high on steep outcrops like the nest of an eagle, they say. Even then, they build their houses high, with no window holes to let in the light, so I hear. They are an old enemy of my people and so we are unlikely to find any friends amongst them, I am sure of that. No, better that we go around to the west coast, away from their ships of war. There we should safely make land with the blessing of the gods.'

Soon enough in the afternoon they came to a sheltered bay where a few fishermen's huts lay. The men were still out in their boats it seemed, for no-one appeared to challenge them as Talakh swam ashore to check for submerged rocks. Soon after they were beached, two small fishing boats rowed in and it was only then that the fishermen's wives and children dared to peer from their ragged huts. Once Kharopinos had reassured them that they meant no harm, one of the older fishermen sat down to talk, but the man spoke only a little of the Greek tongue, so there was not much to be learned from him. Kharopinos once again gifted the fishermen some wine to ensure their goodwill and they in return made him a gift of some freshly caught fish, though after this they returned to their huts with no thoughts of entertaining their visitors.

The fish, Talakhonsu roasted on sticks over a small fire, and when they were cooked the crew of the Zosime washed them down with wine, though Kharopinos drank more than the his share. Soon the captain's words grew slow with drink.

'We will set off early again tomorrow... while the weather holds fine,' he said lazily as he gazed into the fire embers.

'Aye,' Akrisios nodded. 'It will be good to be heading back home. Much further north and we will drop off the edge of the world.'

'We have a way to go yet,' Kharopinos said flatly.

'A way to go?' Akrisios protested. 'We have already met our part of the bargain, have we not?'

'Your kinsman is right,' Talakhonsu turned to the captain. 'The journey north is ours alone now, mine and Huell's. You should return to your own land and watch over your families. After all, who knows if Carthage might decide to attack Sikelia again?'

'Aye, we should go no further,' said Periphetes now. He had hardly spoken at all in the presence of Talakh and Huell, but now that he did, there was a hard edge to his voice. 'We should turn back Kharopinos.'

'We are from the Greek line,' Kharopinos grunted, his eyes set narrow in his wine-flushed face. 'Our forefathers settled these shores. Why should we be afraid to follow their footsteps?'

'Tell that to your wife when you meet her in the afterlife,' Akrisios said testily.

'Why not let the gods decide?' Talakh shrugged. 'Let's throw a coin for it. Which side do you call?'

Kharopinos looked angry at this, but after looking from face to face around the fire, he relented. 'I will call the head,' he agreed.

'Then if you lose,' Talakh answered, 'the gods have decided and you can return home knowing that is their will.'

'Aye cousin,' Periphetes said, placing his hand on the shoulder of Kharopinos. 'Let the gods decide, eh?'

Talakh flicked his silver coin into the air and it flashed briefly in the last of the fire light before landing in the sand.

'Ach, the gods send us home,' Kharopinos frowned. 'Perhaps it is no bad thing.'

'Aye,' Talakh nodded. 'I will sleep better tonight I think my friend, knowing that you will return to your loved ones.'

'Sleep would do us all good,' Periphetes agreed, and wrapped his cloak around himself as he lay down in the soft sand.

It grew late and before too long Kharopinos and Akrisios had joined their kinsman in the land of sleep, so that only Talakhonsu and Huell were left awake.

'A wolf do you think?' Talakh asked after a distant cry had broken the still of the night.

'Aye perhaps,' the red man answered quietly. He had been lost in his own thoughts all evening, but now he stirred himself to speak a little.

'That was a clever thing you did with Kharopinos. "Let the gods decide", yes that was good, though perhaps not wise. We could have saved ourselves some time and trouble along the coast if they had taken us on. Still, all the same I am glad to have my feet back on dry land for a while.'

The next morning, Talakh and Huell helped to push the Zosime back into the shallows for the last time, and said goodbye to the Messenians with good wishes for their long journey back to the far distant island of Sikelia. Talakh watched as the boat rowed back out into the bay, turned about and then slowly pulled away, for there was no favourable wind to fill her sail. Would she rest her prow once more on the sands of Messenia, or would she too be lost to a storm on some distant rocks? That he would never know and it saddened the Napatan not a little to think that life for him had become a long line of such goodbyes and uncertainties.

Even before the Zosime finally passed from their sight, the two travellers had already gathered up their belongings and set off north along the rugged coast, for now they were truly on their own on this strange island, with only the little food and water they could carry to sustain them. There was no time for them to waste, for though the sun still blazed fiercely in the sky, the year was starting to wear on.

For the next few days, the progress of Talakhonsu and Huell along the coast of the island of Cyrnus was painfully slow. The paths were faint and easily lost as they passed through a dense scrub of low bushes, whose aromatic scent hung heavy on the breeze. The rocky nature of the coastline was also against them, with high headland crags to be climbed over and scrambled down. Soon they had little food left and their efforts quickly drove them to hunger, though they at least found a small stream to quench their thirst and refill their water skins. Of other folk there was no sign, not even the scent of smoke on the wind, so that they wondered if the land was now barren of people. Here and there were the massive stone tombs of ancient giants and this only added to the foreboding air of the island of Cyrnus.

On their arduous trek north, Talakhonsu and Huell very soon came to realise that if things did not change, their hunger would turn to starvation. Always then their eyes were open for berries, nuts and any other food they could find. Luckily for them both, Huell at least knew how to make fire with a bow and spindle, though it was a difficult thing for him to do, even with the good tinder they found all about them and his knowledge of the fire craft. In the evenings they gathered a few clams from the beach, feeling for their hard shells under the sands with thin sticks, and these they cooked gently in the cooler ashes of the fire until the shells opened. Frogs too they roasted and ate, when they could find them amongst the rocks at the edge of streams. Yet these things were too few and too small to sate their appetites, so they looked to hunt for the small deer that they had seen all too briefly before they crashed off through the thick brush. The trouble was that the wind was not their friend, for in the daytime it always blew in from the sea, taking their own scent far inland so that there was little chance of them surprising their quarry. As they struggled north, their prayers to the gods went unanswered and their frustration grew with their hunger.

It was only after five days of this that their luck finally changed for the better, when the breeze swung round to blow out hard to sea, taking their scent with it. When they broke their camp on the beach in the early morning light, Huell saw a chance for them to take a deer.

'We will carry a torch with us and see what we can flush out with fire,' he said, the glint of the hunt in his eye.

While the morning sun was still low, they came to a narrowing stretch of wooded land that stuck out into the sea.

'Here, take this,' Huell said quietly now, offering Talakh a second branch he had lit from his torch. 'If we turn inland we can split up and try to flush any deer we see toward that headland. Set a fire here and there amongst the brush and we will let the smoke do the driving for us. It will cover our scent too.'

'A good plan,' Talakh nodded.

'Let us hope so. You have a sharp spear Talakh, and a good throw. Try to work round the edge of the cliffs and if any deer are about, I will drive them on to you. We can meet at the tip of the headland, if not before.'

The two men crept a good way inland as quietly as they could and circled around, both of them lighting the dry brush now and again, so that the smoke drifted off toward the sea. Huell was soon lost from Talakh's sight and, enough fires lit, the young Napatan quietly retraced his steps and made for the headland to lie in wait. It was only then that Talakh thought of his own danger as the smoke carried to him and he heard the crackle of fire in the distance. Still he crouched, spear at his side, throwing stick in his hand. Then he saw it, a blur of movement off to his left, before it was gone in a flash. He cursed under his breath, but did not stir for the deer had already vanished into the undergrowth. But where one deer comes, others often follow and so he waited quietly, patiently, for what seemed an age.

Suddenly there was a rustle off to his left again and then he saw it, a small, horned buck running straight toward him, its dark eyes staring straight into his. Talakh thought it surely must have seen him and yet still it came on even as he stood up. With a grunt of effort, he unwound his long arm and the heavy throwing stick span end over end, its iron wood glancing off the beast's brow with a hollow thud. The deer's legs buckled for a moment as if it might go down, but it regained its strength and ran on, heedless of the tall man who now stood in front of it wielding his spear. At the last moment the stunned buck saw its danger and veered off, but by then it was too late. Talakh ran at it hard, lunging with his spear into its flank with such force that he knocked the beast onto its side. He was on it in a flash, pushing the spear shaft in until the beast was skewered right through and into the stony ground. The buck's dark eye stared up at him, white around the edges, full of fear and pain for a moment before the life started to leave it. Talakhonsu knelt on its bloody flank and drew his small knife quickly across the buck's throat as the blood ran out warm over his hands. The beast jerked with the last of its life and then was still.

'Be quiet now and sleep,' Talakh said gently in his own Napatan tongue as he covered the deer's eye with his hand. 'When you waken, your spirit will run again in the shadow world.'

'Talakh, you got it!' Huell shouted as he came up at a breathless run. 'Well done there, well done! We will feast well tonight.'

'Aye we will,' Talakh answered, managing a smile. Though hunger gnawed at his belly, still there was always a little sadness in him when he had taken an animal's life.

'We must hurry,' Huell said as Talakh twisted his spear free. 'The fire is at our backs. Here, I will carry the buck.'

After Talakh had found his throwing stick, he quickly followed Huell away and out of the line of the fire that was bearing down on the headland. They made for a nearby beach and quickly began to butcher the buck there on a flat rock away from the flies.

'You hunt well Talakh,' Huell said as they roasted the animal's liver and heart over a small fire.

'Well it was your idea after all,' Talakh grinned, as he tried to ignore the delicious smell of the cooking meat.

'You were the hunter and I was the dog, driving the deer onto your spear,' Huell laughed to himself, though after a pause his face became more thoughtful. 'I mean no offence by this, but what was it you were saying back there?'

'Saying?'

'Aye. I heard your words as I came up, but I did not understand them. Was that your own tongue?'

'It was,' Talakh nodded. 'I thanked our friend here for his gift and wished his spirit a good life in the shadow world. It is the custom amongst the Greeks of Kriti, and I think also with my own people as far as I can remember.'

'With my people too,' Huell said. 'When the skull of a boar has been picked clean by the crows and bleached white by the sun, we hang it in the chieftain's hall, or some other place of honour. In this way we remember the beast's bravery before it fell, and the skill of the hunter who claimed it too.'

After the two men had feasted until their bellies felt like they might burst, and after Huell had fallen into a deep sleep as the evening drew in, Talakh set up a small bed of stones by the trunk of a tree that grew a little way from the beach. Upon this he laid a piece of the deer flesh as an offering to his great god Amun, saying his words of thanks for the gift of the buck.

When he awoke the next morning the offering of meat had gone, though whether this was by the cause of the god, or by some animal or bird as was more likely, it was not for him to know, nor to say. On this lonely island of Cyrnus, the Napatan was so far from his own lands now that he could not be sure that the great god still heard him anymore, still less that Amun had the power to help him. Still, he offered his thanks to the god again all the same. After eating what they could manage, the two men carried with them the rest of the roasted meat as they went on their way, though the flies soon buzzed after them whenever the sea breeze dropped. At least for the moment hunger was behind them, yet still they were no closer to leaving the island, or so it seemed.

Then finally on the afternoon of the following day, their luck changed at last whilst they sheltered under a tree from the scorching sun.

'A ship!' Huell suddenly shouted, waking Talakhonsu from his stupor.

Sure enough when Talakh blinked his eyes open against the brightness of the day, there far out to sea in front of them a small sail had appeared. The two men watched in silence as it seemed not to move, and Talakh could only wonder who sailed that ship and where they were going. After a while the sail disappeared.

'It has gone over the horizon,' Talakh said, a heaviness in his heart.

Huell stared intently into the distance for a moment in silence. 'No Talakh! Look, she has only struck her sail.'

'Your eyes are better than mine, red man. What does she do now?'

'She has oars enough to row...' Huell said thoughtfully. 'Perhaps they plan to beach for the night?'

The two men watched on, trying to see whether the ship was to come in, or carry on her way. For a long time Huell said nothing, but then at last he spoke.

'She definitely means to come in Talakh, though to the north of us I think. You see?'

Sure enough Talakh could now clearly see the vessel and as it came closer to the shore he could just make out the movement of her oars as they dipped rhythmically into the water.

'Five banks of oars I think,' Huell said thoughtfully. 'Ten men plus their captain at least. What should we do?'

Talakh could see that Huell was wary of this ship of strangers, as well he might be after his long captivity on the ship of Meketra. Yet still they needed a ship to take them off this island of Cyrnus and this one might well be the best chance they would get.

'We follow them along the coast until they come in,' Talakh said firmly. 'Then we watch them. Hopefully we will see who they are and learn where they are from.'

'Aye,' Huell agreed, though his jaw was set. 'We must try our luck.'

'So it will have to be many times I think, if we are to make it to your isles of tin,' Talakh nodded.

The two men set off north again, losing the ship from time to time behind a hill or a headland, only to see it reappear again, each time a little closer until finally it turned about and ran straight for the coast ahead of them. Talakhonsu and Huell approached warily, using the cover of the scrub that ran down to the sea until they came to a low cliff above a small sheltered bay. Below them, two men were already in the water, wading a rope ashore to make sure there were no rocks for the vessel to ground on. At the stern of the ship a very short, yet very stout figure stood giving orders.

'What does he say?' Huell whispered.

'I don't know, but they don't speak Greek, I know that. Are they Phoenicians?'

'I can't be sure from here, but I think not,' Huell shook his head.

They crept a little closer while the crew were beaching the high prow of the ship on the sands, Talakh counting silently on his fingers.

'Twelve of them,' he whispered. 'They look like a trading ship to me.'

'Aye, but still... Maybe we should wait a while I think. See? Traders or not, they are all armed.'

'As we are,' Talakh whispered back. 'But yes, we'll wait and see what they do next'

So they hid and watched, while some of the crew went off with jugs and skins in search of fresh water and others gathered wood for a fire. The wait for Talakh and Huell was long and dull, but eventually luck smiled on them. Whilst one of the ship's crew, a tall dark, bearded man with a balding head took a piss a little way off from the rest, one of the others called out a joke to him.

'Listen!' Talakh whispered. 'The bald one answers the other in Greek. No true Greek would side with the Phoenicians.'

'Aye, more likely than not,' Huell had to agree.

'So, we either make ourselves known to them now, or we will have to wait 'til the morning. For when it gets dark, they would not welcome strangers, of that we can be sure.'

'Still...,' Huell hesitated.

'What other choice do we have?' Talakh hissed, his patience wearing thin. 'Sooner or later we will have to trust in others if we're ever to leave this place.'

'Ach, you are right Napatan,' the red man resolved himself at last. 'However they receive us, we will gain nothing from hiding ourselves.'

'Come on then,' Talakh managed a grin in spite of his own unease. 'We'll see what adventures the gods have in store for us next.'

The two of them walked onto the sands of the beach, Talakh talking to Huell in Greek as if nothing was amiss, until one of the ship's crew called out something to his captain and all of the men who had been sitting around talking and laughing suddenly stood up, their arms at the ready.

'Welcome to Cyrnus strangers!' Talakh called out cheerfully in the Greek tongue.

For a moment the ship's crew said nothing and a menacing silence hung in the air, before their stout captain stomped forward and looked them up and down with his skewed eyes. He was an odd looking one, Talakh thought, with a long dark moustache that hung over his mouth, though the rest of his jowly face was clean shaven.

'You don't look like a Greek,' the short man said in a heavy accent. 'Still, you speak their tongue well enough,' he added, a curious look on his face as one of his eyes fixed them whilst the other looked out to sea.

Talakhonsu did not know which of the captain's eyes he should look at as they flitted about, but finally he fixed on one of them and answered.

'I was born in a place called Napata, far to the south of the Kemet lands,' Talakh answered. 'I sailed with the crew of a Greek captain, Leontios of Kriti.'

One of the men who had spoken Greek, a taller one with fair hair, said something to his captain then, though he spoke in a strange tongue that Talakh could not understand.

'Kriti is far away,' the captain shook his head. 'Far away,' he repeated again. 'How came you to be here?'

'Our ship was wrecked on the far coast of the land of Iapygia,' Huell answered. 'We two were the only survivors.'

'Not good, not good,' the captain shook his head. 'I am Longback,' he said, as he strode forward and offered his hand to the two travellers who towered above him. 'Not my father's name for me,' he grinned, 'but all the same this is what they call me now.'

It was a strange name, Talakh thought, yet one that fitted him well, for his back was indeed long compared to his short limbs.

'I am Talakhonsu and this is my friend Huell,' he introduced himself.

'Hmm,' Longback nodded, his lazy eye wandering again. 'You are a strange one. Tall. Very tall.'

Talakh could not be sure if Longback looked at him now or at Huell, but he answered for himself anyway.

'We travel north,' he said boldly. 'We look for a ship that might take us off this island of Cyrnus.'

Longback exchanged a few more words with his crewman, before he spoke again. 'I am sure that you do. You are warriors, by Teutates!' he gestured at the Napatan's spear.

'A sailor first, but yes a warrior too if I am pressed to it,' Talakh answered proudly. 'As we both are.'

'Ah,' the short one stroked his whiskers thoughtfully as his eye wandered again for what seemed an age. At last he muttered something to his crewman and then bade the man to speak for him.

'I am Coryptos,' the fair haired one spoke. 'My captain asks what you would offer if he were to take you from here?'

Talakh could feel Huell's eyes upon him, for the red man was ever wary. 'Tell your captain that we offer good company and stories of our adventures across strange and distant lands.'

'That is all?' the man Coryptos looked at them doubtfully 'I will tell the captain what you say, but if that is all you can offer...'

'Tell him also that we will pay him a fair price in the silver coin of the Sikelians, if he can take us to the place they call Massalia.'

'I hear your words,' Longback said in his rough accent, after Coryptos had spoken with him. 'Come. Sit with my men, young strangers. We will hear your story and if it is a good one, well then we can talk of the silver price.'

-φ-

'So, by luck and the favour of the gods, my father Talakhonsu and Huell came to know this man Longback,' Pelia smiled. 'And a good friend to them he proved to be, as things turned out.'

'He was a dwarf then, the captain Longback?' Cerian asked with a puzzled look on her face.

'He was, yes. Oh, I can see what you are thinking. How could a man so small win the respect of men who were longer in limb than he?'

'He had lots of silver? Lots of gold?'

'He had these things, that is true, because he was a successful trader. He brought furs, animal skins and amber from the northern lands to places like Sardos, then took oil and wine back the other way. In this way he grew rich with silver.'

'But how did he gain a ship? How did he master a crew?'

'Well, he was a man who made friends easily, despite his crossed eyes and his height. He had a way about him my father said that was bold and fearless, yet friendly as well and he could make people laugh which is a gift in itself. He was very

198

wise too and these things won people over to him, because they knew he was an honest man who could be trusted.

'His younger brother Acichorius was much bigger than Longback, and so it was Acichorius who came to have their father's ship when he died. Yet Acichorius knew that where he had the brawn, Longback had the brains, so they sailed together and amassed a great wealth between them. So much wealth that Longback was able to build a ship for himself, and so while Acichorius traded his wares up and down the western coasts of the Gaulish lands, Longback had his own ship to trade with across the Middle Sea.'

'And so he came to meet your father,' Cerian nodded, a thoughtful look on her face as she imagined these far off places and people.

'And so he did. Captain Longback listened to the stories of my father and Huell with great interest, and it was their good luck that he decided to take them across the Middle Seas to the land of the Gaulish tribes, though he would take no silver as payment for this when he heard of Huell's quest to reclaim his father's lands.'

Cerian leaned back on her elbows as she sat next to Pelia, looking up at the fine, fishbone clouds that shone gold in the evening sky. 'What are the chances that they should meet captain Longback and that he should want to help them?' she wondered almost to herself.

'All the more so when it turned out that Longback's ship had been driven to the west coast of Cyrnus by a storm and so he had not meant to be in those waters at all,' Pelia nodded. 'Yes, the gods smiled on them in this and in other things besides, in their long journey to our own land. It was their fate.'

'Like me and Tyrnon?' Cerian asked innocently, the setting sun twinkling in her green eyes.

'Yes, like the two of you,' Pelia rolled her eyes.

'Like you and Aneurin also,' Cerian grinned.

'No!' Pelia protested. 'It is not the same at all. Yours is a young love, the love of a boy and a girl. I have known Aneurin too long for that.'

'But you love him all the same.'

'Of course, but not the love you speak of,' Pelia scolded the younger girl. 'Ach, who can say?' she relented. 'Perhaps one day I will feel differently.'

'Oh, Pelia,' Cerian sighed. 'Perhaps one day it will be too late. Sooner or later another will catch his eye and he will tire of waiting'

'He is a hunter. He never tires of waiting, that is his way,' Pelia answered with defiance in her voice. But in her heart there was a doubt. She had heard Niamh sing to him at his passing, while Tanith smiled at him often. They knew he would make them a good husband and so Pelia knew that there was some truth in Cerian's fears.

'He will take your hand if you go to him,' Cerian persisted. 'At the Samhain feast, we could share the day together and ask the goddess to bless both of our weddings.'

'Honestly Cerian,' Pelia shook her head. 'Sometimes you are like my mother.'

'But you will go to him soon?'

'No, the time is not yet right.'

Cerian stretched out her hand and held Pelia's.

'You know,' she said gently, 'you are the wisest person I know of, and yet still you don't know your own heart.'

'I know it well enough,' Pelia looked down at her lap.

'Perhaps. I think you are afraid of giving up those freedoms you have now.'

Pelia's eyes shone green and gold as they glistened with quickening tears.

'Ach, I don't want a life of babies and children,' she cried. 'Is that so wrong of me?'

'For you, no. But for Aneurin? You must talk to him. Ask him if this is enough.'

'Men always want strong sons to follow them,' Pelia shook her head.

'They do, but Aneurin is not like the others. Perhaps he will be different. If not tonight, then speak to him tomorrow.'

The two friends grew silent now, listening to the bird song

high overhead. In the distance the axes of Tyrnon and his father rang out, echoing amongst the trees as they felled some poles for the new hut that Tyrnon was soon to start building for Cerian.

It was a sad sound Pelia thought, for it signalled not only the coming end of Cerian's time with her, but also the diminishing of the forest. With each passing year the trees grew a little farther away from Llan Huell as the people of the village cleared and burnt new fields to grow their crops. The trees were her old friends and though she knew that some must fall in order to feed the hearth and mend the roof, still she wished it were not so.

'Will you continue your father's story,' Cerian asked, holding her friend's hand again.

'I'm not sure I'm in the mood now,' said Pelia, wiping her eyes dry.

'Come on, tell me more about Longback and his men,' Cerian cajoled her, anxious to break the spell of sadness that had come down upon her friend.

Though Pelia did not feel like it, still she knew that talking of her father's adventures usually cheered her. The story of his life had its share of sadness, but it was the story of her own life too and how she came to be. And so she started up again the tale of how Talakhonsu and Huell sailed away from the wild island of Cyrnus with Longback and his crew, and of what happened to them next.

-φ-

From the last of Cyrnus, four days passed until the ship of Longback finally sighted the coast of the mysterious and distant mainland of the Gauls. Four long days where Huell's mood grew increasingly dour with a new fear of the sea and shipwreck which had taken a hold on his mind. Such fears came sometimes to Talakhonsu as well when the sea grew rough, but still for all the discomforts aboard the trading ship, at least Longback was generous with his wine and bread. Such was the hospitality of Longback, who would take no silver from them, but asked only that they pull at the oar when need be and share the tales of their adventures with him through the fluent Greek speakers amongst his crew.

'By the all gods!' Longback would say when he heard of a brave deed or a terrible fate in their tales. Talakhonsu listened in turn to the Gaulish crewmen as they spoke amongst themselves and strange indeed were the sounds of their tongue to him, though Huell could grasp at least some of their meaning. Soon Talakh learned a few of their words too, with his gift for such things. Words of water and of wine, of bread, of fish, of stars, of sun and of moon, and a great many other things besides. Other words still he learnt from Huell, so that by the time the ship of Longback ran along the mainland coast, he could speak of a few simple things of life with the captain and his men.

'I feel a change in the air Talakh,' Huell said to him as they shadowed the coast, heading west past forested hills and distant mountains tinged with blue. 'It reminds me a little of my own lands.'

Talakhonsu felt it too, the crossing of another new threshold. As a child he had known only his mother's house, the Great River where he played with his friends, the mighty temple and the sacred seat of the god Amun that sat atop the barren mountain above it.

Since then he had felt the yoke of slavery, witnessed the murder of his father Korkamani and then found his freedom aboard the Kallisto, only to suffer the loss of Leontios, who had been as a second father to him. Now a new land awaited, the gateway to another world of things strange and new. So far away on the other side of the great Middle Sea which parted the lands of North and South from each other, Hippolytos and Pamphilos waited for the Kallisto to return. And little Ketet and Isek too. Not for the first or last time he wondered if he would ever see any of them again?

All things now moved toward their end, an end that perhaps not even the gods knew, far less a young man such as Talakhonsu. He had come a long way, but there was a long way still to go.

Chapter 7

Wolves of Land and Sea

Short or not, the man Longback was one to be reckoned with, Talakhonsu thought to himself. For though his long black moustaches and straight lank hair sat ill on his overly large head, and though his eyes wandered in different directions as if he were drunk, still he had a broad smile, a shrewd mind and a clever way with words.

A wise man makes many friends and few enemies they say, and so it was with captain Longback. When he had brought his ship safely into the shelter of the coast, the captain called Talakh and Huell to him and spoke to them of where there path now lay.

'The port of Massalia lies a good day's sailing to the west,' he explained through the words of one of his crewmen. 'When we reach there, I will send you on with one of the fur traders, to my brother Acichorius who plies his own trade along the western coast of the Gaulish lands. It will take you perhaps ten days hard walking to reach him, if I can find you a guide that is. Even then, Acichorius may be there or he may be not. But when he does come, you will go aboard his ship and so you will be taken at last within a spit of your own northern land.'

'How will he know you sent us?' Huell asked, ever cautious.

'Here,' Longback offered him a short, crude knife that was clipped onto his belt. 'The carving of the handle is my brother's work and he will know it is mine. Give it to him and he will have it sent back to me, for I value it well.'

Talakhonsu looked at the knife as Huell took it from the rough hand of Longback. It was small and blunt ended, the kind of knife that a boy might have for paring and skinning. Perhaps it was from his childhood. Huell slid it safely into the hide sheath that held his own long knife.

'We thank you again for your kindness captain,' Talakh bowed his head.

So it was that when at last they came to the great port of Massalia, the two travellers owed Longback a great debt of gratitude for his generosity toward them.

Once the ship had moored up, Talakh and Huell went ashore, each of them eager to put their feet on dry land once more, and so whilst they waited for the arrival of the fur trader whom Longback had mentioned, they wandered along the storehouses that lined the harbour of Massalia.

After the solitude of Cyrnus, Talakh was glad to be in a peopled land again, full of strange voices, faces and smells. From doorways and stalls a great many wares were being traded by rich and poor alike. Here were cloaks of fine wool, leather sandals, baskets and fired clay wares of all shapes and sizes. There were traders in herbs, wine, nuts and nut oil. Traders also in seeds, spices, fruit, honey from the mountain meadows and forests, and a great many other good things besides. Then there were farmers with their pigs, goats and fowl to trade. From one of these, Talakh bought a young kid goat for a little of his silver and this they took back to the ship of Longback, for the captain had mentioned it was his favourite amongst meats.

As the cool night drew down, Talakh and Huell made a feast for Longback and his men on the shore. After they had slaughtered the goat and poured its blood into the sea as an offering to Poseidon for his protection of Longback's ship, they laid out bread, wine and cakes sweetened with honey, to eat while the meat roasted over a fire. There was laughter and joking amongst them all as they ate and shared stories of their mishaps, but after they had finished feasting, the face of captain Longback lost a little of its cheerfulness as he spoke of what awaited them next.

'You are a brave man Huell, to try to take back your right after all these years,' he nodded, his wandering eyes managing to fix both of the travellers at once. 'And you Talakhonsu, you are perhaps braver still for following your friend where you need not, at a great danger to yourself. Brave or foolhardy! Ah, but either way, may Teutates be always watching your backs!' he raised his wine cup to them and drained it dry.

When the fire and the talk had died down, they slept that night in their cloaks on the fine sands of the beach, though Longback himself went to lodge with a woman he knew. Whilst not his wife, she let him sleep in her arms for a small price of silver whenever his ship came to Massalia. When he came to find them the next morning, the grin had returned to his broad face.

'Ah!' he greeted them with a yawn and a stretch. 'You have slept well?'

'Not as well as you I think,' Talakh grinned.

'Hmm,' Longback nodded. 'She wants me to tie my hand with hers, but as a wife she would soon grow tired of my ways. One day perhaps, when I turn my back on the sea.

'Ah, but now I must take a final farewell of you my friends,' Longback grasped their hands in turn. 'A man called Viriathus will come to you in a while. He looks like a murderer, but do not worry about him! Viriathus knows these lands better than the back of his hand. He will guide you safely to the western coast and my brother. Be sure to reward him well for it.'

'Thank you, O captain,' Talakh said in Longback's own Gaulish tongue, bowing his head low. 'May the gods always smile upon you.'

'And may Teutates keep your ship safe,' Huell added with a bow of his own.

'A good man,' Talakh said quietly as Longback stomped off. 'We would have been lost if the gods had not crossed our path with his.'

'Aye,' Huell nodded. 'But the gods are fickle too, Talakh. First they wreck the Kallisto and our friends perish. Then they send Xenagoras, and then Longback to help us. What will they do next I wonder?'

Talakh shrugged, but kept his thoughts to himself, for there was nothing that could be said without tempting the fates.

After some while of waiting a man came walking toward

them.

'Viriathus I would guess,' Huell raised his eyebrows.

'Aye,' Talakh nodded as the man came closer.

The Napatan had never seen a bear himself, though Leontios had told him of those feared creatures that lived in the mountains of Attica. Yet still as the man's great feet padded toward them at a brisk pace, Talakh felt sure he had seen a bear now. This one was full as tall as he, far broader, and had a dark beard and thick hair that showed little of his face. His limbs and his broad chest too, where it showed through his tunic, were covered in the same thick, dark hair. Longback had been right. This man looked one not to cross, unless you were careless of life itself.

'I am Viriathus. You are the friends of Longback?' he asked gruffly in the Greek tongue.

'Aye, we are,' Talakh answered raising himself up to see if he could make himself a little taller. 'I am Talakhonsu of Napata.'

'And I am Huell, a chieftain of the northern isles,'

'Then we will be good friends!' the face of Viriathus split into a wide grin as he shook each of their hands with his great paw. 'Come, we have a long journey ahead of us.'

After they had stocked themselves well with water, bread, some baked eggs and dried boar meat, Viriathus led them away from Massalia along the coast to the west.

The walk was long and for the first few days they passed many a fishing village that would not have looked out of place around the coast of Kriti, until the hills to the north of them slowly receded. The land grew flat and pocketed with salt marshes and lagoons. Here amongst the creeks and inlets, Viriathus had them on their guard, for the tall grasses of the marsh could conceal cutthroats, thieves and huge, horned cattle, so he said.

Just the same, there were also good folk there who lived from the plentiful fish and fowl, or from the salt they gathered at the edge of the many shallow pools that sat inland from the coastline. When the evenings came and the red sun dipped low in the west, great clouds of biting midges rose up out of the reeds to plague the travellers, so that they had to wrap their cloaks around their faces. Even so, their legs were harshly treated by the pests, so that soon they were covered with many bites, though Viriathus seemed not to notice.

By and by they came to the banks of a river, too wide and deep to think of fording, though they were able to persuade a fisherman to ferry them across. Viriathus was no stranger to these lands and so he knew where to find fresh water, where to ford the rivers and where to turn inland. It was just as well, for otherwise Talakh and Huell might have wandered on, lost amongst those featureless marshes for all of time.

At last the Gaul led them away from the waterlogged lands as the coastline turned south away from their westerly path. Here the land changed again, the marshes giving way to flat plains, then to forested hills where narrow tracks led them through thick woodland. The going was hard for them, for though the trees provided shade from the hot sun, there was little breeze and the air was stiflingly hot. Now and again they would emerge onto a bald hilltop, where Viriathus would point to some distant peak or valley as being their next waypoint, but in between times all Talakh and Huell could do was to blindly trust in the Gaul's lead.

So their days passed and their nights too, sleeping under starlit skies where the air could grow suddenly cold, so that when they woke in the morning they could see their breath and their cloaks glistened with the dew. Mists filled the valleys on these mornings and while the sun took time to gather its strength, the air was cool and clear. One such morning the three travellers came upon some blackberry bushes full of ripe fruit, sweet to the taste.

'This is a beautiful land of yours,' Talakh said to Viriathus as they stopped to eat the berries.

'Aye, it is,' the Gaul nodded. 'Make the most of it while you can my friend. Soon the leaves will turn to gold and then it will not be long before winter comes.'

'True enough,' Huell agreed. 'In my lands it is beautiful too when the snow lies on the ground, but it is a terrible beauty that takes the old and the young alike to their graves under the cold earth. It will be hard for you, Talakh. Hard for me too, after so long under the southern sun.'

'Your hide will thank you for it though,' Talakh grinned cheerfully. For though the red man was not as burnt as he had been, the sun's fires still antagonised his skin.

'True enough again,' Huell chuckled, a rare enough thing for him to do, as the weight of his coming task bore down a little more on him each day.

They carried on along their way, finding food where they could to add to their dwindling store of dried boar, their bread long eaten. Here and there toadstools sprouted from the ground, whilst on the trunks of a few trees grew their cousins, those ones that some think of as the seats of the fairy folk. Viriathus was a Gaul who knew these lands well and so knew which of these could be eaten and which were poisonous. With the good ones that he picked, he made a little broth over the fire in a small bronze pan which he carried with him. Things such as these, together with the nuts and berries they gathered along the way helped stave off their hunger a little.

Unerringly Viriathus led them west toward the setting sun until one day they came to a woodland stream which ran into a series of deep, dark pools, each one beckoning the weary men to cool off in its waters.

'Wait!' Viriathus said, staying Talakh with his hand as the Napatan put down his spear.

'What is it?' Huell whispered.

Viriathus beckoned to the others to crouch down with him. 'If we are lucky, I will have a fish for us. Stay here.'

So, Talakh and Huell watched as the big man crept around under some low trees until he came to the edge of a smaller pool, where he lay down on his stomach in the grass and dipped his brawny arm gently into the water.

'What is he doing,' Talakh asked aloud.

'I have seen this amongst my own people when I was a boy, though I could never do it,' Huell said quietly. 'He is tickling a fish. A trout I would think.'

'Tickling a fish?'

'Aye, Talakh. Watch.'

And so the two men looked on. At first Viriathus' brow furrowed as he concentrated his mind on the task in hand. Then a smile came slowly to his face and with a sudden movement he pulled out his arm. There in his hand a small fish wriggled, its flanks silver in the dappled sunlight.

'Ha ha!' the big man beamed, as he got to his feet. 'A trout!'

'You have a quick hand,' Talakh said when Viriathus showed them his catch. 'How did you do it?'

'Ah, I have caught fish in this very same place before, my young friend,' Viriathus chuckled. 'You see they like to rest under the overhangs of the rocks, where they feel safe from the heron's beak. All you have to do is find a likely spot where one might be hiding, then gently search for it with your fingers. Sometimes they will swim away as swift as an arrow, but others stay where they are and if you stroke their bellies they fall asleep. Then it is a simple thing to grasp them and pull them out.'

'Simple enough with a hand as big as yours,' Huell laughed. 'I have tried many times and the fish has always been too quick for me.'

'I will try,' Talakh said, for this thing he had seen was almost like magic to him.

'Ah well, try if you like, but I doubt you will find another trout today. The other fish seem to know when one of them is taken and so they swim away to another part of the stream.'

So this proved to be and Talakh searched in vain for a trout of his own, until at last he gave up and plunged into the chill waters himself to cool off.

The travellers had seen hardly a soul as they walked the wild lands, but a while later as they settled on a grassy clearing to make their camp near some standing stones of the old people, they heard a distant shout. Slowly the voices of men approached, echoing through the darkening woods.

'Should we not hide?' Huell said urgently.

'No, there is no need to fear,' Viriathus said cheerfully. 'They will be friendly enough, you will see.'

'But how do you know that?' Huell answered, a trace of mistrust in his voice.

'Thieves and murderers always go quietly,' Viriathus laughed, shaking his head. 'These ones make enough noise to wake the dead!'

Huell said no more, but he kept his hand on his long knife just the same.

'As I thought, a packhorse train,' Viriathus said as a man emerged into the clearing, leading one of the stout ponies. 'Maglorix, you old dog!' he called out in the Gaulish tongue.

'Viriathus!' the man called back. 'Why am I not surprised to see your ugly face?'

Despite their insults, it was obvious as they embraced and slapped each other's backs that the two men were old friends. Their words ran fast, too fast for Talakhonsu to follow them, but when Viriathus pointed to him and Huell, the man Maglorix introduced himself in a few words of Greek, though his accent was terrible. He said something else in the strange tongue of the Gauls that Talakh could not grasp.

'He says that we are far from home,' Huell translated, 'but that we have the best guide there is. We need have no fear, Viriathus will take us to the great ocean.'

There were three other Gauls in the band of Maglorix, each of them with their long moustaches and oiled, dark hair that seemed the mark of the folk in that land. They bore the arms of men who knew how to fight as well as hunt, but they said little, saving their attention for the line of rough haired ponies that they now brought up in a circle, tying the first to the last before they dragged the heavy packs from the backs of the beasts. It seemed that they were all to make camp together that night and so this proved to be.

After they had gathered wood for a fire, they sat down to eat and Viriathus offered Maglorix the trout he had caught as a mark of their long friendship. He was wilier than Talakh had thought in this, for Maglorix and his men had speared a young boar earlier that day and were happy for it to be shared by all. After many days with scarce food, the roasting boar drove Talakhonsu almost mad with hunger as the juices ran from it and spat on the hot embers, while the men talked of their hunt.

But though Huell joined in with the talk now and again, it was all Talakh could do to follow even a part of their meaning and many times he lost it altogether. The Gaulish tongue was a difficult one to follow, sounding to him like the slurring of a man who had drunk too much wine.

Little by little though, he learnt that Maglorix was a trader in furs and skins from the north. It was this cargo that their pack animals carried on to the port of Massalia, where they would sell them to sea traders like Longback. Mostly these were great bear skins, wolf pelts and the fine furs of the beaver, which were the most valued in this trade and would bring much silver to Maglorix. In time, they would warm the wives of powerful men when the winter nights came to places like Sikelia. Even there, snow could still fall up on the slopes of the smoking mountain.

It struck Talakh now how strange the world was in these things. Always the rich seemed to want what was not around them, and so those things which they desired were carried to them from far off lands by traders like Maglorix and Longback, whilst other things were carried back the other way. These strands of trade joined the world's far flung corners together to the north and the south, to the east and the west, and all points in between it seemed. Long after he had eaten, and long after the talk was done and the others were fast asleep, Talakh lay awake with these thoughts for some time as he watched the vast night sky for the stars that sometimes fell to earth. There were many of them that night and so he had the chance to ask many favours of the gods, before he fell asleep at last.

The next morning they said their farewells to Maglorix and his band in the early morning. A mist had come down again in the night, dampening not only their bones but also the sounds about them, so that they trod warily for fear of surprising a tusked boar, or worse still a bear. When the sun's rays finally burnt off the mist, it was a relief to them all, for there was a cold bite in the air these mornings as they journeyed further into the Gaulish heartlands.

So it was for the next few days with them until at last they came to a gentle slope leading down to a wide river. This was called the Garona, and it flowed swift and deep said Viriathus. It would be along this river with any luck that they would sail west toward the great western ocean itself. As a heavy, red sun set behind the far distant horizon that evening, they came to a large settlement on the river. Tolosa, this place was called, and it had a great many timber and stone houses. Even though the day was almost done, still there were traders aplenty and soon they had eaten so much bread and cheese that Talakh was full to burst.

Viriathus was well known in this place of Tolosa, as well he might be, for few were as tall as he was. Before the night drew in, he had arranged for them to sleep as guests with a friend of his. For the first time since they had left Sikelia, Talakh and Huell now had a roof over their head and fresh harvested straw to lie down on. Without the fear of wolf and bear, without the need to keep a high fire or listen out for thieves, Talakh kept the dead company that night, so deeply did he sleep. Viriathus woke him the next morning, long after the misty sun had risen.

'I have found a boat that will take you on for a fair price,' he said as he handed them each a loaf of warm bread, a gift from his friend's wife.

'But not you?' Talakh guessed.

'No, not me,' the big man replied. 'The river will be your guide to the west now my friends.'

'Then we must thank you Viriathus for bringing us safely here,' Talakh said and with that he took off the cloth belt he wore over his shoulder and unpicked a number of silver coins that were roughly stitched into it. 'Here,' he said, 'this is a fair trade for your help I think.'

'More than fair,' Viriathus said as he counted the coin. 'You are a generous man O Talakhonsu, but where you are going you will need your silver. I will take only half then half again from you.'

'As you wish,' Talakh bowed his head in respect for the Gaul's gesture. 'May your Teutates watch over you and your kin.'

'And may your gods watch over the pair of you, whoever they are,' Viriathus grinned, gripping each of their hands in turn.

After they had eaten their bread, the Gaul took them down to the river bank, where a small boat was hauled up on a gravel beach. A sun wizened, balding man sat nearby mending his fishing nets with his young son.

'His name is Tarvos,' Viriathus said. 'I have rewarded him already for taking you down the river, but if you feel you want to make him a gift, that is for you to decide my friends. Now I must leave you. Good luck follow you in your venture.'

'And you, Gaul,' Huell answered him in his own tongue.

After they had said their final farewells and watched Viriathus out of sight, the fisherman Tarvos beckoned them aboard as he launched his small craft. There was not much room aboard the boat and it stank of fish, but it was watertight and had a small mast and sail, as well as a pair of oars. It was plain that Tarvos and his son had no other tongue than their own, so there was not much talk to be had with them.

Even so, by sign as much as by word they learned that he fished in the wide mouth of the river where it met the sea, and that he had brought a cargo of salt fish up the river to sell in Tolosa. The three men and the boy, all took turns to row, though it was no great effort. Even though the breeze did not favour them, still the river's gentle current carried them along the muddy waters, past islands great and small. Huell grew steadily more ill tempered as the day wore on, but perhaps this was no surprise. After all, the boat was stained with old fish blood, and her nets glinted with scales, while large flies buzzed lazily around them. The fish scales got on Huell and Talakh too, so that when Tarvos ran his boat ashore for the night on an island, the two travellers wasted no time in swimming in the river to cool off and wash themselves clean. That night the mosquitoes came to plague them again, even though Tarvos made the fire smoke with some pungent herbs to keep them at bay.

The land slowly changed as they drifted on, growing flatter as the winding river grew wider and more sluggish, so that they hardly seemed to make any progress at all, but at last on their second morning aboard the boat, a fresh breeze sprung up at their backs, filling the small sail to speed them on their way. The man Tarvos knew these waters well and caught fresh fish for them in the shallows with his nets every evening so that at least they were not hungry. He knew too where fresher streams ran into the river, so that they could fill their skins. For the waters of the Garona herself were muddy and not good for a man to drink, so Tarvos told them.

These flat lands had fewer trees, and the signs of the tribes who lived there were plain to see all around them. From time to time they would pass by a man with his cattle, or another boat out hunting fowl, or a boy fishing. Whoever the folk were that they passed, young or old, warrior or wife, always they stared as if they doubted their own eyes. Likely, Talakh thought to himself, they had never seen a man's skin as dark as his before. Once they saw a small band of horsemen, who jeered and cursed at them, waving their spears from the riverbank before they kicked their steeds on again. The wide river was their protector at times such as this.

Vast islands of mud and wide, shallow shoals slid by them as the river grew broader and broader still with each day, until the water at last took rough with the wind and grew salt with the sea. Finally they had come to the beginning of a long, wide sound, ahead of which somewhere over the horizon there stretched the endless expanse of the great ocean of the west. These things Tarvos told them as he began to steer his boat off the river and into a wide and muddy creek. They rowed up this creek until they reached a ramshackle settlement on a low rise of drier ground surrounded by marshes. It was here that Huell and Talakh said their farewell to the fisherman and his son, as this was the place he assured them they would meet the ship of

Acichorius, brother of Longback. Talakh had grown more practised in the Gaulish tongue along the way and so he found enough words to thank Tarvos, as he split a silver coin in two and handed half to the fisherman.

Tarvos was known in this place, though not well known and he had no kin there for Talakh and Huell to stay with. But all the same, grateful as he was for the gift of silver, he spoke to another fisherman who finally agreed at length that the two men could stay in a low shelter where he hung his nets, until the ship of Acichorius arrived from the north. The two men watched Tarvos row off down the creek toward the wide sound of the river beyond, until the small boat was out of sight, each of them silent with their own thoughts and fears for what might happen next. It was an uncomfortable night that they passed on the dank floor of the net hut, with only reeds on the ground for any comfort. Mosquitoes droned around them in the dark seeking their blood, so that the next day could not come soon enough for Talakhonsu and Huell.

The dawn brought a grey sky and so it remained for the next three days that followed, for there was no wind to shift along the sombre blanket of cloud. This place of Lannion, as its folk called it, was a miserable one for Talakh and Huell to have to idle away their time in, waiting for Acichorius to come. By day most of the men of the settlement would go out in their boats to fish, though the strangers were not welcome to go with them, nor were they welcome amongst those others who hunted the marshes for fowl. The women folk too shunned them and the children taunted them when they were brave enough, or just hid themselves in fear when the dark man and his friend walked by carrying their spears. The days passed ever slowly as they hunted fruitlessly on their own in the marshy land, and the mood of the red man grew dark.

'You must try to keep your spirits up,' Talakh said to him one day. 'Whether the boat comes today or tomorrow, we have come this far. One way or another, we will come to your homeland in the end.'

'Ach, I do not like to stand still for long,' Huell frowned, his words cold like stone. 'It gives me too much time to think on things. If Acichorius' ship never comes, what then?'

'Then we will find another way. The gods did not bring us this far just to leave us to rot in this place.'

Huell nodded at that, but all the same it did not lift his mood.

Yet they did not have to wait much longer, for at last the next day, while they were walking along the creek close to the river, the two men saw through the morning mist a dark sail coming upstream on the sea breeze. They had seen others before, but this one was larger, a seagoing ship, and she came up swiftly and silently with the rising tide. When the vessel drew close to the mouth of the creek, over the tips of the tall reeds they could make out her crew running out the oars as they furled her sail. Talakh and Huell looked at each other now, both hoping that at last Acichorius had come. Their hopes soared again when the ship's prow swung around to face her squarely into the creek. And yet Talakh had a knot in his gut. Something was not right.

'I have a bad feeling about that ship,' Huell muttered, echoing the Napatan's own thoughts.

Without saying another word to each other the two men crouched down low behind a clump of reeds and waited, as the sound of oars dipping rhythmically in and out of the water came slowly toward them.

'They row quietly,' Huell spoke under his breath.

'Aye, as quiet as death,' Talakh whispered back.

The ship slipped past them all too silent, her crew hidden by the reeds for the most part, except for two thick set and heavily bearded steersmen who worked the long steering oars to keep her course true. Their faces were grim and filled with menace.

'Raiders!' Huell hissed. 'The wolves of the sea.'

'You are sure?' Talakh whispered back.

'Aye, I can smell them from here. I have seen them in my own lands, their ships come always from the east and the north. This one is a ship of war, a raiding ship, not a trader.'

'Then they will take the villagers as slaves?'

'No,' Huell shook his head. 'They are too far from their own lands here I would think, and they don't need more mouths to feed. They will take what they want, goats, grain, furs, though they will find little silver in Lannion. They will kill all they can of the old and the young. The women too, once they have had their way with them.'

'Then we must warn the fisher folk!'

'Are you mad?' Huell hissed. 'There will be two score men or more on that ship Talakh. We can't face that many!'

But Talakh had already made up his mind, or rather his legs had, for in an instant he was running along a track that led back across the marshes toward the settlement. He did not look back to see if Huell followed, though over the pounding of his heart in his throat he thought he heard the footfall of another behind him.

Now, Talakhonsu was a fast runner, faster than any ship could row, and the sea wolves also had to round a wide bend in the creek before they could fall upon the settlement, but still he ran as if a spear point was at his back, ran until his lungs burned with the effort. The taste of blood was at his throat.

'Spears!' he shouted in the Gaulish tongue as he saw an old man of the village. 'Spears come!'

'What?' the old man started to say.

'Men! Spears!' Talakh shouted full in the old man's face. 'Look!'

But the old man's eyes were as weak as his ears and he could not see the ship's mast as it started to round the bend in the creek toward the settlement.

'A ship?' one of the fisher women asked as she came from her hut to see what the noise was about.

'A ship of spears!' Talakh shouted at her in his frustration at his poor words.

At last the woman saw the danger and now she ran about summoning all to her. Talakh looked about him, but there was no Huell, so he ran to the net hut and retrieved both of their spears and the other few scant belongings of the both of them. Outside, the fisher woman had gathered her kin about her and was leading them off quickly into the marshes. Talakh's heart pounded in his chest now as he looked to his left, for the ship of the sea wolves was closing fast, its oars dipping cleanly in and out of the muddy waters of the creek. A bearded man with a great mass of hair stood in the prow, plumbing the shallows. The ship slowed now as the creek narrowed, but still, it could be only a matter of moments before it beached.

Talakh ran hard after the fleeing villagers, not daring to look back, and soon caught up with them despite the burden of the spears and other possessions he carried. For the old ones were slow, whilst the youngest children had to be carried in their mothers arms through the sodden ways of the marsh. Their only hope now was that the raiders would not follow them into the maze of paths that led away between the high reeds towards the drowned lands beyond. Talakh edged along the stream of folk until he reached the woman he had first shouted at. Her blunt, stern face dripped with sweat, but she ploughed on regardless, dragging a young boy by the hand as he struggled to keep up.

'Where do you go?' Talakh asked her as best as he could.

The woman spoke quickly, breathlessly, so that Talakh picked out only a few words that made any sense to him.

'The tide,' she said again, gesturing with her free hand to show that the rising waters would come up to their necks.

Talakh shook his head, for he did not understand how this could help them.

'This way,' the woman gasped, pointing ahead.

But all that Talakh could see was a wall of reeds all around them that seemed to have no end. Still the path divided in many places and so as they turned first left, then right, then left again, Talakh thought that perhaps there was a way for them to evade the raiders. He dropped back to watch over the stragglers as the old ones fell further behind.

It was only then that Talakh heard the first of their pursuers.

'Hai, hai, hai!' came a high pitched cry, not far behind them. The tall Napatan stopped in his tracks and listened, his dark knuckles showing yellow as he gripped the two spears tightly.

Another cry called out a way off to his right, and that was followed by a further one out on his left. The pack of sea wolves had fanned out in their pursuit of the poor fisher folk and now they hunted their quarry as they would a wounded deer. The first voice called again, closer now and Talakh knew there was no choice for him but to stand and fight, or die running with a spear in his back.

He stepped off the track and crouched down in the reeds, closing the parting he had made in them so that he was hidden. With his heart in his throat, Talakh waited, one spear at his side, the other in the firm grip of both of his hands for what seemed an age, until he heard the heavy padding of a man's feet running toward him.

Now, Talakh meant to jump out in front of the raider and let him run onto his spear, but in this he was too late. He forced himself to stand and leap out just as the man ran swiftly past in a blur of dark leather and glinting iron. It was then that he realised his mistake, for another man followed the first, a huge brute with a thick, dark beard and a tangled mass of thick hair, like a great boar running on two legs. Instinct and the speed of the young helped him then as he turned his spear quickly and ran at the giant, whose eyes opened wide in his ugly face with a mixture of surprise and fear at this shadow of a man who had sprung from nowhere.

In the blink of an eye the spear pierced the raider's broad chest, splitting bone and flesh as it ran straight to his heart, but though Talakh leant forward with all of his might, the weight of his foe brought him on yet. The sea wolf swung an axe with the last of his strength and the Napatan just managed to duck away from the blow in time, the bloodied spear slipping from his grip so that the wounded man fell upon it, snapping the shaft in two with his great bulk. For a moment Talakhonsu was left sprawled on the ground, but just as quickly he sprang to his feet again, for at the edge of his battle-clouded mind he heard the shout of another. Even as the sea wolf dying at his feet moaned his last, so his comrade came running back, an axe in his hand and a battle cry rising in his throat.

Before Talakhonsu had even thought it, his old throwing stick was in his hand and his long arm was snapping forward. A strange calm came upon him as it left his hand, the effort measured well, and he watched as if in a dream as the weapon flew straight and true, as swift almost as an arrow. The cruel edge of the heavy throwing stick struck the slim warrior's hand as he tried to block it and with a crack of bone it glanced up under his jaw with a dull thud, just as the man's own axe flew low and buried its blade in his own dead crewmate's shoulder.

Talakh was seized with the rage of battle now, a rage born of fear as much as of anger and he took up the big man's axe and ran at his fallen opponent, who lay on his back trying to breathe. The sea wolf's lips were moving as though words should come, but his throat had been crushed by the heavy stick and instead all that came from his mouth was sputtering blood and a strange whistle that made the hairs stand up on the back of Talakhonsu's neck. Again the raider tried to speak, or perhaps curse, and his eyes stared wide in his head at the man of shadow looming tall over him. Whether or not he could have survived such an injury Talakhonsu would never know, for without thinking he closed his own eyes and brought the axe down with both hands and all of his strength. The axe cleaved into the sea wolf's skull as if it were a piece of rotten wood, killing him in an instant with a terrible noise that made Talakh's stomach churn.

Chill fear gripped the Napatan once more. He had killed two of the raiders and his hands dripped with their blood. Their kinsmen would seek a terrible revenge if they caught him, of that he was sure. Talakhonsu uttered an oath under his breath as he quickly retrieved his throwing stick and the spear of Huell. The bloodied axes, he left where they had fallen in the mud as he started off again after the fisher folk.

Yet after he had gone only a few paces, another thought came into Talakhonsu's head and he checked himself. If he could not find the trail that they had taken, what then? He might be caught out on the mud flats that lay beyond the reeds as the tide came up and drowned the land. Or he might find himself facing more of the sea wolves as they gathered in their pursuit of the others.

'Amun protect me,' he whispered under his breath as he closed his eyes and strained his ears to listen for more voices on the wind.

The marsh was quiet now but for the gentle rustling of the reeds and the song of small birds, their innocent warbling at odds with the grim death around them. No doubt, even if there were cries for help from the hunted fisher folk, the breeze would carry them away to where none would hear. None save their murderers.

Talakh saw now that he had done all he could for them and that there was little choice for him but to go back the way he had come. The fate of the villagers was in the hands of their gods now.

Retracing his steps, it did not take the Napatan long to reach the settlement by the creek, though the path was far from clear. A pall of smoke was rising up into the sky to guide his way and the acrid smell of burning thatch hung in the air, no doubt from the torched huts of the fishermen. Slowly, carefully, he crept forward between the reeds, ever watchful for more of the raiders. There was no plan in his head then, only the thought that perhaps he would find Huell somewhere nearby.

Yet when Talakhonsu saw what the sea wolves had done, putting fire to those simple homes and wantonly destroying all in their paths, he was filled with anger again. The image of Leontios came to his mind and he wished with all his heart that the crew of the Kallisto could be by his side, so that together they could wreak a heavy price upon the sea wolves' foul hearts. He crept closer still, circling around the settlement under cover of the choking smoke, to where the raider's ship lay a little way off. The raiders had beached her on the creek's muddy banks but there were only two men standing guard over her on the nearby bank side. Young men with sparse, fair beards that flecked their tanned faces, their hair tied behind their heads in long tails.

As Talakhonsu watched them from behind a clump of reeds,

unsure of what to do next, a shiver went down his spine and he felt suddenly that he was not alone. He turned quickly, his spear at the ready, only to find to his relief that it was Huell himself, that same spear's owner, who crept up next to him.

'You have been in a fight,' the red man whispered, a grim smile creasing his eyes. 'Are you wounded?'

'No,' Talakh whispered back. 'I killed two of them.'

'Two?'

'Aye, two. One took my spear in his chest. The other's skull I split with an axe after I had knocked him down with my throwing stick.'

He did not mean to boast, but as the words left Talakh's mouth he felt a strange pride anyway, all the more because he had done these things alone whilst Huell skulked in hiding.

'Ah,' Huell nodded. 'You have my spear still though?'

'Aye,' said Talakh, handing it back to the red man. 'And you Huell? Where were you?'

'You were too quick!' Huell hissed, angry at Talakhonsu's jibe. 'You ran off like a madman before I could follow you.'

Talakh held his finger to his lips for Huell to be quiet, but it was too late. The guards had heard the red man, or at least they had heard something. They spoke quickly in their strange northern tongue, hefting their heavy axes in both hands, but still it was plain that they were unsure what to do. First one started forward and then the other grabbed his arm and pulled him back.

'That one is rash,' Talakh whispered.

'Aye, and the other is a coward,' said Huell.

'Or a wiser man. Their captain will have told them to guard the ship at all costs, not to go racing off after shadows.'

'Aye,' Huell nodded.

'They will do nothing until the others return,' Talakh whispered as he and Huell crouched out of sight. 'We should take them now, whilst they are full of fear.'

'Take them?' Huell hissed angrily. 'Are you mad?'

Talakhonsu wondered then if he was, for the words that he said next did not seem to come from his own mouth.

'What would you do?' he said hotly. 'Wait for the rest of them to return and hunt us down for killing their crewmates? No, we should take them while the odds are even. Look at them Huell, they are full of fear.'

'Aye and you have no spear,' Huell shook his head dismissively.

'Maybe not, but I have this,' Talakh whispered back, unwrapping the sword of Leontios from its oiled leather cover.

'No, we should be away while we still can!'

'And the fishermen who sheltered us Huell? We will abandon them? Their wives? Their children?'

'We owe them little enough,' said the red man, contempt in his voice.

'What of Longback's brother? Where will we find Acichorius if not here? How will you go on to your own lands then, without him and his ship?'

Huell hung his head, but said nothing. Perhaps only now did he feel his shame.

For Talakhonsu this was too much after all he had endured in Huell's cause and he clenched a fist in front of the red man's face, the anger in him rising up.

'We have made it this far as men,' he said bluntly. 'Let us act now while we still can and push these wolf men back to the sea where they came from.'

For a moment Huell hesitated, but then he at last found his own resolve.

'The gods be with us,' he said through gritted teeth. 'We will fight them come what may, though I think you are touched by the moon, Napatan.'

'Then you take the one on the right and I will take the other. Have your battle cry ready, red man,' Talakh urged him, as he stood up and ran forward a few steps into the open, still not sure if Huell would follow. Only the great god could know what would happen next.

The two raiders cried an alarm at the sight of the tall, shadow man who bounded out of the reeds, but though they stepped back, still they did not run.

In an instant, Talakhonsu stuck his sword in the soft ground and stretched his long, sinewy arm back over his shoulder whilst his enemies stood rooted like trees to the spot. As he took aim and threw hard, the two of them were so close together that he thought he could not miss. Yet this time of all times, he pulled his throw and the stick clattered harmlessly into the ground at their feet.

Talakhonsu swore loudly, but there was now nothing to be done in these fleeting moments but attack, or flee and be hunted down. He pulled the sword of the lost captain of the Kallisto from the earth and raised it up.

'For Leontios and great Amun!' Talakh cried as he bounded forward in great strides, not daring to think if his life would end there on the wicked blades of his enemies axes.

One of the men, the fairer of the two, threw his arm forward and in the blink of an eye an axe flew past Talakhonsu's ear whistling as it went, whilst its owner turned and fled toward the ship.

Talakh came on toward the other, who though young stood his ground and roared an oath of his own, swinging his axe in a broad sweep in front of him just as Talakh brought the sword of Leontios down, its bright, oiled blade glinting in the sun. When it bit into the haft of the axe with a shudder, the force almost took the sword handle from Talakh's grip, but though his fingers were half numb from the blow, still he renewed his hold on its leather-bound handle and put all of his weight into his shoulder as he charged on forward. The young raider was still to find the full strength of manhood and he fell to the ground, knocked off balance by Talakhonsu's baulk.

Out of nowhere then, the point of a spear rammed forward into the fallen raider's arm pit as Huell, a keen cry in his throat, skewered him through. The wounded sea wolf bravely tried to raise up his axe to defend himself, but Huell leant on the spear from a safe distance and the young man's spirit flew from his body with one last gasp of pain as the spear point pierced his heart.

As quickly as he had come up, the red man let go of the

spear and ran off to chase down the other raider, his long knife drawn. Talakhonsu looked on as Huell cornered his foe in the muddy shallows against the ship's side, raining stabbing blow after stabbing blow down, until his hands were as red as his face with the blood of the fair raider. Even then, in his fury Huell did not stop until Talakhonsu had yelled his name three times. By then the sea wolf's cold, blue eyes stared only in death at the grey sky, as his body sank limp and lifeless into the bloodied creek.

'What?' Huell yelled in his rage as he turned on Talakh with wild eyes that boiled with rage, for now it was he that was truly the madman.

'You wanted their blood Napatan!' he screamed. 'And now you have it. But there is more to be done.' With that he waded ashore and ran to a nearby hut that blazed fiercely, plucking up a burning clump of thatch. This he threw onto the ship, and then seized up more of the same, throwing it after the first.

'Come on!' the red man bellowed. 'Burn it! Burn the ship!'

Something in his heart nagged at Talakhonsu as he stood rooted to the spot. To burn a ship, except in a funeral pyre to its captain, that was not an easy thing for a man of the seas to do.

'Come on!' Huell raged again and this time Talakhonsu could not ignore him, for to do so he knew would only make their danger worse. What was done was already done, without heed to the fates, or to the wisdom of the deed. The two men sweated amongst the flames, pulling out timber after timber from the burning huts and hurling them aboard until the ship's sail caught and her timbers began to blaze fiercely, bubbling with the pitch that sealed them.

'It is done!' Talakh shouted, grabbing Huell by the arm. 'Come on, we should be away.'

'And the fisher folk?' Huell's words came full of bile as he washed the sticky blood and black soot from his hands in the muddy waters.

'We will go to the mouth of the creek and wait for their men to come back from the fishing,' Talakh spoke coolly. 'Perhaps then something can be done against the raiders.'

'The fishermen are no fighters! What chance will they have against these murdering dogs?'

'There are four less of them now, and fear will take them when they find their dead friends and their own ship in flames.'

'Yet now they have no way of fleeing. They will fight all the more fiercely for that,' Huell answered coldly.

Talakhonsu bit his tongue, even though he wanted to say that it was Huell's doing that the ship was burning. 'What is done is done,' he said quietly as he picked his throwing stick up and wiped the dirt off it.

'Done and done for the worst.'

Again Talakh bit his tongue. 'Perhaps,' he said. 'But for now we should go all the same if we want to see another sunrise.'

And so, with the acrid smell of burning pitch in their nostrils, the two men ran for their lives to hide themselves in the reeds before the sea wolves could return.

Chill night followed the grey evening, as Talakh and Huell hid near the mouth of the creek. But though they were tired, and though there were reeds enough to make a bed of sorts, every night sound sent a chill of fear into their bones that the sea wolves might be coming for them.

When at last the dawn broke, the sea mist drifted in to shroud the drowning land in a silent, grey cloak. Yet all they could do was wait all over again.

'It is strange that none of the fishermen have passed this way,' Huell said as he licked the cool dew from the blade of a reed, careful not to cut his tongue. The two men were thirsty and aside from the dew, there was no other water away from the village but the muddy brack of the creek mouth.

'Aye,' said Talakh quietly. 'They should have come up the river well before nightfall.'

'Perhaps they saw the raiders ship coming in, or the smoke from the fires? But surely they would not have abandoned their own people? Surely they would not have fled?'

Talakh thought of what Huell might have done in their place, but he did not like the answer, and so he said nothing.

'If no-one comes by the noon, we should make our way

north,' Huell muttered.

And so they waited. Yet they did not wait long, for even as the mist thickened with the rising of the sun, Talakh heard a dull splash like a fish rolling on the surface of the water.

'Listen!' he whispered urgently.

They heard another more subtle noise, and then another, like the sound an otter makes when it slips into the river.

'Oar strokes!' Huell hissed.

'Aye, but friend or foe?'

They waited for that answer as the oars paddled slowly closer. A small fishing boat slipped past them in the mist followed by another. Talakh made out Guaire, the headman of the settlement of Lannion and called out low to him. The boats disappeared into the mist for a moment before turning around and steering into the shore. Others were aboard, Talakh saw, others he did not know, armed with bow and spear.

'Where are our women? Where are the children?' Guaire demanded as he jumped ashore from his grounded boat. He was a small, slight man, but there was iron in his grey eyes then.

'They are not with you?' he demanded again.

'No, and not with you either,' Huell said bluntly, his hothead temper rising again. 'Where were you when the raiders came?'

Though the Gaulish tongue was still new to him, Talakh understood enough of these words to know that many more of them would lead to blood.

'Enough!' he held up his hand calmly. 'I led your women away into the marshes and then we killed four of the raiders and burned their ship.'

'And the rest of them?' Guaire asked anxiously as more of the small boats drew up. 'Where are they? Where are our people now?'

'After we had burned the raider's ship, we did not wait to find out,' Huell answered, his anger cooling. 'Where the women are, where the raiders are, we do not know.'

'Aye,' Talakh added. 'The women said they would go to one

of the secret places in the marsh. But for the sea wolves, there were too many of them for us to fight alone. I mean no offence, but you Guaire, why do you come only now?'

'We were too few and too scattered to have fought them.' Guaire hung his head. 'I came up the river after the noon, only to see smoke from the village and then the mast of the raider's ship. My home was afire and I thought all would be dead, so I went back to wait for the others to come back from their fishing.

'None of us knew what to do, but then the ship of Acichorius was sighted and after we had told him of our plight we hatched a plan with him for our revenge on the murderers. Here the Cardixa comes now.'

Out of the mist came a high prow, and behind it a ship the sight of which brought a tear to the eye of Talakhonsu. It might have been the Kallisto and Leontios sailing it too, for the shipwrights who built both ships surely had a like mind. Her oars dipped rhythmically in and out of the muddy water with hardly a sound and Talakh could see by this that her crew knew their task well, as the Cardixa slowed to a stop and then held her station in the slight current. Her captain, a hulking, blunt faced man, hailed one of the fishermen to ferry him to the bank.

'You are Acichorius?' Talakh held out a hand of friendship.

Acichorius eyed him up and down with suspicion until a flicker of recognition brought a grin to his face. 'Ah, but you two are the travellers that Viriathus sent down the river, yes?'

'Aye, but how did you know? We last saw him in Tolosa,' Huell asked.

'Why, Guaire told me of you,' Acichorius said, a puzzled look on his broad face.

'Ah,' Huell said, a little embarrassed. 'It is good to meet you at last Acichorius. We have a token for you from your brother,' he offered the small knife of Captain Longback.

Acichorius looked the knife over and over until finally he knew it as his brother's. He was not a quick man, just as Longback had said of him.

'Your brother said to tell you he wants it back when you see him,' Huell said, half joking.

'Of course I will!' Acichorius answered gruffly. 'But first we must root out these raiders. Unless we stamp on these dogs and defend our lands, they will come back twice as many and that is bad for trade. Bad for everybody.'

In those words Talakh could see that though his mind might not turn a problem over quickly, still Acichorius was not stupid.

'We will help you in this if we can,' he said, though Huell shot him an angry glance. 'But if we live to tell the tale, you will agree to take us to the north in your ship?'

'Hmm,' Acichorius rubbed his chin. 'I have heard this from Viriathus. Yes, if he and my brother Longback vouch for you, then I will give you passage north aboard the Cardixa. But first we must deal with these raiding dogs and send them to the shadow lands where they belong! I accept your help in this.'

And so in his own slow yet forceful way, Acichorius stood in counsel with Talakhonsu, Huell and the headman Guaire, as they hatched a plan for how they would put an end to the raiders. It was not long before the plan was agreed, simple as it was, and then while Acichorius and his men boarded the Cardixa, Guaire the grey-eyed and Talakhonsu led a small band of the fishermen along the shore. As the Cardixa slowly got under way, the men crept like ghosts through the mists of the early morning back toward the settlement, not sure of what they would find there other than the ruin of their homes.

'We should circle around behind them,' Talakh whispered when they sighted the raiders stirring themselves around the hulk of their ship. Though it was burnt out, the ruined vessel still floated in the shallows while her crew milled around her like bees around a broken nest, not knowing what to do. Two of them started to bicker with each other in their strange tongue.

'Northlanders,' Guaire said bitterly, testing the edge of his newly sharpened long knife with his thumb. It was sharp enough to draw his blood, though in his fear and anger he did not feel it.

'Wait,' Talakh held up his hand, though in truth he did not need to. 'We must do nothing until they see the Cardixa. Maybe they will rush toward her, maybe they will run away, but we will see and only then will we act.'

So they waited in the damp mist for what seemed an age, looking for the ship they knew was coming, while the Northlanders argued amongst themselves.

At last the ship of Acichorius appeared, just as the mist was lifting, her prow golden in the sunlight and bristling with men. Talakh heard a hissed curse behind him. One of the fishermen had soiled himself in his fear, knowing that the moment had come. Yet still they had to wait, for the raiders did not notice the oncoming ship that spelt their doom.

'Acichorius will be on them before they realise it,' Talakh muttered under his breath, but just as the thought came to his lips, a cry went up from one of the raiders.

'Wait,' Talakh whispered again through gritted teeth as his dark knuckles yellowed around the hilt of his sword. 'Wait...'

Now the raiders were unsure of what to do. Some ran forward a few paces shouting and yelling, while others retreated. A stocky man, their leader, shouted roundly at them and they fell into some sort of order, beating their shields with their battle axes in a show of strength. Still the ship of Acichorius came on, and still the raiders stood their ground until an arrow flew from the ship's prow and buried itself in the thigh of one of their number. As he cried out in his pain the other Northlanders ran forward screaming out their war cry.

Talakh threw the heavy throwing stick hard at them and as it scythed into the throng, 'Now!' he roared, waving the fishermen forward. 'For your wives, and your homes!'

In truth there was little of fighting in the fishermen, only a quiet pride in their skills upon the sea, and yet they conquered their fear that day all the same, running after Talakh as his long legs took him bounding ahead. The cry went up from behind him as he ran on, a cry of hatred and spite that rose into a howl that named revenge.

Now the raiders knew fear themselves as more arrows flew into them from the front and they started to fall. Talakh and the fishermen fell upon them from behind, heedless of the danger of the arrows of Acichorius' men in their rage. And where once he might have hesitated, Talakhonsu now drove the point of the sword of Leontios into a scrawny Northlander's backbone without a second thought. The blade cleaved through bone and muscle with an awful, hollow crunching sound, spilling much blood. It stuck fast, but Talakh had already drawn his long knife and slashed a wide arc with it across the bearded face of another of the raiders. All around him, men roared and bright metal flashed as axe and knife rose and fell with terrible speed. It might have been over for the fishermen very quickly then if the men of Acichorius had not leapt from their ship and joined the fray. As the raiders were hemmed in, fighting as best as they could from behind their shields, they found themselves outreached by the jabbing spears of the Cardixa's men and many were soon wounded in their feet and legs.

It was then that the sea wolves made one last desperate charge to try to break out of the killing trap. From out of nowhere, an axe shaft knocked the long knife from Talakh's hand, but he was quick and he caught a hold of the axe man's arm, dodging inside his barging shield to fasten his hands around the raider's throat. For a moment they struggled as the man tried to butt him with his head, but Talakh was the stronger and the man, who was past his youth, could not break his grip. Talakh kneed him in the stomach and the Northlander staggered backwards onto the knife of the fisherman Guaire, who had found his own courage.

As the raider fell to the ground, Talakhonsu wrenched the heavy axe from the dying man's grip and turned away, sensing another danger behind him. It was Huell, almost upon him now, the red man's spear point aimed squarely at his side. A savage roar rose from Huell's throat and Talakhonsu saw now that his life must surely end here at the hands of one he had counted as a friend.

'No,' he started to mouth, yet as Huell thrust the spear forward it skimmed past his side and then came to a juddering halt, burying itself in the belly of the man who was about to strike Talakh down from behind. The axe that would have scythed into his back now fell harmlessly to the ground and Talakhonsu knew in that moment that once again the red man had saved his life. There was no time to thank Huell, only time to swing the axe he had seized, down into the leg of another raider.

The fight was at its fiercest now, yet already the time of the Northlanders amongst the land of the living was coming to an end as they were attacked and hacked down on all sides. In a few more moments, all but three of them lay dead or dying under the merciless assault. It was the fishermen themselves who finished the last of the sea wolves with the axes of their own crewmates, for they would leave none of them alive in their lust for blood. To do so would have invited a terrible revenge from the kin of the raiders if even one of them had escaped.

Talakh had seen enough and turned his eyes away from the bloodshed, his rage replaced with sadness. There was no other way than this, but still his heart was as heavy and tired as his sword arm. Heavy with the weight of the spirits of the slain, for there was much blood on his hands even if there had been good cause.

When the fishermen's anger was at last spent, the unwounded amongst them went off in search of their wives and their kin, who for all they knew might lie murdered in the sodden marshes. Their joy was untold then when they returned with their loved ones, who had hidden themselves well, though there also was great sorrow amongst the kin of a fisherman who had died of his wounds.

Acichorius had the bloodied bodies of the sea wolves piled into their burnt out ship and, her hull still being more or less watertight, they towed her behind the Cardixa down the creek, into the river and then to the sea beyond. They sank her there, or rather she sank herself, bodies and all, captain Acichorius told Talakh when he returned that evening. Out on the open sea, the spirits of the dead raiders would not trouble the living, though the fishermen would mark the wreck in their minds and would no longer fish near that place.

'More sea wolves will come in time,' the captain said as he chewed on a roasted duck leg that night, while the wounded rubbed salt into their wounds. 'It is in their minds only to wander the seas and take what they find.'

The next morning, the Cardixa left the fishermen and their families to their grieving. Almost all of the fishermen's homes had been burned to the ground, pots, furs and all. It would be a long, cold winter for them in this bitter world of the north, Talakhonsu thought to himself as the ship turned her prow out of the mouth of the creek and back up the wide reaches of the river Garona. Much to Huell's annoyance, Acichorius still had a full cargo of furs to trade before he would sail back out to sea and the northern lands beyond, so the red man's return to his own lands would have to wait.

So it was that over a week passed by before the ship of Acichorius, now free of her cargo of furs but instead laden with jars of oil and wine, sailed past the mouth of the creek of Lannion again. They did not stop, but only asked a passing fisherman what he knew of his neighbours.

'Things will be hard for them,' the man said. 'But they already rebuild their houses as we speak with what they can find.'

'In the same place?' Acichorius called back.

'No, further away from the creek this time, so people tell me, in a place well hidden. They have no wish to be surprised again by the north men. We are all in your debt captain for what you did,' the fisherman said humbly. 'Your name will long be remembered in these parts.'

Captain Acichorius nodded, but said nothing, for he was a plain man who did not look for the praise of others. With that the Cardixa was at last free to drift onward on the gentle current until the wide river mouth emptied the Garona's waters into the vastness of the great ocean of the west. The sun hid behind thin grey clouds and the waters of the ocean were dark and forbidding as the ship set out her oars and rowed out beyond the landward breeze. At last she turned north to follow the coast, riding the swells with a chill breeze in her sail.

Talakhonsu loved to be upon the sea again, even though it had claimed the lives of so many who were dear to him and even though it had almost taken his own. Yet this was not the great Middle Sea he had known and sailed upon with Leontios and Hippolytos. No, this was the great ocean herself, a realm beyond the legends of his friend Pamphilos, beyond even the imaginings of those men he had once known so well. He was now seeing what they had never seen, nor would they ever. As he looked out to the western horizon a shiver of excitement went up his spine at the thought of that. None knew what lay out there, nor where the great ocean ended. If it ended at all.

Chapter 8

Across the Sound

The Cardixa, ship of Acichorius, was a seaworthy enough craft. Still, though her raised sides would keep out most seas, her captain put her into shore every night without fail. For as Acichorius said, great walls of water could come from nowhere on the western ocean, even when the weather seemed fine. There were islands too, and a great many hidden rocks and reefs around them, eager to tear out the belly of any passing ship that drew to close.

All in all this was a dangerous enough coast when the sun shone. It was one not to be ventured at all when darkness and foul weather came down. Due to these things, it was a slow voyage for the Cardixa and her crew as she made her way northwards toward the land of Armorica. The nights grew cooler and mists came more often to the morning, so that each dawn Talakh awoke on an often pebbly shore, cold and stiff despite his thick cloak.

'The winter will come early this year,' blunt Acichorius said one such morning. 'I feel it in my bones.'

'Aye,' one of his trusted men pulled on his moustaches thoughtfully. 'Time to return to our homes at last, no? I must plough my land over, before the frosts come.'

Such talk put Talakhonsu on edge. He had no home and no kin to shelter with. Soon enough it would be him and Huell against who knew what odds? And the harsh spirits of ice and frost, they would lay their white breath upon the land until nothing stirred in the bitter cold. He did not look forward to that at all.

Huell too grew darker in mood by the day as if a thunder cloud hung above his head, so that though Talakh joined in with the rowing chants of the crew, the red man never did. No doubt the slaughter at Lannion had put Huell in mind of what might await him when he reached his own lands, so Talakh could not blame him for that.

By and by they came to a place where the coast ran out to the west as far as the eye could see and it was here that the Cardixa sailed through a narrow inlet and into a vast sheltered lagoon. The Morbihan, so Acichorius called it, was almost completely cut off from the sea with many green islands dotted here and there and gentle hills of rich pasture rising away from the turquoise waters. It was a place of such great beauty that Talakh wished with all his heart that his Ketet could be by his side to see it.

'The Morbihan is as far north as ever I sail,' Acichorius told Talakhonsu and Huell in his blunt way, as he steered the Cardixa across the great lake of the sea until they came to a small settlement of farmsteads and fishermen.

'Then what would you suggest?' Huell asked.

'To get to your own lands? Well, there are perhaps a few fishermen who would take you around Armorica for the right price, but you should not go that way. That coast is a wrathful place in a storm, with no shelter but jagged rocks.

'No, it is better for you to follow the tracks north from here over the land until you reach the far coast. Ask for Coriallo, a place of many traders, and there perhaps you can find a boat that will take you across the water before the autumn gales come. Ah, but for me I am home at last. Here the Cardixa will have her winter rest.'

They beached the ship near the settlement and after the work of unloading the cargo and ballast stones, the crew used log rollers to haul her up away from the sea with the help of the local fishermen, who were all friends of Acichorius. It was a melancholy task for Talakhonsu as he remembered hauling the Kallisto out onto the beach for the winter at far off Roussolakos with his lost crewmates. His voyages with Leontios and the others seemed a lifetime ago now.

That night the local chieftain, who was a good friend of Acichorius, feasted them all well in his long house and clapped his hands many times when he heard of their battle with the sea wolves, for those raiders had also troubled his own people in the past. Wine and mead enough were drunk, so that all were soon merry. For a while at least, the trials of Huell and Talakhonsu were forgotten.

When morning came, Huell was impatient to set off inland as soon as he could, but to the red man's annoyance Talakhonsu was in no such hurry. There were groggy heads all around and the sleep that came with them, so the Napatan waited instead until both Acichorius and their host the chieftain had risen, so that he could say his last farewell to them. Yet when Talakhonsu offered his final thanks and two of his silver coin to Acichorius, the captain looked surprised at this.

'I will take one only of your coins Talakhonsu,' he said slowly so that Talakh could better understand his words. 'But here, I will give you one of my own in return. You and Huell fought for those who were not your kin, when you could have just fled.'

Talakh bowed his head and said nothing more of that, for he was not proud of the blood on his hands whatever the cause.

'What will you do now that your ship is laid up for the winter?' he asked, to change the subject.

'I will build up a stock of furs again, from the trappers and hunters who bring them to me here,' Acichorius rubbed his chin. 'But first there is my cargo of oil and wine to move on. Men will come from far and wide to trade with me against these things through the long winter. The chieftains have a taste for good wine in these parts,' he grinned, 'though it is just to show their wealth.

'But there is also my ship to care for,' he looked fondly upon the dark hulk of the Cardixa, lying off down the beach. Her mast was already lowered and her oars stored away

'She is a fine one captain,' Talakh said holding out his hand in farewell. 'Perhaps we will meet again one day.'

'Aye, perhaps we will. I always have need of good men Talakhonsu, remember that,' Acichorius said, gripping his hand firmly. 'Men who can sail. Men with strength at the oar. Men who can fight if need be. Be sure to come and see me if you pass this way again.'

'I will captain.'

'Well, good luck then. And may Teutates protect you.'

With that, Acichorius went back to the wooden hall of the chieftain where he was lodged as an honoured guest, while Talakh took up the bundle of bread and dried fish that the chieftain had gifted him for his bravery.

'A good man, that one,' Talakh breathed hard as he caught up with Huell, who was already started on the steep path up away from the settlement. 'Wiser too than Longback gave him credit for.'

The red man said nothing, for now that his goal was almost within reach, he had only dark thoughts of revenge on his mind. Talakhonsu glanced at Huell's cold, blue eyes and looked quickly away again. In spite of all that they had endured side by side, Huell was lost to him as a friend. But still, he owed the red man his life twice over now. Until that debt was repaid in full, Talakhonsu had no choice but to serve the cause of Huell as best he could, come what may. With each passing step now, the Napatan cursed his misfortune.

And yet there was always still the faint hope that one day he would see his old friends Pamphilos and Hippolytos again. Perhaps even that he might yet return to the side of the girl Ketet and her father Isek in far off Kemet. A faint hope yes, but a hope nonetheless to keep his spirits up on this long and dangerous journey.

The path north through the rolling hills and woods of Armorica was a well trodden one they found, though others they passed along the way always eyed them warily, as well they might two such strange warriors. Others still ran from their approach and hid themselves away until the shadow man and the wild eyed one had passed by.

Of settlements there were many, but these were small and fenced about with sharpened timbers that offered no welcome to strangers. Of great standing stones there were many too, some of them as tall as trees, rising like giants into the grey sky.

'It reminds me of my own lands,' Huell said thoughtfully. 'The look of the people, their customs... it all seems much the same.'

The few people who greeted them sounded like Huell too, though when Talakh mentioned this, the red man was quick to say otherwise.

'No, they use many of the same words, but they kill them with their tongues,' he said dismissively.

After a cold night spent trying to sleep, a drizzle began to fall on the travellers in the dawn light. Heavy rain followed, harrying them for the next two days, so that they were soaked through despite their heavy woollen cloaks. At night they made simple shelters up against the widest tree trunk they could find, though some rain always reached them all the same.

At last the weather relented on the third day of their path north, yet still when they found themselves come to a low plain by the coast, they were already weakening again with hunger and tiredness. What directions they had took them another day east and then another two days north as the coast swung around to face west onto the great ocean.

Finally their weary path brought them at last to Coriallo, a large settlement gathered around one side of the mouth of a river. Even if there was no welcome for them there they thought, at least there might be food and shelter to be bought for their silver coin. In the fading light of a grey evening they came to the settlement's banked and stockaded walls which were further defended by a deep ditch. When they crossed the causeway over it, Talakh and Huell found the high gates barred to them.

'What do you want?' a man's voice called down to them from a lookout platform above.

'We are travellers,' Huell answered back. 'We seek only food and shelter.'

'Strangers then,' the man said, his head appearing

cautiously above the stockades spikes. 'Can any man vouch for you here?'

'No, but we have silver coin,' Huell replied curtly, his impatience rising.

'Who is it?' another man's voice asked the lookout.

'Two men. One from across the sea by the sound of him. The other... the other is a dark skin. They say they have silver, but they look like troublemakers.'

'Troublemakers eh?' the voice from within said. 'We will give them trouble enough to be going on with!'

There were shouts now from within the walls as other men were called to their arms.

'We should go,' Talakh urged Huell. He had understood enough of what had been said to know that these people were not friendly.

'Go?' Huell spat, angrily. 'No, I will not run from these bastards. They will have to deal with me whether they like it or not!'

While they argued, the heavy gates creaked open and six warriors armed with spear and shield strode out to face them. All of them wore the breeches of the northern peoples, woven in dull patterns of green and russet, as were their tunics and cloaks. Their leader, a big man with long plaits in both his dark hair and his moustaches, looked them up and down in silence, daring them to speak first. His bare arms were tattooed and bore the scars of battle. Talakh saw too that he wore many iron finger rings, the mark of a warrior.

Huell stared back, his cold blue eyes boring into the other man, and still nothing was said. This was a fight, Talakh saw as he looked between the two men, a fight of the eyes.

The Gaul swallowed but he did not look away and finally, after what seemed an age he spoke boldly.

'Who are you, and what do you want here?'

'Who I am is no concern of yours,' Huell answered curtly. 'But who then are you?'

The big Gaul blinked again and his face reddened with anger. 'You northern dog!' he spat back. 'You come across the narrows to our lands and expect to treat them as your own? You should go back to the fishwife that whelped you and hide under her skirts!'

Huell spat at his feet, but before he could reply Talakhonsu spoke up.

'He is Huell and I am Talakhonsu,' he said as calmly as he could in the tricky tongue of the Gauls. 'We travel back across the seas.'

'Across the Sound to Albion, eh? You should choose your friends more wisely, dark skin.'

'He is not my friend,' Talakh answered.

Huell looked at him then as if he had just seen the sun swallowed up, his face dark with anger.

'Not your friend?' the Gaul frowned. 'Then you should be on your way. Go on, clear off before I change my mind!'

'No,' Talakh said bluntly.

'No?' the warrior scowled, as his companions shifted edgily.

'No,' Talakh shook his head. 'Twice he saved my life. So I fight by his side if I have to.'

'Hmm,' the big man said, pulling his moustache plait thoughtfully. 'The blood debt, eh? And how much of your blood will you shed to pay us for his rash words?' he gestured at Huell.

Talakhonsu felt the taste of iron in the back of his throat, as he always did in a time of danger, but he forced down his fear and raised himself up to his full height before he answered.

'Our journey was long and hard from the southern mountains, and the Middle Sea beyond,' he said boldly. 'We fought with the Gauls against the wolves of the sea, so we are not your enemy. Still if you fight my friend, you fight me too.'

This is what Talakhonsu strove to say, though his words were simple and clumsy in the strange tongue. Somehow the Gaul seemed to understand him well enough though and he grinned broadly, his yellow teeth showing behind the long whiskers of his moustache.

'Hah!' he laughed at last, 'You're a brave man, dark skin. You could have walked away and left this one to his fate, but instead you choose to stay at his side,' he nodded with satisfaction. 'There will be no fight between us, for I see that you are a man of honour and of pride. You will be my guest tonight, but as for this one...'

What happened next surprised Talakhonsu. He expected Huell to rail with anger, but instead the red man stepped forward and for once he spoke with his head rather than his heart.

'I meant no offence to you and your men,' Huell bowed his head humbly. 'I am so weary from hunger and the rain that I don't know myself. But if you would let me, I will remain outside of your walls until my friend returns.'

The man pulled his long moustache plaits again while he thought on this.

'Give up your weapons to my men and you will both be my guests tonight,' he said at last. 'I will hear the tales of your travels.'

'I would prefer to keep them...,' Huell started to say. 'But then if I put myself in your place, I would ask the same. I agree to it.'

'Good. Your weapons will be returned to you when you leave in the morning, you have my word on that,' the Gaul said, as he set aside his own spear and offered his hand in welcome. 'I am Luatha, foremost of the warriors here and these are my men. You will be under my protection whilst you are within our walls. Now come, a warm hearth awaits your stories.'

So at last the two weary travellers came to their rest in the chieftain's long wooden hall, where they were sat at the hearth opposite Luatha, feasting on roasted boar, bread and greens of the forest. While the grey bearded and ancient chieftain of Coriallo looked on sleepily from his fur covered shield-seat, Huell told the gathered warriors the tale of his betrayal at the hands of Dubhain, and then of the many hardships he had endured at the hands of the Phoenicians, until he was at last freed by the ship of Leontios.

'So you come back now to reclaim your birthright,' Luatha nodded.

'Aye,' Huell answered, a dark look on his face in the flickering firelight at the thought of those who had betrayed him.

'Well, you will find your lands much changed I think for the years that you have been away. More ships come to Albion from the east now, my friend. Ships full of murderers and desperate men. The landless sea wolves of the north, who take what they can and settle here and there along the coast if they get the chance. They drive out those too weak to fight them off.'

'My own people are strong and they are far inland,' Huell shook his head.

'I hope you will find them still so,' Luatha said, pulling his moustache plaits thoughtfully. 'I say these things only to warn you that you may find many new enemies there over the sea to add to those of your own tribe.'

'Then what should I do? Give up the land of my father and his father? Wander landless until someone sticks a spear in my back? No, that is not for me. I will go back. I must go back,' Huell answered grimly.

'Aye, there is no easy path for you,' said Luatha. 'But whatever happens, right is on your side. I will offer to my god, Taranis who makes the thunder, that he will look well on your cause.'

'And I will not forget your hospitality, O Luatha,' Huell bowed his head. 'We will be brothers across the sea and if you are in need, then I will support your cause when I have gathered my own warriors about me. And of course the cause of your chieftain,' he added, so as not to offend the old man.

Talakh felt strangely contented as he sat watching Huell and Luatha make their pledges of allegiance with one another while he himself sat in the warmth of the fire, eating his fill. The skin of the boar was crisp, the fat beneath succulent and the meat tender. Now at last it seemed that, with his destiny at hand, Huell had finally come to his senses. Perhaps now he would put aside the rashness that too often drove him to make enemies of those who would be his friends.

Much later, when the feasting and talking were done at last, sleep came easily to the travellers as the embers of the fire cast a warm glow up into the high roof of the chieftain's hall.

The next morning dawned dry and bright. While they ate some warm bread and barley gruel, Luatha gave Huell and Talakh the news that, like as not, two boats would cross the water that day if the weather was fair. Sooner than he had dared hope, Huell might find himself back in the land of Albion once more. With their weapons returned to them, they talked further with Luatha, while his men sat idly polishing their blades, as is the way with warriors.

These ones were full of curiosity about Talakhonsu, and through Huell they asked him a great many questions about his homeland among the seas of sand in far off Napata. They were curious too about his throwing stick, so Talakh proudly showed them his skill with it by throwing against a shield that one of them propped up against the stockade wall. The watching children clapped and cheered when the weapon clattered loudly against the shield.

'I will keep my spear all the same,' Luatha grinned when he saw the small dent the heavy stick had made in the shield's painted surface.

Before they left, Talakhonsu and Huell both traded some of their silver for finely woven thick Gaulish cloaks under the guidance of Luatha. Huell traded for some leggings too, though Talakh would not bring himself to do the same.

'I have never worn anything on my legs,' he maintained. 'Surely it will not grow that cold?'

'You will change your mind soon enough,' Luatha shook his head. 'When the snow falls and the river freezes over for days on end, then you will see why we cover our legs!'

With the noon, the tide started to ebb and a favourable wind picked up, so they said a grateful farewell to Luatha and his warriors and set off across the seas in company of a large trading boat from Albion itself. Just as with Luatha, the captain would not allow them to keep their weapons with them and he had them wrapped in a cloak and put out of reach in the vessel's prow as a precaution. For this he could not be blamed, since although his men outnumbered Huell and Talakh, they were none of them fighters.

'My people say there is always a third time for things if there is a second,' Huell said tensely as they braced themselves against the rolling of the boat on the swelling seas. 'Twice I have survived the wreck of a ship. Twice, Talakh! When next we touch land I will not chance my luck again upon the sea,' he shook his head. 'Whatever comes next, it is dry land for me from now on. Only dry land...'

Talakhonsu could not blame the red man for that, though in his own heart he was glad to be back upon the sea once again, for it was another home to him. As the ship made a good headway on the cold breeze, they talked of Huell's tribe with the captain, but though the man had travelled far and wide in his time, still he knew nothing of them, nor of the other inland tribes that Huell spoke of as their neighbours. Dusk gathered in about the vessel with still not a sign of land, though the captain was not worried by this with the sea as calm as it was.

As darkness fell, the broken clouds gave way to a starlit night and the following wind took on a bitter chill that made for a cold and comfortless night for all aboard. Talakhonsu drifted in and out of a restless sleep, huddled in his cloak at the foot of the steering deck. After one such spell he awoke to feel that the ship had stopped her progress and now only rose and fell gently with the small swell. The captain had furled the sail, yet there was no sign of a storm.

'You see land captain?' he guessed, forcing his stiff limbs upright.

'Aye land it is, off to the left of us there stranger.'

Talakh followed the captain's finger to where he could just make out a dim line, pale blue against the dark horizon.

'The Dark Isle, we call it,' the captain said quietly. 'A place of restless spirits.'

'Dark, but yet it seems to glow,' Huell muttered as he roused himself from his sleep. 'How did it come by such a name?'

'Ah, the waters about it are troubled by treacherous

currents,' the man answered. 'When the tide is low and the storm winds blow, great banks of sand and gravel rise up from the deep to snare unwary ships in the crashing waves. Many are drowned in such a way each year, and so you see it is their spirits which haunt the island.

'This is why it has this dark name amongst us, though when you see it in the light of day it looks harmless enough. It is all white cliffs and green top,' he nodded. 'But there! A good piece of seamanship, no?'

'What do you mean?' Talakh asked.

'Well, this is the point I had in mind when we set out from Coriallo and here we are. Straight across the dark seas, to exactly the right mark!'

'So dangerous and yet you chose to sail here?' Huell asked, half mocking the captain.

'Aye, still we come, inlander. From here I can sail easily into the mouth of the Afon Wey, a safe enough inlet. But just a little further to the west where the Dark Isle waits? Ah, then we might have had a battle with the sea my friend!'

As the line of the coast slowly revealed itself in the dawn light, the captain had his men unfurl the sail again and the ship resumed her way, all aboard her impatient to go ashore and stretch their stiff limbs. While Huell and Talakhonsu warily eyed the high cliffs of white rock that formed the place called the Dark Isle, the ship skirted steadily around it at a safe distance under the chill breeze. Still, even though the conditions were all in their favour, all the same they felt the invisible currents the captain had spoken of, pushing the craft strongly across her beam.

It was not long before they came round into a sheltered bay out of the wind, and with the sun barely above the eastern horizon, the captain broke out some oars to row them into the mouth of a river. This they ran up a little way until they came to a bend where a small settlement stood by a beach of shingle and mud. Here at last they drew up in the shallows and dropped some anchor stones so that they would not drift.

Huell jumped over the side into the shallow water and

waded ashore, moved almost to tears that at last his feet rested on the shores of Albion, his own land.

'This is a day I never thought to see,' he said, shaking his head. 'I could die a contented man right here and yet there are other things I still must do. Come on Talakh, there is no time to waste.'

After they had taken their farewell of the captain and ferried their weapons ashore, the two men wandered through the settlement, Huell asking after his own people amongst any folk they came across. But though he gave his people's name and the names of those around them, still none had heard of them. The eyes of these folk were turned only to their neighbours along the coast and across the sea in Gaul, not to those deep away inland. The best direction that could be had was from a frail old man who had outlived his sight.

'Follow the river inland and make your way to the fortress of Mai Dun,' he told them in a voice as dry as a crow. 'The chieftain there is the greatest in all of the land they say.'

He looked both ways about him then, though his sightless eyes would not have told him who might be nearby.

'Yes he is the greatest by far,' he whispered behind his hand, 'though the people there hate him. Mind you, he has the wisest of men for his advisors. Perhaps one of them can help you find your way?'

Talakh was not convinced and he looked from the old man to Huell and silently shook his head.

'What else can we do?' the red man shrugged his shoulders after he had thanked the old man. 'His is the best advice we have had. The only advice come to that. We can do little else but follow it until we have something better.'

So they took the well trodden riverside path, past a calm lake where small fisher boats were just setting out for the day. A grey heron fishing for his breakfast amongst the reeds, flapped his great wings slowly up into the deep blue autumn sky as they passed by, a good omen Talakh hoped, though he said nothing.

The river soon narrowed to a clear, shallow stream and by

the noon it had already become little more than a trickle as they approached the springs that were its source. The water here was sweet and cool and the two men drank their fill, gathering handfuls of cobnuts and berries to ease their hunger a little. Here, the head of the valley was skirted about by low hills, clad in woods of beech and oak. The leaves already ran to yellow and gold here and there, a sure sign that the year was running on and that soon the warmth of summer would be far behind them as the winter approached.

'I think I have heard of this place of Mai Dun before, Talakh,' Huell said thoughtfully as they climbed a winding path that led them over a saddle in the surrounding hills, just as the old man had said.

'When I was a lad my father told me of it, but I thought it was just a story. It only comes to me now, but never did I think I would see Mai Dun with my own eyes.'

'It is built of stone, this fortress?' Talakh asked as he tried to imagine what it would look like.

'Stone?' Huell laughed. 'No, I don't think so. In these lands we build only our hut walls of stone and then only if it lies about in the fields waiting to be gathered up. Most huts hereabouts will be of timber, and there is plenty enough of that.'

Talakh thought of the great temples and palaces of the land of Kemet and shook his head. 'You have no temples of stone?'

'Only those standing stones left by the old people who once lived here, but they were giants so the elders say.'

Talakhonsu nodded, but said nothing more. Though he had heard legends of giants in many of the lands he had travelled through, still he had never seen one. There had never been giants in the land of Kemet, nor of his own Napata, of that he was sure. And yet the strength and cunning of ordinary men and their faith in the gods had been enough to raise up temples great enough almost to touch the roof of the sky itself.

Soon the track they followed led them out of a wood and onto gentle down land, where the rough stubble fields showed that the harvest had already been gathered in.

'There!' Huell pointed to the great long hump of a hill that reared up on the horizon. 'That will be Mai Dun, I think.'

Talakh followed the red man's gaze and took in this strange sight. All along the hillside deep gouges and high banks had been cut into the green flanks of the hill of Mai Dun, whilst along the uppermost bank there stood an immense dark wall of sharpened wooden pales. 'They build it still,' he said as he screwed his eyes up to make out the small figures of men who worked along a freshly dug stretch in one of the banks.

'Aye, it must be a great chief indeed who has his hall there!' Huell nodded. 'It looks like they mean to ring the whole length of the hill with their stockade.'

They walked on toward the great hill, the path taking them around to the west, where it seemed there must be a causeway up onto the top, for they could see people and carts making their way to and fro from that end.

'Let me do the talking,' Huell said quietly as they at last joined the main track that led from the west up onto the fortress hill.

'Why would I not? This is your land,' Talakh shrugged. In truth, he was only too happy for Huell to speak for them both, as long as he held his temper.

Up ahead the path rose up, weaving between high banks of freshly dug earth, white with the chalk that lay beneath the thin soil.

'We will wait here and talk to the next passerby,' Huell said, unsure of himself.

'Aye, that is wise,' Talakhonsu agreed. 'They may not welcome a stranger like me in there.'

It was not long before a man and his young son trod wearily past down the causeway, but he knew nothing of Huell's people, having himself come from the coast only a few days before. Talakh felt the man's eyes staring at him and knew that of course he had never seen someone with black skin before.

'But what goes on there?' Huell asked, pointing up to the men who were digging into the hillside.

'They strengthen the defences still more, stranger,' the man said gloomily. 'Once the harvest is gathered in we are all called to labour here, and have been for many a year, for when Odhrain summons us, all must obey him. All but the other chieftains and their warriors of course. But even they must give him their oath and bring their spears when he calls on them.'

'Odhrain? Who is he?'

'He is high chieftain, overlord for as far as his eye can see from his great hall up there, and further still besides. Between here and the sea and to all the four winds, all must kneel to him. Odhrain protects us from the sea raiders in return for the best of our harvests, which are stored in his granaries.'

'Up there?' Huell glanced up beyond the earth and timber ramparts.'

'Up there, aye. For safekeeping,' the man nodded, bitterness in his voice.

'It is the same the world over,' Talakhonsu shook his head. 'The strong live off the weak.'

The man's mouth gaped wide in surprise as if he had thought the dark man could not speak.

'He is my friend,' Huell said, 'you don't need to fear him. He is a man just the same as us and a good one at that.'

'Then you should not stay in this place,' the man whispered, leaning close. 'There are men here who would cut you open for looking at them the wrong way.'

'The men of Odhrain?' Huell asked.

'Aye, the same. Do not linger!' the man urged them again, the words strained thin with fear against his throat.

Talakhonsu watched after him as the man hurried away down the hill, clutching his son to his side.

'There will be no welcome for us here, Huell,' he said, turning to the red man. 'We should look for another way.'

Yet before Huell could give his answer, they heard the hooves of horses pounding hollow against the earth from up the hill above them. Around the earthen rampart they came, a file of a dozen men or so, warriors all, riding large ponies and riding them well. Each of them carried a short spear through their arms and they came on heedless of those who scattered in their path.

Huell and Talakh stepped back out of their way to avoid the trampling hooves, though rash Huell called something after them, half under his breath. Talakh did not need to understand the words to know that they voiced a curse and he felt the blood fear rise in the back of his throat again. For a moment it seemed the warriors had not heard Huell as they rode on, but then one of their number urged his horse on to the front and wheeled the band around as one.

'Amun protect us,' Talakhonsu muttered under his breath, for he knew what would surely come next. There was no running from the pack of horsemen who bore down upon them at speed, forming their mounts into a broad line that bristled with spears.

'Do nothing!' Talakh held up his hand, as the red man readied his spear.

'Nothing?' Huell spat.

'Aye, nothing,' said Talakhonsu quietly. 'If we try to fight them, we will die soon enough.'

Still the riders came on, the ground thundering under their hooves, but just when it seemed they would ride over the two travellers, they pulled up sharp, kicking up clods of earth and dust over Talakhonsu and Huell.

'Who are you?' their leader demanded at the point of his spear, his baleful, iron-grey eyes fixing them. He was a great bear of a man with a thick red beard that stood at odds against his balding head and wispy fair hair. 'Who are you!' he demanded again.

'My name is Huell of Gorthyn's people. Chieftain Gorthyn was my father...' Huell started to say, but the warrior cut him off.

'You!' he bellowed at Talakhonsu, as one of his men whispered in his ear. 'You, burnt man! You think to curse my men and still keep your tongue?'

'I said nothing,' Talakh shook his head.

The red bearded one's pony shifted nervously under his weight, shaking its head.

'So, my brother here is a liar then, is that it?' he sneered, making a show of spitting at Talakh's feet to show his contempt.

'He barely knows our words,' Huell said, stepping forward. 'I was the one who cursed.'

'Then after I have cut his tongue out, I will take yours as well to feed my hounds,' the warrior spat again.

Huell stepped closer still.

'Your words are brave from up there, with your men behind you,' he said. 'But I have not come this far to die so easily. If you want to take my tongue, then come down from your horse and fight me man to man.'

'Ha, ha, ha!' the red beard laughed harshly, as he handed his spear to his brother and dismounted. 'I will squash you like a fly with my bare hands, little man. And then I'll have your tongue alright. I'll rip it from your dead throat. Ha!' he clapped his heavy hands together.

Talakhonsu looked from the red bearded one to Huell and then back again. It was an unequal match, for the other was far taller and stronger than the skinny red man, his arms thick like the hams of a boar and covered in the dark patterns of a warrior's tattoos. Before he had even thought it, Talakhonsu pushed Huell roughly aside.

'Fight me instead,' the words came boldly from his mouth, as if another had said them.

Now the red beard's brother nudged his pony forward and thrust his spear at Talakh, who slipped sideways, and grasped it firmly with both hands.

'Leave him!' red beard waved his brother away. 'Am I not a generous man my friends?

'Aye, Mabon' his war band raised their spears.

'Then I will grant your wish, burnt skin. Let us see if your blood is as black as your hide, eh?'

'Stay your arm, Mabon,' a thin, reedy voice called out from the ramparts above.

A look of fury came across the warrior's face. 'Don't interfere old one,' he roared back. 'Nothing here is your concern.'

'The spirits make it my concern,' the thin voice came again. 'I have seen these ones before in a waking dream.'

'You see nothing but shadows old man,' the warrior Mabon muttered under his breath.

'Be careful how you choose your words, Mabon,' the reedy voice came again. 'My ears are as keen as any man's.'

'You threaten me Caentigern?'

'I? Threaten you? Come now, how could a white haired old man threaten a mighty warrior such as you?' the voice said. But though his words were gentle enough, still there was contempt to be read in them.

'Yet,' the old one Caentigern continued, 'just as your sword acts for our high chieftain, so does my counsel. I must hear of the travels of these men. I wish to know what they know, and this they cannot tell me if they lose their tongues to your hounds! Unless the beasts can speak to me with them?' he chuckled to himself.

'So, this is how it shall be. You two, come,' he called to Talakh and Huell. 'You will be my guests, under my protection, such as it is.'

'They insulted me,' Mabon roared, spittle flecking his beard as his face turned red with rage. 'No-one does that and escapes so lightly, old man. I will have blood from them, do you hear me? Blood!'

His men roared their agreement at this. The lust for violence was on them too.

'Blood you want?' the thin voice of Caentigern came again, this time from near at hand. 'Then blood you shall have Mabon. You, dark one, give me your hand.'

Talakhonsu stole a sideways glance and saw the old man, tall and thin standing next to him, his wispy, white hair blowing in the breeze where it hung from under his cap of dark felt. Like Mabon and his men he also wore a tunic and trousers of tawny wool, but the cloth was finer and his cloak had a collar of rich fur, clasped at his neck with a jewelled broach. There were the lines of many years in his face, and yet he was strangely unbowed by them, his back as straight as a spear.

'Give me your hand!' Caentigern snapped again.

Caentigern's cold, bony hand gripped Talakhonsu's wrist, trying to pull his arm forward.

'That would not be wise,' the old one said, his clear, grey eyes turning on Talakh with a piercing stare that seemed to search amongst his very thoughts.

Talakhonsu saw then that he had no choice but to let Caentigern draw his arm out, though he had no idea what would happen next.

'Now Mabon, your spear may drink,' the old one gestured as he turned Talakh's palm upwards.

Mabon muttered something under his breath again, but did as he was bid and held his spear forward so that the old one could grasp it.

The bright spear head's flat sides had been sharpened to a wicked edge that glinted in the sun and Talakh knew now what was to come. Sure enough as he tried not to flinch, the old man drew the blade edge across the palm of his hand, slowly and deliberately. There was a sharp pain, but Talakh gritted his teeth and held the gaze of the leering Mabon as the blood pooled dark red against the pink of his cupped hand.

'There is your blood!' the old one announced, turning Talakh's hand over so that it dripped dark red over the spear point of Mabon.

'Now you!' he turned to Huell. 'Give me your hand.'

For a moment, Huell looked as if he might refuse, but then he too offered his hand for the spear of Mabon to drink from.

'What is a little blood to me?' he started to say, though he could not help but flinch as the spear scored his palm. 'A tickle,' he scowled unwisely.

Mabon grinned and twisted his spear at that, so that its cut was ragged and deep. 'A tickle eh?' he snarled, his grey eyes as cold as a winter's day. 'Where is your laughter then, eh? Weakling!'

'That is enough,' Caentigern said, pushing the spear away. 'These men have given their blood freely to you, O Mabon in payment for their hasty words. As counsel to high chieftain Odhrain, who is wise in all things, I judge in his absence that the debt they owe you is therefore paid in full. We will let you and your men be on your way, for I know you have important business to attend to, protecting the high chieftain's lands.'

Mabon stomped back to his pony, still seething with dark rage, and hauled himself astride with a grunt and a loud belch that he did not seek to cover.

'You won't always have Odhrain's ear old man,' he sneered.

'Everything and everyone passes,' Caentigern nodded his head as if in agreement. 'Everything and everyone. This much I know. This much we should all remember.'

'I will remember all right,' Mabon said darkly, spitting on the ground as he and his war band reined the heads of their steeds around and galloped off, roaring at all who lay in their path as they rode to the west.

'Aah!' the old man breathed out deeply, clapping his hands together. 'Victories like these are few and far between when you reach my age, my friends,' he grinned. 'Once I was a young man, a warrior like the two of you, but now I have to look to my wits for protection.'

'Thank you. I am called Talakhonsu,' Talakh said simply holding out his good hand.

The old one waved it away and instead held up the wounded hands of the two men. 'So, your blood is not black after all,' he smiled with teeth that were still good despite his great age. 'I am Caentigern, counsel to the high chieftain, and in return for saving your hides you will tell me all that you know. That is a fair trade, would you not say?'

They followed the old man as he strode swiftly up the chalk path that wound uphill between the earthen ramparts, where yet more hidden defences lay. These banks were cunningly made Talakh could see, so that any attackers had no straight way through and could be attacked in turn from the heights above them. It was a foreboding place, all the more so when he saw that the windblown rags fixed to a tall pole atop the ramparts were the remains of a man.

'A mark of the justice of Odhrain,' Caentigern said, following his gaze.

'What was his crime?' Huell asked.

The old man gave a long, low laugh that rattled deep in his chest as he shook his head.

'There does not have to be a crime in the fortress of Mai Dun for a man to be punished so by Odhrain! But do not worry yourselves, he is away from here, off to the east. You will be gone long before he returns, if you have any sense in your heads.'

They came now to a high gate set between a narrow gap in the ramparts. A row of boar skulls were fixed to the wooden bar that crossed above the gateway, their tusks sharp and curved.

'The spirit animal of the high chieftain,' Caentigern looked up. 'He runs with them in his dreams, so he says.'

'He sounds like a mad man,' Huell said sourly, staring back at two guards who were eyeing them suspiciously.

'Perhaps he is,' the old man nodded with a curious smile. 'But still he is chieftain here, so who will call him that? No, like many a war lord he is vain first and mad only second.'

In spite of the pain from his wounded hand, Talakhonsu's eyes widened as they left the ramparts behind and wandered further onto the vast, flat enclosure of the hilltop. All around its circumference a wall of high earthen banks had been raised over what must have been a great many years. A cluster of large square huts stood close by, curiously raised up on rocks and heavy wooden stumps so that they sat a few feet above the ground. These too were guarded by a warrior, who leant on his spear looking bored.

'The granaries of Odhrain,' Caentigern explained. 'In them is a wealth that in times of hunger becomes as great almost as that of his cattle.'

'He has not many of those then,' Huell said dismissively.

'On the contrary, his herds are greater than any man's in these lands. Yet the grain is what keeps the people tied to him, not the cattle, nor his sheep. If the harvest fails, then the people look to their chieftains, who in turn look to Odhrain. So you see at certain times, the grain can exert great power over men.'

'And yet your high chieftain needs to make this place stronger still,' Huell said.

Caentigern gave him the kind of look that a father might give a foolish child.

'No, he has made it bigger, rather than stronger,' the old man said. 'Even before it is finished, Mai Dun is now the greatest fortress in all of the lands, here or across the sea. A sign of Odhrain's strength.'

'And your people labour out of love for him?' Huell asked sarcastically.

'Ha!' Caentigern laughed. 'You are a prickly one! Huell did you say your name was? I will call you hedgehog I think. That one is your spirit animal!'

'When I find my own clan, I will lead them only by their choice, not through fear of me,' Huell said, ignoring Caentigern's jibe.

'Then you may not rule long, if at all,' the old man poked a bony finger in Huell's chest. 'In these lands only the ruthless prosper. You should remember that, Huell,' he said, fixing the red man with his grey, hooded eyes.

Talakh could see Huell's hackles rising, his temper ever quick.

'What is that place?' he asked, pointing out an enclosure of sharpened pales that lay a way ahead, so as to divert the crossed words between the two men.

'That? Ah, it is the enclosure of the high chieftain. None may enter there, not even I, unless he bids it. My hut is over there,' he pointed to a much smaller enclosure nearby. 'Now come, we have much to discuss before I set you on your way again.'

The round hut of Caentigern lay in a circle of five others behind the low pales of the smaller enclosure, the timbers of which were more for show than defence, being little higher than a man's chest. Huell and Talakhonsu followed Caentigern through the low entrance to his home, where a woman perhaps half his age was baking some flat bread on the hearth stone.

After she had washed and bound their hands for them with some healing herbs, cobwebs and strips of young, damp bark, Caentigern asked her to leave.

'Even an old man must have some comforts,' he said to them in a low voice as she ducked out of the doorway, 'but she has a loose tongue that one. Now sit and have some bread. Then we will talk.'

The hot bread had risen well and both Talakh and Huell ate it down greedily as they sat by the fireside, burning their mouths in their haste.

'Hungry, I see?' Caentigern chuckled, not needing their answer. 'Now you, Talakhonsu,' he struggled with the name as he poured some water into a cup and passed it to the Napatan. 'Tell me of your own lands and how you came to be here. Leave nothing out, for I must know it all.'

And so, with the help of Huell when the strange words failed him, as they often did, Talakhonsu told the old man of his distant childhood in Napata. He told too of the raid of Khaemwaset and how he was taken into captivity by that evil one, along with the man Korkamani, who he later came to know as his father. There was also his time in Kemet, the land of the black earth to relate of course, so he told of the holy city of Waset that stood nearby to Siamun's farm. Waset, the pride of Kemet, where the gods dwelt in their vast temples, or so the priests said.

There came in turn the sad tale of the murder of Korkamani at the hands of the evil one and Talakh's own escape to the Great River where his wits found him a place amongst the crew of Leontios. He spoke too of his revenge against Khaemwaset and the death of Meketra, then of how he came to meet Huell.

Many times the words choked in his throat as Talakh spoke of these things, so that strange as the tale was, Caentigern knew it to be the truth. At the telling of the wreck of the Kallisto and the death of her captain and crew, a tear of sadness came to the old man's eyes.

The day drew to a close and dusk descended before Talakh had done with his story. Even then he had only touched the surface of his adventures and all that he had seen.

Of Huell's story, Caentigern was not so keen to learn and instead he returned time and again to the things which Talakhonsu had told him of, until the Napatan was hoarse with talking.

'Tell me...,' the old one said dreamily as he stirred the fire embers. 'Tell me again of this giant lizard. It lives sometimes in the water and sometimes upon the land? As an otter would?'

It seemed a strange request, but Talakhonsu told once more of the crocodile's great teeth and long scaly tail that could break a man's legs with one thrash.

'But even though it often kills children,' he added, 'still in some parts of Kemet, it is worshiped as a god. In those places they give offerings of food for the beasts and bow down to them at their passing.'

'But why do you want to know of things such as these?' Talakh asked after a pause. 'Why did you risk your life to help us?'

'Risk my life? At the hands of that blustering fool Mabon? Pah! That whelp can no more do me harm than can a fly buzzing around a horse. He is an annoyance, nothing more,' he waved his hand dismissively.

'But as to why I want to know of the places you have passed by and their people, well that is simple enough. I am an old man, despite my youthful looks', he grinned. 'The gathering of knowledge is all that is left for me in this world. When I pass on, then I will take that knowledge with me to the spirit lands that shadow our own. Who knows what use it may be to me then in that other place?

'But enough of these things!' Caentigern clapped his hands suddenly so that Talakh and Huell started from their tiredness. 'You have told me much that I could not even dream to know and I am grateful for that. But now we must think of your escape from here.'

'What of Mabon then?' Huell asked.

'Ach, that wooden head will be drunk on mead by now and snoring like a boar!' Caentigern clapped his thigh. 'But all the same he will have told the men on the gate not to let you out, you can be sure of that.'

'Then how are we to escape from this fortress?' Huell asked irritably.

'Ah, patience my young friend, patience. We will wait an hour or two, for by then the moon will have set and all but the guards at the gate will be asleep. Then I will take you to a place where it will be nothing to a pair of fine warriors like you to go over the wall.'

'But where should we go then?' Huell asked. 'To the north? To the west?'

Caentigern blinked as if a little surprised. 'You ask where you must go and yet you are a man of these lands? If you don't know your own way home, how am I to tell you?'

'Then you have wasted our time old man!' Huell said his quick temper rising again.

'And yet without my intervention, you would be spitted on Mabon's spears by now and his hounds would be chewing on your tongue,' Caentigern answered simply. 'Think on that, rash one.'

'Is there nothing you can tell us?' Talakh asked.

'Yes. I can tell you that my woman Una will never speak to me again if I do not go and bring her back from her sister's hut soon,' the old man chuckled.

'But there is something perhaps in your voice, Huell,' he said when he had recovered himself. 'We get many from the east here and you are not from that stock by the sound of you, that much I know. By the way you speak you were raised further north or perhaps even west.

'Ah, but not the far west I think. The land of Belerion, has the sea all around it and you say the sea was strange to you until you were enslaved. So, it is plain then that you are not from the west after all.'

'We head north then?' Huell asked impatiently.

'Yes, prickly one. To the east and the west is where Mabon and his men usually ride out and you do not want to cross paths with him again, of that I am sure. So head north and keep north, until you have left Odhrain's lands far behind you, that is my advice.

'Ah but still, something in my mind tells me that you should head for the Maen y Lleu. The journey will take you three days, perhaps less as you are young and strong. You will soon be beyond the reach of Mabon that way.'

'I don't remember any place by that name,' Huell said doubtfully. 'How will we know it?'

'Hah! You have not heard of the Maen y Lleu? Truly you are an ignorant man Huell. Did your father teach you nothing, dunderhead? Had you no elders in your tribe?'

'I know it not, just as you knew nothing of the places we spoke of,' Huell said through gritted teeth.

'Be that as it may, you will know it when you come to it,' Caentigern answered, ignoring the red man's slight. 'Surely even you will have seen the circles of stone that the old ones left upon the land?'

'Yes, I have seen them, of course.'

'Well, the Maen y Lleu is one such place,' Caentigern said, a distant look in his eye as he stroked his short white beard.

'Ah, but this one was not raised by the old ones, oh no. Only a giant, or perhaps even the gods themselves, could have accomplished such a feat. Be sure to pass around the great stones nine times sunwise to seek the blessing of great Lleu, god of the sun.'

The old man nodded in agreement with himself as he sat silent in his thoughts for a moment as if in a trance, the firelight flickering in his grey, unblinking eyes. There was something about him then that sent a shiver down Talakhonsu's spine.

'You are cold?' Caentigern asked him, a smile returning to his thin lips.

'No, no.'

'Well you soon will be when you get out into the night, so be careful not catch the chill my young friend. These things are as dangerous when the winter comes as any man's sword. Get yourself some leggings, that is my advice!

'Now,' he turned back to Huell. 'From one sacred place, you

will go to another. Follow the way west a long day's walk from the sun stones to the place they call Teyrnas yr Hynafiad. You will find there a great many sacred places of the old ones and a circle of stones bigger by far than even the Maen y Lleu! Pass around this circle nine times too and ask for the guidance of the ancestors in the search for your kin.

'From there the avenues of the dead lead to the tombs of the old ones and also to a great sacred mound that reaches into the sky, but do not climb upon it! That is forbidden to all but the seers and the holy men. If you climb there, you will know only madness forever afterwards, so think on that!' Caentigern said grimly before growing silent again.

'And then what?' Huell asked sceptically.

'Then? I can offer only this,' the old man said. 'Go to the great circle a final time and close your eyes. Listen then for one stone that calls to you. When you know it, rest your forehead against the stone that has chosen you and ask it your question. But if the spirits choose not to speak to you, it will be for you to find your own way.'

'I have no other choice then?'

'None that I know of,' Caentigern said, peering at Huell from under his heavy eyelids. 'I may be wrong in all that I have said, but these things are what my mind's eye sees, and it rarely fails me. That is why I have the ear of Odhrain.'

'Then I will follow your guidance,' Huell said with a heavy heart.

'And I will make an offering to the gods for you,' Caentigern said, a little lightness at last returning to his face. 'But now gather up your things, for you must go. Talakhonsu, take up my old spear over there. The head will sharpen again easily enough and the shaft is of ash, as hard now as iron. It will serve you well enough, since you have not one of your own.'

To Huell he gave some thin strips of buck meat which had been drying on a wand by the fire and a little hard cheese for the journey. Then the old man led them out of the hut, cautiously looking about him as he went. All was quiet and still as Talakh and Huell followed him out into the chill night air, the cold not pleasant to the Napatan.

'A raw night, eh?' Caentigern whispered. 'The first frost will come early this year I think. Now stay close and mind your feet.'

The three of them strode quickly out of the enclosure and made for the dark outline of the wall. It was not far, but fearing they might be attacked by Mabon's men at any moment, it was farther than Talakh would have liked. When they climbed the bank to reach the shelter of the wall of pales, they saw that here it was little more than a fence, barely as high as a man's chest and easy enough to climb over despite the sharpened tip of each pale that stuck through the woven willows.

'Be careful as you climb over,' Caentigern warned them. 'There is a steep bank on the other side where the ditch is cut, and then another beyond that.'

Talakh offered Huell a stirrup of his hands so that he could climb over, but instead of heeding Caentigern's advice the red man used the stirrup to vault over and so lost his footing on the slippery grass of the ditch beyond. How he hissed and cursed under his breath as he tumbled down the steep slope and into the bottom of the ditch.

Caentigern folded in half as if someone had punched him in the belly, laughing silently as he clutched his sides.

'I am a wicked man,' he whispered when he had recovered. 'But I did warn him, did I not?'

'Aye, you did,' Talakh grinned as he lowered the spears and the sword of Leontios over the wall. 'Thank you again O Caentigern for your kindness.'

'It is nothing, friend. In return I have learnt much from you about the world beyond these shores. Now, when I close my eyes, my thoughts will take me to the far off places you spoke of and I will see them in my imaginings. That is a rare gift.'

Talakh nodded and shook the other's bony hand.

'Go well,' the old man whispered quietly after him as the tall Napatan scaled the wall and lowered himself carefully down the other side.

Talakh looked for the old seer when he had clambered up

the far bank to join Huell, but Caentigern was already gone.

With the North Star that remains always fixed in the sky as their guide, the two men picked their way up and down through the deep maze of ditches surrounding the Mai Dun, then struck out as fast as they could into the darkened lands beyond, making all haste for fear of the wrath of Mabon.

Chapter 9

The Whispering Stones

Outside the hut of Pelia, the rain came down in a flood as claps of thunder shook the roof, causing both her and Cerian to jump in their fright. The rain dripped from the smoke hole hissing on the low fire, and Pelia made a silent wish that whatever had angered the thunder god would not draw one of his bolts down upon Llan Huell.

'The old man Caentigern, I suppose he is long dead now,' Cerian thought aloud as the skies quietened again. 'He sounds very funny in his way, calling Huell a hedgehog,' she laughed. 'Was he right do you think, to mark Huell ignorant?'

'Well,' said Pelia, 'that depends. We only know the things we know, either because we see something with our own eyes, or because someone tells us of it.

'But Huell's father, he had not been a man with a thoughtful mind. For him the defending of his land was all there was. He didn't trouble himself with thoughts of the sacred places, as long as the spirits left him alone.'

'So Huell knew no better then?'

'Aye. But then of course we must remember he was only young when he was taken away. He returned a man and by then Huell had learnt the value of knowing. His travels and his hardships had taught him that much at least. This is why he was a strong leader of our people while he lived, even if his temper was often quick.'

'He was lucky his rashness didn't get him and Talakhonsu killed when he insulted Mabon though.'

'Yes, lucky indeed. Still, it gave him a livid scar on his hand to remember Mabon by. Perhaps that reminded him afterwards that there are times when even a chieftain must bite his tongue.'

'Did Mabon come after them? Did they have to fight him

and his men?'

'Ah, that is another story for another day, Cerian.'

'Well, you say that, but there are not many days left for us Pelia in your hut. Soon I will spend my nights with Tyrnon...'

'You speak of it as if it is a bad thing,' Pelia frowned. 'Do you not love him?'

'Of course, yes. But still I will miss these times. I hope that whatever happens we can still sit like this in each other's company.'

'Perhaps we will sometimes, but you know that when you have a husband he will want your attention. So will your children too, in time. You and I will still be friends Cerian, but it will not be like it is now.'

'I know,' Cerian nodded sadly. Although she had a wise head on her shoulders, she was in many ways still very young.

'You are right though,' Pelia patted the young woman's arm. 'The day of your hand fasting will be here soon enough, and so the story of my father's adventures must draw to its end. I will tell you a little more tonight.'

'Yes! It gets to the part I know soon,' Cerian said excitedly. 'How Talakh and Huell fought side by side to take back Huell's birthright.'

'Ah well, you may think you know this part,' Pelia said shrewdly, 'but really people remember things in a way of their own choosing, Cerian. If you want to know what really happened, forget the things others have told you before and listen again with an open mind.'

And so Pelia told of how Talakhonsu and Huell made their way north to the great stone circle of the Maen y Lleu, the reckoning now close at hand between the red man and those who had betrayed him so many hard years before.

-ϕ-

From the fortress of the Mai Dun, the two travellers headed

north as Caentigern had told them, always on their guard for fear that Mabon and his riders might fall upon them. In the darkness, they lost the track many times, but luck was with them and always they somehow found it again.

At last, their path joined another and that led them to a small settlement by a river, though this was too wide and uncertain to ford at night. A watch dog started to bark at them, but this again was their good fortune, when a ferry man appeared warily from his small hut. He was sour faced at his sleep being broken, but for a shaving of silver coin he paddled them each across quickly enough in his coracle. They hastened quickly away on the other side, for even with the river between them, there was no doubt in their minds that Mabon and his horsemen would try to hunt them down if they could. As soon as the dawn broke, the two men sought the cover of a wood for most of the next day, resting there rather than risk being caught in the open.

Talakhonsu slept fitfully through to the afternoon, wrapped in his cloak on the newly fallen leaves, awakening only as the day was evening toward dusk. Huell was already on his feet, his spear in hand.

'We should go now,' he said dourly.

'It will soon be dark,' Talakhonsu yawned as he stretched out his stiff limbs. 'There will be no-one to ask the way of,'

'Aye, and no-one to give us away to Mabon either,' said Huell.

They set off under the gathering cloak of darkness, though that had dangers of its own too as they scaled hills and crossed small streams under the light only of the stars. Long was the night and cold for them too, so that Talakhonsu's fingers and bare toes ached from it, and not for the first time or the last, he longed then for the warmth of his homeland, where the sands were so hot they might blister a man's feet.

When the dawn at last came to the eastern hills there were no woods nearby to hide them and so, though they were ill at ease, there was nothing to be done but to press on in the hope that Mabon still snored in his bed.

The sun had barely crested the horizon the next morning when a thick mist rose up, the damp air stealing away what little warmth remained in Talakhonsu's body so that he shivered miserably. As the two travellers wandered on, they caught the scent of wood smoke in the air, the tell tale sign of a settlement up ahead of them. Sure enough, as they followed the track warily into a gentle combe, a ditched enclosure emerged from the mists, girt about with a thick thorn hedge that wore the last of its leaves. Within it stood a few huts, whilst without there were stubble fields where the barley had been harvested.

A young man was turning out a few pigs and sheep onto the fields for the day, but when he saw Talakhonsu and Huell looming out of the mist, he cried out a warning and ran back into the enclosure.

'We will wait here and let them come to us,' Huell said quietly, and so they did.

The young lad reappeared with four men, all of them carrying spears. A large hound loped at their side as they strode forward together a way, though not so far that they couldn't retreat back to the safety of their enclosure if need be.

'Who are you? What do you want?' a gruff voice called out from the oldest amongst them.

'We are travellers, bound for the circle of stones called the Maen y Lleu,' Huell called back, his voice echoing around the hollow. 'We wish only to pass by your lands in peace.'

'You should go back the way you came then. Find yourself another path!' the gruff voice called back.

'That we cannot easily do,' Huell said, biting his tongue. 'We are strangers here.'

'Then pass on and don't come back,' the man said firmly.

'Perhaps you could set us on the right path?' Huell asked as politely as his shortening temper would allow.

'The great stones are many days walk away,' another of the men called back, 'but you should follow the high ridge, not the valleys. That way you will keep off land where you have no place to be. Now be on your way!'

The face of Huell grew red, this time not from the heat of

any sun, but with an anger that blazed just as fiercely. Yet there was nothing to be done about it. They were outnumbered and had made enough enemies already through his careless words, so without another word they turned aside and started up the steep side of the combe. The grass was slippery under their sandaled feet, so that they had to lean heavily on their spears. Always they were under the watch of the clan below, and always the echoing bark of the dog harried them until at last they were lost in the mist again.

'Are all the people of this land so friendly?' Talakh asked in between deep breaths.

'Perhaps they have cause to be wary,' Huell grunted back, ignoring the joke. 'Things will be better the further we get from the coast.'

When they had gained the broad ridge above the combe, the mists finally started to melt away under the gentle warmth of the low morning sun. A clear track worn white into the chalk led off to the north-east ahead of them and so they decided to follow this, resolving to keep to the high ground. Yet tired as they now were, they dared not stop. Up on the ridge there were few enough woods to hide or sleep in.

The wind picked up and clouds blew in to cover the sun as the day wore on. In his weariness and hunger, Talakh's heart sank when the first few spots of drizzle started to fall on his face. When the rain began in earnest, there was nothing the two men could do but seek the shelter of a small wood up ahead. Here, sat on a dry carpet of spent needles under the thick, low branches of a yew tree, they escaped the worst of the weather. Huell sank into a deep sleep almost as soon as he had wrapped himself in his cloak.

But for Talakhonsu sleep did not come so easily, even with the gentle pattering of the last of the rain. He could see now that these northern lands were a harsh place, troubled by landless men who came to steal and murder. He had seen enough of that in his own land.

When nightfall came at last, the two men ate between them the last few pieces of their dried meat before setting off again through the dark land, seeking what shelter they could when more showers blew in from the west. The hills slowly gave way to flatter ground and thick forest where the trail constantly branched and so was almost impossible to follow with any certainty in the dark of the night. With no North Star to guide them, all Talakhonsu and Huell could do was trust to their instincts.

The next morning, dark storm clouds rolled in low on the south-westerly wind, threatening more rain, but the two weary travellers could do nothing in this open land but trudge onwards, for the Maen y Lleu called them now. A few others appeared on the track as it crossed other paths, until at last up ahead they heard a shout just as the rain began to fall in earnest. At the crest of a slight rise, finally the massive and broken circle of the Maen y Lleu lay before them. It was plain that this was a sacred place of the old people, its massive hewn stones showing light against the darkening sky.

'The Stones of Lleu, the sun god,' Huell spoke in the Greek tongue, so that Talakh could better understand. 'Never was a place so ill named.'

Lightning flashed across the sky, followed by a great crack of thunder that boomed and echoed across the wide, treeless plains as if it might split the earth apart.

'Amun protect us,' Talakhonsu said quietly, though he knew that surely now they were far beyond the realm of his own god of the four winds. He drew his cloak over his head and trudged on, eyes down in case the angered gods of the sky should look into them.

In this way, Talakhonsu did not see the full might of the stones until he was almost upon them. There they stood in a great circle within a ditched enclosure, the sacred stones of the sun. Each of them was the height of three men at least and linked across their broad tops by other slabs almost as massive, while more stones lay broken on the ground as if a giant's hand had swept them aside. Another lightning bolt lit up the land, throwing the shadows of the handful of folk gathered there against the mighty stones, and a great moan of dread went up from them in fear of the god's rage.

'Nine times around, that is what Caentigern said,' Huell spoke through gritted teeth, as much to himself as to Talakh.

So they began, and they did not finish their service to the god Lleu until they had passed sunwise around the stones nine times, though it took what seemed like forever before they were done.

The rain fell hard with hail and the thunder hammered the black clouds above them as they at last passed through the outer stones and into the sacred inner cove of yet larger pillars. Here they found a few others sheltering from the worst of the wind and rain under the towering huddle of stones. Some stood, but others cowered on their haunches with their heads in their hands, gripped by the madness of the spirits as the god of the sky shook his mighty fist again. When they saw Talakhonsu's dark face under his cloak, their fear was complete and many ran away screaming, thinking him a spirit from the otherworld.

'Can you feel it?' Huell said, reaching out with both hands to touch one of the giants. 'The power of the stones.'

'Aye, I can. The hair stands out on the back of my neck! The gods are angry Huell, we should not linger here.'

'The gods are angry, yes. But I will take that as a good sign,' Huell said, his face catching the rain as he gazed up into the roiling sky, a wild look on him.

The red man stood there for a moment in silence as if seeking the will of the gods and then raised his spear to the sky. Roaring oath after oath, he swore that he would have his vengeance upon those who had wronged him, the glint of madness once more in those cold blue eyes of his.

Talakh left Huell to his curses then and sought what shelter he could under one of the crossing stones that bridged the massive uprights of the sacred cove. Here the stones were so close in on each other that they blocked the worst of the wind and rain, but still it was a miserable place to be. He peered in vain past the outer stones and across the treeless plain for a sign that the storm might yet abate.

'You are very tall,' a soft voice from behind gave him a start.

Talakhonsu turned around to see the slight figure of a young woman, her face in shadow under a fawn hat of felt from which the rain dripped past her nose. As he looked down she looked up, so that their faces were revealed to each other dimly in the gloom.

'A strange one too,' she said, a curious smile on her pale lips. 'Though not as odd as your friend over there,' she gestured. 'The warrior's rage is in him.'

For a moment Talakh stood there, frozen as he tried to arrange her strange words in his mind.

'He has cause,' he said haltingly as he looked into her startling green eyes.

'Ah,' the girl nodded. 'Our tongue is strange to you. What is your name stranger?' she asked, her words slow and deliberate.

'Name? Ah, I am called Talakhonsu.'

'And I am Liath. Well come then stranger, well come to this sacred place on this sacred day,' she smiled again.

The corners of her mouth creased a little in a way that made Talakh smile back in spite of his weariness. She had a certain gentle beauty about her, but was perhaps not as young as he had first thought. Fine lines crossed her forehead and her skin was freckled from the sun, though still she looked pale in the chill of the rain and the hail.

'Sacred?' Talakh asked, as she came and leant against the stone opposite him, out of the weather.

'It is Samhain Eve, of course,' she laughed. 'Tonight the dead cross over from the shadow world into our own. The stones will whisper their mysteries to those who can listen.'

'The dead? You are not scared?'

'Not I,' she laughed. 'Only fear is to be feared. Those spirits who want to make trouble will look for those who are afraid, but they will pass me by. Are you afraid, man of shadow?'

Before Talakh could answer, Huell came up to find him. The red man looked exhausted and yet strangely happy, as if he had ridden himself of a great burden through his raging.

'I am Liath,' the girl introduced herself again.

'She waits for the dead,' Talakhonsu added.

'She will join them, as will we if we stay here my friend,' Huell said, a rare grin on his face. 'You should be off now to your own kin,' he turned to Liath, 'as we too should be on our way.'

'Off? Why would I do that?' Liath shrugged. 'It is Samhain Eve and I wait here for the wisdom of the spirits.'

'You are a wise woman?' Huell frowned. 'You don't look old enough for that.'

'The age of the wise is not in the skin, but what is in here,' Liath tapped her temple with her finger. 'I was taught well by the one who came before me and when she passed on, so her healing powers came to me.'

'You have the power of seeing too?'

'Sometimes I have waking dreams,' she shrugged her shoulders again.

'And they come true?'

'Sometimes they may, sometimes not.'

'I am Huell. What do you see for me and my friend here?'

Liath gave a wry smile.

'Your friend,' she said, looking Talakhonsu up and down, 'he is from a far off land. You have both newly come here through many hardships and much unhappiness. But I do not need to be a seer to tell you that. It is there plain in your faces for any who choose to look.'

'The skin of my friend gives him away...' Huell paused as another boom of thunder beat upon the clouds. 'But for me? How is it you know of my travels?'

'Your skin is bitten by an angrier sun than shines here,' Liath grinned. 'I have heard that there is a scorched land in the west where the disc of the sun sets. Perhaps that is where you have been?'

'Not the west, but the far south. Beyond any land you would know of anyway,' Huell said with a certain pride. 'I have sailed the seas for many years and so this is why my skin is red.'

'And now you return to settle a score.'

'Aye. That is why I have come back to this land... my land.'

'And what binds you two together?' she turned to Talakh. 'Why follow him so far from your own lands?'

'I will do what I must to help him,' Talakhonsu said simply. 'Twice he saved my life,'

'Hmm,' Liath nodded. 'And so I have a last question. What brings you to this sacred place when you did not even know that it is the eve of Samhain?'

'I was taken from my people many years ago when I was just a boy,' said Huell bitterly. 'But now that I return I do not know where they can be found. A wise man told me to come here, but I think he knew nothing of Gorthyn's people.'

'Gorthyn's people you say? Now Dubhain's people?'

'Dubhain?' Huell spat. 'What do you know of Dubhain?'

'He is chieftain now,' Liath answered. 'At least that is what I hear.'

'You can tell us where to find Huell's kin?' Talakhonsu asked.

'I will do better than that,' Liath grinned. 'I can take you to the edge of their lands if you can wait until tomorrow.'

'Wait? In this rain?' Huell snapped.

'Yes, wait. Where else would you go?'

'West to the ancestor stones, that is where.'

'Teyrnas yr Hynafiad?'

'Aye, that is what they are called,' Huell answered testily.

'Go there if you like,' said Liath as she stared hard at the red man from under the brim of her hat. 'But you will not find your people that way. They lie north of west.'

'You are sure?'

'I am sure. Gossip travels far and wide, Huell. All the more when the story is of a son dispossessed of his father's lands by his own brother. You would not know, but your brother is dead now they say, killed by Dubhain.'

'Dead?'

'Yes. If you are the son of Gorthyn, as I think you must be, then you are alone in the world now,' Liath said gently. 'Now, come with me and I will tell you what else I know of these things.'

'You are not afraid of us?' Huell asked, sourly.

'Afraid?' Liath laughed. 'Why should I be afraid? Your friend will see that no harm comes to me. I see it in his eyes.'

'His eyes are the eyes of a warrior. He has killed many men.'

'Perhaps, but still there is gentleness behind them all the same,' Liath answered. 'Now, do you want my help or not?'

'But where would you take us in this desolate place?'

'Ah, to a secret shelter I know of, you will see. So come now.'

So they trudged after Liath through the gloom and the driving rain, Talakhonsu thinking on how the fates had again taken a hand in his life and those about him. The world was wide and strange, one thing bound to another by the fates, so that try as a man might, the way was already decided for him for better or for worse. An image came to his mind of the farm of Siamun in the distant land of Kemet and his life as a slave there. It seemed to him he was almost a slave again, doomed to serve Huell until his debt was repaid or he died in the red man's cause.

'Where do your thoughts take you Talakhonsu?' Liath asked, seeing the distant look in his eyes as they walked through the downpour.

'To things I have known,' he answered quietly.

'Places? People? How I would like to hear about them,' Liath said, her green eyes lit up for an instant by a distant flash of lightning. 'For I do not doubt you have seen things I never will.'

Suddenly the fierce barking of a dog rose up as they approached a rough tumble of great stones. As Liath led them closer, Talakh saw that a large slab of stone lay perched on top of three others set into a bank of earth, so as to make a kind of rough shelter. It was in this gloomy place that a great shaggy hound stood tethered, so fearsome to look at that the two men held back, their spears at the ready.

'Do not fear Arthfael,' Liath laughed, walking up to the beast. 'His bark is worse than his bite, at least for those who are kind to me.'

'He is yours then?' Huell asked as Liath crouched low and put her arms around the hound's neck.

'Yes, since he was a pup,' she smiled. 'Now come, there is room for us all under the stone, though it will be a tight fit.'

'It is safe?' Huell asked, trying not to sound uneasy.

'One day it will fall, as all things do, even the mightiest tree,' Liath shrugged her shoulders. 'I will take my chance to get out of this storm. Will you not?'

So the two travellers joined Liath and her hound under the great slab of stone. While the thunder crashed and the lightning forked across the dark sky, the wise woman told them of what she knew of the fate of the people of Gorthyn. How Cadno, the brother of Huell had plotted with Dubhain to be rid of him. And how, once Huell had been disappeared away, Cadno in his turn had been driven off and then hunted down by Dubhain.

All the while the hound Arthfael growled low at the red man, for he had taken a dislike to him as dogs sometimes do for no good reason. It was long into the afternoon before finally the winds slackened, the rain eased and the storm at last moved off to leave the sky clear.

'There will be a great fire tonight to welcome the spirits of the dead,' Liath said as they ventured outside of the cramped shelter to stretch their damp bones. 'Will you help me to gather wood?'

'I will come,' Talakh answered. He liked the young woman's company and so was happy to help.

'I did not come all this way to throw twigs on a fire,' Huell said scornfully. 'I will wait here.'

'He is a quick tempered one,' Liath said once she and Talakhonsu were away, out of Huell's earshot. 'It seems to me your friend makes an enemy of himself,'

'Aye, he is like that.'

'He is lucky then to have a friend like you.'

'I owe him my life,' Talakh said simply.

'Perhaps, but then you must not trade your own life for his.'

She took off her hat now that the rain had passed, and let down her plaits of ash blonde hair that had been coiled under it, before putting it on again.

Talakh stole a glance at her as she walked with the hound Arthfael at her side and saw that the plaits were thick and frizzy rather than long. In his mind's eye a picture of her came to him with her hair freed, a mass of flowing curls covering her neck.

Liath looked back at him, her eyes of green locking with his so that he had to quickly look away again once more. Though he was cold, tired and hungry, still he was happy to be away from Huell and in her company instead as they walked along together.

By and by they came to a rise where a small wood lay, and gathered there some fallen wood, of which there was plenty enough from the force of the storm winds. When they had piled as much as they could carry, they wandered slowly back with their load.

'Your hand is hurt?' Liath asked when she saw Talakh wince as he cradled the wood.

'It is nothing.'

'All the same, you must let me look at it when we get back. The cut is deep?'

'Deep enough,' Talakh answered.

'And Huell too? I noticed his hand was bound as well? Ah well, it is none of my business all the same. I will bind your hands anew with some healing things I carry in my bag.'

'You are kind.'

'To those who deserve my kindness, I am kind,' she nodded. 'It is my path in life. Just as it is yours.'

'Me?' Talakh shook his head. 'No, I am not kind. There are things I have done...'

'Who has not?' Liath smiled gently. 'But you have a good heart Talakhonsu. You would stay with your friend and help him despite the danger to yourself, so to me you are still a good man.'

Talakh understood enough of what she had said for his heart to be warmed by the kind words of Liath and he smiled too, his thoughts for once on something other than the hard times been and those still to come. He still smiled when they returned to Huell, and he laughed aloud when Arthfael straight away growled at the red man again. Huell growled back at the hound, his own mood lifted a little by their return.

That night after Liath had wiped the two men's wounded palms clean with damp moss and bound them with cobwebs and healing herbs, the three of them gathered together with those others who remained at the stones, bringing their wood to add to the fire that had been started beyond the ditch circle of the Maen y Lleu. The ground was far too wet to sit, so Talakh and Huell could only squat on their haunches around the fire, warming and drying themselves as best they could while it blazed and crackled in the darkness. Liath stayed with them a while, until in the deep of the night the time came for her to return to the stones.

'What are those?' Talakh asked as she began to eat something from a small pouch of leather.

'They are a kind of mushroom,' Liath answered him after she had swallowed them down with some water from a skin. 'They have within them a gift of magic from deep within the earth goddess herself.'

'Ah,' Talakh said, though he did not really understand.

'Through them, your dreams and thoughts take shape in the real world,' she said. 'If the magic is good and there is enough of it, then the stones will talk to me so that I hear the wisdom of the ages. The magic opens the way to other places beyond what we normally see.'

Liath swallowed down the rest of the mushrooms and then sat quietly with her thoughts, while Huell talked with a gnarled old man who sat by the fire. Talakh grew quiet too, listening as he always did to try to pick out new words from this strange tongue.

In this way they all dwelt in the warmth of the fire for some while, until quite suddenly Liath got unsteadily to her feet and leaning over, gently kissed both men on the forehead. Without a word she wandered off into the great circle of stones, the hound Arthfael loping along at her heel.

'Should we follow her?' Talakh asked as Liath was lost from sight in the darkness.

'Ach, let her go and do her rites,' Huell waved his hand dismissively, his spirits low again with tiredness and hunger. 'No-one will touch her with that hound at her heel.

The cold night wore slowly on, but eventually the fire's heat dried the ground enough for Huell to lie down wrapped in his cloak as weariness overcame him. Soon the red man had fallen into a deep sleep, but though Talakh too was exhausted, he could not put the girl Liath from his mind. Thoughts of her kept him awake long into the night while he listened to the distant voices on the wind.

When at last she returned a long while later, a tired smile played on her face in the dim light of the embers. She looked as if she had just awoken from a dream.

'Did you hear your stones?' Talakh asked as she sat down next to him.

'I heard many things,' she said, with a contented sigh. 'The stones, the trees... all things have a voice you know Talakhonsu, if you can only let go your grip on this world and listen for them. But you!' she giggled. 'Look at your hair!'

'My hair?' he patted his head to see what could be wrong. 'I do not understand,'

'It is springy, like a pillow of moss,' she giggled, pushing her fingers into his hair. 'And your beard too. Are all of your people like you?'

'My people?' Talakh frowned as he struggled to understand her meaning. 'Ah, my people, like me, yes. My father though... he was different.'

'There is sadness in your face, even though you smile. You have lost those who were dear to you,' she placed the warm palm of her hand against his cheek. 'Here, I will hold you until the morning comes,' she said, shuffling next to him. 'There is a bitter chill in the air.'

Liath lifted his arm around her shoulder and leant against him, her head resting against his chest as the hound Arthfael settled at their feet. It was not comfortable for Talakhonsu to sit in this way, but he did not care even so. When at last her eyes closed and her breathing grew deep and slow, he laid her down on his cloak and he too fell asleep by her side.

When the first light of the day slowly came into the sky the next morning, Talakh found himself lying next to the grey ashes of the fire as Huell shook him awake. They were alone now, with Liath nowhere to be seen.

'Where is the girl?' Talakh mumbled, rubbing his eyes as he looked for her in the grey morning.

'Away with the little folk for all I know,' Huell said dully. 'The magic in those mushrooms she ate, it can turn the mind. Drive you to madness, so I have heard.'

'She was fine when she came back here last night. She sat right here next to me.'

'Perhaps you had a dream of her?' Huell grinned, mockery in his voice.

'And perhaps I did not!' Talakh grunted as he got slowly to his feet, trying to rub the stiffness from his knees. 'She was here, just as sure as you are.'

The two men gathered their things together and waited awhile, but when still the wise woman did not appear Huell's patience came to an end.

'We cannot stay here forever,' he said, getting to his feet. 'If that old man back at Mai Dun tells Mabon where he has sent us...'

'Caentigern would not do that, I am sure of it He is a man of his word,' Talakh shook his head.

'Perhaps he would not tell willingly,' Huell conceded, 'but all the same I would rather not wait here to find out. Anyway, maybe your friend has gone on ahead? Maybe we will catch up with her still?'

And so the two travellers set off again, one more reluctantly than the other as they followed a track to the west. They had not gone far when they heard a familiar bark as Arthfael the hound came bounding up from behind them at speed. The beast loped around them, playfully snapping at Talakh's hand, as he tried to ruffle its ears.

'Wait for me!' Liath called out as she ran to catch them up.

'It is good to see you again,' Talakh smiled.

'Aye,' Huell joined in. 'We thought you might have got scared at the thought of travelling alone with two strange warriors.'

'Scared?' Liath laughed. 'Why would I be scared of the pair of you? More likely that you would be scared of me I think.'

'And why would that be?' Huell goaded her.

'Your arm may be stronger than mine Huell, but I have my own strength.'

'Aye, well,' said Huell, less sure of himself now.

'Aye, well enough,' Liath grinned and clapped him on the shoulder as another man might have. Chieftain's son or not, she had made it clear she thought herself his equal.

So, Talakh and Huell resumed their journey westward with their guide, slowly leaving behind the grassy plains for a land of hill and forest as Liath set them a rapid pace. Here there were many streams to be forded and many a steep sided valley to be descended and climbed, until at last they came tired and hungry in the evening light to a small enclosed settlement of no more than a few huts.

'Here is my home amongst these good people,' Liath smiled. 'The shelter of those stakes keeps the wolf from my door and in my turn I heal the clan when they are sick and help their children into the world.'

'You are all kin?' Huell asked.

'No, they are not mine by blood,' Liath shook her head. 'I have no kin that I know of. You see I was found as a baby alone in the woods, left there by my true mother it seems. But my foster mother, she was raised here. She never took a man, so she was glad for me to come to her and here I grew up, loved by her kin even though I am not truly their own.'

'Liath is that you?' a woman's voice called out as Arthfael ran off ahead of them, barking his own greeting. 'Are you safe?' she called again.

'I am well Seadna,' Liath answered. 'Don't worry about

these two, they are friends.'

The men and boys of the settlement came out with their spears and wood axes all the same, despite Liath's words. They were wary of strangers, as all in these northern lands seemed to be.

'This one is Huell, son of the old chief Gorthyn,' Liath said to calm their fears. 'And the dark one is his friend Talakhonsu.'

'Huell?' one of the older men said, stepping forward. 'I remember a boy called Huell. Can it be you?'

'I do not know you,' Huell said as the man drew face to face with him. 'At least, I don't remember...'

'Perhaps not. It seems a lifetime ago since last I saw you boy. Besides I am old now and my hair is long gone. Ah, but I remember you all the same I think! My name is Tadoc, I was a friend of your father's.'

'Tadoc? That name means something to me, Yes!' Huell beamed as he gripped the older man's shoulders. 'My father talked of you often. You and he hunted together when you were boys, he told me.'

'Aye, that is right. Your father was fostered to my father for a while, to make him a man, and so we became as brothers, he and I. He was a good man, Gorthyn and I was sad indeed at his passing. Sadder still when I heard what happened next. But you, you were just a stripling when I last saw you lad!' Tadoc laughed, though there was a tear in his eye as he hugged the red man. 'And now here you are come back to us at last, when all thought you long dead. Well come Huell, well come to you and your friend. Ah, but you are worn with travelling man. Come to my home and warm yourselves by the hearth.'

So they went to the round hut of Tadoc, which was far bigger than the others of course, since he was headman with the responsibilities that this brought.

Talakhonsu followed Huell through the high doorway into the dim interior, where Tadoc bade them sit by the hearth, while his wife scooped each of them out a bowl of meat broth from a large cauldron that hung just above the ashes. This he and Huell ate down greedily in their great hunger, while

Arthfael whined outside.

'Get your hound a meat bone Liath, before he eats one of the children,' Tadoc joked with her. 'There is more than enough for us all left over from the Samhain feast.'

'Thank you,' Liath smiled at him as a daughter would for her father.

'And then you must tell us of the omens for the year to come, if any you saw at the Maen y Lleu,' Tadoc said.

'Aye, I will that.'

Tadoc leaned forward once Liath had gone outside. 'We were all worried for her in the storm yesterday,' he whispered, not wanting her to hear. 'Liath is a dear one to us, though she is headstrong as any man. It was well that she met the two of you it seems.'

'Aye, that it was,' Huell nodded. 'Without her I would not have found my way to my father's lands so easily.'

'Ah yes,' Tadoc sighed a deep sigh. 'Your father, your father... a great man. You will try for your birthright against Dubhain?'

'That is why I have returned,' Huell said solemnly, as Liath joined them again.

'Then in your father's memory I will give what help I can,' Tadoc said solemnly, as he leant over again and gripped Huell's shoulder. 'But first you must tell me all that has passed since you were taken off.'

Huell told his tale as briefly as he could, while Tadoc and his close kin listened on intently.

'So,' said Tadoc when the tale was done. 'As Liath told you, it seems it was your own brother Cadno who plotted with Dubhain to be rid of you, though it did him no good in the end. Where the little wretch's bones lie I do not know, but I think you will agree he got the fate he deserved.'

'Aye,' Huell answered, his voice cold with bitterness. 'And Dubhain? How many men can that treacherous dog count on?'

'Perhaps only a dozen, though he would think he has more. He is the chieftain, for none are strong enough to challenge him. Ah, but he is not trusted by our people.'

'What are his weaknesses?' Huell asked, his cold blue eyes glinting in the firelight.

'They are much the same as his strengths. By this I mean that while he is ruthless and feared, all the same he is also hated. As you know, the betrayer Dubhain came to your father as an outcast from his own people, so blood does not bind us to him. Whilst he has men to call on, they have no love for him and none of them would give up their lives for Dubhain's sake, of that you can be sure. Of course though, they might still fight for their pride all the same. They are his oath men after all.'

Talakhonsu had listened to all of this as best as he could, but now he felt it was time that he should speak.

'I will say my words,' he said haltingly.

'Aye stranger,' Tadoc nodded. 'Speak your mind.'

'Then I say the fight with Dubhain's men will be bloody, whether they love him or not,' Talakh said in the Greek tongue.

'He says we should not fight!' Huell seethed as he translated the words for Tadoc. 'Why should we not fight?' he turned back to Talakh angrily.

'I mean only that we should fight him in our way, not his.'

'How so?' Tadoc frowned.

'As the hunter hunts, so we must be patient and wait for our moment.'

'Hmm,' Tadoc rubbed his chin, thinking on Talakh's words after Huell had repeated them. 'But how would you do this? Dubhain does not venture far from his warriors.'

'Then we must bide our time,' Huell said quietly, the simple wisdom in Talakhonsu's words for once quelling his rashness. 'Will you give us shelter until then Tadoc?'

'Aye, I will lad. My hearth is your hearth until it is done, and the gods grant that it be done soon. Until then, you can trust that no one here will betray you.'

'I thank you for that, loyal friend of my father,' Huell bowed his head.

'Aye well,' Tadoc said with a thin smile that stretched the skin taught over his bony cheeks. 'We will set things right, if they can be set right. I owe your father that Huell. Now come, let us drink against our pledges. There is mead enough left from last night!'

The mead of Tadoc's hut was good and strong, and it warmed Talakhonsu's heart as much as did the kind words of their host. At last he knew that come what may, the fate of Huell could take him no further than this place and these people. So, in spite of the danger they all now faced, Talakh sat and stared into the cheerful flames of the fire with a strange contentment as Huell and Tadoc talked on.

Chapter 10

The Reckoning

After all of the hardships he had known on the long journey north, the hut of Tadoc was a cheerful place for Talakhonsu. The hearth was warm to sleep by and the company of others cheered him, though Huell was as prickly as ever. The time when Talakh had thought the red man a friend seemed long, long ago. Still, as the shortening days began to slip by and winter approached with no news of Dubhain, Talakh too began to feel his own mood darken.

By day the two men did what they could to occupy their minds by clearing trees away from the forest edge to add to Tadoc's lands little by little, so as to repay their host as best as they could for his hospitality. When their axe arms tired, they tilled Tadoc's fields too, ready for the crops of the year yet to come.

For Talakh, at least there was bright Liath to lift his spirits with her talk as the days grew still darker and the cold of winter set in. Of an evening, she invited him into her small hut to sit with her, so that she could hear more of his strange tales of far off lands. And though Talakh's words were halting, little by little he learned her tongue well enough. Of course he was often stuck, but somehow they always seemed to make each other understand.

Talakh saw too the ways of the wise woman and her craft. Liath's hut was full of a great many things, far beyond what one person might usually have about them. Small bundles of dried herbs were tucked amongst the eaves, whilst around the low walls sat pots of all shapes and sizes, each one carefully sealed with a lid of hide or beeswax.

'That one is honey,' she explained, making the sound of a bee to help him understand. 'That one also, but a different kind.

287

As is that one, which is a darker honey still. Over there, the big jar is sap, gathered from the birch tree. It helps to make the sick strong again when the winter chills come.'

Many other things she explained, but how she remembered all of the charms and potions, Talakh could not guess.

Somehow Liath seemed to understand and remember everything that Talakh told her of his own life too. The memories were often old wounds to him, though still there were others enough that brought him happiness, so that both tears and laughter came to him in the telling. There were tears in Liath's eyes too when he spoke of the deaths of Korkamani and Leontios, so that Talakhonsu saw she had come to care for him a great deal. It was not long before she took to embracing him and gently kissing his cheek when he returned to Tadoc's hut each night.

Yet for Huell, Liath had little time. He was always restless and tense as he waited, thirsting for vengeance. The days passed slowly for the red man with no sign or word of Dubhain, and so no possibility of catching his enemy off guard. For Talakh too, the waiting for the fight to come grew unbearable, though he at least had the company of Liath to take his mind from this.

One chill evening Talakh went to the edge of the woods beyond the settlement gates to be alone there, so that he might put aside his worries for a moment and remember his distant god, Amun of the winds. When the fight with Dubhain and his men came, he knew he would surely need the god's help. Talakh had been standing with his palms facing upwards, his eyes closed to the blood red sun as it sank quickly below the hills, when the voice of Liath came from behind him.

'What do you do Talakh?'

'I make an offering to my god,' he answered awkwardly, turning to see her pale face there, framed by her blonde plaits in the last of the evening light.

'I'm sorry. I did not mean to interrupt you.'

'No, no, I had said all that I needed.'

'You speak to your Amun?'

'I speak his name so that the great god knows I do not forget,' Talakh said quietly. 'My people believe he travels the earth on the winds, high up in the sky. But here, I am so far from my own lands...'

'You are strong in your belief in the god,' she smiled, as she came to stand beside him. 'He will hear your words Talakhonsu, I am sure of it.'

'Perhaps.'

The two of them stood for a while in silence and watched the last of the sun as it slipped away behind the hills.

'The sky is beautiful tonight, is it not?' Liath smiled up at him. 'The colour of the black bird's egg.'

'Aye, it is,' Talakh smiled back. 'If only the sun lingered longer though...'

'We all wish for that,' Liath sighed. 'But it is still a month until the midwinter, so the days will grow shorter yet before they ever lengthen again.'

'In my land the power of the sun god is always strong. The days are never short, nor cold.'

'You long to return there.'

'Yes...' Talakh frowned. 'And yet I have travelled so far... it may be that my feet will always wander now.'

Liath put her hand on his shoulder. 'Sometimes it is best not to think too much on these things Talakh. Let them be what they will be. Everything will become clear to you when the time is right.'

'Aye, you are right Liath,' Talakh smiled wryly as he put his hand on hers. 'Always you are right, wise one.'

The following day, Talakh and Huell took themselves off again to enlarge a clearing that Tadoc wanted to join to his own wheat fields. They took their weapons with them too, for they were ever watchful for Dubhain and his men. Soon the woods rang out with the mournful echo of axe on wood as they felled the smaller trees and cleared the scrub. It was hard work, even for two men used to straining at the oar, so the words between them were few as they toiled in the drab winter woods. Yet despite their labours, when they did rest it was not for long. The leaden sky above the leafless trees was dark with the threat of rain, so both men worked on, stopping only for their bread and cheese until the light began to fade from the day.

'I will never raise an axe to another tree when I have my father's hall back,' Huell said wearily, resting on his axe shaft.

'Aye,' Talakh agreed, standing himself up straight to stretch his arms to the sky. 'While Tadoc puts a roof over my head and shares his bread, I will gladly do what I can for him and his kin. But when you are done with Dubhain, then I will hand back his axe and be on my way. That is, if I still live.'

'Be on your way?' Huell glowered as he swung his axe round in a wide arc to stretch his stiff shoulders. 'What do you mean by that?'

'If I live to see Dubhain dead, my oath to you will be released. Then I will return to Kemet,' Talakh said bluntly.

'Return? I thought perhaps that you and Liath...'

'I do not belong here in your northern lands Huell, where the sun never shines and the damp is always at your bones. Besides another girl waits for me and she also has my oath.'

'A girl?' Huell smiled thinly. 'Ah yes, the one you told me of. But what is one girl to a man like you, after all you have seen and done?'

'I gave her my word, and her father too. That I would come back for her. That she would be my wife.'

'And yet now without Leontios to prosper under, you have little enough to offer them,' Huell said coldly. 'Stay here. Take Liath instead.'

'Liath is a fine girl,' Talakh said, taking his axe to the trunk of a tree he had half-felled, to vent his growing anger. 'But still my mind is made up. I have some silver coin left and I know the sea,' he grunted as he swung the axe again. 'I know the ways of trade and I will do well enough with Ketet and her father, so do not trouble yourself for me.'

'When I am chieftain you will be my trusted man, Talakh, think of that!' Huell said, his own anger rising. 'You will stand on my right side. Be my counsel in all things. Surely what I offer is better than risking your life on such a journey again?'

Talakhonsu rested on his axe and turned to look the red man in his cold blue eyes. 'We have fought side by side and endured much together, but I can never be what you ask Huell,' he shook his head. 'Tadoc is shrewd and trustworthy. He will be a better man than I to have at your side.'

'Tadoc?' Huell waved his hand dismissively. 'He is an old man.'

'He is a wise man too and a loyal one, don't forget that. If he backs you, then so will others.'

'But are we not friends, Napatan?'

'It is true that fate brought our paths together, but I can't be the friend you seek now.'

'No? What do you mean by that?' Huell said, his face reddening.

'You are always quick to anger when others oppose you, Huell,' Talakh said as calmly as he could. 'I have seen a side of you I don't much like at times, a bitter side, though the gods know you have cause enough for that.

'It comes down to this: you have your way while I have another. If I stayed here, when all your enemies are dead it would be me you would quarrel with. No, when Dubhain is gone I will leave you in peace to rule your father's lands as you see fit.'

Before the two men could argue further, a deep barking suddenly rent the silent woods.

'Arthfael,' Talakh said under his breath, turning his ear to listen.

'Dogs bark, what of it?' Huell said sullenly.

'There is something wrong, I feel it in my guts. We should go back.'

'He is just off chasing something,' Huell spat again, but Arthfael barked on.

'Stay here if you want, I will go on my own,' Talakh said, quickly strapping the sword of Leontios to his belt and taking up his spear. He took the axe in his left hand too and bearing these weapons the tall Napatan looked a fearsome sight as his long legs carried him at a run back towards the settlement of Tadoc. Behind him Huell cursed loudly, but whether the red man followed or not, Talakh could not tell, for all that he could hear was the sound of his heart pounding and the rustle of the leaves under his feet.

When he came to the edge of the woods he instinctively dropped low and crept forward until he had a clear view of the farmstead of Tadoc. A band of strangers bearing spears stood by the gateway of the enclosure, one of them poking his spear through the eye socket of one of the pair of great ox skulls that were hung on the posts there. Spears had come to Tadoc's land and it was clear that they meant ill.

Talakh crept up as silently as he could and hid himself behind the massive trunk of an old oak that had been too big to be felled. When he peered around the tree, he could hear one of the men talking to Tadoc, whilst Tadoc's younger son looked on nervously, a worried look on his face. Seven of them Talakh counted, all big men, all with the hair plaits and long moustaches that were the mark of the warriors of the north. All that is except one.

'Dubhain,' Talakh hissed under his breath, for the chieftain matched well Tadoc's description of him. Dubhain, the dark-haired one, so his name meant, though now he was bald and kept his head shaved bare. All the same, his face was dark as a storm, his eyes black as forest pools. He was a big man, a heavy man, but he carried his bulk well. A man who would be hard to beat in a fight, that much was plain to Talakh. Yet his thoughts were not on these things alone, for once again he heard the deep bark of Arthfael and he knew that Liath must be somewhere there in the enclosure with the other women.

'Don't try to deceive me, you know why I come here,' Dubhain said, a slyness in his voice as he talked down to Tadoc, poking his finger at the smaller man.

Tadoc said something then that Talakh did not catch, and Dubhain struck him hard across the face with the back of his hand, but still Tadoc did not flinch and he looked back at Dubhain with iron in his eyes.

'Strike me again and you will not see tomorrow,' Tadoc said through gritted teeth as his son started to sob.

'Shut up boy!' he shouted at his son, but as he did so Dubhain hit him hard in the temple and Tadoc fell to the ground, dazed.

'You threaten me, you worm?' Dubhain cursed him as he kicked Tadoc in the side. 'Now where is he? Where is that whelp Huell?'

'How should I know that?' Tadoc said hoarsely, his breath short. 'The son of the chieftain is long dead.'

'I thought so too,' Dubhain laughed harshly. 'And yet now I hear tell of a red haired one and his black skinned friend, come from afar to your hall. You are a lying turd, Tadoc. You shelter these men, I know it. Now where are they? Answer me!'

'You are wrong,' Tadoc rasped as he got to his feet. 'Now leave my land, you are not welcome here.'

'Your land?' Dubhain mocked. 'Only yours with my good will Tadoc. I see that you have cleared more of the forest for your sons to farm? Well unless you give up Huell to me they will have no father and the land will come to me and those that I favour.'

At that Dubhain drew his sword and pressed its point against Tadoc's chest, but though he winced as the iron pinched his skin against his breastbone, still Tadoc did not move. His wife Seadna, a blunt faced, sturdy woman, drew her weeping son close to her, muttering curses under her breath whilst the men of Dubhain shuffled their feet.

'You are brave with these men around you and a sword at my chest, Dubhain,' Tadoc growled. 'Are you brave enough then to fight me on your own, man to man? Let all here see the man that you are!'

'Hah!' Dubhain gloated. 'You think yourself still a warrior? Your best days are long done, old man, but still I will grant your wish. After I have wrung the name of Huell from your scrawny neck, then will I crush the life out of you with my bare hands. When the last of your breath leaves your body Tadoc, you will welcome death!'

'Your talk bores me,' Tadoc said grimly, spitting on the ground at Dubhain's feet. 'Now will you let the wind blow your tongue around in your head all day, or will you fight?'

The colour rose in Dubhain's face at that insult and for a moment Talakh thought he would run Tadoc through with his sword there and then, but one of his own men stayed his hand.

'It would be too quick for him, Dubhain chieftain,' the warrior said quietly.

As Talakhonsu looked on, knowing he must either act or watch the slaughter of Tadoc, Dubhain laughed again and stuck his sword in the ground.

'Now, throw down your knife, Tadoc,' Dubhain gestured slyly.

'Whilst you still have yours? I think not. If you want my knife, you take it from me. I will put it in your eye, you treacherous dog!'

Dubhain roared at this insult, his temper snapped like a twig as he rushed at Tadoc with his own knife drawn. For a big man he moved quickly, but Tadoc still had the wits of a warrior and he was quick too. Feinting as if he would go one way, he stepped aside so that Dubhain's long blade glanced from his own in a flash of sparks. As Dubhain sprawled past him off balance, Tadoc's knife flashed again but did no more than scratch the back of the false chieftain's neck.

Dubhain quickly turned to face his opponent, but now that he had a fight on his hands, he edged round back toward his own men.

'My sword!' he bellowed, his eyes searching the ground for his blade.

Dubhain could not see it, but Talakh knew where it was. The man who had advised him to give it up now held the sword unseen behind his back. For a moment Dubhain hesitated before wrenching a spear from the grasp of another of his men. As he advanced on Tadoc again, Talakhonsu knew that the older man's pride and the fate of his family would not let him run. He was as good as dead now against a man with a spear.

'Yah!' Dubhain cried, a twisted grin on his evil face as he

thrust the spear at Tadoc's side. The older man dodged the blow, but Dubhain was now just using him for sport. He feinted, then jabbed again and this time the bright iron spear tip tore a hole in the sleeve of Tadoc's jerkin as he sought to evade it. With Tadoc off balance, Dubhain leapt forward and brought the heavy shaft of the spear down squarely on his head with a crack so that he fell to the ground on his knees.

'Now worm,' Dubhain gloated, his tongue fat in his throat as he pressed the spear point against Tadoc's shoulder. 'Tell me where Huell is and perhaps I will give you a quick death. Where is he?'

Talakhonsu's heart pounded in his chest as he looked on. For him to act would mean certain death and yet he could not look on and do nothing while Tadoc met the same fate as Korkamani all those years past.

Arthfael barked again then and the great hound came bounding forward at Dubhain just as Talakh broke cover from the tree, his heavy throwing stick drawn back above his head ready to throw. Shouts went up from Dubhain's men as they turned their spears on Arthfael, but they did not see the dark warrior's throw.

Sure the stick flew, silently scything the damp winter air for a moment, before it took one of the men full in the back with a heavy thud. The warrior gasped in pain and his knees gave way, yet still unnoticed Talakhonsu picked up his spear and axe from the ground and came on at a run behind them all. As his long legs covered the last of the ground, Talakhonsu kept a grim silence and only when he was almost upon them did he roar Amun's name to invoke the great god's protection.

Before they could turn to face him, Talakhonsu swung the heavy axe at the tallest of them and though in his haste he struck the man on the head with the flat of the blade, still it felled him like a tree all the same. Even as this one dropped to his knees, Talakhonsu dropped the unwieldy axe and bored his spear point forward, straight at the false chieftain's belly as the broad man turned to face him. With a lunge that belied his brawn, Dubhain somehow saved himself, but his balance lost,

Tadoc desperately grappled him to the ground with all the strength that he had left.

Talakhonsu felt the danger behind him then and instead of trying to finish Dubhain, he ran on a few steps, then turned quickly to face the warriors again. There was no time for him to think, no time for him to fear, for his death was on their lips and they would have killed him easily if he had hesitated. He did the only thing he could do and ran at the four warriors who stood before him, the hound Arthfael snarling alongside him, fangs bared and sharp.

Now it was one spear against four and yet Talakhonsu saw fear in the faces of these men to match his own. He was the shadow-man to them, a dark spirit of the night come for their lives and they were afraid. Talakh roared Amun's name again as he rammed the spear into the shoulder of one of the warriors, leaning forward with all his strength as the iron tip cleaved through muscle and scrapped over bone. In the blink of an eye, a bright spear point was coming straight at his face and he leapt back, pushing himself off of his own spear shaft to escape the blow.

The great god saved him then, he later thought, for though he slipped in the mud, it was as though an invisible hand steadied him so that he recovered his balance. A strange calm came over Talakh as he drew his sword, the sword of Leontios, and came forward again.

'What are you waiting for?' Kill him!' Dubhain spluttered, though he had problems of his own for the arm of Tadoc was now wrapped around his throat as the two men grappled on their backs in the mud.

One of Dubhain's men had been singled out by fearless Arthfael, who kept him at bay, but the other two stood their ground, their spears jabbing forward. Talakhonsu blocked a spear thrust with his sword and then swept the blade again to block another, but he knew he was fighting for his life now against their longer reach. A searing pain raked across his thigh as a sharp edge found its mark and he knew then that the next spear thrust or the one after that would end him. Yet just as he began to falter under the ceaseless attack, he saw from the corner of his eye a figure run from the trees, the spear in his hand poised above his shoulder. It was Huell and never had Talakhonsu been more glad to see him.

The red man ran swiftly in a curve, so that he came up behind the warriors and then threw his spear from close range, taking one of them in the back as a hunter might take down a boar. The blow threw the warrior onto his knees, a look of both sadness and surprise on his face as blood ran from his choking mouth.

Now the two remaining men of Dubhain saw the odds were turned against them and they backed away, dread in their faces, before running as fast as their legs could carry them while Arthfael snapped at their heels.

'That's it, run you cowards!' Huell shouted out after them as Arthfael chased them off into the trees. 'When I have killed Dubhain I will come for you and run you down like the rats that you are.'

Somehow Tadoc had found the strength to keep his choke hold on Dubhain, but with his men all either fled, wounded, or dead, the fight now went out of the big man completely.

'What will we do with these others?' Talakh asked as he held his sword point at Dubhain's throat.

'Kill them of course,' Huell said harshly. 'Kill them all. They deserve no better.'

'You know them?'

'I remember them, despite the years that have passed,' Huell said bitterly. 'The one I killed there, he is Imar. That one with your spear in his shoulder is Hywel. Age can't hide these other two from me either, I know them. All of them my own people. All betrayers of my father's trust. All oath breakers!'

With that he kicked Dubhain hard in the face, breaking the big man's nose.

'No...' groaned the speared man Hywel through gritted teeth. 'I was always loyal to your father... I had no part in any of it.'

'Yet you came looking for me all the same,' Huell said over

his shoulder, aiming another kick at Dubhain that knocked his senses from him, even as Tadoc still held him fast. 'You would have killed me if you'd had the chance, Hywel. Don't deny it.'

'We all swore an oath to Dubhain, even Tadoc there,' the man Hywel grimaced as he held the spear that was stuck fast in his shoulder. 'I had no choice but to follow him, or it would not have gone well for me or my kin... Dubhain would have thought nothing of murdering us all in our sleep.'

Huell turned on Hywel then and put his foot on the man's wounded shoulder so that he howled with pain.

'Never mind Tadoc. You squeal like a pig,' the red man sneered, gripping the spear shaft while Hywel clung onto it weakly with his good hand, vainly trying to halt the pain. 'You want me to draw the spear? I will draw it alright you dog, and then I will...'

'It is not his fault Huell,' Tadoc interrupted him as he released his hold on Dubhain and wearily got to his feet. 'This is all Dubhain's doing, isn't it you shit-sack?' he roared, aiming a kick of his own at the false chieftain's ribs.

'Yet these men stood by him and so I am due my revenge on them. Do you hear me?' he bellowed at Hywel. 'You will all pay! You will all suffer as I have suffered.'

The man whom Talakh had felled with his throwing stick moaned in pain, but the other one he had brained with the side of the axe head was still out cold, perhaps even dead. Even though these men would have killed him given the chance, still Talakh felt uneasy at the blood he had spilt and the bones he had cracked. Yet Huell was still in a blood rage, his face as red as his hair now, his eyes bulging as if they might fly from his head. He went around all of the fallen men of Dubhain, kicking their ribs in turn as he snarled like an animal. Even the hound Arthfael, who had now returned from his chase, could only look on meekly, his brow furrowed and his tail between his legs.

'Huell,' Tadoc started to say, but the red man was deaf to his words as he kicked and spat at the fallen men.

'Huell, enough!' Talakhonsu grabbed his arm.

The red man turned and glared at him, his blue eyes stormy as the sea against his ruddy face. 'This is no business of yours,' he hissed, wrenching his arm free. 'I am chieftain here, not Dubhain and not you.'

'You will make yourself chieftain only of dead men then, if you kill all who followed Dubhain.'

'What would you have me do then Napatan? Thank them for coming here to kill me? Let them keep their spears and their land?'

'If you make enemies of their kin, then you will not live long before you find a knife in your back. Think Huell! Don't let vengeance rule your head.'

Tadoc did not know the Greek words of Talakhonsu, but he guessed their meaning all the same.

'Talakh is right,' he grunted as he bound the still groaning Dubhain's hands behind his back with a tether his wife had brought him. 'If you kill these men, then the killing will never stop and our people will be divided and weak. Others will come then to challenge our right to the land. That is why we must mend the wounds we have, not open up new ones,' he said wearily as he got to his feet and placed a gentle hand on Huell's shoulder. 'Ask yourself what your father would have done in your place.'

Huell's cold, unblinking eyes stared hard at Tadoc for a moment as if he might strike his father's old friend, but then at last the fire of his temper finally burnt itself out and he breathed a deep sigh.

'You are both right,' he said at last, rubbing his eyes as if he had just woken from a dream. 'I will go to my father's hall and claim my right there among my people.'

'The two that ran off could come back here with others,' Tadoc said grimly, rubbing flakes of dried blood from his face. 'Yet if I know them, they will stay by their wives. They will not fight on for Dubhain's sake.'

'You will come with me then?'

'Yes, I will willingly come with you to assert your right. Now, what would you do with these ones?'

'They will stay here with Talakhonsu, as hostages.' Huell answered.

'Aye, that is as well. Liath will look after their wounds, but we will bind them all just in case.

'And Dubhain?' Talakhonsu said as the defeated chieftain came too with a deep groan.

'He will come with us so that all can see him defeated at my hands,' Huell gloated, kicking Dubhain again in the ribs.

'Whatever you do, you should not let him live,' Tadoc said gravely. 'He will always be a bane to you if you do.'

'Do not worry on that, he will die soon enough, but he will not die well. No, he will suffer and suffer again, you can be sure of that!'

Talakhonsu looked into Huell's eyes for a sign of the man he had first met what seemed so long ago now, but that man was no longer there. Huell's fate had been cruel to be sure and he deserved his vengeance. But now he was a bitter man with a quick temper, untrusting of those around him. As Talakh clutched his leg to staunch the flow of blood that oozed from the angry cut on his thigh, he saw more clearly than ever that he must leave this place behind and return to the world he had known before the wreck of the Kallisto.

Now that the danger to the children was over, Liath and the other women came to help then, their hearts full of joy that they were all safe again.

'You are hurt,' Liath said, her smile turning to a worried frown as she saw the bloody wound on Talakh's thigh.

'It is nothing,' he lied, holding his hand over it. 'We must see to this man Hywel first.'

So, after they had bound the arms of Dubhain's men behind their backs and hobbled their legs with tethers so that they could not run, Tadoc took a heated knife to cut the spear point from the shoulder of Hywel, whilst Huell and Talakh held him down. The man's screams were a terrible thing, but it was done soon enough at Tadoc's skilled hand and then Liath tended to him. Talakhonsu watched as Liath first washed the gore and splinters of bone from the deep wound with water that one of the boys brought from a spring. Next she dribbled honey from a jar into it, to soothe the flesh that was burnt from the knife, she said. The blood still oozed, but then Liath gathered a clump of old spider webs from the smoky roof of her hut and laid these on Hywel's wound. The magic worked well and though the blood showed through the webs, it was soon staunched as a dark clot formed.

They dragged the other men to Tadoc's hut and sat them near the fire, though they would say nothing in their shame. There was Hywel, his teeth gritted against the pain and Ruadhan whose ribs Talakh's throwing stick had cracked it seemed, for every breath was an agony to him. Then there was tall Mongan whom Talakh had knocked out with the flat of his axe. Far from being dead as Talakh had thought, his senses were slowly returning to him, though he was still dazed and dark blood caked his matted brown hair.

'Here, chew on this bitter bark,' Liath said, giving a piece to each of the three men. 'The magic of a strong willow tree is in it. It will help ease your pain.'

'They will live?' Talakhonsu whispered in her ear, whilst she tended his own wound.

'I cannot say,' Liath said quietly, avoiding his eyes. I have seen men with worse wounds get better, while others die from nothing more than a scratch. They are not evil men so I will do my best for them, but their fates are in the hands of the gods.'

Talakh winced as she used a slender wand of stripped hazel to work some dark honey deep into the wound on his thigh. The spear had sliced over an old scar he had received when fighting Meketra's men alongside his old captain, and this brought memories once again of Leontios and his old friends. Many were dead now and those others that remained were scattered to the four winds amongst their homes in the thousand isles of the Greeks. Perhaps one day he might again see Hippolytos and Pamphilos. That was as much as he might hope for.

'Here,' Liath offered him a bowl. 'Drink this. Then you must sleep. You have lost a lot of blood.'

As he sipped the steaming broth, Talakh could hear the voice of Huell outside, gloating over Dubhain in his victory, while the others who were now their captives groaned in their pain, spears held over them by the women and their boys. A great weariness came over him then, despite the sharp sting from his wound and he slipped into a deep sleep while Liath sang softly to herself, her voice like a cool breeze to his brow as the evening gathered in.

-ϕ-

Pelia paused in her story awhile and poured a cup of water for herself. She looked suddenly sad in spite of the lovely summer evening, as if tears might easily come to her eyes.

'Are you alright?' Cerian asked her.

'It is nothing,' Pelia forced a smile. 'My story draws to a close, that is all and there is no happy ending to it when all is said and all is done.'

'And yet once again your father survived the battle to live another day, and all these years later here you are because of him,' Cerian said, trying to cheer her friend. 'He was a brave man and a wise one too. But Liath, your mother... did she save Dubhain's men?'

'I will tell you all of that next. But first, Talakhonsu. My father had lost more blood in the fight than even Liath had realised and this weakened him greatly, though neither he nor my mother could know it then. Whilst he slept a terrible fever overtook him that could not be shaken. He came through the dangers of battle, but death was soon close at his shoulder again.

'But still,' Pelia continued, 'as you say, I am here so it is plain to you that he survived his illness. He was young and he was strong and this alone kept death from him as the days passed.

'When at last my mother's healing ways helped bring him

back from the spirit world where his sleeping self had once again strayed, almost a week had passed. He awoke to find himself not in the hut of Tadoc, but in Liath's.'

'So at last then your mother and he were together alone,' Cerian said with a knowing smile.

'You mean they become lovers? No, not then, nor soon after,' Pelia tutted. 'He was sick almost to the point of death itself, he had no strength for love then.'

Cerian grew silent for a while before she spoke again, a frown furrowing her brow. 'But you know that the elders tell a different story to this when they talk of Huell? They say...'

'Yes I know what they say,' Pelia interrupted her. 'They say that the evil Dubhain led an army of foreigners to take over our lands, and that Huell returned to rout them all, with the help only of loyal Tadoc and the dark skinned outlander. They say that Huell killed ten men on one hand and ten men on the other before the rest of them fled, but it is all lies.

'Huell was selfish and bitter too in those days and his truth was the kind a man remembers best when he is drunk,' Pelia sighed with a shake of her head. 'Men like him think of things as they wish they had been, not the way they actually were.'

'Not all men are like that though,' Cerian said gently. 'Not my Tyrnon. Not your Aneurin.'

'No, you are right, not all men. Only those with something to prove. Men with an axe to grind, like Huell.'

'And what of Dubhain then?' Cerian asked. 'Did he die as they say he did?'

'Oh yes,' Pelia answered grimly, 'that much is the truth, I have no doubt of it. Huell did as Tadoc had advised him and they came the next day to this place that we now call Llan Huell. They beat Dubhain before them as they went, goading him at the end of their spears and when Huell claimed his birthright, none opposed him.

'They made Dubhain's woman disown him to his face and then Huell made all of the men break their oaths to him and spit in his face. This they could do without losing face, as he had no right to be chieftain in the first place. All of the men swore a new oath to Huell then, while he ground Dubhain's nose into the dirt with his foot. Each one of them Huell looked in the eye, they say, and then to prove their oath he ordered the foremost men amongst them to each cut off one of Dubhain's fingers. Terrible they say were, Dubhain's screams, and worse they were still when Huell turned him over on his back and cut off his bloody nose. Dark hearted these things were that Huell did to Dubhain, even though he deserved his fate to be sure.'

'I heard that they drowned him in a mere,' Cerian shuddered again.

'And so they did. Huell said that it was to be done this way as an offering to the gods, but Tadoc saw through that. In truth Huell had so much hate in him that he wanted Dubhain's death to be as slow as possible. Later he gloated to my father that they tied Dubhain's legs, but not his hands. They threw him into the mere then, but when he somehow struggled to the surface they cast a cord out to him. Of course with his fingers gone, he could not pull himself free and so the cord slipped from him and he drowned, gasping for breath in the dark waters.'

'A horrible death,' Cerian shuddered. 'Even for what Dubhain did.'

'Aye, Dubhain was an evil man full of spite and violence, but was Huell any better in the end? Vengeance is a bitter thing,' Pelia sighed again and was alone in her thoughts for a moment.

'So Huell was made evil by his hate for Dubhain? But he became a great chief all the same though, didn't he?'

'He grew to be a feared chief that is true. Yes, he was powerful and he protected our people well, so we remember him well, especially compared to the rule of Heilyn, his son. Ah, but still Huell's rages were the downfall of him in the end. That is why his heart gave way, so my mother thought.'

'Was it because of Huell that your father went away from here back to his own lands?'

'That is not the whole reason, but yes it is at least a part of it,' Pelia nodded.

Cerian took up her friend's hand and squeezed it gently.

'More than ever I wish you could see your father,' she said.

Pelia closed her eyes then as she looked into her mind.

'He is here with me always, wherever I go,' she said. 'Somehow although I never saw him still I seem to know his face.

'Now,' she said, her mood brightening a little. 'Tomorrow, you will take Tyrnon for your husband and just in time the story of Talakhonsu comes almost to its end. Listen one last time and I will tell you all that is left to tell.'

-ϕ-

Talakhonsu saw many strange things as his mind wandered the dream lands for what seemed a lifetime, while the fever racked his body just as it had many years before in his boyhood. Much he forgot but always his fevered dreams found him amongst the desert sands with a chill wind on his skin. Sometimes distant words came to him, calling his name in a strange tongue he did not know, but he could not tell from where the voices came and so he wandered on.

He was lost. Lost under a sun that was always on the horizon but neither set, nor rose. Slowly, ever slowly, the roaring of the wind eased and then at last he heard another voice, one that he thought he knew, though still it was very faint. Talakhonsu turned to listen, and knew at last the voice of Liath, calling to him from across the barren sands.

'Talakh,' Liath's voice came to him again, and he felt a cool hand on his forehead. At last the dream world faded away and he opened his eyes on the land of the living once again.

'You are safe,' Liath said softly as her pale face came slowly into focus. It was dark, but still in the gloom he could make out her golden hair.

'Liath... it is you,' he said, though the words were like sand in his dry throat.

'It is,' she said, stroking his cheek tenderly. 'You cried out, but don't worry, you are safe here in my hut.'

'Your hut? But I should not be here. Not like this...' he started to say.

'Hush now. You have been very sick with a sweating fever, so that is why you are here. Now, try to drink a little water and then you must rest.'

'My body aches,' Talakhonsu groaned. 'I should get up Liath, I've lain here too long already.'

'Aye, you have,' Liath smiled. 'Almost a week. But you must rest a while yet until your strength returns.'

'Huell will need me,' Talakh said as he tried to raise himself up on his elbows.

'Not any more. Now rest yourself knowing that Dubhain is dead and Huell is rightful chieftain. All is well,' Liath said as she dipped a piece of moss into some water and squeezed it gently so that the water dripped into his mouth. 'That's it drink down what you can.'

The water was the sweetest that Talakh had ever tasted and it soothed his parched throat.

'The fighting is done?' he asked.

Liath gave a wry smile. 'Is the fighting ever done? But no, it is for now at least. All that there is for you to do is to rest and get better. Now close your eyes and I will sing you to your dreams.'

'Dreams? I have had my fill of them.'

'Then I will sing you only to your sleep,' Liath smiled.

So things passed for the next few days with Talakhonsu. He would wake when he was thirsty and Liath would give him water from a healing spring of magic deep in the forest, which she sweetened with honey. Then he would sink wearily to sleep again.

Slowly his hunger returned as his wound healed, so that he could eat a little bread and some barley broth made with meat bones, but still he was too weak to do much more than venture outside to visit the midden. When he did this last thing, it seemed colder than ever to him in those northern lands and he was always glad to regain the smoky warmth of the hearth.

But still, all was quiet at Tadoc's farmstead. The dead and wounded of the battle had been taken back to their own kin, while Tadoc was still away at Huell's right hand in case of any further trouble. But though Huell had heard of Talakhonsu's grave illness, he was too busy asserting his place as chieftain to return to see him.

The days passed and Talakhonsu's strength returned little by little, until he could walk a while with Liath. He played with the young children of the settlement too, though he was still easily tired and felt the cold, even wrapped in Liath's furs. His hair had grown wild and bushy, but Liath cut it for him and shaved his beard with a sharp blade too. He felt better for that at least.

'It is time I should go back to Tadoc's hut, now I am getting better,' he said one evening as he washed out Liath's cooking pot after they had eaten.

'There is no need,' she looked up at him.

'The others will talk, if they don't already.'

'Let them talk if they want,' Liath said. 'Whatever comes between us would be no shame to me.'

'Liath,' he started to say, but she put her finger to his lips.

'Hush,' she said. 'Talakh, I know you will leave here soon and I know you will not come back, but before that happens let us have one night together.'

'Liath,' he said again, but this time she kissed him on the lips and he felt himself stirring despite his better thoughts that this would be wrong. In his still young life, he had never known a woman and he felt clumsy, unsure of himself as he touched her cheek with his fingers.

'Share my bed,' she said gently, her soft lips lingering on his. 'Share it until the time comes when you must leave.'

So that night their lovemaking started and Talakhonsu truly felt then that he had became a man. The next night too, their sweating bodies locked together and so it continued between them as the grip of winter over the land grew stronger still. After each short day, they would spend the long evenings lying together on Liath's furs, holding each other while they talked of the things that were the same and the things that were different between their two worlds.

All the while Talakh received no word from Huell, but at last on the midwinter's eve the red man summoned him to a feast the next day at the place of his people, which was now called Llan Huell after himself.

The next morning, as was the custom amongst the northern peoples, Talakh first went with Liath and Tadoc's kin to celebrate the midwinter sunrise. On the summit of a hill, a few low stones of the ancestors were cast in a rough circle near a mound, and from this place of old magic they watched for a first glimpse of the returning sun god, though the dawn was stubbornly grey and overcast. Despite their singing and chants the sun remained hidden, but still all were in good spirits. From this day on all knew that though the coldest days of the winter were yet to come, and though snow might soon cover the land, still the days would grow longer all the same.

Liath and Talakh walked back to Tadoc's farmstead then and warmed some broth over a low fire, to drive the chill from their bones.

'I should not leave you here alone,' Talakh said as he sipped from the steaming broth. Still, he knew well enough that if he didn't go this would be taken as a slight by Huell. Liath knew it too.

'Don't worry about me,' she said, 'I don't need a man to protect me when I have Arthfael on the one hand and Seadna at the other.'

'She is a fierce one right enough,' Talakh smiled.

'All the more so with Tadoc still away. You must bring him back to her Talakh. Huell has had Tadoc at his side long enough.'

'I will do my best. Why not come with me Liath?'

'Like you, I have no great love for Huell,' Liath shook her head. 'Besides it will be no place for me, talking about battles and enemies and land. I will wait for you here.'

They kissed and held each other close for a long while and

though she at last pushed him away, still he looked into her eyes and held her close again.

'You should go, Huell will be waiting for you,' she said, pushing him away a last time. 'Now, be sure to keep to your own pace as you go, not the boy's. Remember you still don't have your full strength yet.'

'I have strength enough for you, Liath,' he smiled as he picked up his spear.

'Then save it for when you come back to me,' she returned his smile, her hair golden in the dull midwinter light as she led him outside.

Talakhonsu kissed her forehead a last time and then Liath watched as he strode away with one of Tadoc's sons to lead the way. His long limbs seemed to move slowly, she thought to herself, though they covered the ground just the same and he easily kept up as the young boy ran on ahead.

With a final wave, Talakhonsu disappeared from her sight amongst the trees of the forest. Liath could not know then that she would never see his face again.

-ϕ-

With her story at last told, Pelia sat still and silent, her hands folded in her lap.

'But what happened then?' Cerian said urgently. 'What became of him? Why did he not come back? Why did he go away when he loved Liath?'

'So many questions,' Pelia sighed. 'I wish I could answer them all for myself, but in the end all that we know for sure is what Tadoc told my mother. You see, two things came from the death of Dubhain. First there was the matter of a blood price.'

'A blood price? For Dubhain's head?'

'Yes. When his own people in the north heard of his death they took it as a murder. You see, even though he was outcast from them, he was bound and unarmed when his life was taken, and they were insulted by this. So they sent men to demand cattle in payment for their loss. They asked only for two calves, as they knew Dubhain had been in the wrong. This they asked so that their honour would be satisfied.

'Even so, Huell's temper was as quick to rise as ever and he refused these kin of Dubhain, slighting them still further with his angry words. My father could see what would come next and he said he would fight no more for Huell if a feud came.'

'So Talakhonsu went away so that he did not have to fight?'

'That is part of it, yes. But not because he was afraid. He just did not want any more blood on his hands because of Huell's pride. This was not his land and these were not his battles to fight.'

'I understand,' Cerian said sadly. 'You said there were two things that came from Dubhain's death.'

'Yes. The other was the matter of Dubhain's wife.'

'His wife?'

'Aye. The power of being chieftain had already gone to Huell's head and he declared that Talakhonsu should take her for his wife, to secure the loyalty of her children as they grew up. According to Tadoc they quarrelled on this so angrily that he thought they would come to blows. Then early one morning when everyone still slept, Talakhonsu left this place. No-one ever saw him again.'

'He did not return to Liath?'

'No,' Pelia said distantly. 'I think he could see that without land or cattle of his own, he would always depend in some way on the good favour of Huell. And what use would a landless man be to one such as my mother, who had no land of her own either?'

'But did he not love her? Would that not have been enough for them?'

'Perhaps it might if Huell had been prepared to leave my father in peace, but he would not. And so, Talakhonsu went away, not knowing that I already grew in my mother's womb.'

'It must have broken her heart,' said Cerian sadly. 'They were meant to be together and yet they were not.'

'She was strong in herself, my mother, so when she heard what had happened from Tadoc, she forgave Talakhonsu in the end and was at peace. Besides you see, very soon she had me to occupy all of her thoughts. But still she did not want me to forget Talakhonsu as he was my father and a great man. After all, he is the reason that my skin is dusky and my hair hangs in these ringlets.'

'And he would have been proud of you,' Cerian smiled, tears in her eyes. 'If he had known Liath bore you, then he would not have gone away, you know that. I wonder what became of him?'

'Something in my heart tells me he still lives, somewhere out in the vastness of the world,' Pelia nodded to herself. 'I will never see him with my own eyes, I know that, but still I hope that his god Amun would have guided him back across the seas to his past life. Perhaps he found his old friends and took up his love again with Isek's daughter Ketet. Perhaps they have children. I will never know, but I will tell his story again I think, to any who will listen. There is a wide world which lies far beyond our own, Cerian. Even in our strangest dreams we cannot imagine all that is to be found there.'

And yet that was not how it was to be. After the joining of Cerian to Tyrnon, Pelia grew lonely without her constant companion and she spent more time again with Aneurin, her old friend. Soon a different love blossomed between them at last and then came also the tying of hands between Pelia and Aneurin, the one to the other until death chose to part them.

On their first morning together as she lay in his darkened hut, the hound Sealgair woke Pelia, washing her face with his rough tongue.

'Sealgair!' she spluttered, shooing him away. 'Your breath is foul! Go to your bed.'

Aneurin lay next to her, deep in the dream world, not stirring at all. She gazed at his sleeping face, wondering where his spirit wandered and gently stroked his cheek, her fingers dark against his skin. Already the stubble of his beard grew back, although he had only shaved it clean with the edge of his small knife the day before. He looked so at peace as he lay there, his bare chest slowly rising and falling, and Pelia felt a deep love for him then. At last she had stepped from the long shadow of her father's memory and into a life that was truly her own.

Though she would remember the stories of Talakhonsu well in her heart, she resolved then that she would speak of them no more. When the last breath left her body and she passed on into the shadow world to join Liath, her mother, so the story would pass over with her. None then would know of the life of the Napatan. None save the gods who see and know all.

The gods do not forget.

Author's note on the Greco - Persian wars

'Beyond The Pyrene' concludes the chronicles of Talakhonsu begun in 'Beyond the Black Earth'. Following the return of the Persians to Kemet and the fall of the Kemet nobles, Talakhonsu, had escaped from a life of toil as a slave on the farm of Siamun the overseer and found a place on the ship of a Greek trading captain at a time when the ancient world found itself once again on the brink of war.

After the defeat of Darius the Great of Persia at the battle of Marathon, his son and heir Xerxes thirsted for revenge against the Athenians. In the momentous year 480 BC, aided by the ships of his Phoenician allies, he launched a massive invasion across the narrow reaches of the Hellespont, to march on Athens and end the opposition of the Greeks once and for all. Athens and her chief allies, the Spartans of Lacedaemon, looked for help to the powerful Greek colony of Syracusa on the distant western isle of Sikelia (Sicily), but Gelon the dictator of Syracusa had his own problems. Under Hamilcar, the Phoenicians of Carthage in North Africa invaded western Sikelia at just the same time as the Persian invasion of Greece (probably more by coincidence than by any formal military collusion with Xerxes).

Gelon and his allies quickly defeated Hamilcar in a series of battles, but the fate of the eastern Greeks hung in the balance through a series of battles on land and sea. First, the Persians defeated and killed the Spartan king Leonidas at the battle of the Thermopylae pass, before marching on Athens. The Athenians had already abandoned their city, which was put to the torch by Xerxes. At the same time, the Persians drove back the ships of the Greek allies at the battle of Artemesium, though they lost many of their own fleet to violent storms, both before and afterwards.

Soon the Persians had conquered most of eastern Greece, yet when they finally cornered the Greek fleet in the bay of Salamis a month later, the Greek allies led by the Athenians overcame the odds and defeated the Persian fleet outright in a great sea battle. With his supply lines now under threat from the Greek fleet, Xerxes retreated back to his own Persian lands, but left a large army behind in Thessaly over the winter under his general Mardonius.

The following spring of 479 BC, Mardonius advanced back into Attica, retook Athens and then made peace overtures to the Athenians, hoping to split the Greek alliance. When this failed and Mardonius heard that the combined Greek armies were on the march, he retreated again, only to be brought to battle at Platea in Beotia. This time Mardonius was defeated and killed, while on the same day the Greek fleet finally destroyed that of the Persians at Mycale. This spelled the end of Xerxes' ambitions in Greece, marking the start of the decline of the Persian Empire and the beginning of the ascendancy of the Greeks in the eastern Mediterranean and beyond.

Glossary of place names

Afon Wey

A small settlement at the mouth of the river Wey in Albion
(now known as Weymouth)

Albion

The island of Britain

Armorica

Brittany

Asia

In the context of this book, what is now the country of Turkey

Athens

The chief city of Attica, a city state on the Greek mainland

Belerion

Land's End, Cornwall

Belgae

The people of the god Bel
(The lands of the Belgae corresponded roughly to Belgium, although coastal settlements would also have existed in Albion and perhaps elsewhere)

Carthage

A powerful Phoenician city-state, located on the North African coast

Coriallo

A port in north western Gaul
(now known as Cherbourg)

Corinth	A powerful city state, strategically located at the isthmus of the Greek Peloponnese
Cyrnus	Corsica
The Dark Isle	A small island, adjoined to the southern coast of Albion (now known as the Isle of Portland)
Ériu	Ireland
Garona (river)	The river Garonne in southern Gaul
Gaul	The land of the Gaulish peoples, corresponding roughly to modern day France
The Great Middle Sea	The Mediterranean Sea
The Great River	The Nile
Iapygia	The southern part of the peninsula now known as Italy
Iberia	The Iberian peninsula.
Itanos	A major port on the island of Kriti (still known by the same name)
Kemet	'The land of the black earth' - later called Egypt by the Ancient Greeks

Kriti	Crete
Kush	An ancient kingdom in what is now northern Sudan
Kypros	Cyprus
Lacedaemon	Land of the Lacedaemonians; the most powerful city-state within the Greek Peloponnese, with the city of Sparta at its head
Lannion	A small fishing settlement at the mouth of the Garona river, in western Gaul
Llan Huell	A farming settlement in Albion
Maen y Lleu	The Stones of the Sun (Stonehenge, in the south of Albion)
Mai Dun	Maiden Castle hill fort, in the south of Albion
Massalia	A Greek colony on the southern coast of Gaul (now known as Marseilles)
Messene	A port on the north-eastern tip of Sikelia (now known as Messena)
The Morbihan	An enclosed bay on the southern coast of Armorica

Naukratis	A Greek colony in the Nile delta, later lost to history.
Napata	The northern capital of the Kushite Kings (near the modern day town of Karima in Sudan)
Olbia	A port in the north –eastern corner of Sardos (still known by the same name)
Persia	The Persian Empire, which stretched through the Middle East as far as the Indus, Turkey, the Ionian Islands, Cyprus and Egypt
Phoenicia	The colonies and lands of the sea-going Phoenician peoples, chief allies of Persia and historic enemies of the Greeks. The Phoenician trading empire spanned parts of North Africa, Sicily, Spain, Lebanon, and Syria.
The Pyrene	A chain of high mountains at the southern frontier of the Gaulish lands. (known today as the Pyrenees)
Roussolakos	A small port near to Itanos in Kriti – home of Captain Leontios

Sardos	Sardinia
Sikelia	Sicily
The Sound (of Albion)	The English Channel
Sparta	Chief city of Lacedaemon, in the Greek Peloponnese
Syracusa	Powerful Greek city-state in eastern Sikelia
Thebes	The Ancient Greek name for Waset
Tolosa	A large trading settlement on the Garona river in Gaul (known today as Toulouse)
Teyrnas yr Hynafiad	The Kingdom of the Ancestors (Avebury stone circle (including Silbury Hill and other Neolithic landscape monuments) in the south of Albion)
Tyrrhenia	Land of the Tyrhennians, in Iapygia; the Tyrhennians were traditional enemies of the Greeks

(cont. over)

Waset	Capital of Upper Kemet; home of the greatest temple of Amun (Waset was known to the ancient Greeks as Thebes and is located within the modern day city of Luxor in Egypt)

Acknowledgements

The author would like to thank fellow author Peter Knyte for his immeasurable advice and support in the editing of both 'Beyond the Black Earth' and 'Beyond the Pyrene'.

Thanks are also due to Peter Harding, Zigi du Toit, Michael Blake and Peter Boardman for their advice on archaeological, anthropological and historical matters in connection with this book.

Also, to my wife, friends and family for their support and encouragement.